Day Of The Spiders

By

Brian O'Gorman

Text copyright© 2017 Brian O'Gorman.
All Rights Reserved.

This book is a work of fiction. Any resemblance to real people or situations is purely coincidental

Dedicated to the memory of
Gemma O'Gorman
1942-2013

"How egotistical can you be, to have a camera trained on your face and you're watching it on the telly?"

For my long-suffering wife Zoe. It ain't easy, I know, but it will be worth it in the end.

Contents

Prologue 8

1. 9

2. 21

The Break of Day 25

1. 26

2. 47

3. 62

4. 74

5. 86

6. 109

7. 119

8. 133

9. 145

10. 157

11. 174

12. 182

13 197

14 214

15. 227

16. 244

17. 251

18. 272

19. 291

20. 300

21. 315

22. 327

23. 339

24. 355

25. 364

26. 376

27. 392

The Plague of the Whisperer 412

1. 413

2. 425

3. 433

4. 452

5. 469

6. 480

7. 534

8. 548

9. 562

10. 567

11. 570

12. 577

13. 583

14. 590

Epilogue. 594

A Quick Word.

Could you indulge me for just a moment? Please? Thanks. Pull up a chair if you wish.

So, what's all this Day of the spiders stuff? Didn't you write a sequel called Land of the Spiders?

Yeah, I did. I really did. But you have to understand a little something. I was utterly taken by surprise by the success of Dawn. It did far better than I ever would have predicted, which was why I hastily wrote a sequel. When I say hastily, I mean it. Land was written in just four weeks, and I hate to tell you, it absolutely shows. It was simply a reworking of the same story but in a tower block instead. I had to kill my darling, wipe the slate clean and start all over again. Land was pants, absolute pants. Day is my way of setting things right again.

Besides, after the success that those eight-legged buggers brought me, I thought it would be the kindest thing I could do.

I hope you enjoy it, and thanks for coming on another journey into the darker side of things.

How's that chair?

Comfy?

Then let us begin....

Prologue

"In the beginning, God made the heaven and the earth. He created man in his own image. At some point along the way, he made spiders. What was he thinking?"

1.

Jenny Roberts had lost her stupid cat again. She might just be worrying about the damn thing too much, but she hadn't had the best luck when it came to cats. This had been the fifth one that she had owned since she moved onto Corsica Road seven years ago to be with her boyfriend-now-husband, Alan. For her it had been an upgrade, moving from a bedsit into a full-blown house. Not that she had ever really been poor but she was a stickler for saving her money. Any unnecessary expense was just not her bag, baby. That's why living in that little bedsit had done her just fine. As long as she had a roof over her head, she really didn't give a shit about the quality. That bedsit, part of a six-bedroomed house over the other side of town hadn't actually been too bad. It had been pretty clean and well lit, not like some of the other places that she had looked at whilst she had been hunting for digs. Some of them weren't fit to house farmyard animals, let alone a young professional such as herself. Jenny was a mobile hairdresser. But she had the best reputation in the whole county, only because she wasn't a time waster. She was never one for making an appointment last longer than it needed to. She had just the right amount of chit-chat and leading questions to keep her customers engaged whilst she snipped, blow dried and added colour or bleaches. She worked more hours than all of the other mobile hairdressers could ever do. She had built the business up from nothing much at all. She had learned her craft at college and then set right out to make her mark. The idea of going and working for someone else just didn't sit with her at all, she needed to go out and make it on her own. At first, she did it just for her friends and family, charging them discounted rates whilst she got her shit together and then she was off and running. The advent of social media and word-of-mouth had got her name out there and ever since she had been grafting hard and earning some good money.

Jenny had been taught her most valuable life-lesson pretty early on by her father who had died of lung cancer when she was fifteen years of age. As a child, she had found a stray ten-pound note sitting under the bench at the local park. Her father liked to bring their dog Laddie to the playground. There were some nice big fields surrounding the play area where Laddie could go charging around in big circles, his tongue hanging out of his mouth and flapping in the wind as he ran. Stan could sit on the bench, smoke his pipe and watch Jenny play in the park for a good hour or so. He had called Jenny over ready to set off for home and she had climbed off the swing and thundered over to him. Her eyes had darted downwards under the bench where her father was sat and she had seen the note. At first, she thought that her father had dropped it and she bent down, picked it up and handed it to him.

"Well, what have you found here?" said Stan, taking the note off her.

"You dropped it, Daddy," said Jenny.

Stan unfolded the note. "It's not mine Jen, someone else must have dropped it."

"Oh," said Jenny, her forehead furrowed into a frown, "Shall I put it back?"

Stan laughed. "No, my dear, we should put it to some good use," he said. He stood up and began to rummage around in his trouser pocket. Eventually, he pulled his hand out with a crumpled five-pound note. He handed it to Jenny who took it from him, her head still wrinkled in that little frown that made her look so much like her mother.

"That's your half. Keep it safe Jenny. Remember that with money, it's not how much you make, it's how much you are willing to save," he said.

Jenny nodded, "Ok Daddy," she said.

"Now, what's say we get this silly dog home and have ourselves a hot chocolate," said Stan, a grin spreading across his face.

"Yay," said Jenny. She grabbed hold of her father's hand and let him lead her all the way home.

Jenny never spent the five pounds her father gave her. She took him at his word and saved it. After he died, she mounted the note onto a piece of white card and had it framed. She hung that picture in every place she lived from that day forward as a reminder to be careful with her money.

It was just a shame that she couldn't be as careful with her cats. Every time she got herself a new one, be it a rescue cat or a brand-new kitten she would always end up in exactly the same position that she was in right now, standing by the open back door in her vest top and jogging bottoms and shaking a box of cat treats in an effort to get the fluffy shitbag back into the house. It was bitingly cold this evening as well, which made her impatience even more short-fused. She wanted to get the little fucker inside before it got to rush hour.

"Come *on, Tigger,*"

Shake-shake-shake

She listened for anything that might sound like a cat approaching, perhaps a bang on the wooden fence as he scaled it, a bark from next door's dog as he bounded past their back window, but there was nothing, just the sounds of silence rolling in through the darkness towards her. She sighed, mentally kicking herself for continuing to have faith that a cat would have any loyalty whatsoever. Granted, the last two had fallen victim to Hemmington Road which ran right past the back of the house. It was the main road through the town and it used up a lot of pets, especially on a Friday and a Saturday night when the takeaways that were dotted up and down the road put their rubbish out for the local wildlife to rummage through, including most of the neighborhood cats. The problem for them was that the road never really went quiet, even at all hours of the night. It was the primary route from central Hemmington to the M56 motorway which ensured that there were, at the very least, a high number of delivery vans and lorries roaring up and down all night. It was just a sad fact that it was far easier and much less dangerous for a driver to just mow an unsuspecting animal down if they chose to run out into the road. Cats were the number two victims on that road, only outnumbered by urban foxes.

She had lost another three cats to straying. One, in particular, a white socks cat that she had named Nibbles had gone out for his evening constitutional never to return. Two months later she had seen Nibbles happily sitting in the window of a house five doors down. The cat looked right at her as she stared at him open mouthed and if he recognized her at all then he didn't give any indication whatsoever.

She shook the box of biscuits one more time. Some of them jumped out of the little serving hole in the side of the box and clicked onto the flagstone porch.

"Come on Tigger, you little fuck nuts," she said, probably a little too loud. She craned an ear to the garden which was lit up by the security light. There was nothing but silence, and more silence, and then….

Bang

Jenny recoiled a little. The bang had come from the garden fence to her left-hand side. It was followed by a thud and then the unmistakable scrabbling of claws.

"Tigger, thank Christ for that," said Jenny and she took a step forward to grab hold of him as he got to the top of the fence. She didn't want him running away again. It was bedtime for cats. As she got to the fence, Tigger's front paws appeared over the top. Jenny stopped dead in her tracks, her hand going up to her mouth. Then the cat pulled himself up to the top of the fence and she staggered backward and screamed her husband's name as hard as her lungs would allow her to.

Alan Roberts had entrenched himself into the sofa, ready to watch the football and he was pulling his first can off his six-pack of beers when Jenny had screamed. The act of her screaming was a shock in itself, it wasn't something that he was used to hearing from her. In Alan's mind, Jenny was a pretty tough nut. She wasn't one to be easily spooked by a horror film or a bug in the bathroom sink, nor was she one of those people that would take any shit from anyone. She was never rude, but she was assertive and bloody-minded when it came to getting what she wanted, and it didn't matter what it was, a return on an item of clothing she had bought but found fault with, or haggling the best price she could get for anything expensive that they had bought. She had managed to get a seventy-pound discount off the forty-two-inch television that was sat in their front room right now just by haggling with the young shop assistant. She had managed to get the assistant manager and then the manager involved and ran them around in circles until she got what she wanted. He hadn't interjected himself in the haggle at any time. He had just stood back and watched her serve the shop workers their arses, and then they left with the television they wanted and the price that she wanted. It really was a thing of beauty to watch. Their marriage worked better than a well-oiled machine. They both knew exactly what they wanted and needed from each other, there was no bullshit, there was very little needed in the way of compromise. Since the day that they first met they had fitted together like a foot in an old leather shoe. He knew that she would be working her tail off to keep her business going so he made sure that she didn't have to worry about the trivial shit such as food shopping or paying bills. He took care of all of that in between his shifts at the card factory running the folding presses. She would leave him to his football and wouldn't bug him about how many beers he would drink or how loudly he would bellow at the television. He could have even brought friends around to watch the game with him if he wanted to, but he didn't like to make chit-chat or be distracted in any way when the game was on. Tonight was a little different to the norm. Tonight she had shrieked his name in such a way that he knew something was terribly wrong. He was out of his seat before the scream had even come to an end. He ran straight through into the kitchen and he saw

Jenny backing up through the back door, her hands clapped to her cheeks. Her head was shaking from side to side and she was making a low moaning noise in the back of her throat.

"Jenny? What the fu...." The words died on his tongue.

Their pet cat Tigger was weaving and wobbling on top of the garden fence. Every few seconds he was letting out a gravelly, guttural wail that sounded nothing like the healthy and happy sound of a cat. Tigger's ginger and white fur, or what was left of it was matted in wild patches. Every visible piece of skin was covered in angry blisters. Some of them had broken open allowing a white, milky fluid to ooze out and cake the pieces of remaining fuzz. The worst affected area was Tigger's face. The left side of it looked unharmed, but the right side wasn't even recognizable anymore. The right eye looked like it had been blown right out of the cat's skull. The shredded pieces of it were plastered to his swollen and savaged cheek. The lower right jaw was hanging down as if it had been torn out of place. Tigger's tongue poked through the mess of flesh and exposed bone.

"Oh….oh…….oh…" was all Alan could come out with. He had never seen such a vision of horror in his life. He didn't know how the animal could possibly have still been alive in such a state. As he looked on, Tigger swayed back and forth on the fence and then he pitched forwards. He fell to the concrete floor with a nauseating wet slap. As his body struck the flags most of the sores on his back broke open sending an arc of milky and bloody fluid spraying up the fence and across the porch. He lay on the floor shaking and growling and looking to Jenny and Alan with his one good eye for help that they couldn't give him. Jenny turned and tried to get away, but the strength went out of her legs and she went to her knees in the middle of the kitchen floor.

"God, dear sweet God, oh Christ Alan, what happened to him?" she wailed.

Alan opened his mouth to answer and then he brought up the mash potatoes, onion gravy, and sausages that he had spent an hour cooking earlier that evening. The grotesque concoction roared out of his mouth and coated his bare feet and a decent area of the floor beneath him.

As Alan was dry retching and Jenny was biting the back of her hand to stop herself from fainting, Tigger breathed his last shaking breath right there on the porch. After what he had been subjected to in the last few hours, he felt nothing but the faintest hint of relief when the end finally came.

2.

The jerking reaction to the nightmare had caused Briggs to sit bolt upright on his bunk. The light from the overhead spots hurt his eyes, even though they were constantly on low. His body was slick with sweat, pinning his vest top to his body in a slimy coating. His chest heaved, tearing a breath into his lungs. He sat there for a moment, panting, feeling the terrible vision that he had just been subjected to beginning to fade away, at least for now. It wasn't the first time he had been thrown from his sleep by that nightmare. He had lost count of the number of times he had replayed that moment over and over again. He looked around his room. The same room he had as his own for so long now. How long had it been? Three years? Four years? The fog of his chemically induced sleep was still coating his mind.

The small blind on his window suddenly clicked open. There was a pair of deep blue eyes looking in at him. It was one of the nurses. Her name was momentarily lost in the swirling mist of his mind right now. It would come back to him.

Blue eyes looked in at him for around five seconds and then the blind clicked back up again, shutting out some of the light from the corridor. They checked up on him every two hours or so, just to make sure he wasn't trying to take his own life. They called it *'Protecting you from yourself Mike. I can call you Mike, can't I?'*

He didn't want to be called Mike, but they called him Mike anyway. That wasn't the only thing they had called him.

They had called him *insane.*

They had called him a *terrorist.*

They had called him a *murderer.*

Of course, they had wanted to pin the blame for Newtown on him, it was a nice, tidy way to put the whole thing to bed. He was pretty sure that he had been tried and sentenced by the media and the powers that be without him having to lift a finger. But, he would be damned if he was going to make it easy for them. He knew what the truth of the matter was. It was only a matter of time before it would all come back to haunt them, then they would change their tune, then they would see that there was nothing he, or they, could have done to stop what happened in Newtown.

So, they had sent him here, inside the walls of this hospital.

They had called him *insane.*

He swung his legs off the bed and placed his bare feet on the cold wooden floor. He looked around the sterile room that had been his home for such a long time now. He had an idea that it was around five years since he had first been brought here and sedated day after day. He had fought them at first, thrashing his body around, trying to stop the needle being buried in his buttock, but they always won. He would feel the sting on his skin and then a few moments later his strength would float away...

Five years? Has it really been that long?

It was easy to lose track. Every day was exactly the same. The routine never changed. Some of the others couldn't cope if the routine altered, the others that came and went. Some of them fought, some of them screamed, and in the end, all of them fell into the silence, shuffling around the corridors, a glazed look in their eye. The right hit of medications at the right time of day kept them quiet, kept them under control. Some of them stayed a while, some of them vanished without a trace, but they all fell to the silence. All of them.

But he hadn't fallen. He still had hope. He still had a little fight left inside of him. Plus, he was no dummy. He knew he wasn't going to just walk out of the door.

They wouldn't just let him go.

Even through the residual fear that the dream had left him with and even with the knowledge that he was facing another day in this hole, another week, another month, perhaps even another year, a smile broke out on his face.

It was just a matter of time, after all.

The Break of Day

"There is nothing finer than the birth of a new day. Be it full of hope and opportunity for thee. For some that walk this mortal coil, the coming of a new day signals their time is soon to be over. For all, their day will come."

1.

Braden Benson made it home with two minutes to spare. He burst through the door with his arms out and a big cheesy grin on his face which was partially hidden behind six weeks of beard growth.

"Ta-daaah" he sang, knowing full well that his ten-year-old daughter Jaqueline (or Jax for short) would be sat in the living room watching the clock to make sure that he made good on his promise. She looked over at him, trying in vain to give him a grouchy look. The moment she saw his stupid looking face with the silly beard and toothy grin she was done. The mock frown smoothed out and a smile broke out on her face, no matter how hard she tried to keep it pulled in. There was something about her Dad that just made her laugh. No matter how many times he broke a promise, or forgot something important (like picking her up from school which had happened on more than one occasion) she couldn't help but love every moment that he was around. She jumped out of her seat and charged over to him. She crashed into his mid-section, causing all the air in his lungs to be involuntarily expelled. He let out a loud *Huuh* and enveloped her in his arms. She began to jump up and down like a frog in a box.

"Daddydaddydaddy," she sang over and over.

"JaxJaxJax," he sang back and joined in with the jumping up and down. They jumped around in a big circle until Braden got too near to the coat hooks that were on the wall next to the front door and hit his head on one of them. He bellowed in pain and clutched at his head. Jax shrieked with laughter.

"Hey, that ain't funny knucklehead," he said and brought his hand down so he could rub his knuckles into her hair. She yelped and squirmed away from him.

"It is funny, you banged your big thick head," said Jax and laughed again.

Braden put on his mock-serious face and began to advance on her. Jax knew what was coming next and she ran for the sofa.

"Now you're gonna get it kiddo," he growled with a terrible American accent.

He threw off his overcoat and dived onto the sofa. He dug the point of his elbow into

Jax's left leg just above the knee and began to grind it a little. Jax screamed with laughter and then drove her own elbow into Braden's collarbone. Braden roared and fell backward clutching at his pretend injury.

"Arrrgh, you got me kiddo, you got me good," he growled and then he played dead with his eyes crossed and his tongue hanging out. Jax responded by yanking his shirt up and blowing a huge raspberry on his belly. Braden flopped his limbs around as if he was being electrocuted. Jax tried to hit another belly raspberry but she was laughing too much. She collapsed back on the sofa holding her belly and giggling.

"Have you two quite finished now?" said Mary Benson coming through from the kitchen.

Braden put up his hands. "Yes ma'am, I have conceded defeat to my worthy opponent."

"Thank God for that, you were giving me a headache," she said.

Braden jumped up off the sofa and went over to Mary. He planted a kiss on her lips and gave her a hug. She resisted a little at first but she soon warmed to him. She was just like Jax, she knew that Braden was a pain in the arse and unreliable, it came with the job after all, but when he did come home, there was no person on this earth that she would rather be with. He was one of those people that could light up a room just by being there. It was such a double-edged sword that she loved him as much as she did because no matter how badly he fucked up she would always forgive him.

"What shall we eat tonight oh-not-so-virgin Mary," he said. A wise-guy grin spreading across his face.

"Well, it is Friday night and I don't feel like cooking," said Mary, her arms going up to the back of his neck.

Jax jumped up on the back of the sofa. "Pizza, pizza, can we have pizza Dad, *pleeeese,*" she crowed.

Braden looked over at her. She pulled out her bottom lip and opened her eyes as wide as possible. This had become known as the 'Dad-face' in the Benson household. It was the face that Jax used when she wanted to get her own way. Most of the time it worked just fine.

"Weeeeell, I suppose we could stretch to a little bit of pizza," said Braden.

"Yay," said Jax.

"And perhaps a slice or two of garlic bread."

"Yay."

"We could even go mad and have onion rings," said Braden his smile spreading out into a grin.

"Can we have a bottle of coke too?" yelled Jax, jumping up and down on the sofa.

"Let's not go crazy eh?" said Braden dropping his grin into a pretend-serious look.

The Dad-face re-appeared. Braden let it ride for a few moments before he relented. "Oh, go on then."

Jax shrieked with delight and jumped up and down on the sofa again.

"You have to promise not to break the couch, that's my only price," said Braden. Jax leaped up one more time and dropped back down into a perfect cross-legged sitting position. She saluted him and then went back to her cartoons on the television. Mary kissed him on the lips, not minding the little tickle of beard that went with it. She made fun of his beard, but secretly she rather liked it. It made him look more grown up.

"You spoil us, you know that," she said.

"Well, if I can't spoil you two, who can I spoil?" he said. "Is there beer in our fridge, or have you drunk it all again?"

Mary gave him a light slap across the cheek, "Cheeky bastard. Yes, there is. Shall we?" she said gesturing towards the kitchen. She went through and he followed her. She opened the fridge and brought two cans out. She handed one to Braden and then popped the tab on her own. Braden followed suit and they both drank in silence for a moment. Braden let out a loud belch.

"Pig," said Mary and then she let one fly which was longer and louder than Braden's. They both laughed.

"So, what's been the big story today?" said Mary. She always asked him whenever he came home, be it at a regular time or in the middle of the night.

"Well, we have a missing teenager that has already gone on the website and everywhere else, and a murdered cat," he said and raised his can again.

Mary's face crumpled into a frown, "A missing teenager? Jeez, another runaway?"

Braden shrugged, "Not very likely, she is only thirteen. She never made it home from school yesterday. There is no other information at the moment. The police thought that it might have been her father because they are separated, but apparently, he is just as much of a mess as the girl's mother, so they don't think that he had anything to do with it, plus, his place has already been searched and there is nothing there."

"God, how awful," said Mary and shuddered. She took a long drink from her can. Braden knew that she was thinking exactly the same thing that he had thought when he heard the story for the first time. He was just thankful that it wasn't their daughter. The very idea of someone taking Jax away like that made his blood run cold. It wasn't much of a stretch for him to knock off and get his backside home this evening. He had felt a terrible guilt come over him about how little time he spent with his family. They could just as easily have been snatched away from him just the same as the missing girl. He had felt for the first time in many years a sense of relief and joy in coming home tonight instead of the usual nagging itch to go fact-finding and writing more reports before any other newspaper got hold of it. Tonight the competition could eat it all up with his glad tidings whilst he ate pizza with his wife and daughter.

"It is," he said "But the story about the cat is not much better," he said.

"Oh?"

"Yeah, it's pretty grim," he said. He had a sudden maddening urge for a cigarette, but he had given that shit up more than ten years ago. He would have that crazy urge rise up in him every so often, the same way that an amputee might feel the itch of an arm or a leg that had long since departed.

"Really?"

"Yep. About three hours after the girl had gone missing, a resident on Corsica Road had her cat come back home horribly mutilated. I saw the pictures and I can tell you I have never seen anything that gross in all my life. I nearly lost my lunch."

"Urgh, what did it look like?" said Mary. He was about to tell her when she put her hand up to stop him. "Don't tell me, I don't really want to know."

Braden laughed. "Shall we get more supplies and head for the sofa?" he said waving his can at her.

"Sounds like a good idea. Are you working tomorrow?" she said, expecting him to say yes. Historically, he worked every Saturday, most Sundays too.

"No. I'm having the weekend off to spend with my two favourite girls," he said.

Mary felt a jolt of happiness which quickly melted. She had heard him say this before and the next morning he had been up and gone before she had woken up. She looked at him and saw something in his face and his eyes that she hadn't seen for a long time.

He meant it.

She felt a goofy smile pulling at her cheeks. She stepped forward and kissed his beardy mouth. "That sounds lovely," she said. "Now, you grab the beers and I'll order the food. I promised Jax that she could choose a film for us to watch tonight."

Braden grimaced. He knew it would be 'Mama-Mia' again. The child had developed an obsession with that film. Still, if he had enough beers he wouldn't care what he was watching.

"Yeah, I know. But you love to listen to Pierce Brosnan singing, and you know it," said Mary. They both laughed and then set about making their nest on the sofa for the evening. Braden suddenly noticed that there was something different about the room. There were two new floating shelves hanging above the television set.

"How did those get there?" he asked.

Mary opened her mouth to speak but Jax cut her off.

"Trent came 'round and did 'em," she said.

Braden looked at Mary, there was a tinge of colour in her cheeks. Trent was their next door neighbour. Very handsome he was too and divorced. Braden had a lot of reasons to hate Trent and there was two of them right there.

"I didn't know when you would be home. He… he just offered…" Mary spluttered.

Braden held his hand up, "It's fine, I understand." Although he didn't like the idea of that muscle head being in his home with his freshly signed divorce papers and his big posh Land Rover, he didn't want to argue about it, not tonight. He took Mary's hand and kissed it. She looked relieved.

"I should go 'round and thank him," said Braden, slipping the needle in just a little.

"Don't you fucking dare," said Mary.

"*MUM!*" yelled Jax. That was another twenty pence for the swear jar.

An hour later, Braden was four beers and six pizza slices in. He felt wonderfully buzzed and full of junk food. Every so often he would glance to his right at the faces of his wife and daughter. There was no doubting that

Jax was her mother's daughter. They were both sat with their eyes on the television screen twiddling their hair in exactly the same way. He smiled to himself. He felt like today's little excursion into the dark and nasty side of the world had really struck a chord with him. He didn't know why, after all these years of reporting all of this nasty shit, that it was suddenly getting to him? He was thirty-eight years of age now, not the fresh-faced and hungry kid he had been when he had started at the Daily News. Back then, the nastier the story, the more dramatic the report and the more money he would earn in bonuses, especially if he got the story to press before anyone else. That shit had got more difficult these days with the advent of the internet and the rise of social media. Now, you had to be razor sharp, and even faster than you were before. One moment of hesitation and your story would have already broken on the 'net. It was a cut-throat way to make living and in his younger years, that kind of challenge didn't bother him. But, sitting here now, he had begun to think about perhaps not being at the forefront of everything. Perhaps he could let some of the younger and fresh-faced reporters have their day in the sun. He glanced over at his family again. By Christ, they were beautiful. And more to the point they were still here when he came home. He had given Mary a ton of reasons to go and find love and companionship elsewhere on many occasions, but she had always stayed with him. At his worst, he hadn't come home for four days. Jax had only been four months old at that time and when he had finally poked his head around the door Mary had been ready to pack up and walk out. They had rowed, they had fought, but in the end, they had worked it out. Braden had practically begged her to stay, promising her that he would spend more time at home and he had done for a while, but the old habits had started to creep back up. He couldn't for the life of him think why Mary had put up with him for such a long time. Then it occurred to him that this woman must really love him.

His train of thought was interrupted by Jax ripping off a huge fart which rippled against Braden's leg. Jax began to shriek with laughter, her cheeks turning red with the effort.

"Jax!" yelled Mary, but she was laughing too.

"Wow, that smells like pizza," said Braden making the girls laugh even more. Eventually, they settled back down again. The film was approaching the home straight.

Yes, Braden had been a workaholic for fifteen years, and now he was thinking about shifting the gears down and moving into the cruising lane. Was that really possible? He had an idea that it was. After all, the buzz that he used to get off hitting on a good story had been partially derailed when he had written a piece on the Newtown Incident (as it had been christened.) That was the story that had started the shift. He had actually been thrown into a month-long depression after covering that one. Really, he shouldn't have covered it, but he felt that he needed to close that one off by finding out just exactly what had happened that day. After all, his father had lived in Newtown and he was listed as one of the dead. Of course, there were no bodies and very little in the way of remains after the army had blown the whole town to shit. There had been a funeral of course and a coffin that had some little bits of memorabilia related to his father. None of his buddies had contributed anything, but then again how could they, they had all lived in Newtown. As soon as he had finished writing that story he put it to bed. There were all sorts of conspiracy nuts on the internet offering lots and lots of bullshit theories about what had happened. But Braden always went with the philosophy that an opinion was like an arse hole, everyone had one. After all of that, his enthusiasm had waned somewhat. He wasn't putting in the same effort to find the story as he once used to. There was a deep subconscious part of him that didn't really want to know anymore. The world was fast becoming an ugly place to live in and he didn't want to be reminded of it.

That's your story and you're sticking to it eh?

He nodded to himself and took a long drink from his can of beer. It was going down pretty well at the moment, but at the back of his mind, he was beginning to fancy ditching the beer in favor of a nice cup of strong tea. He decided that he would wait until Jax had gone to bed before he made one, otherwise, she would want one too and the caffeine content would have kept her going for another couple of hours. He would have ended up sitting up and playing endless games of rock, paper, scissors or slaps, which he was particularly bad at. He loved his dear daughter very much, but he wanted to be alone with Mary for a little while. This new chapter in his life was just beginning and he wanted to kick it off in the right way. The film came to a merciful end and Mary announced to Jax that it was late and it was time for bed. Jax groaned, but her slightly flushed cheeks and half-lidded eyes gave the game away.

"Can I have a story Dad? Pleeeease," she said and then pulled the Dad Face again.

"Oh, go on then, just the one though, ok?"

She nodded, jumped up off the sofa and took off out of the room and up the stairs at a hundred miles per hour.

"I don't know where she gets her energy from," said Mary. She looked like she could have done with a story and bed herself.

"I'll go and give madam a story and then we can have a nice cup of tea, what do you say?" said Braden.

Mary stretched and yawned, "Sounds perfect."

Braden leaned over and kissed her on the end of her nose. "Catch you in two."

Mary clapped him on the backside as he was leaving. By the time he got upstairs, Jax had already chosen a book. It was 'When a Monster is Born' One of her favorites ever since she had been a youngster. She liked Braden to read this one because he would put silly voices on to entertain her. It seemed that she never got bored of his bad comedy, not ever. He read the book in his silly voices whilst Jax bellowed with laughter and afterward, he tucked her up in her bed. He leaned in and gave her a kiss goodnight and she blew a raspberry in his face (as per usual.) As he was walking out of her bedroom door she said:

"I love you Dad."

He stopped in his tracks. He felt like he had been punched in the guts. She had never said that to him before, not ever. He was floored. He turned around and smiled at her. "Love you too horror bag."

Jax turned over and put her thumb in her mouth, a habit which she had been unable to leave behind no matter how old she was.

Braden turned away and went downstairs with a big goofy grin on his face.

He went into the kitchen and made tea for the both of them. He came into the living room carrying the mugs and set one down on the coffee table. Mary had put the ten o'clock news on. That usually meant that there was nothing else on the television worth watching. Braden set his own mug down and crashed down on the sofa next to Mary. She shuffled along the cushions and rearranged herself so that she was leaning on him. Braden put an arm around her and she leaned her head on his chest. They sat in a comfortable silence for a little while, just enjoying the peace and quiet after Jax had gone to bed. The local news came on and the stories of the missing teenager and the murdered cat were the first two stories out.

"I just can't imagine what her parents are going through," said Mary.

"Hell, I would guess," said Braden.

They fell silent again. The local news went through a few more stories and then the weather report came on. For once it was good news, it was going to be cold, but sunny.

"Are you really not going to work this weekend?" said Mary suddenly. Braden had an idea that she was working herself up to asking the question. Perhaps she was slightly fearful that she was going to piss him off.

"No, I'm not working this weekend," he said. He felt a mild irritation, but he couldn't really blame her for having doubts about his conviction. She sat up and looked at him.

"What's changed?" she said.

"I guess that I'm just beginning to realize what is more important to me," he said.

Mary smiled. It lit up her face. "Why don't we drink this tea and get ourselves an early night."

Now it was his turn to smile. "Sounds perfect," he said.

They drank tea, went to bed and made love. It had been too long, far too long. Mary was asleep soon afterward. Braden tried, but something was nagging him at the back of his mind. He tried everything in his power to shrug it off but it wouldn't go. He had seen the picture of the mutilated cat. He didn't know how on earth it could have survived long enough to get home with the injuries it had, nor did he know what kind of a human being could have inflicted such terrible injuries on an innocent animal.

Unless it wasn't human.

He wanted to get out of bed and go and power up his computer so he could do a little research on the area around Corsica Road. But, another part of him wanted to stay in bed with his wife where he belonged. That part of him just wanted to let it go. Even if he found the answer to his questions, what good would it do now?

He fought with himself for another hour and then he fell into a restless and shallow sleep. By the time that morning came around and Jax was jumping up and down on the bed to get him up, he felt more tired than he had done the night before. He decided that when there were a quiet few minutes he would have a quick look on the laptop, just to satisfy his curiosity and then that would be it, no more.

In the meantime, he had to be the perfect husband and the perfect father, nothing less would do.

2.

Meep-meep

Meep-meep

Mee....

Gerald Thompson groped for the radio alarm on the side of his bed. He fumbled around, knocking his paperback and his reading glasses on the floor in the process. He managed to find the button and gave it a healthy slap. The *Meep-meep* got cut right off in mid-flow. He let out a heavy sigh.

"Is it seven already?" said Cindy, in a weary, sleep-thickened voice.

"'Fraid so," said Gerald, falling back down onto his pillow. There was a greasy spot just under his right ear where he had probably been drooling again. His mouth was parched and his vocal cords felt dry and creaky. They needed some good, strong coffee to grease them right up again. "I think I might call in sick," he said to Cindy, his wife of the last thirty years. The corners of his mouth ghosted with a grin in anticipation of her response.

"Bullshit, Mr. Policeman," she muttered.

Gerald wheezed laughter. She had called him Mr. Policeman since the first day she had seen him put on a uniform a million years ago. He didn't have a uniform now, not since he had been promoted to D.C.I. fifteen years ago. Now all he had to worry about was a decent shirt and tie, of which he had plenty.

"I could stay home and make love to you all day," he said to Cindy, still grinning.

"Bull-*shit,* Mr. Policeman," she said, louder this time. She lifted her head off the pillow. Even at age fifty-two, and first thing in the morning, Cindy Thompson looked like a pretty fine woman to him. He turned towards her and planted a kiss on her cheek.

"Very smooth, now get out of here and make me coffee," she said, slapping him on his bare shoulder. She knew that it would be her who would make it downstairs first, such was the length of time it took Gerald to get himself ready to go. It was only on his off-days that she would enjoy the fruits of his kettle related labour, and if she was honest about it, she preferred her own. Gerald always made it just that little bit too strong.

"Yes, my love," he said and rolled over. He stood up out of bed and stretched, feeling his joints click and crackle. He wasn't in bad shape for a man of his age. He was only two years older than Cindy, and his waistline was still within the acceptable boundaries of good health. He had been blessed with a pretty solid metabolism and an inbuilt hatred of junk food that had served him well over the years. He was the pristine example of a well-balanced and healthy individual, a real goody-two-shoes, as his brother Eric had told him over and over again as they were growing up.

He went into the bathroom and closed the door behind him. He hated the morning shower, but it had become ingrained into his routine like a cigarette addiction. If he skipped it, then he would be sluggish and half-witted all day because he psychologically hadn't woken himself up with a good wash. Crazy, yes, but he couldn't break the habit. He *daren't* break the habit. He turned the shower on and watched it splutter into life with a sigh. He looked at himself in the mirror which was over the bathroom sink. He saw the semi-permanent wrinkles in his brow and the crow's feet around his eyes. He still had his hair, but it was mostly grey now, and it was starting to recede. He stuck his tongue out at his reflection and pushed the tip of his nose upwards.

"You are a silly old fart, you need to hang up your badge and go and do something else," he told himself. He let go of his nose and it pinged back into its normal shape.

"Did you say something dear?" said Cindy from outside of the door, startling him a little. She was heading past to go and get the kettle boiling so she could have a reasonable strength to her morning cup.

"Nothing, just singing to myself," he called back.

"It's too early to be jolly," she called and then made her way downstairs. He smiled to himself and began to undress ready for the shower. He hoped today would be a nice easy one. He had a week off booked as soon as his slate was clear enough for him to do so. He had been carefully doling out the workload so that it would happen sooner rather than later. He hadn't taken Cindy away on holiday for over a year now, and he knew that she was beginning to get itchy feet. She needed a change of location, and if he was honest about it, so did he. He fancied going somewhere hot and sunny so he could slob around and catch up on his reading. He remembered the last few times they had been away. They had gone over to the Costa Brava in North-East Spain and spent two weeks each time lazing around in the sun and going out every night to eat. When they had sat in the sun they had both spent most of it asleep as if they were catching up on all the extra sleep that they had been missing out on, such was the price of modern day living. He fancied some of that lifestyle. He couldn't wait for it. For now, however, it was business as usual. He stepped into the shower cubicle and gritted his teeth against the hot water that was cascading from the shower head.

Once he was washed, shaved and suited up he went downstairs and found Cindy at the table reading the morning paper. She was slowly chewing a piece of brown toast, pausing only to wipe crumbs from the corner of her mouth. In his place was a tall cup of coffee with a dash of milk, just as he liked it. He wasn't a breakfast man at all. He didn't usually start to get hungry until well past ten o'clock and it was a habit that he had never been able to change in all the years he had been getting up early. His long hours usually meant that he had to just grab food whenever the urge took him. It was a waste of time trying to have a routine during the day, anything could come up at any given moment and throw the whole thing right to the dogs.

He pulled up his seat and took a sip of the coffee. It hit his taste buds like a blessing from heaven above. Cindy looked up at him and gave him a smile.

"What?" said Gerald.

"Oh, I don't know. I was thinking that we should go out tonight," she said and wiped away the crumbs again.

"Anywhere in particular?" he said.

"Pub crawl, nightclub, fish and chips afterward," she said, still with that cheeky smile spread across her face.

"Do you have any idea how long it has been since either of us saw the inside of a nightclub? Or stayed out past eleven? Are you having a mid-life crisis, my love?"

"Oh, you old spoilsport," she said and returned her eyes to the newspaper. Gerald sipped more coffee.

"How about a nice dinner and a trip to the cinema. I might even pay if you're good," he said.

"Ooh, you old charmer. I'll tell you what, if you pay then I might put out too. Might being the operative word," she said, her eyes still on the newspaper. That little smile was twitching around the corners of her mouth again. Gerald got up from his stool and moved over to her. He scooped her up out of her seat, his arms going around her waist. He loved the feel of her body in her silk dressing gown, it got his motor turning over every time. He kissed her neck just below her ear.

"Well, I might put out too. Might being the operative word," he mumbled in her ear. He felt her skin break out in goosepimples, the same way it did every time he whispered in her ear. She let out a giggle and then planted a warm kiss on his lips.

"You're a bad boy, Mr. Policeman," she said. "Now get lost before I get crumbs on your nice suit."

He kissed her again and then he let her go back to her newspaper. He picked up his coffee and went through to the living room. His mobile phone was on the top of the fireplace on its charger. He always switched the damn thing off the moment he got home, he didn't like to be disturbed when he was on his downtime. He also hated the idea that anyone could reach him when he was off duty. There had to be a distinct time of day when he could say that enough was enough and he was going to spend some time being human instead. He powered the phone up and drew the curtains back so he could have a look out of the window.

They had moved to Layton Town nine years ago. The moment that they had come to look at the house that he was now standing in, they both knew it was the perfect place for them to go. The house was on the very outskirts of the town on the road that led right out towards Layton Valley. Once you got to the outskirts of the town the road climbed upwards very quickly, affording you a view of the rest of the town that was absolutely breath-taking. The view from the front windows was stunning. The whole town looked like it was laid out right before them, with the church spire poking up right in the middle of it all like a holy exclamation point.

This morning, the sun was just above the horizon, setting most of the town in a silhouette. There was a light mist rising with the warmth of the new day making the sunbeams radiate a golden colour all over the scene in front of him. The sunlight washed into the room warming Gerald as he stood drinking his coffee and taking in the scenery in front of him. He didn't mind helping to police this town. There wasn't that much in the way of trouble anyway. It was only when he was called over to Hemmington City that there would usually be something to get his teeth into. There had been a fair few murders there over the years. Not a lot when you compared it to other areas of the country, but enough to keep him in work. There were a few snatched children, a couple of pedophiles and other assorted dregs of society that he had to deal with, but most of it had been pretty plain sailing. Superintendent Carl Roberts was his immediate superior. He really didn't care for the man, but he had enough respect for him to be able to work with him effectively. They were just from different sides of the same coin, both of them just as passionate about police work. But Roberts was a fair few years younger than him and he didn't quite have the instincts that Gerald had built up over the years, and he never had hunches. Gerald had them, more and more as the years crept on by. Nine times out of ten, his hunches would prove to be absolutely on the money. But Roberts never wanted to hear about them. He always reminded him just to deal with the facts, or risk getting himself in hot water. Gerald usually would nod and say 'yes sir' in the right places and then go about things his own way anyway. His way hadn't steered him wrong in the past.

The most important hunch of his life was about moving to this house. They had a perfectly nice home before they had moved to Layton. It was a house that had a two-car garage, a great big garden at the back and enough local amenities so that you wouldn't ever have to get in the car for anything if you didn't want to. The old house had been in Newtown which was a good twenty miles in the opposite direction to where they were now. They had lived there for fifteen years before he started to get the creeps every time he walked in the door at the end of the day. Cindy would question him about it, but he could never quite put a finger on what it was that was bothering him. It got so bad that he stopped sleeping at night. He would lie awake in bed, listening to Cindy snoring gently next to him, his skin crawling all over as if it had a life of its own. He would try and go over everything in his mind that could possibly be making him feel like he was in any way unsafe. Did the windows have locks? Yes, they did, nobody could get through those without waking the dead. Did all the doors have the right locks? Yes, they had bolts at the top and bottom on the front and the back. Any potential intruder would have had to use a power tool to get inside, and that wasn't going to happen without attracting a hell of a lot of attention. Why did he feel this way? What was making him so uneasy? It was the same way that he would feel if he was interviewing a suspect he just *knew* was guilty despite the evidence that said otherwise. It was the same feeling every time he walked into the house. The warmth seemed to go out of the room, his stomach would churn and something inside of his head would begin to itch. It was a hunch. Plain and simple, it was one of his hunches.

He had talked to Cindy about how he was feeling about the house. They had argued (something that they didn't do very often) and then gone to their respective corners to lick their wounds. When the heat had gone out of the situation Cindy had told him that it wouldn't do any harm to at least have a look at what was available in the surrounding area. She was pissed off at him for wanting to leave their perfect house, but she knew to trust his hunches. She saw that look in his eye, that look that turned him from being a strong, able man to a frightened little boy every time he came home. He could barely sit still, unable to read the paper, or watch television without getting up every twenty minutes or so to go through to the kitchen and then return a moment later with nothing in his hands.

He had a hunch about the house. Something bad was going to happen here. He told her so, and she believed him. Before long, neither of them could settle. Both of them would jump out of their skins if something creaked late at night and if anyone knocked at the door….

So they had found the house in Layton and they had moved. Cindy couldn't have been happier with the new place if it had been constructed out of gold. Whether his hunch had been right or not, it had led them to this house, and she loved their new home.

It turned out his hunch had been absolutely spot on, because just three weeks after they had signed off on the new place, Newtown was wiped off the face of the earth. Bioterrorism, the news was saying. Playing God with Mother Nature to hold the government to ransom, that was the big story here. That and the plague of spiders that had swarmed all over the town.

When he had seen it on the news, his blood had turned to ice and his mouth had hung open. There was Newtown in ruins and the face of the man that had done it splashed all over the screen. Cindy had been calling him into the kitchen to come and get his cup of coffee that she had made for him. She had given up shouting him and had come into the living room to see why he had suddenly gone deaf. When she saw the images on the television screen, the cup that she had brought in fell from her hand as the strength had gone from her fingers. It had hit the floor like a bomb spraying both of them with hot coffee.

Not that either of them felt it. They were too busy taking in what they were seeing and the implications of Gerald's hunch.

Since that moment, Gerald had always trusted his hunches without question, and so had Cindy.

"Are you still here?" said Cindy coming into the front room. She had snapped him out of his little daydream. He looked at the clock and realised that he had been standing at the window for over twenty minutes. The sun was now fully up in the sky and the town was now fully visible out of the living room window. His coffee was now room temperature, still warm enough for him to drain the cup in two big swallows.

"I had better get a shift on. I'll be getting in trouble," he said. He went over to Cindy and gave her a kiss. She took his mug from him.

"Have a good day Mr. Policeman. Don't forget, you owe me a date tonight," she said and then kissed him again.

"Message received and understood," said Gerald. He turned to go and get his overcoat out of the cupboard and Cindy slapped him on the butt.

"I'm doing the food shop this afternoon, do you want anything?" she said as he pulled his coat over his arms.

"Nah, just the usual," he said.

"Have a good day sir. Love you," she said. He blew her a kiss and then she went through to the kitchen. He peeked another look at her rear end as she went.

Christ kiddo, I hate to see you leave, but I love to watch you go, he thought to himself. He checked his pockets (keys, wallet, phone) and then he went out of the door.

It was a beautiful day outside. It was still early autumn so the temperature was a little on the cool side. He thought that by the time midday came around he would be shedding his coat. He couldn't think of a single thing in his life that was bad, not right now. This was as good as life could ever be.

He caught himself singing along to his car radio as he drove to the station.

3.

Lilly Richmond was trying as hard as she could to get her shit together. She only had an hour before she was due to arrive at work and her daughter Lottie was playing merry hell this morning. Granted, she was only three years old, and what three-year-old child *didn't* play merry hell in the mornings? The thing about Lottie was, she seemed to only start when Lilly had got up late or had some other stressor affecting her general mood. It was almost as if Lottie knew, and she decided to see just how far Mummy could be pushed before she lost her rag and began yelling.

This morning, Lottie wanted to go and play in the garden on her new climbing frame and slide. It had been her birthday a week ago and her father had bought her the damn thing as a great big surprise. Ever since the monstrosity had been built in the garden Lottie had picked the most randomly strange times to want to go and play on it. The night before last she had been awake at two in the morning wanting to go outside and play, the denial of which had resulted in a full on screaming tantrum that had lasted until three thirty. Lilly had shown up at the solicitors, where she had worked for the last six years, with dark circles under her eyes and a temper that was on very thin ice for the duration of the day. It was no picnic being a single parent, that was for damn sure. There seemed to be no rest bite from it at all, other than when Lottie was asleep or staying at her Nana's house (which she did once a month at the insistence of Lilly's mother. She needed to find a new mate after all, didn't she? Those were the exact words that she had used too and it had made Lilly cringe with embarrassment.) But, Lilly was just about as stubborn as they got. She was determined to make it work for both her and Lottie.

Robert (her soon to be ex-husband) had told her that she wouldn't be able to cope, not only without his guiding light but with a young child *and* a full-time job. She had never been violent in her entire life, but she had come very close to slapping the taste right out of his mouth when he had passed such a judgement on her. Instead, she had bottled it up and used it to give her a steely determination to make him eat his own words. Yes, she would do it, and make a success of it, if nothing else, just to shove it up his arse. That would show him that, not only that he was wrong, but he would see what an awesome marriage he had thrown away on a one-night-stand that he couldn't even blame the drink for. She took no prisoners on that one, none whatsoever. If he had been so easily led astray, then he couldn't have thought too much about his wife or his family. He was out straight away, no messing around. He had apologised, he had pleaded, and she had almost cracked, but the image in her mind of him lying on top of his bloated, ugly ex-girlfriend Penny and pumping away was too much for her to tolerate. Every time she looked at him the same image would be there. He had chosen a fuck over his marriage, so it was done, game over finished.

He had tried to make things difficult for her. He had tried to deny his adultery, but Lilly had proof.

Proof? What Proof? he had roared.

She had picked up her mobile phone and with a few taps of her long fingernails, a message was buzzing its arrival in Robert's pocket. He pulled out his mobile, opened the message and found a screenshot taken from his very own phone, the words that he had sent, and the words he had got back with the picture of Penny's enormous droopy breast. He looked at the picture, a dark crimson working its way up from his collar to his cheeks. He had nothing left to say. He was done, game over finished.

After a few weeks, when the dust had settled a little, she had sat down with him and negotiated with him. She had told him that there was no way she could ever trust him again and it was really as simple as that. He had to accept it and he had to move on, not just for the sake of his own mental health, but for the sake of keeping a relationship with his daughter. He had relented, apologised again and again, and then they had worked out a deal. He could come and spent time with Lottie whenever he wanted, and when he was set up in his own place he could have her stay overnight. That had been seven months ago and he still hadn't got his shit together enough to get his own place to live. He did, however, show up and spend time with Lottie a few days out of the week. Lilly never doubted his ability as a Dad, and Lottie would squeal with delight every time he knocked on the door. Lilly suspected that he hadn't worked out his own place to live just so he could spend more time in the family home. She didn't begrudge him either.

He had arrived on her birthday dead on five o'clock with the huge box that contained that goddamn climbing frame. Lottie had been delighted. Lilly was a little less enamoured with the whole thing. She couldn't wait for the day when she finally got bored of it and left it alone in the garden to rot. That time couldn't come soon enough, especially this morning.

"I wanna play ooouuuuut," Lottie was wailing.

Lilly's head was beginning to ache. She had misplaced a letter from her bank, telling her that she needed to get in touch to tell them why she had gone over her overdraft this month. She was going to sort it out on her dinner hour today, even though the idea of having to fawn and apologise to them filled her with utter revulsion. She had only gone overdrawn to pay for Lottie's birthday, so she was hardly reaping the benefits of the money herself. Still, it needed to be sorted out. She liked to be organised, it reduced the stress in her life, or at least that was the theory. But the letter had apparently grown legs and had gone off to hide somewhere just to make her morning even more of a hassle than it was already.

"Muuuuuuuuuuummmmeeeeeeeeee"

She closed her eyes for a moment, feeling the anger building up in her system. She was pretty close to just flipping out and roaring at Lottie at the top of her voice to get the hell away from her. But the reasonable and logical part of her mind told her to get Lottie outside to play on the climbing frame, and then she could look for the letter and get everything else ready for the off without being hounded. It was certainly the better option. If she yelled, then Lottie wouldn't want to go to nursery. She would cry the whole way there and then she wouldn't go in. Then she would be late for work, a symphony of catastrophe to kick the day off. Her mood would be sullen and grouchy when she showed up at work and that would be reflected in her attitude towards the customers who, because of their own stress from being tangled up in a variety of legal haranguing would be just as short and impatient as she was. Basically, the day would be pretty much knackered before it had even begun to stretch its legs. This way, Lottie could go out and play and there would possibly be only one more mild fight to get her off the damn thing so they could get going. It wasn't perfect, but it was a more palatable outcome.

"Go and get your coat on, it's cold outside," she said.

"*Yaaay, fankoo mummy,*" yelled Lottie and she hugged Lilly's legs. Even with the stress of the morning, she couldn't help but smile. Soon she was outside climbing to the top of the bulky plastic frame and bellowing to anyone that would listen that she was the king of the castle in her high-pitched baby voice.

Lilly managed to find the letter down the back of the toaster. How the hell it had got there she had no idea, but at least it had been found and she would be able to proceed with her day as planned. She needed to go and fix herself up. As much as she hated it, she needed to look the part for her job, which meant applying makeup and getting her hair in a presentable fashion. She made her way upstairs.

She knew that she would be able to keep an eye on Lottie from the bedroom window which looked out over the garden. She went into the bedroom and over to the window. Lottie was still standing on the frame singing an unintelligible song. Lilly opened the window and shouted down to her to let her know that she was upstairs. Lottie waved at her and then carried on her improvised verse. Lilly stood in front of the mirror and began to put herself together. She docked her phone into her speaker and started up her playlist. She fixed her hair and then her make-up listening to the music. She began to sing along, not well but with lusty enjoyment. She felt that the day, which had started off on such a downer was beginning to pick up. She felt that she could possibly turn this one around if she didn't have too much of a fight to get Lottie to go to nursery. She was certainly better equipped to deal with another bout of stamping feet and sulking, perhaps with a little bribery.

She checked her reflection again. It looked pretty good.

Robert really dropped the ball here, she thought to herself with a smile. She wondered to herself if she would ever go after another man. It certainly wasn't on the radar at the moment. She had everything she needed right here and right now.

"Lottie, time to get ready," she called, going over to the open window. Her hand paused on the handle as she prepared to pull it closed and her second shout for Lottie stopped in her throat. She wasn't on the frame anymore. Lilly poked her head out of the window and looked down to try and see if she was in the garden anywhere. There was no sign of her. A little spring of fear began to well in her insides. She tried to put it to bed by telling herself that she must have come inside the house to either get herself a snack or to get herself ready for the off. Lilly pulled the window closed and hurried downstairs calling Lottie's name, but there was no reply. The fear began to grow in her. Lottie sometimes decided to play an impromptu game of hide-and-seek every now and again. Lilly hated it when she did it, and she was so good at it too. She had spent a fair few minutes looking for her in the supermarket a few weeks ago, only to find her standing right behind her. Lottie had managed to stay out of her eyeline just long enough for her to get a serious amount of panic going through her system. When she had seen her standing behind her, a cheeky little grin spread out over her face, she had yelled at her right in front of all the other shoppers who stopped to watch the spectacle. Lottie had cried, the fun of hiding from Mummy crumpling from her face and Lilly had immediately felt bad. They had hot chocolate and a cake when they had got home and she had explained to Lottie as best she could that what she had done had scared Mummy and that she shouldn't do it again. They had spent the rest of the evening watching Disney films and eating far too much junk food. All-in-all that day had ended on a high and a valuable lesson had been learned.

Right now, she was bubbling with a combination of anger and fear. If she was hiding from her then she was going to tell her off again which was going to end in tears, if she wasn't…….

She tore the back door open and shouted her name. Her voice was getting higher and more panicky each time she yelled.

"Please don't hide from Mummy," she called out into the garden.

Nothing.

She stepped out of the door and went over to where the climbing frame was stood. She looked all around it to see if there was any sign of her.

Nothing.

She was in full panic mode now. Her heart was crashing in her chest and a huge glut of emotion was rising in her throat. Where could she be? Where could she have gone? Where?.......

"Muuuummmeeeeeeeeeeee"

Lilly craned her head around the back of the climbing frame. Lottie was on the floor, her legs splayed out on the grass and the rest of her half propped up on the back of the climbing frame. She yelled out again, her voice strangled and gargling. Her cheeks were burning red and her eyes twitched and rolled unnaturally in their sockets. A steady stream of foam was running out of her mouth.

"Oh dear *God*," yelled Lilly. What had happened to her? Had she fallen? Had she broken something? She bent down to Lottie, holding her face in her hands. "What's happened, baby? Tell Mummy what happened."

Lottie's eyes met her for a moment. There was a fleeting recognition and then they rolled over white. Lottie began to convulse, her arms and legs drumming the grassy floor and her head thrashing from one side to the other.

"Jesus," whimpered Lilly. She scooped up her baby, tears spilling down her face. She took her inside, laid her on the sofa and grabbed the house phone so she could phone an ambulance.

By the time the flashing lights appeared outside Lilly Richmond's house on Corsica Road, she was standing out the front, holding her daughter's lifeless body in her arms. She was screaming for somebody to help her, please would *somebody help her.*

But Lottie Richmond was already dead.

4.

Three doors down from where Lilly Richmond lived was the home of Boris Nelson. Every single one of the houses on Corsica Road was almost identical, as most terraced houses in the west side of Layton were. The layouts inside mirrored each other almost perfectly. If you felt at home in one of the houses on Corsica Road then there was a pretty good chance that you would feel at home inside *any* of the houses on the street, they were so similar. The layout of Boris's house was just the same, however, you would be hard pushed to feel at home inside it unless of course, you were Boris Nelson. He wasn't high on decorating, or maintenance, or even general tidiness. His living room was awash with old newspapers, empty beer cans, and ashtrays that were full to the brim of old dog-ends. The kitchen wasn't much better. He hadn't washed a single plate or dish in months and months. Nor had he cleaned any of his clothes for twice as long. His washing machine had died in a spectacularly underwhelming way. It had clicked the door lock on, filled itself, refused to rotate and had pissed its supply of soapy, lavender smelling water onto the floor. After that, it had failed to respond. It was stone dead. The clothes that had been put into it when it had decided to commit suicide were still in there. But now they had turned into a furry-green collection of mold that obscured the glass window. The smell in the house overall was pretty overpowering to anyone that would be brave enough to go inside. But, nobody other than Boris had set foot in the place for over three years.

That was just the way that Boris liked it. He didn't want to engage with anyone in conversation. He didn't want to have to put up with boring, meaningless chit-chat or anything else that would waste his valuable time. Boris's pre-occupation for now and for the foreseeable future was to wallow, no, to actually *drown* in his own pathetic self-pity. Boris had got on the proverbial bus to self-pity land when his wife of just over six years had been killed as she lay in the accident and emergency department of Wythenshawe hospital on the day that it was invaded by the Newtown Spiders.

She had been coming down the stairs and using her mobile phone as she descended.

He had *told* her about it on many occasions. He *said* that she would hurt herself, and guess what? She had missed her footing right on the last step. There had been a noise that sounded a large stick being snapped inside a wet towel, and wouldn't you know it, she was sat on the floor with her left foot turned all the way around. There had been a ride in an ambulance for her and he told her that he would follow in the car and bring some of her stuff. There was no way that she was going to be out of there in just a few hours, not with an injury like that, so he had stayed back and packed her a few days' worth of clothing and her current battered paperback into a small bag. He was just about to go out of the front door to drive to the hospital and he saw that he had left the television on. He went to turn it off and his hand was stayed by the breaking news report that was playing on the screen. There had been a suspected terrorist attack inside Wythenshawe hospital. He sat down slowly on the edge of his armchair, unable to process that the building that was being shown on the screen was the same place that Joanne had been carted off to just an hour earlier. There was a reported rambling on about the situation and that they had very little information to go on blah, blah, blah. Boris had watched it for around five minutes and then he decided that he was going to go down there anyway. His hand was reaching for the remote control when there was suddenly a loud crash from the television. Some of the windows on the upper floors had burst through and there was something oozing through the broken panes. At first, Boris thought that it was some kind of sludge running down the sides of the building, but then one of the cameras zoomed in and he saw that it wasn't sludge, it was hundreds of very ugly looking spiders slipping and crawling down the walls. He had never seen anything like it before in his life. It looked like he was watching a cheap-ass b-movie from the mid-eighties. The river of spiders quickly became a torrent and then he saw something that made him clap his hand over his mouth. There were dead bodies being dragged out of the windows. One of them had his chest torn open, a deep cavity of red and splintered ribs in the place of his heart and his lungs. The picture on the screen suddenly cut off. He headed for the hospital anyway but was stopped in his tracks by a roadblock that was preventing anyone getting anywhere near the area.

None of it mattered anyway. There was nothing he could do about it. They had a mock funeral for her, not that they could find a body, only shredded pieces of the woman that he loved. The casket had been a full sized one, and when he had carried it with three pallbearers he had felt how light it was and that only added to the sense that none of this was really happening. She wasn't *really* dead, was she?

After the dust had settled, he had taken to staying at home, not bothering with going to work anymore, happy to put in a claim for sickness benefits, happy to send away anyone who wanted to interfere with his life, until they just stopped bothering. He knew what he was doing. He was going to stay at home and wait for Joanne to come back. One day she would breeze through the door and shout his name. Then they could get on with their lives and forget that any of this spider business had ever happened.

Of course, Joanne was dead. She had been bitten over a half a dozen times and then used to breed more of the mutated horrors that made their way to Newtown, but Boris was never going to accept it, never. His wife was alive and well somewhere and she *would* come home one day.

Until then, Boris moped around the house, eating beans straight out of the can and any other tinned food that he would go and buy from the shop at the bottom end of the road. He used to watch television too until his repeated failure to pay the electricity bill led to him being cut off. He didn't care. He was happy to sit in the dark once the sun had gone down, lost inside his own repeating thoughts that would eventually lead him down the road of taking his own life, he was dead certain of that. But he would always tell himself to give it one more day, just to see if Joanne was going to walk through the door and save him from his torment.

Today was an especially bad day. His utter misery and self-contempt had been hounding him from the moment he had opened his eyes. Normally he would have a blessed few seconds as he rose from his sleep where his brain hadn't fully booted back up. It was as if it had gone back to a time before all of this had happened and none of the negative processes that had dogged him for so long now were even present. But, then he would open his eyes. He would see the mess surrounding his bed, the piles of rubbish that were building up all around him, and the crushing weight of his broken life would come crashing back down on him, flattening out the little spirit that he had left. Today there had been no rest-bite. There was no small piece of hope for him. It was upon him before his eyes had even become unglued. He was pretty sure that this was going to be the day. This was going to be the moment that he had been working up to. This was going to be the end of the line.

    He got up and climbed over the junk that was between his bed and the door to the landing. Trash crumpled and crunched under his feet sending savage waves of decaying odours up to his nostrils. He went across the landing, kicking rubbish as he went along, no longer caring about any of it, no longer feeling anything except the hollow place in his guts where he used to keep all of those horrible human feelings, the love, the hope and the need for life, all of them now history to him.

    To compound his misery, even more, his stomach felt like it was twisting and knotting into a ball. He must have eaten something that hadn't agreed with him at all. He picked up the broken toilet seat off the floor of the bathroom and he balanced it on the bowl, He dropped his pants and sat on the less-than-secure ring and a huge diarrhea movement rushed out of him, making him lower his head into his hands and groan. He stayed there for a few minutes waiting to see if there was anything to add to this moment of foulness. When he was satisfied that it was all over, at least for now, he looked over at the little table he had set up for his reading material and toilet paper, hoping that he had remembered to restock the latter. He was relieved to see that there was still half a roll there waiting for him and he reached out and grabbed it. The roll was halfway towards him when he felt something sharp puncture the tips of his fingers. He yelped and let the roll fall from his hand. It bounced on the grubby floor and partially unrolled. It came to rest next to the radiator on the wall. He looked at his wounded fingers and saw that there were two tiny sets of pinpricks on his forefinger and his middle finger.

What the hell could have done that? He thought to himself.

Whatever it was, the tips of his needled fingers were beginning to swell up right in front of his eyes. He leaned forwards, the seat wobbling precariously underneath him, and grabbed the fallen toilet roll. He held it up so he could have a look down the middle to see what had spiked his fingers.

Suddenly a spider emerged from the middle of the roll. It was the biggest goddamn spider he had ever set eyes on in his life. The spider shot out of the toilet roll and ran upwards onto his wrist. He bellowed and shook his hands as violently as he could, sending the toilet roll and the spider skywards. The toilet roll hit the floor again, but the spider came right back down on his naked left leg. It sank its fangs into his exposed flesh. He felt the hot needles penetrate his skin for the second time and he roared again. He batted the spider away, his skin crawling with revulsion and utter terror. It flew across the room and hit the door frame. He heard the tiny splat of its body smacking against the wood. It fell to the floor on its back and it lay still. Boris watched it carefully, hoping on top of hope that the impact with the wall had killed it. It lay in a crumpled little heap with some of its legs curled up and some of them spread out flat against the floor.

"Yeah, that's wha' you get if ye fuck wi' me," said Boris.

The spider suddenly flexed its legs and stood up again. Boris was frozen to the spot, his breaths coming in short, shallow snaps. He thought that the spider would run for it, go and find somewhere dark to hide just like all the others that he had chased and failed to kill. But it shuffled itself around to look at him. It stayed there for a moment and then it charged full pelt at him. This time he shrieked and jumped up off the toilet. He charged for the landing, holding his trousers up as best he could. He went backward out of the door and was horrified to see that the spider had turned around and was charging at him again. He groped blindly behind him and found one of his empty cans of deodorant sitting on the banister rail. He gripped it in a shaking hand and brought it down on the spider as hard as he could. He struck it dead center and yellow gunk splattered from its ruptured body in all directions. Some of it caught Boris right in his eyes. They immediately began to burn as if he had pepper spray blasted into his retinas. He screamed, bringing both his hands up to try and wipe the fluid away. His trousers fell to the ground and ensnared his ankles again. His balance started to go. His left foot went down the first step of his stairs and then he fell, his arms shooting outwards in vain to try and catch himself. He fell backward, his back striking one of the outcrops of the stairs. The impact immediately blew out one of the discs in his spine. His legs flipped over his head, and he half rolled, half bounced down the rest of the stairs. He hit the floor of the hallway on top of his head, breaking his neck so severely that a slice of bone punctured through his windpipe. He folded into a heap on the litter covered floor trying with everything he had to try and get air into his lungs. He wanted to claw at his throat, but his ability to move any of his limbs had been ripped away by his savage injuries.

Boris had killed the spider. But, in the wet darkness of his front room, piled high with junk and stinking rubbish, more of them were hiding. They had been waiting for their chance and now it had come. The discarded newspapers began to rustle and patter with the movement of hairy legs of all shapes and sizes. They had a job to do.

Boris got his wish that day, finally. Just before he finally lost consciousness, lying there in a broken heap on the floor, he felt the faintest hint of gratitude. His pain was coming to an end, finally. The last vision before his eyes was of Joanne. She was walking in through the doorway, a smile spreading across her face. She was home. They were both finally home.

5.

Thompson had an inkling that this day was going to go his way. Normally he would hit some pretty bad traffic as he hit the junction of Hemmington Way and Lowbridge Road. There were no traffic lights and no roundabout to control the constant flow of vehicles, so it was basically a free-for-all every single day. He had witnessed some of the most prominent cases of dumbfuckery he had ever seen at that junction, including people taking that hellacious right turn directly into oncoming traffic causing a screeching of brakes and a blaring horn. Sometimes a set of curses and some choice hand gestures would be exchanged. On one occasion it had resulted in two middle-aged men squaring off in the middle of the crowded road, ready to wage war on their way to the office over an inch of road space. Thompson had intervened on that occasion, waving his badge at the two men and threatening to run them both in if they didn't knock off the shit and return to their cars. It normally happened when a driver had got to the point of frustration that they stopped giving a toss any more. Some days it was bad, other days it was bloody awful. However, when he had pulled up to the junction *this* morning he had got the right turn without even having to wait. It was a welcome bonus, and probably one that wouldn't be repeated anytime soon.

He went into the station, swiped his card and took the stairs up to the second floor. There was a lift but he had never used it in all the years that he had been here. He would have told you that it was to help him stay in shape, but the fact of the matter was that he had a fear of the damn things. He couldn't for one minute imagine working in a skyscraper and having to get to the one-hundredth floor every single day. It would probably be the undoing of his entire career. Still, the daily trips up and down the stairs *did* help him to stay in shape, so it was never an inconvenience to him. He arrived on the second floor, swiped his card again to get through the main office door and walked inside. Almost everyone who worked in there greeted him in turn with a cheery hello. They all seemed to like him and they called him by his first name. He made his way through to his office and closed the door behind him, muffling the conversation, ringing phones and tapping of keyboards. He took off his coat and hung it on the hook on the back of the door. He went to his desk and fired up the computer. The damn thing was so old that he wondered if it had a key in the back that he needed to wind up a couple of times to make it perform better. He smacked his lips, wondering if another cup of coffee would go down well whilst he waited for the computer to finish waking up. He decided that it was a good idea and he took himself off to the modest kitchen area halfway down the office floor. He went in and he found John Wells, his partner of the last two years pouring himself a cup from the filter machine.

"You must have read my mind," he said. Wells jumped as if he had been goosed.

"Christ Ged, you gave me a start," he said. He pulled another mug off the hook and filled it for Thompson.

"So, what's new today?" said Thompson.

"I'm gonna quit. I swear on my mother's cracked old arse that I'm gonna quit," said Wells.

Thompson rolled his eyes. Wells had been talking about quitting since day one. "Roberts giving you grief?"

"Grief? How about giving me shit to walk in every day of the fucking week. Has he got nothing to do but sift through the scum pile and give me all the crap that's at the bottom? Jesus. It's enough to drive you mad."

"Got you typing his reports has he?" said Thompson. He was purposefully needling him. There was nothing finer on this earth than listening to Wells rant and rave. For him, it was an art form.

"You would think that he learned how to fuckin' type by now wouldn't you. He's in charge of our collective destiny and he doesn't have the brains that God gave to a gopher. I'm tempted just to fuck them all up so that he gets in trouble, but I would never hear the end of it. In fact, on the day I do get out of here, I'm gonna stand on his desk, drop my pants and take a big dump right on his laptop. Let's see if he can figure out how to deal with that one. Stupid arsehole."

Wells fell silent, milked the coffees and took a sip out of his cup whilst Thompson stifled a laugh.

"Why don't I have a word, see if there's anything brewing for us to go and have a look at. I think we could both do with some time out on the road, what do you say?" said Thompson.

"I say yes please, chief," said Wells and handed Thompson his cup.

"Leave him to me. In the meantime, stop griping and get typing," said Thompson with a grin.

"Fuck you and the horse you rode in on chief," said Wells. He left on Thompson's laughter and made his way to his desk. Thompson took a sip of coffee. It was a little too hot to be enjoyed properly. It needed to sit for a little while. He slowly made his way to Robert's office and tapped on the door. The door was made of clear glass, save for Robert's name emblazoned on it in large black letters. Thompson had told Wells that he had that done just so he could have something to wank over. Wells had sprayed his mouthful of ham and cheese panini all over his desk when he had heard that one. Roberts had come out of his office to ask him what the hell he was playing at? The two men had roared with laughter until Roberts had left them be, shaking his head as he went back into his little room.

He waved to Roberts, who was busy on the phone. Robert saw him and beckoned him inside. Thompson pushed through the door, mindful to not let his hand touch the glass. Roberts hated finger marks on his beloved door. He sat in the seat opposite Roberts' desk and tried another sip from his mug. There was a high flush on Roberts' cheeks that Thompson had seen many times before. It usually meant that he wasn't having the best of mornings. He was sounding off to whoever was on the other end of the phone.

"Don't keep phoning me every time another department wets its pants, ok? Deal with it for Christ's sake," he growled and then he slammed the handset down. He regarded Thompson for a moment.

"Good day?" said Thompson, knowing that he was poking a hornet's nest. Roberts was right up there with Wells for sounding off.

Out of the frying Wells and into the Roberts. He thought to himself and suppressed a smirk.

"No, it's not a good day," said Roberts with a deep tone of sarcasm in his voice. "It seems that our jurisdiction is now awash with dim-witted, imbecilic perpetrators of crimes which baffle me beyond measure. Already this morning, five people have been sectioned under the mental health act, one of whom was rabbit-hopping down the bonnets of a line of parked cars. He was as naked as the day he was born and he had a set of keys sticking out of his rectum. Good day? How about a smash and grab over on the east side of Hemmington City, except these jokers backed a car into an ATM and tried to drag it away with elasticated climbing ropes. Needless to say, one of them broke and somehow managed to blind one of the suspects in his left eye and he's talking about compensation. I ask you, compensation! The whole world around us is going mad and you are asking me if I'm having a good day. Jesus H. Christ. I hope that you are in a state of mind to do some real police work today Detective Thompson because the mood has most definitely been set."

Thompson shrugged, "That's what I'm here for."

Roberts sighed and he threw a skinny file at him. "Here's something for you. A three-year-old girl was killed in her back garden. Uniform is already down there and they have the area sealed off. We are waiting for a post-mortem and as you can probably understand the parents are pretty distraught."

Thompson nodded. "I'm guessing that the details are a little sketchy."

"Correct. I need you to get down there and have a look around, see if you can see any clues as to what happened. Once you have assessed then you can get forensics in should there be a need. Any questions?" said Roberts.

"Is this a two-man job, as per protocol?"

Roberts stuck his tongue into his cheek and raised an eyebrow at him. "I take it you want to get Wells off his desk and out into the real world?"

"It's all good experience for him, isn't it? After all, he might be replacing me one day soon," said Thompson.

"You're not thinking of leaving us, are you?"

"Only since I met you," said Thompson.

Roberts managed a smile. "You got a big mouth Thompson, I won't miss it one bit. Do you really want that little weasel on the road with you?"

Thompson nodded.

"Then be gone, Thompson. Take the weasel. See if you can teach him some table manners whilst you are out and about or at least teach him to chew with his mouth closed. Now, if you will excuse me, I have other fires to put out," said Roberts snatching the phone up again and dialing.

Thompson took the file, stood up and went out of the room. Yes, he didn't care for Roberts, but somehow his blunt style saved him a lot of wasted time. There was certainly no bullshit from the man and that had to be a good thing. He drank off the rest of his coffee and returned the cup to the kitchen before heading over to Wells' desk. Wells was tapping away on his computer keyboard and frowning deeply at his screen. He had on a set of reading glasses that aged him by about twenty years. He wasn't even sure he needed them and that he only wore them to try and make himself look a whole lot smarter than he actually was.

He looked up when Thompson approached his desk.

"Please tell me you have a gig for us. If I have to stay at this desk all week I will take up alcoholism on a professional scale," said Wells.

Thompson smiled. "Get your coat Johnny boy."

Wells stood up, sending his chair rolling backward until it struck one of the electric heaters that were attached to the wall. It made a soft metallic clang as it hit. He snatched his coat off the hook near to his desk. "Let's go," he said.

**

Wells began to relax the moment that they stepped out of the station. Thompson hated to dampen his apparent good mood by telling him the subject of their latest case. He could see Wells' face falling as he relayed the story of Lottie Richmond to him. He knew this case could hit Wells pretty hard because he had a young family. His sons were only eight and four years old. It must have been a tough thing for him to have to do in his line of duty and he guessed that it never got any easier the more that you did it. Thompson had no idea exactly how it felt because he had never been blessed with children. They had wanted a family all along but for some reason, Cindy had never been caught. She had gone to the doctors and there had been test after test, which showed no abnormalities. He had been tested too, having to endure the indignity of pulling himself a hand shandy in a little room and leaving his deposit in a little plastic cup. Cindy had teased him endlessly about it over the course of the following two weeks, accusing him of having a passionate affair with a cup and stopping him every time he put the kettle on just to make sure he was shagging one of the coffee mugs. By the time the joking had worn off he had come close to yelling at her. Everything had come back normal; his swimmers were in fine shape. They had put it down to, what they had called, unexplained infertility. They had talked about adopting, but they had never approached the subject with any real purpose. It was almost as if Cindy had resigned herself to never having kids, and as time went by they appreciated the fact that they had their lives all to themselves. A lot of their couple friends would always cancel on them because of a child being ill, or not being able to find a babysitter. They had none of these problems, and eventually, they started to enjoy the fact that there was nothing really tying them down. Their talks began to steer towards things like exotic holidays whenever he could get the time off and the long-term plans for when he hung up his badge for the last time. He had all of that to look forward to if he could stay in one piece in the meantime.

"I hate these weird ones," said Wells, snapping him out of his thoughts.

"Yeah, me too. Let's try and get this one out of the way as quickly as possible and then we can go back to our usual drink induced crimes," said Thompson

The drove on in silence for a moment until Wells snapped on the radio. It was the top of the hour and the news was just starting. The top story was all about the dead child that they were on their way to investigate.

"Jesus, how did they get a hold of this already?" said Wells.

"I'm guessing that someone must have told them," said Thompson.

"Do you think the press will be at the site?"

"Oh yes, they'll be there alright. Don't worry, we'll set uniform on them, that'll keep them off our backs whilst we try to find out what happened."

Thompson was an old veteran when it came to handling the press. They had been a thorn in his side for as long as he had been a D.C.I. He handled their questions the same way each time, with a cheeky smile and a 'no comment.' It drove them nuts and he took great pleasure in it. To him, the press were nothing but vultures swooping in to pick over the bones of broken lives, he had no time for them at all. As they approached the turning for Corsica Road, Thompson could already see the news vans lining the streets, right on the doorstep of the crime scene. He was going to have to flex a little muscle here. He usually didn't like to throw his weight around, but with these jackals, he was only too happy to make an exception. Wells pulled the car over a few doors down from the house. There were two uniforms outside the door and the ginnel that ran down the side of the house had yellow tape pulled across it. The uniforms had done their job pretty well from what Thompson could see. They got out of the car and Wells immediately lit a cigarette. The change in the law that prevented him from smoking in the car had kept him in moans for at least six months. Thompson could almost recite his moans word for word he had heard them so often. Whilst Wells smoked, Thompson went over to the news vans one by one and told them to go to the top end of the street. Some of them protested, citing the freedom of the press, but Thompson gently reminded them that a child had died which shut them right up. They begrudgingly packed their cameras up and started to move up to the top of the road. Thompson went over to one of the uniformed officers that were standing outside the house and told them to set up a roadblock at the top of the road. He nodded and gave him a polite 'Yes sir' and began to talk into his radio. Thompson waved Wells over, who pitched his cigarette into the gutter.

"Let's get on with it, shall we?" said Thompson.

Wells shrugged, "Can't put it off forever."

They headed to the ginnel down the side of the house. Thompson lifted the yellow tape so that they could both duck under it and they made their way towards the back of the house. For Thompson, the feeling he got of walking into a scene where someone had died never changed, no matter how many times he had done it. It felt to him almost like the place was unreal, as if it was a film set that had been set up for him and he was an actor, meant to say the right lines at the right time. Perhaps he should have been wearing a long overcoat, a Trilby and have a smoke hanging out of the corner of his mouth. Oh, and the hip flask full of booze so that he could blot out the horror of it all. Perhaps he would change his name to Jack Daniels, right Chief? He thought not. He had yet to meet a D.C.I that fitted that description, although he knew a fair few that would shake hands with Mr. Daniels after a long shift. The reality was that an investigation like this was as far removed from the almost romanticised version that you would see in a film or a television show, but if you didn't harden to it quickly then Mr. Daniels would start to set up shop.

The garden looked like any other average garden. He scanned it, looking for something to jump out at him to indicate what the hell had gone on. But, everything looked quiet and normal. He walked forwards slowly, Wells following just behind him also looking around for anything obvious.

"What do you think boss?" said Wells.

Thompson shrugged. "Nothing out of place here."

"Shall we take a look inside?" said Wells.

"Sure," said Thompson and they started to walk towards the back door. They were nearly at the door when Thompson felt something pop under his foot. He stopped in his tracks and lifted his shoe from the floor. On the floor was a crunched-up spider. It looked like a pretty impressive house spider, the sort of spider that would send Cindy screaming from the room. The mashed body was lying in a small pool of yellowing goo that had burst from its body when Gerald's foot came down on it.

"That's gross," said Wells, peering over his shoulder. "I hate spiders, I fuckin' hate them."

"They don't speak too highly of you either," said Gerald. He wiped his foot on the grass and then he turned back towards the back door. He started to move forwards again and something caught his eye. He stopped in his tracks and turned to look at the manhole to his left. The cover looked as though it had been displaced, only slightly, but Thompson saw it. Curiosity began to pinch at the back of his mind. What this had to do with their investigation, he had no idea, but….

Just a hunch….

"We should get forensics in here," said Wells.

"We will," said Gerald. He was fumbling a pack of latex gloves from his pocket. "But I want to see what's under that manhole before we do. Get your phone camera out, I want you to document everything. Got to keep our necks covered."

Wells brought out his mobile phone and tapped the screen. "Ready when you are," he said.

Thompson worked his fingers around the recessed handles on the manhole cover and he pulled, expecting it to be heavier than it was. It pulled up easily, almost causing Thompson to throw the damn thing over his head. He nearly lost his balance too but he managed to steady himself and he set the lid to one side. When he saw what was down the manhole, he jumped to his feet almost knocking the phone out of Wells' hand. "Jesus," he said.

"Fuck me," said Wells, fumbling the phone and accidentally taking a picture of himself in the process.

Down the manhole, dotted around the deep grooves that made up the waste channels, were the bodies of dead spiders similar to the one that Thompson had stood on a moment before.

"Did you get some shots?" he said. There was silence from Wells. He gave him a dig in the shoulder.

"Shit," said Wells. He pointed the phone in the right direction and began to push the button. He caught half a dozen shots of the drain below them.

"You got it?"

"Yeah, I got it," said Wells. His face was wrinkled up in disgust. The smell of shit emanating from the drain wasn't helping matters at all. Thompson hesitated a moment and then he went to his pocket again. This time he brought out a plastic evidence bag.

"I need to get one of those spiders," he said.

"What in the hell for?" said Wells, although deep down he knew the answer. It was for a reason that people around here didn't like to talk about. Thompson gave him a look.

"You know the reason as well as I do, and you know the rules too. Unusual activity? That's what I would call this," said Thompson. He squatted beside the drain. "Are you going to volunteer?"

"Not a chance," said Wells.

Thompson positioned himself on the edge of the drain and then he lowered himself in, his feet straddling the sides of the channels. He bent down to one of the spiders and picked it up using the bag as a glove. Wells looked on, his phone still in his hand.

"Careful boss," said Wells suddenly, causing Thompson to almost jump out of his skin. The spider dropped out of his hand and fell into the sloppy, damp mess at the bottom of the drain

"Christ on a bike," roared Thompson, and shot Wells a disapproving look.

"Sorry boss," said Wells.

Thompson reached down again and pinched the limp spider by its leg. He lifted it halfway out of the drain and pulled the bag inside out so that the spider was caught inside. He sealed it up before it could get out of his grasp again and then he clambered out of the drain. He wiped a sweat off his forehead with his sleeve.

"Are we going inside?" said Wells.

"No, I don't think we need to. We should call this one in and get our little friend in here sent off for analysis. Do you want to give him a kiss before he goes?" said Thompson waving the bag in front of Wells. John took a couple of steps backward and his heels caught the edge of the low wall that was behind him. He sat down on it hard and his phone fell from his hand and clattered to the floor.

"Shit on it," said Wells.

Thompson laughed, "No kiss?" he said. Wells gave him the finger and then he reached down to get his phone. He paused for a moment because there was another spider sprawled out on the concrete next to it. He went to snatch the phone up and just as his hand went near, the spider suddenly sprang into life and ran with incredible speed towards him. It managed to climb onto the back of Wells' hand before he had a chance to draw it away. He uttered a high-pitched and very unmanly shriek and flailed his hand around to try and get the spider off. The spider lost its grip and flew away into the grass behind him. He jumped up and down for a moment bellowing curses and then he held out his hand in front of him.

"It bit me. I swear to God, the little bastard bit me," he exclaimed in a voice that was reedy and close to cracking.

Thompson looked at Wells' hand. There were two small pinpricks, both of them oozing a tiny amount of blood, just below the knuckles. "I think we should get out of here, and you need to have that looked at."

Wells rubbed at the bite with his other hand. "I'll be fine, don't you worry about me," he said.

Thompson barely heard him. He was looking out over the garden towards the garish plastic climbing frame in the middle of the garden. Lottie had been playing on it when the accident

(Incident)

happened. Something began to churn in his guts and tickle the back of his mind. He had a hunch. He had an idea of what had happened here, but he needed more to go on. If he spread word of his hunch, even to Wells, then the whole thing could blow up right in his face. He was about to nudge Wells and start heading back for the front of the house again when he saw movement out of the corner of his eye. The spider that Wells had launched off his hand and into the grass was emerging from the edge of the lawn. It scuttled towards them.

"Watch out," said Thompson, pulling Wells backward by his sleeve. Wells caught sight of the spider and let out another curse. Thompson stepped forwards and stamped on the spider as hard as he could. The spider was obliterated under the weight of his foot. He pulled his leg back and the rolled-up corpse of the spider came out from under the front of his shoe. It was followed by a nasty trail of bloody pus from the spiders' innards.

"Come on, let's get the hell out of here," said Wells

"I think you're right," said Thompson

They walked quickly across the backyard and down the side of the house. By the time they made it back to the front, they were both out of breath.

6.

The itch of the laptop had started the moment that Braden had been woken by Jax. He took her downstairs and put her some Coco Pops out for her breakfast (with two tablespoons of sugar, dentist be damned) and got her settled in front of the television. He made himself and Mary a coffee and took hers up and set it down on the bedside table. She opened her eyes for a moment and thanked him before snuggling back down in the bed again. Braden knew quite well that that cup of coffee would still be sitting there an hour from now absolutely stone cold. But as Mary had told him on more than one occasion it was the thought that counted. He went back down and got his own cup and brought it to the couch where Jax was sitting. She was still half asleep, despite the fact that the Pops had gone down pretty fast. There was a zany American cartoon (as Braden referred to them) on the television. It made Braden hark back to the days of Saturday morning television when custard pies and casual racism were the order of the day. He wished that he could engage with the vast array of colorful and noisy characters on the screen just to keep his mind off the reports that had come in last night. It was terrible. It was like fighting a drug addiction. Every so often his mind would whisper to him.

Just one little look, what harm could it do?

But he could see it now. Mary would get up and come down to find him pawing over his laptop, that faraway look in his eyes that he got when he was on to a particularly juicy story, or Jax telling her mum that Dad had been working when he had promised not to. He could see the look on Mary's face, that one that he had seen a hundred times before. The crushed, disapproving look that made him feel like the biggest piece of shit in the world. The only way he could ever cope with that look was to be as far away from home as he could get, to be throwing himself headlong into more gossip and rumors, more devastated lives and broken dreams. He couldn't do that to her again, he just couldn't. He decided right there and then, whilst sipping his coffee and listening to his daughter guffawing at the television that he needed to get them, and himself out of the house for the day. That way, when he did eventually look at his laptop (which was a certainty) it would be too late in the day to do anything about it. It was the perfect plan. He just had to come up with something for them to do. The last time they had been out as a family they had done bowling, food, and the cinema to round things off. It had been so long since they had last done it that it seemed like it was due a revival. He kept the idea in his head for when Mary got up. Instead of the look of despair and dread of him being on his laptop, he was going to make her face light up instead. That had to better didn't it? Surely it did. He thought about how excited that Jax would be at the prospect of a day of messing around and eating. Yes, that was absolutely better than a news story, even if it was one about a teen going missing and animals being mutilated. He drank more of his coffee, content for a moment that he had himself a pretty good plan. All thoughts of the news story went to the back of his mind. He managed to feel that warm buzz of contentment for all of two minutes before the questions started to buzz around his head again. If there was someone out there that had snatched that girl, then what the hell had he done to her? Whoever it was certainly was following the modus operandi of a serial killer. Most of them start with something smaller, like a bird, or a mouse and then their kills would get progressively bigger and more violent as they got a taste for it. Who would be next? Would anyone on Corsica Road be safe from them? Perhaps the killer/kidnapper was a resident of Corsica Road. Perhaps they were in the act of shitting right on their own doorstep. Perhaps the lifeless body of that girl was residing in one of their cupboards right now or had been buried somewhere out in those woods at the back of the housing estate. What on earth was the motive? Had they been forced to put up with an evening of loud music coming through the paper-thin walls one time too many. Had there been any disputes over boundaries or poor maintenance, or too many piles of stinking rubbish that hadn't been moved despite numerous polite requests to do so? Start with a cat, or a dog or something just to get the taste of violence in their mouths, then perhaps they would move on to a bigger target.

Like a teenage girl.

That could be the connection. That could be the big story. Braden Benson could solve the case before Gerald Thompson. Wouldn't that be something? He needed more evidence. He needed to look these things up. He could find out if there had been any court hearings in the last few months and then he could perhaps get some names to check up on. He could have a full profile of the killer/kidnapper before the police even caught the bastard ready to hit the front page. Then there would be the slaps on the back, the hearty handshakes from the Editor-in-Chief Peter Farlow, and more importantly, there would be that big fat bonus that he would get for a job well done. A story like that would spike the sales of the newspaper from the tens of thousands into the millions, all because he had done his homework at the right time. Then perhaps he could retire from the race completely, then he could spend all the time with his family that he wanted. And wouldn't it be nice to do it with a big fat pile of money in the account? Hell yes, it would.

He was halfway to the laptop when he heard footsteps on the ceiling above him. By some merciful act, Mary had got out of bed before her coffee had gone cold. Any other time she would have stayed in bed for at least another two hours. Perhaps her subconscious radar had detected him falling from grace. He doubled back into the lounge and grabbed his empty mug from the coffee table thereby giving himself an alibi. *Laptop? What laptop? No laptops here your honor.*

He went through to the kitchen and snapped the kettle on for his second coffee that he didn't really want all that badly. He was just filling his mug when Mary made it down to the bottom of the stairs and came through to say good morning to him. She was in the process of wrapping her cream dressing gown around her middle. She had on her favorite pink fluffy slippers that she had owned since the beginning of time. He had bought her new ones on many different occasions but they would always end up lined up at the bottom of the wardrobe in favor of the moth-eaten pinkies as she called them.

"'Morning handsome," she said as she came into the room.

Braden looked behind him and then back at Mary "Oh, you mean *me*," he said.

"You really are a pain in the arse," said Mary, a little smile breaking on her lips. Braden stepped forwards and slipped his arms around her waist. He kissed her gently on her lips and pulled her in close for a hug.

"So, what have you got planned today?" she said in his ear. The feel of her warm breath on his lobe got that motor cranking up. He slid a hand down across a cotton-covered buttock and gave a little squeeze.

"Well, I might just take you back to bed for a start," he said.

"Ooh, sounds pretty good to me," said Mary.

Braden was about to go for the other buttock when Jax came into the kitchen. She saw them hugging and started to work her way between them. Braden looked down at her and she offered him a big toothy smile. It was just impossible to be mad at the girl, ever.

"So, now that our plan has been killed stone dead, what shall we *really* do today?" said Mary.

Braden's motor had gone into a full-on stall. It was true what he had heard from parents of young children when he had still been a bachelor, that the best form of contraception was children. He laid out his big plan for bowling, food, and cinema to his girls. Mary smiled and clasped her hands together and Jax jumped up and down whilst pumping her fists in the air.

"Where are we going to go?" said Mary.

"Well, I thought we could go over to Hemmington, their cinema is much better than the one near Layton Valley, and there is more choice of eating venues," said Braden.

"Burgers, burgers, burrrrrrrgers," shouted Jax.

"Yeah, let's go and have great big burgers," said Braden, making Jax jump up and down even more.

"What time shall we go?" said Mary.

"No time like the present. Let's go and get ourselves ready, shall we?" said Braden. Jax took off up the stairs so fast that she stumbled over the first three of them. Mary planted a big kiss on Braden's lips. "Don't forget our original plan, I'm going to hold you to it later, I promise," she said and headed out of the kitchen to go upstairs.

I've been spending far too much time away from home, he thought to himself as he watched her rear end work underneath the cotton. Mary blew him a kiss at the foot of the stairs and then headed up. He took his mug of coffee and dumped it down the sink. He went towards the stairs and caught sight of the laptop sitting on the table. He couldn't possibly get away with it, not for a moment. Then a thought blossomed in his head.

You could have a sneaky little look on your phone.

Now, that would be the ideal solution, wouldn't it? Mary wouldn't even know what he was up to. He could have the best of both worlds right there. He closed his eyes for a moment feeling a little nauseous. Did he really have this much of a problem letting it all go? Could he really not just give this shit up and do something good with his life instead?

But, if he really was going to stop, if he really was going to go from workaholic to doting father and perfect husband then surely he should give it up slowly. Perhaps if he did things this way then he wouldn't be going cold turkey and he would have a better chance of success.

If Mary catches you, then it will all be ruined. She will never believe you ever again. You know what happens if you beat a timid dog one time too many, it turns around and tears out your throat. Are you prepared to risk it? Are you really going to take that chance?

Closely followed by;

I'm an addict.

He made his way slowly up the stairs where his wife and daughter were getting themselves dressed. Mary was already in the bathroom cleaning her teeth and Jax was playing some bloody awful dance music on her mp3 player in her room. Braden made his way into the bedroom and closed the door behind him. He picked out a long-sleeved shirt and some dark jeans to wear. He also made sure that his mobile phone was tucked into his pocket ready for his research.

She'll never know. She'll never find out…..

7.

Katie Underwood had only been awake an hour before the police vans and reporters had begun turning up at the end of the road. She had heard a fuss going on outside whilst she was lying in bed, trying to decide if she was actually going to go to work today. She was having one of those internal monologues that usually went on in her head first thing in the morning. It was no secret that Katie hated her job with a deep and resounding passion and she complained relentlessly to anyone who would listen. She could never find the vocabulary to explain just how utterly shitty it really was. In her mind, working in a call center trying to sell insurance to people that really didn't want it was just about the worst job in the world. Of course, the plus side to it was that when she did take a sick day she felt absolutely no guilt about it whatsoever. The number of sick days that she had already taken was getting to the point where she was losing count of them, and she had already suffered the indignity of having to listen to a stern telling off from her line manager Chris Poynton about her *'negative attitude to her performance and punctuality.'*

Poynton was a wanker. He was a wanker in every way possible. From his stupid, wanker haircut (which had a left side parting actually shaved into it,) to his ridiculously tight-fitting wanker suits, and his constant wanker catchphrases (*There's no 'I' in team, bucko,*) which grated on her nerves like fingernails on a chalkboard. Yes, he was a wanker. A top-class wanker. An uber-wanker. A wanker for the ages. When it came to wankers, Poynton set the bar, and he set it high.

She had managed to turn up every day since, but today was beginning to feel like the day that she was going to finally fall from grace again. However, at the last moment, just before she turned over and went back to sleep, she managed to motivate herself to put up with it for just one more day, perhaps even two. She wanted to have just long enough to try and think what she would do if she decided to up sticks and walk out. She was thinking along the lines of perhaps going back to college and getting back into the education that she had largely given up on when she was sixteen. All she knew was that there had to be something more to her life than just this. She knew that it was out there, she just had to find the guts to go and get it. Change was pretty scary to her, but not as scary as the prospect of living the life that she was living right now for the next fifty years.

She swung her legs out of bed and got up with a sigh of indignation. She went and picked some acceptable work wear out of her pile of discarded clothes on the drawers. Her boyfriend Perry kept on getting on her case about keeping the clothes pile to a minimum, and she always promised to sort it out, but she never did. It was an old habit that she just couldn't break. Besides she didn't want to spend all of her free time washing and ironing, it just wasn't her style. Perry was generally a good guy, but he didn't half fuss over trivial nonsense. The moment he started going on with himself, she would switch right off, nodding and 'uh-huh'ing in all the right places. Most of the time he was good-natured and well-mannered, the kind of man that you could take home to meet your parents. Sometimes it wasn't very exciting, but it was as steady as a rock…..and given that the early years of her life had been anything but, she needed to be with someone that she could rely on and Perry was the man that fitted the bill.

She pondered on whether or not she should have a shower, but if she opted not to then she would have more time to lounge around and have a second cup of coffee before she set off for the call center. Plus, Perry would be home from his night shift soon and she could spend half-an-hour with him before she left the house. It was the curse of being on opposing shifts, but Perry's money was exceptionally good and he worked a four-on four-off pattern which gave them enough time to spend together. Everything seemed to work well for them in the basic sense. She would have ideally liked to have a little more spontaneous excitement thrown into the mix, but that was probably just being a little petty.

She decided to go for the shower, after all, just a quick wash-rinse and repeat, just so she could at the very least look like she was putting in a little effort. She went into the bathroom, pulled the power cord and then hit the button to switch the thing on. There was a momentary gurgle from the pipes and then the water began to roar out of the shower head and into the bathtub below. She stripped off her night clothes, checked that there were enough towels for her and then she stepped into the running water. She always washed her hair first, just so she could coat it with conditioner and let it soak. She wet her hair through until it was hanging down just above the swell of her breasts and then she lathered it up with the shampoo. She put the bottle back down on the small shelf just above the shower head when she felt something nip at her hand. It wasn't a terribly big pain, but it was enough for her to draw her hand away and hiss in a breath over her teeth. She tried to see what had caused the pain, but the soap was beginning to run into her eyes and they began to sting. She ran her hair under the water, washing off the shampoo as quickly as she could. There was an uncomfortable throbbing in her right forefinger where the stabbing had occurred. The soap from her hair felt like it was getting inside the injury and making it more painful. She gritted her teeth as best she could and got rid of the last of the shampoo from her hair and face. She rinsed her eyes one more time and then inspected her finger. There was a single needle prick right on the top of the finger. It was an angry red colour and had a large white swelling all around it. Curious, she pressed her thumb and forefinger on it and applied a little pressure. To her utter disgust, a jet of almost solid green pus burst from the tiny wound and sprayed the tiles in front of her. She screwed up her face in disgust and then squeezed her finger again. More green pus came out, this time without the same ferocity. It oozed out of the hole and splattered at her feet. The water from the shower began to disperse the green shit around her toes. She grabbed for the shower head so that she could wash the nauseating gunk that was slowly sliding down the tiles in front of her. She gripped the shower head and pulled it free, turning it over in her hand so she could aim the jet of water towards the soiled tiles. Something caught her eye and she let out an ear-piercing scream and dropped the shower head, sending it clattering to the floor of the bath. There was a large black spider sitting right there on top of the shower head. She didn't know if it was just her imagination but it seemed like the creature had started to run up the shower head towards her hand. She took several precautionary steps backward until her calves were touching the edge of the bath. The shower head was turning over slowly spraying the shower curtain and parts of the ceiling with water. She couldn't see any sign of the spider anywhere. Perhaps she imagined it. Perhaps it had just been a piece of dust or a cobweb that had accumulated on top of the shower head. It must have been, it must...

The spider pulled itself out from underneath the shower head and began to scramble up the side of the bath. Katie screamed again and instinctively tried to step away from it again. She fell backward out of the bath and landed hard on her backside. All of the wind in her body was knocked right out of her. Her teeth had clicked together, catching the edge of her tongue between them. The coppery taste of her own blood began to fill her mouth, making her instinctively want to spit. She took a huge whooping gasp of air into her bruised lungs and began to cough. Small tendrils of bloody spit flew out of her mouth and landed on her bare legs. The pain from her fall from the bathtub was put to one side quickly by the realisation that there was still a hell of a spider in there. She scrambled away from the tub and then tried her best to get to her feet as quickly as she could. Every movement brought a fresh stab of pain across her chest and her lower back which had taken the brunt of her fall. She got herself into a half-standing, half-stooping position using the closed toilet seat for leverage. She stayed there for a moment, taking in a few more breaths until the worst of the pain began to ebb away.

She decided that the first thing she needed to do was to get rid of that spider, flush it down the plughole just like she had done with many of them before. That bastard thing could drown down there in the sewers for giving her such a scare. She grabbed a towel from the rail that was hanging over the radiator. She didn't want to battle the spider naked, there were too many areas of bare skin that it could get to for her liking. She wrapped the towel around herself and tucked it in to prevent it from falling open. Then she grabbed the toilet brush from down the side of the bowl to use as a weapon against the offending creature. The pain in her finger flashed again as she tried to pick the brush up. It throbbed like a broken tooth. She inspected it for a moment, wondering just what the hell could have caused it. She started to suspect that it could have come from that spider. Well, the little eight-legged shit was going to pay whether it was guilty or not. Judge, jury and executioner right here, baby.

She was snapped out of her thoughts by movement out of the corner of her eye. The spider had managed to get itself onto the shower curtain and was trying to scramble its way onto the edge of the bathtub. The water from the shower was still spraying upwards in an almost perfect upward fountain. The damp on the shower curtain was slowing the spider's progress, but it still managed to maneuver itself from the curtain onto the edge of the bath. Katie thought that she was probably imagining things, but she could have sworn on a stack of holy books that the ugly little fucker was looking right at her. It stayed there for a moment, one of its legs still twitching as it slipped on the porcelain edge of the bath. To Katie it felt like a stand-off at high noon, both of them ready to draw their guns when the clock-tower bell tolled its twelfth chime. The heat in the room, coupled with the pains in her lower back, chest and her finger was putting a generous sweat upon Katie's head and face. She was breathing hard and gripping the toilet brush tight, ready to take two big running steps forwards and knock that eight-legged shithouse into the middle of next week. She had almost plucked up the courage to do it, her lips pulled back in a snarl to show her bloody teeth when the spider suddenly started to run forwards towards her. She let out a reflexive scream and took a step forward, swinging the toilet brush wildly as she did so. Her foot slid from under her, having stood in the wet patch that had been put there from her fall from the bathtub. The excess soapy water from her body and more predominantly her hair had turned the bathroom floor into an ice rink. The toilet brush flew from her hand and clattered harmlessly into the bath. Her right leg went sideways and socked against the edge of the bath. She felt something splinter, something deep inside the flesh of her thigh. A raging fire of agony shot up from leg that made the previous pain that she had been feeling seem like a massage session in comparison. The pain was white hot, burning, torturous, utterly sickening in every way she could think of. She went down to the floor, screaming so hard that her vocal cords felt like they were being sand-blasted out of her throat. She took some fast breaths, trying to get herself back under some sort of control. She knew she was hurt and she was hurt bad.

The pain subsided a little, just enough to stop her from tearing out another scream from her ruined throat. She managed to half-turn herself onto her right elbow and the pain flared again. She gritted her teeth together and squeezed her eyes shut until the flare passed. She opened her eyes again and as tears rolled down her flushed cheeks and mingled with the sweat, she saw that the top part of her right leg had been clearly broken in half. There was a huge dent in the skin that was beginning to swell up and turn black right in front of her eyes. She was going to have to do something about it, get help somehow. She needed to get to the hospital she needed to….

The spider was sitting on the edge of the bath right above where she had fallen. Again, it seemed to her highly strung out mind that it was looking at her as if it was reveling in the fact that she was now lying on the floor with her leg all fucked up. She suddenly felt furious at the little bastard. This was all that damn spiders' fault. She had chosen to do the right thing and get herself up and out to work today and now look at her, just because of that horrible little creature.

"Just *fuck right off*," she brayed at it, the last remnants of her voice cracking and breaking as she shouted. The spider didn't move. It stayed exactly where it was. She was sure that it was going to run away and hide somewhere where it could come out of hiding again and torment her another day, another day long in the future after her leg had been fixed. There would be a big old cast put on it, that was for sure. Perhaps she could choose the colour of the plaster. Perhaps she could get all her friends at work to sign it with a big black marker pen. Perhaps Diane, her closest confidant, would draw a big ol' cock and bollocks on it just to annoy her and give them both a cheap laugh, perhaps….

The spider jumped. It actually jumped off the edge of the bath. Katie saw it happen. For a split second the spider was in mid-air with its legs spread out like a grotesque skydiver and then it was sitting on the upper thigh of her good leg. Despite the pain, despite everything that she was going through, she felt its tiny body make an impact with her skin. She let out another horse shriek and reflexively jerked her body, trying to get the spider off her skin. But the pain flared again, worse this time.

She felt a crunch from underneath the swollen and discoloured skin and then she felt as if a knife had been driven into the flesh on the inside of her right thigh. The world began to spin in front of her eyes. She was going to faint, she knew she was going to faint, but she didn't want to until she had pounded that spider into oblivion. She could feel something wet and sticky pooling underneath her. She wondered if she was losing control of her bladder as a parting gift before she went into a shock-induced sleep. Her eyes caught sight of the inside of her right thigh where the latest flash of pain had come from. There was a piece of bone, splintered and shockingly white sticking out of the bloated skin of her leg. A steady trail of crimson red blood was running from the wound onto the floor and pooling all around her. She wanted to shout for help, try and get someone from next door perhaps, or anyone that might be nearby. The final bolt of shock at seeing the open fracture rushed through her body and the world as she knew it spun away. The back of her head thudded against the tiled floor and she began to hitch in one snoring breath after another.

The spider made its way up her lifeless body, acting on the only instinct that it knew. It had to hide. It had to hide and wait for its next victim.

Exactly four minutes later, Perry arrived home.

8.

Thompson and Wells were sitting in the relative safety of their car. Thompson was on the phone to the hospital and Wells was nursing the bite on his hand. It didn't hurt so much, but the damn thing was itching him like crazy. It took everything he had to stop rubbing at the damn thing and making it worse. He even licked it and blew on it in an effort to cool the skin down a little, but none of it seemed to help at all. He lowered his hand and tried to listen in on Thompson's phone call. He fidgeted, not knowing quite what to do with himself. Thompson gave him a look that wouldn't have been out of place at a four-year-old asking if they were there yet. Thompson went back to his phone call, offered a thank-you and then hung up.

"Well, what a nice little turd storm we have walked in on," said Thompson.

"What do you mean chief?" said Wells. He was dying to scratch at his hand again, but instead, he stuck it under his leg where he couldn't get to it.

"The little girl, Lottie Richmond. They are saying that she died of anaphylactic shock. She was allergic to stings. They found two on her leg" said Thompson. He sighed and rubbed his forehead with his fingers.

"That's not what we saw in that garden," said Wells.

"Nope. Which means we now have an investigation, and one we have to be very careful with. One false word to the wrong person and this one could blow up in our faces."

"So, what's our next move?" said Wells. He couldn't resist scratching at his hand anymore, he pulled it from under his leg and drew his nails back and forth across it. It felt like heaven. Thompson frowned, watching him raking at his hand.

"I want to take you to have that bite examined," said Thompson.

Wells dropped his hands into his lap as if he had been caught doing something nasty. "Why?"

"I want to know if that little girl really was stung or if she was subjected to the same thing as you," said Thompson.

Wells looked down at the angry red skin, suddenly worried. "What if it is?"

"Then we know her death was caused by a spider. Then, we will have to get the Environmental Agency involved, and that means, my dear old friend, that we are going to have to start knocking on doors and fetching their coffee until all of this is resolved. I knew I should have retired early, I just knew it," said Thompson, shaking his head.

"Should I call it in?" said Wells.

"Not yet, we need to make sure that it was a spider that bit Lottie Richmond. If her bite matches yours then we will know for sure," said Thompson. He started the engine and got the car moving.

It only took ten minutes to get to the hospital. The roads were pretty quiet now that the morning rush hour had long since finished. Wells felt an uneasy tension creeping through his body, but there was at least a slight reassurance in the thought that if he was going to roll over and die because of the bite, he would probably have already done so by now. Still, there was a light sweat on his head and a crawling in his guts that probably wouldn't go away until he had seen a doctor.

They entered the A&E department and walked up to the reception desk. Thompson showed his identification.

"And what can we do for you today?" said the receptionist with practiced politeness and a painted-on smile.

"I'm afraid I can't discuss it with anyone other than a doctor. It is a highly sensitive and classified issue and I hope I can count on your cooperation," said Thompson. His tone was a little blunt which was out of character for him. He was normally polite almost to a fault.

The receptionist's smile faltered a little and then he nodded and got up from his desk. He disappeared from view for a few moments and then came back. He leaned over the desk slightly so he could talk quietly to Thompson.

"You can go straight through. Doctor Wilson is waiting for you sir," he said.

Thompson offered his hand and the receptionist shook. "Thank you, that's a big help to us," he said.

The receptionist waved it off, "It's no problem, sir."

They went through the waiting area which was littered with a few people sitting in the uncomfortable plastic seats. Some of them looked up at Thompson and Wells as they went by with a little bitterness in their eyes at having someone jump the queue. They went through the large double doors at the back of the waiting area and into the department. A young woman in a dark blue uniform was waiting for them as they came through. She offered her hand.

"Doctor Wilson. I understand I can be of some assistance to you," she said.

Thompson shook, "Well, I sure hope so," he said.

Wilson nodded politely and led them to one of the side rooms. She offered them a seat on two lightly padded chairs which had looked like they had seen a hell of a lot of action over the years. Wilson took a chair opposite.

"How can I help?" said Wilson.

Thompson showed his identification again. "We are investigating the death of a little girl by the name of..."

"Lottie Richmond," Wilson interrupted.

"You know about it then?" said Thompson.

"I was on call when she came in. The press has been actively trying to get information on the case. I've had to get some of your boys in to help keep them away from Lilly, the child's mother."

"Do you know what killed her?" said Thompson.

"Severe anaphylaxis. It's an allergic reaction. As far as we could tell, she had been stung on her left ankle. Her mother however.....she...."

"What did she say?" said Thompson, leaning forwards slightly.

"Well, it was hard to make it all out. She was hysterical, y'know? As you would be in that kind of a situation. None of us could really get any sense out of her. She is on the psychiatric ward right now dosed up to the eyeballs. I wouldn't even go there for at least a week or so if you want to try and find anything out from her. I can get Doctor Rayton to keep you updated with her progress if you like," said Wilson. She looked almost apologetic.

"That would be great. We will, at some point, need to piece together what happened. Did she sustain any injury?" said Thompson.

"No, nothing. Whatever stung Lottie had already gone by the time that Lilly had got to her."

There was a pregnant pause. Wells knew what the nest question was, he automatically covered the bites near his knuckles with his other hand. He felt like a child trying to hide a piece of chewing gum from the teacher.

"We went to have a look around the scene this morning, my colleague here was… stung on his hand. I need to know if the injury he has is the same as the one on Lottie Richmond," said Thompson.

"By all means," said Wilson. She fished a pair of glasses from her top pocket and perched them on her nose. She leaned forward and reached out her hands towards Wells. He hesitated for a moment and then cautiously offered out his injury. Wilson took hold of it and began to prod around it a little with her thumbs. Wells felt a dull pain shooting up his forearm.

"Hold still a moment," she said, feeling Wells tensing up a little. The area around the bite looked red and angry. The two tiny pinholes were sticking up out of the skin, raised up by a small amount of swelling that had been exacerbated by Wells' scratching and rubbing. Wilson suddenly pushed her thumbs together and a fountain of green and red streaked pus shot upwards from the wound and splattered on Wilson's hand. Thompson jumped backward, nearly overbalancing his chair as he did so.

"Jesus…." said Wells in a strangled voice.

Wilson seemed to be nonplussed by what had just happened. She squeezed again, harder this time and a slug-trail of secondary pus came running out of the bite. A smell began to fill the room. It was like somebody had just opened a month-old bag of fruit that had been left on a radiator. Thompson scrambled his handkerchief out of his pocket and clapped it to his face. Wilson finished squeezing when the fluid from the bites started to run clear. She let go of Wells' hand, stood up and headed towards the door.

"Don't move," she said.

She went out through the door and then a moment later came back into the room pulling a small trolley behind her that was full of bandages and other medical equipment. She brought it back over to Wells, sat back down and began to clean up his hand. She applied a small dressing to the punctures and then sat back in her chair. Wells clutched at the dressed hand, visibly shaking.

"That wound was exactly the same as the wound on Lottie Richmond and it was infected in exactly the same way. In my opinion, whatever stung your friend here was also responsible for the death of Lottie Richmond."

"Are you sure about that?" said Thompson, lowering his handkerchief. His face was still wrinkled into a grimace from the terrible smell in the room.

"I would bet my career on it. Lottie Richmond was allergic to stings, we know that for a fact. She had been in this hospital before with anaphylaxis and we brought her back out of it, no problem. This time she had no reaction to any of the antihistamines or the adrenaline that we administered. It was almost as if she had been poisoned beyond any help that we could give her." said Wilson.

"I see," said Thompson.

"Are you going to tell me exactly what stung your friend?" said Wilson.

Thompson sighed. "He wasn't stung, he was bitten."

Thompson paused, wondering if he should say the words that were hovering in his mouth. He plowed on. "He was bitten by a spider."

Wilson's forehead wrinkled into a frown, "A pet tarantula? Or…..it wasn't…"

"No," said Thompson, cutting her off. "It was nothing like the Newtown spiders. This one looked normal, like any other regular spider."

Wilson sighed. "It looks like we may have a problem on our hands Detective."

"Possibly. I'm hoping that this was a one-off, an anomaly. If there is a problem then I need more to go on before I start declaring an emergency and potentially starting a panic," said Thompson. He leaned forwards. "I need to be able to count on you and your staff to keep all of this quiet and to report to me any other cases that you might see coming here. If we get any more then I will contact the environmental agency, they have measures in place just for this kind of thing."

"Leave me your card. I'll brief everyone that needs to know. If I see anything else I'll give you a call straight away," said Wilson.

Thompson thanked her and pulled a card out of his inside pocket and handed it to her. He looked over at Wells who was just beginning to get the colour back into his cheeks.

"Looks like it's going to be a long day for us my friend," he said.

"Hasn't it been already?" said Wells.

9.

During the time that Thompson and Wells were talking with Doctor Wilson, Katie Underwood arrived at the hospital. She was wheeled into the A&E department with Perry half running alongside her holding her limp hand. The shot of morphine that they had given her on the bathroom floor had put her into a semi-conscious state. Her half-lidded eyes were trying to focus in on what was happening around her, but the effects of the drug made them roll over white, the eyelids flickering for a moment and then close again. Every thirty seconds or so she would offer a weak cough and would croak Perry's name. Every single time, he would give her lifeless hand a squeeze, bend down to her ear and whisper *'I'm here babe, I'm here'*

Her leg was messed up bad. Perry knew that the moment he had found her on the bathroom floor. He had seen a broken bone before, many moons ago when he had been a little over fifteen years of age. His brother John had decided to show off the backflip he had been practicing at the swimming baths. But this time he was going to attempt it off the edge of the bandstand in Centre Park in front of Perry and his small entourage of friends, most of which were girls. John's ego had told him that the backflip would be a piece of cake. It had told him that he would be able to pull it off just as well on the bandstand as he had done at the pool. His ego, however, didn't take into account that every time he had done the flip at the swimming baths that he generally had hit the water knees first. It also failed to note that the distance from the edge of the bandstand to the ground was about a third shorter than the distance from the edge of the pool to the water. He had taken the jump, grinning like a loon at Perry and hoping that the girls he was with would be impressed by his athletic prowess and perhaps would want to hang out with him instead of his dorky brother. He took flight, his head rolling back and his body flipping almost perfectly. At least it did until his forehead caught the edge of the bandstand. The impact nearly knocked him out and it sent his body into a sideways spin. The first thing that ended up hitting the ground was his outstretched right hand which then absorbed the entire weight of John's contorted body. It was a no-contest, and John's forearm broke cleanly in half with a dull crunch and folded up under the rest of him.

Perry had remembered that gobbling scream that his brother had made. He had never forgotten it, nor had he ever forgotten the sight of his mangled arm as he rolled around on the grass, uttering curses that Perry had never even heard before in his life.

'Cuntmugger, fuckgibbon, my arm, you dirty bastard cocklolly, my FUCKIN' ARM.'

He had also remembered how he had stayed awake all night thinking about it, all alone in his house after his mother and father had gone to the hospital to put John back together again. He had thought about the bones breaking, the noise it had made, the sickening grinding noise as he tried to move it. It had gotten too much for him, he had to go and throw up, such was the effect it had on him.

He hadn't thrown up when he had found Katie, but the sight of her leg, all bent out of shape near her hip, and the sliver of bone peeking through the skin had for a moment brought all those nightmares right back again. He had cursed so loud that Katie had started to stir. He had seen her trying to move and he went down to the floor and held her still. He told her what to do, that help was coming, and he was here with her. He had felt a numbing sense of something taking over him, the same thing that had made him run to a phone box just outside the park gates to phone for an ambulance for John. And it was, here again, scrambling his phone out of his pocket, making the call and keeping Katie as still as he could whilst she twitched and writhed and made strangled noises in her throat. The ambulance was there in six minutes, and to Perry, those six minutes were the longest of his life. He had never been so glad to hear the sound of a siren in his life. The moment the two paramedics had made it to the top of the stairs, he felt all of that anxiety, that residual old wound fading away and closing up. Katie would be just fine. A broken leg wasn't going to kill her, he knew that much. Yes, there was a fair bit of blood soaked into the towel that was tied around her, but not enough to put her into any real danger. She would get fixed up just fine, perhaps a little surgery, perhaps a decent sized scar on her leg, perhaps a permanent limp and aches and pains during the winter months, but she would be alive, and that was all that mattered.

When she arrived at the hospital, she was sent straight up to x-ray. Perry had to wait around for her to come back, sitting on the uncomfortable blue plastic chair that was in her cubicle. He drummed his feet nervously. There was a surprising amount of people in the department at this time of day. He logically thought that the department would usually be quiet until a Friday or a Saturday night when the head injuries and bruised ribs from alcohol-induced street fights came to get patched up. But it didn't seem to be the case today. Every other cubicle they had passed had a body in it, some young, some old, one or two with oxygen masks clapped to their faces.

As he sat in the chair, wondering to himself how long it would take for them to take a picture of Katie's leg, a long, braying howl came from the other cubicles which made him almost jump right out of his skin.

'Don't touch it…..don't you touch….no…no…nooooooooo'

The voice rose to a shriek and then fell into a series of low grunts. Perry thought that they had probably had a hit of what Katie had been pumped full of before they had carefully moved her from the bathroom floor. She had still yelled out when they had pulled the leg straight, even the deadening effect of the morphine wasn't enough to kill the pain of the bone being pulled back through the skin. The thought of it made him put his head into his hands and wish that the madness could end. He closed his eyes and listened to the bustle of the department all around him. His mind was going through everything he needed to get done. He would have to talk to Katie's mother and tell her all about the accident. She would then filter it to everybody who needed to know and probably a generous portion of those who didn't need to know.

He didn't care for her mother, not one jot, but he had enough grit inside him to be able to tolerate her presence when he needed to. Hell, he might have to up his game over the next few months whilst Katie got better, he might need dear old Mother-In-Law's help. He even entertained the idea of putting her up in the spare room for a few weeks. Christ, now wouldn't that be something to come home from work to every day.

What other choice did he have? He couldn't count on his own family who had never approved of Katie in the first place. He often wondered how he had turned out the way he had after he had grown up living amongst such utter snobbery. It beggared belief. He had never really noticed it until he had left home and had become increasingly reluctant to attend another garden party or charitable fundraiser which, instead of serving his usual liking of a good strong pint of bitter or stout, would have foolishly named cocktails on the menu and the chance to bid on something that you didn't even want all, in the name of a charity auction. And the people that went to these things. How he had not slapped one of them around their big, wet ears was beyond him.

Both of his parents had enough money to last them well beyond their years on earth. His father had become something of an expert on the stock market. He was pretty much all self-taught too, and didn't he just love to tell people about that one. *I'm a self-made man,* he would crow, his hands out at his sides as if he was waiting for everyone to give him a standing ovation. *Bravo, well played that man.* It was such a lot of old bollocks. His mother was equally annoying. She had been as working class as anyone could have possibly have been without resorting to old clichés such as flat caps and fish and chips. She had grown up in a council house, sharing with four other siblings. She had known everything there was to know about hardship and poverty, and yet to look at her now you would never have known it. She had gone from half-a-lager to gin and tonics almost overnight. Her wardrobe had gone from jeans and t-shirt to trouser-suits and jackets that she never put her arms inside, wearing it balanced on her shoulders like an absurd cape. Now she had an outfit for every occasion, including one for just being at home. She had to get changed into the right clothes whenever they stepped out of the house. Meeting one of Father's golf buddies? She had an outfit. Going to a restaurant? She had an outfit. Just going to the cinema for a little light relief? She had a fucking outfit for that too.

Perry was more than happy to reject the whole damn thing and make it on his own, working his night shift in a wholesaler warehouse to bring home the bacon. It gave him a sense of self, a sense of worth that he had never had living amongst the so-called financial elite. Loading up those vans was backbreaking work, but he enjoyed every moment of it. The people that he worked with were rich in other ways. They were interesting, they were traveled and they didn't live inside a bubble. They liked a joint of an evening (or even a morning if they were on shift with him.) They loved to fuck and drink and tell bullshit stories and bad jokes. It was a whole new colourful and gritty world for Perry, and he lapped it up. He wanted to be entrenched in it, to feel every moment of it, to stink of it and to have the sweat of it come out of his very pores, and Katie had rounded off that package perfectly.

From the moment he had met her he knew right from his balls through to the deepest part of his bones that he wanted to be with her. It had been a chance meeting over in the Ash Tree pub which was, at the time, the most popular place to be in the whole town on a Friday night. Perry had been in the beer garden with some of the boys from work. They all liked to be out there, despite the fact that it was just cold enough to put a shiver down your back. They all liked to smoke and it was just too much hassle to keep going in and out of the pub, especially when it was as busy as it was that night. Perry had been sent to get the drinks in, it was his round after all, and he had been halfway up the stone steps which led to the back door when Katie literally fell into his arms. She had been on her way down, a bottle of Diamond White cider in her hand, when she had mistimed her footing on the second step down. She had gone running forwards, closing her eyes and pursing her lips at the inevitable collision with the stone floor at the bottom of the steps. Her mind was telling her that there was no way that this was going to end well. The next moment she felt something, someone wraps a strong, well-muscled arm around her middle, stopping her descent. The bottle flew from her hands and crashed to the floor, spraying glass and white cider up the wall. She opened her eyes and looked right into Perry's concerned face. He had been asking her if she was alright? She had to get her breath back, but she was fine. She had thanked him and then she had seen the shattered remains of her freshly bought drink spread out all over the floor in front of her.

Don't worry, Perry had said. *I'll grab you another.*

And that was how it had all started. At first, they had sought each other out every Friday night, then it had been twice a week, then three times…..until they had ended up seeing each other pretty much every day. They fit together perfectly, they really did, and one day he was going to marry her….he was…

"Are you Perry Williams?" said a voice from above him, jerking him out of his thoughts.

"Yes," he said standing up. The voice had come from a man in a light blue nurses' uniform. He was wearing spectacles which had ridiculously thick frames.

"Miss Underwood has got a pretty serious break of her upper leg, which you probably guessed. The x-rays confirmed it."

Perry nodded politely.

"She needs to have surgery on the leg just to straighten it out and to add a metal fixator into the bones to hold them in place. Other than that, she is going to be just fine," said the nurse.

Perry stuck out his hand, "Thank you, thank you so much. When is she going for surgery?"

The nurse shook "Oh, you're welcome Mr. Williams. The surgery? Well, there's no time like the present, she is being prepped right now. She will be in the hospital for a little while afterward, so it might be worth you going home and getting some of her things together whilst the surgeon fixes her up."

Perry mulled it over for a moment, "I'd rather wait until I know she's ok," he said, "It just wouldn't feel right……y'know."

The nurse held his hand up, "No need to explain, I understand." I'll show you to the ward where she will be staying. They have better facilities up there, and a vending machine if you need a snack."

Perry nodded and the nurse led him towards the lift.

10.

Braden Benson had made it to the Bowl-a-rama on the Redwick Wood complex on the outer edge of Hemmington city. He was planning the right moment to go and look at his phone, without making it obvious that he was up to something. Jax had wanted to go on the arcade games the moment she had got through the door. Mary had told her that they could play on them after they had finished their game of bowling. Jax had protested a little, but she was smart enough to know that her mother wouldn't go back on the deal if she didn't make a fuss so she kept a lid on it. They had gone to the shoe hire and Braden had handed over his high-top converse that he had been wearing on a casual basis for the past three years. Those shoes were battered and they were worn out, but to his feet, they felt like home. Jax handed over her bright green trainers. Those trainers had lights in the heels that danced a little electronic jig every time she took a step. Braden wondered why the hell they didn't make such fun shoes for adults as he probably would have worn them himself. They were handed their pairs of slippery-soled shoes which were as stiff as boards. After they had squeezed their feet into them, Braden and Jax took turns trying to moonwalk across the carpeted area in front of the bowling lanes. Mary sat tying her shoelaces and smiling at them. Jax was cackling with laughter as she watched her dad trying out some Michael Jackson dance moves. Mary finished putting on her shoes and went over to them.

"I can't take you two anywhere can I," she said with a smirk on her face.

"Hey, you can't do this stuff with regular shoes on. You should give it a go," said Braden.

Mary shook her head at him and then she turned and did a perfect moonwalk, her feet sliding and snapping at all the right moments. Jax roared with infectious laughter again. Braden cheered and clapped her on, a big grin spreading on his face. Mary finished the steps with a twirl and then grabbed her crotch.

"Ooooww."

"Bravo, bravo. Nice moves Mrs. Benson," said Braden, still applauding. Some of the other patrons in the bowling alley had stopped their games to look at what was going on.

"That was *awesome* mum," shouted Jax and wrapped her arms around the top of Mary's legs.

"Now then, are we going to bowl or not. I think I'm going to be on a winning streak today," said Mary.

"The gauntlet has been thrown down. I accept your challenge fair maiden," said Braden bowing to her. He knew quite well that Mary was likely going to thrash both of them. Jax would inevitably want to team up with the person who was winning. Not a bad strategy by any means.

They bowled for a good hour. Jax insisted that the gutter bars be put up so she could at least have a chance to hit some of the pins. Most of her shots ricochet off the bars and sluggishly flattened the bright white pins. Mary bowled the best out of all of them as Braden had accurately thought. She hit four strikes in a row and showed off some more of her dance moves when she did so. Jax joined Mary's team after the first strike. Braden didn't bowl much better than Jax. He hit the middle of the pins a few times but he was cursed with six seven-ten splits that he completely missed every single time. When the game was over Braden changed a twenty-pound note into pound coins and gave Jax ten of them to go and play in the arcade. She usually went to the claw machines that gave out little bags of sweets. These machines weren't as frustratingly hard to beat as the ones that gave out stuffed toys, so she would be kept amused for a little while. Braden and Mary knew better than to hang around Jax whilst she was playing the machines so they left her to it whilst they went and sat at a table and ordered some diet cokes. They could keep an eye on Jax from where they were sat. Every so often, she would turn around and give them the thumbs up to indicate that she had won something. They would return the signal and then she would go back to her game. Braden and Mary sat and held hands, both of them feeling like a couple of teenagers. They had both been in their early twenties when they had first met. They had both been young and reckless and they had nothing but fun times, bar the occasional barn-burning argument. Braden remembered those time as being some of the best of his life. Sitting here now with his wife and watching their daughter playing away on that damn claw machine, he was beginning to think that those times of old, the times of his life when he was young, and Friday night was nothing more than an oversized playground for him and Mary to frolic in, were slowly but surely falling into second place behind the day he was having right now. In fact, it would have been the perfect day if part of his mind wasn't somewhere else. There was that little voice at the back his mind, reminding him over and over that he had his mobile phone stuffed into his inside pocket and that with a few button presses he would be dipping into the story of Corsica Road. It was a war inside of his mind. A war that was making him choose between everything he had right here in front of him and going for that one big scoop. That one last hit that would give him the key to unlocking the door of satisfaction and retirement from the job for good. He could go and do anything he wanted with his life if he got that scoop. He could freelance and charge top whack for his services. He could take a year off and write that novel that he had always wanted to write. He could be at home with his family more. It was a no-brainer. But, that wasn't the worst thing. The worst thing was what would happen if he didn't do it. If he didn't go after the story, he would always be wondering. He would always be thinking at the back of his mind....*What if?*

There was nothing worse in life to Braden Benson than *What ifs?*

Oh, that would nag him. That would nag him and dog him for the rest of his natural life. He would carry it around in his mind like a sack of bricks on his back. Dear lord, it would dog him and nag him until it drove him crazy until he went right out of his fucking mind. He knew it would. He wouldn't be able to let it go, he wouldn't be able to sleep at night. He would lie awake every single night with all of it rolling around his head like marbles on a tray. *What if…..what if….what if…..what if……*

He picked up his glass of coke and took a long drink. As he set his glass down Jax turned and gave them another thumbs up. Braden and Mary gave her the thumbs up right back in perfect unison.

"We should get one of those machines at home and put her dinner in it. At least then she might eat some of it," said Mary.

Braden laughed, "That's not a bad idea."

He picked up his glass again and drank more coke. The glass was nearly empty and Braden saw an opportunity. "I just have to go to the little boy's room," he said standing up.

"Oh Braden, you're getting old. You can't handle your drink with your weak bladder," said Mary.

Braden stuck his tongue out at her and then walked in the direction of the toilets. He went over to Jax on his way.

"How's it going champ?"

"Dad, I won *loads,*" she crowed. She was in the middle of another game, deftly working the claw with the little black joystick. She hit the button and the claw descended. It clamped down and pulled up another helping of cellophane-wrapped treats. The claw returned to its start position and deposited the win down the chute. Jax jumped with joy and grabbed her winnings. She tried to stuff them into her pockets. But they were already full of her previous gains.

"Dad can you look after these?" she said handing the winnings to him.

"No problem," he said. He took the sweets from her and put them in the pocket of his sports coat. He leaned in and kissed her on the cheek. "Be back in a sec. There is a coke on the table for you."

"'K Dad," she said and went back to her game.

Braden went off into the toilets. It was still pretty early so there weren't many people around. The toilets were completely empty and still smelling clean and fresh. He went into one of the cubicles, put the seat down and made himself comfortable. He whipped his phone out of his pocket and began to pummel the screen with his finger. He looked at the local news first, and the story of Lottie Richmond was right at the top in big bold letters.

TODDLER KILLED IN HER BACK GARDEN

"Shit," said Braden, probably a little too loud. He was still alone in the toilets, but it still wouldn't be good for someone to walk in right now and hear him talking to himself. He scrolled through the report, speed reading it and picking out the titbits of information that he needed.

Corsica Road.

Lottie Richmond had lived on Corsica Road.

"Fuckin' bingo," Braden said, again having to check the volume of his voice. His fingers worked the screen as fast as they could go, his eyes skimming the writing for any information that he could get.

He stopped for a moment at the picture of Lottie Richmond's nursery photograph. Her hair was about as blonde as you could get without actually being white. It was tied up in a top ponytail and held in place with a bright pink scrunchy. She was smiling in the picture, her little baby teeth held together in almost a snarl. Her grin looked like one of a child who was somewhat mischievous but at the same time bright as a button, sharp, intelligent, a future genius in the making. Braden shuddered and a wave of disgust ran through him. It was easy for stuff like this to get to him. He had a daughter. If anyone put a hand on her so help him, God, he would….

He shook it off. He had to get to the meat of the problem. What had happened to her? He scrolled again and found the picture of the pale and tear-stained face of Lilly Richmond. He lingered on it for a moment and then moved on, not wanting to imagine how she must have been feeling right now, it was too horrible to imagine, even for a moment.

Insect sting.

He paused at that line and read it again.

….caused by a possible insect sting.

His mind went back to the mutilated cat that had found its way back home. The pictures of its swollen and bitten body, the broken eye hanging out of its socket. Was there a connection? There had to be a connection.

Bingo.

Whatever had injured that cat had to have been the same thing that had put the screws to Lottie Richmond. That was the connection, that was the story. It looked to Braden that nobody had worked it out yet.

You gotta move fast boyo….

He didn't realise it, but his heart rate had picked up and a sweat had broken on his forehead. The thrill of the potential chase was upon him, that same rush that he had got from the very first day he began as a journalist. His fever was short-lived, as the reality of what he was about to do struck him. He was about to go out there and tell his wife and his daughter that their ideal day out was over and he was going to chase the story. There would be the shocked looks upon their faces and then the realisation that he had gone against his word, then there would be the tears from Jax. She would be so upset and she would cry, and that was the sound that jabbed long and sharp daggers into his heart. Then there would be a row with Mary. She would call him all the names under the sun, and she would be perfectly entitled to do so. She didn't understand how much this would change their lives, how much easier it would be after he got his one big payoff. She had no long-term vision for the rest of their lives. She didn't have the worry of what they were going to do for money during the wilderness of middle age. She didn't get that he was just trying to do the best he could for all of them, to ensure that they didn't have to live in the poor house for the rest of their lives. And what about the fact that he had done everything he could for her *and* for Jax the whole time he had been chasing the news. He had to put the hours in he just *had to.* That was the nature of the job after all.

He took a deep breath, trying to get his head to make sense of it all. There was no easy option on this one. If he wanted to go for it then it had to be done now. He had to get back into town which was going to take at least half-an-hour, barring any traffic. Now that the story was breaking, someone would put two-and-two together soon enough. What choice did he have?

There is always a choice kiddo, always. You just have to make sure that you make good ones.

That was the voice of his dead father echoing around his mind. The man that had tried in vain to show him right from wrong. His father and Mary had always got along very well. He understood what a pain in the arse that Braden was, and how he never seemed to put Mary's needs before his own. He hated Braden's line of work, but he had the good sense not to voice his opinion too much, after all, it was Braden's choice to do what he did. There were a thousand other occupations that he could have taken up with the skills and qualifications that he had, but he chose to sensationalise the suffering of others, as he had so eloquently put it. But, his father wasn't here anymore and he couldn't help but think that if someone had got off their backside and done something then those damn spiders would have never made it to Newtown and his father might still be around. Yes, it played heavily on his mind and it had done from the day that it had happened. Perhaps now, with the death of the little girl, that he could perhaps come up with something, just a little something that the police had missed that could blow the whole case wide open.

    He was rationalising again. He was trying as hard as he could to justify his ruining of their perfect day out. The bottom line was he was going to have to sacrifice something. He was either going to have to give up his nest egg or he was going to have to hurt his family again. He was leaning on the side of just letting it go, making good on his promise and then his phone buzzed in his hand. He had an email. It was an email from his informer, his man on the inside. He opened the message and read it through. Then he read it through again. The content of the message changed everything. This wasn't just a story now, it was a mission.

He made his way out of the cubicle, out of the toilets and back over to where Mary was sitting with Jax. They were giggling about something, their smiles almost identical, save for the gaps in Jax's teeth.

"Where have you been, I was just about to send Jax in after you. Are we....." she broke off when she saw the look on his face. A bolt of dread went through her. She had seen that look on his face far too many times. She had really believed that she would never see that look again, especially after last night, especially after today had got off to such a good start.

"Braden?" she said. Perhaps it wasn't what she thought. She was praying to God that she was wrong.

Please, don't let him do this, don't let him.....please, not today....please...

"I have to go," he said in a quiet voice. He couldn't meet her eyes. He couldn't watch her heart break right in front of him, not again.

Stop this....stop it, stopitstopitstopit...

But he couldn't stop it. He couldn't let this one last opportunity go. She would see sense when he came back with his nest egg and his p45. She would forgive him, she would see.

"Daddy? Where are you going?" said Jax. Even she had seen this too many times. The tears were already building in her eyes. Yes, even she knew he was selling them out for one last story.

Mary didn't even spare him the dignity of going outside to chew him out where Jax couldn't witness it. She stood up, bumping the table. The glasses on the surface gossiped briefly.

"You *bastard*. You PROMISED!" she screamed at him. The bowling lanes fell silent and every head turned to look at them.

"I....I...I have to, just this one last time, that will be it, I prom..." He cut it off, he couldn't ever make a promise ever again, not now.

"I don't want to hear another word from you. I've put up with this shit for long enough, *long enough*." Jax covered her eyes and began to sob uncontrollably. Braden put out his hand to try and console her and Mary slapped it away, *hard.* "Don't you *fucking touch her*," Mary shrieked.

Braden opened and closed his mouth. He was at a loss. He wanted to say something, just something that could make her understand. But he saw the blazing fury in her eyes and he knew that she wouldn't listen. He just stood there for a moment and Mary gathered Jax up and held her whilst she cried her little heart out.

"Well, what the fuck are you waiting for? Go and chase your little story. Forget about us, your *family* who have stood by you all these years." She leveled a finger at him, "When you are done playing mister newsman you can come and pick up your things and get out of our house. I won't put my daughter through this anymore. Now *get out of my sight,"* she yelled at him, her cheeks turning a shade of scarlet with the force of her shout. Braden turned and walked towards the exit. The sound of his daughter crying seemed to follow him as he went out of the door.

Braden Benson had never felt so low, so disgusted with himself in his life. He had blown it for the last time and he knew it. But, there was that little voice in his mind again that was talking to him.

Make it worth it. Make it worth it and she will take you back.

He had to believe it, he had to.

11.

Doctor Forbes, the orthopedic surgeon had just finished making his first incision on the broken leg of Katie Underwood when his patient began to have trouble breathing. The ventilator began to sound its alarm, sending Doctor Ochre to the top end of the prone body on the operating table.

"What in the blue hell is going on?" Forbes roared.

Ochre ignored his anger, as she always did. He was a cantankerous old fuck at the best of times. She pulled the ventilator off and shone a light down the tube that was holding Katie's windpipe open.

"I can see something, a blockage. Hold on for a second," said Ochre. Whatever it was down there, it was almost fully blocking Katie's airway. Perhaps it was a piece of chewing gum or a dislodged tooth from her fall that she had sucked down as she went under. It had happened before, she could deal with it, no sweat. She grabbed the thin, long grippers, the same ones she had used for a thousand other problems just like this one and she delved into the tube. She managed to get hold of the object with her first go and a moment later it was lying in a metal dish on the counter. Ochre reconnected the breathing tube and Katie began to take in the correct amount of breath again.

"Can we carry on without a fucking circus now?" said Forbes, the bloody scalpel still in his hand.

"Yes Doctor," said Ochre. She tried to hide her contempt for Forbes in her voice, but she didn't quite pull it off. He shot her a look that could have stopped a clock.

"Sorry Doctor," she said quickly.

Forbes went back to work, with a shake of his head and Ochre took a moment to go and see what it was that she had just pulled from the throat of their patient. She picked up the dish and looked into it with a frown. She couldn't make out what it was exactly. It looked to her like a black date with strings attached to it. She prodded the thing with her thinly gloved finger for a moment, trying to work out exactly what it was. Was it soft or hard? Was it a piece of food or something else? She just couldn't work it out.

Suddenly the thing in the dish came to life. Ochre quickly realised that it wasn't string attached to the thing it was a set of long spindly legs. They waved in the air for a moment and then it flipped over. It was a spider. A big black house-spider. It was covered in slime that had come from the inside of the girl's throat. The spider suddenly ran over the side of the dish and onto Ochre's wrist. She let out a yell and dropped the metal dish to the floor with a loud clatter. At the same moment, a small flash of pain flared in Ochre's wrist, not unlike the sting of a nettle. She shook the spider from her arm and it fell gracelessly to the floor. It lay on the ground, stunned for a moment, just enough time for Ochre to move forward and step on the spider. The small body crackled under the weight of her shoe and she dragged it back just to make sure that the job was done. She turned back to the rest of the crew in the operating theatre. Every masked face was looking directly at her including Forbes whose visible features were contorted into a look of rage.

"Are you done turning my theatre into a circus, Ochre? I'm trying to save this girl's leg if you don't mind," he snapped through the muffle of his mask.

"Sorry Doctor, we had a spider in here, I took care of it," said Ochre.

"A fucking spider. God give me strength," said Forbes and went back to work.

It took three hours to fix Katie's leg. By the time the operation was finished Katie had a beautifully constructed metal brace on the outer side of her leg. The four metal bolts poking into the skin were holding the broken ends of the bones together perfectly. Katie was wheeled out and into recovery.

Doctor Ochre went to clean down, pulling her theatre gown off and dumping it in the bin. She pulled the gloves off and had a look at the wrist that had been bothering her since she had the encounter with the spider. There was a raised lump there and, what looked like, two pinpricks sitting in the middle of the inflamed flesh.

It bit me, she thought, *The little bugger must've bitten me.*

But that was impossible. House spiders didn't bite, they didn't bite at all.

They don't sit in the throats of unconscious girls either.

That was true.

She decided to go and look it up, just to be sure. Research was always the best defence, she had learned that at university. She set off for the office to go and find out about spider bites. Christ, the damn thing itched. Whatever the spider had done to her, it itched like hell. She had to ball up her other hand into a tight fist to stop herself from scratching at it. She walked quickly through the corridors trying to avoid all eye contact with everyone so that she didn't get embroiled in a new patient. She set her face into a deep frown and kept her sight down to the floor. She picked up her walking pace and then the illusion that she was already on her way to do something important and she wasn't to be disturbed was complete. Her little performance got her all the way to the office. She opened the door and froze. The room was full of doctors and most of the nurses that were on shift. They were collected in a semi-circle around Doctor Wilson who was in the middle of talking to them all. She looked over at Ochre and beckoned her into the room.

"Close the door behind you," said Wilson.

Ochre did as she was asked and then stepped forward to join the group. She put her hands into her pockets to keep herself from scratching the wound on her wrist.

"I'll repeat that again, Lottie Richmond, who died here earlier today of anaphylactic shock might have been bitten by a spider. Now, the police officers who are investigating the death came into the hospital earlier. One of them had a bite on his hand that matched very closely the wound on the body of Lottie Richmond. They have asked us to inform them immediately if any other people come into the hospital with similar injuries. If any of you see anything that makes you ask questions then you need to tell me or the senior registrar straight away. Anyone that has a bite must be isolated immediately until a full assessment of their condition can be made. Needless to say, I don't want anyone talking to the press. Just keep your eyes and ears open. Are there any questions?" said Wilson.

Everybody said no, or shook their heads, Ochre included, although there was a sweat prickling her skin. She thrust her bitten wrist deeper into her pocket and felt a shiver of fear ripple through her body. Part of her wanted to speak up, but she was damned if she was going to be put into isolation. Her shift was pretty much over, and she was going to head home and get the information she needed off her own laptop.

"Right then. There are pictures of the bite on Lottie Richmond's body saved to the system if you need to cross-reference. Let's get back to work," said Wilson and everyone started to move with a murmur.

Ochre started to move and Wilson came straight over to her. "How did the surgery go? Any problems?" said Wilson.

"N....no, not at all. It went by the numbers. The girl is going to be just fine," said Ochre.

"Are you alright?" said Wilson, seeing the beads of sweat standing out on Ochre's forehead.

"Fine, just tired. I'm ready for a glass of wine and my slippers," said Ochre. She even managed a smile.

Wilson clapped her on the back. "Well, you get going. Everything is pretty quiet 'round here at the moment."

"Thanks," said Ochre. She set off for the lockers so she could grab her stuff and get the hell away from here as quick as she could. Her mind was racing with thoughts of her keeling over behind the wheel of her car or dropping dead of poisoning in her flat.

I'll make a diagnosis, she thought to herself. *If I start getting sick, I'll phone for an ambulance.*

It gave her a little reassurance, after all, who knew her body better than her?

12.

Thompson and Wells got back into the car and set off again. Wells was clutching his bandaged hand in a way that was beginning to needle Thompson somewhat.

"Leave it alone will you?" he barked.

Wells snatched his hand down to his side, his face coloured a little. "Sorry," he mumbled.

"You're acting as if you have just had a finger off."

"Sorry."

"And…."

"Stop apologising, I know. Sorry," said Wells, a smirk breaking out on his face. It lightened the mood in the car a little. Thompson managed a smile too. They drove on in silence for a few moments.

"Where are we going?" said Wells.

"Back to the station. I have to make sure the Environmental Agency has been informed, and we can hand in the sample we collected. I don't know about you but I don't want to spend the rest of the day walking around with a mashed spider in my pocket," said Thompson.

"What then?"

"Perhaps we'll go knocking on some doors, see if anyone has seen anything out of the ordinary," said Thompson.

"I don't think Roberts will let us go around asking people if they have seen any spiders lurking about. You know what he's like about the paperwork. He couldn't be more anal about it if he had a whole filing system stuck up his arse. Unless we can convince the Environmental Agency to let us help them we will be doing paperwork on this for the next month."

Thompson let out a sarcastic chuckle. "Those fuckers won't let us wipe our own backsides without written permission and neither will Roberts. You know how it is, they don't want a panic on their hands, blah blah. They probably won't even acknowledge that a child has been killed. I'm willing to bet that our involvement in all of this is over the moment I hand that sample over," said Thompson. There was a deep bitterness in his voice, his hatred of the bureaucratic red tape had a habit of grinding his gears.

"Unless…." said Wells cautiously.

"Unless what?"

"Unless we happen to take a little detour on the way back to the station, go and ask our questions anyway," said Wells.

Thompson pulled the car over to the side of the road. One or two other road users honked their horns in anger as they went past.

"Are you suggesting that we *ignore* protocol, that we choose to break those nice little rules that were put in place in an effort to perhaps save more lives?" said Thompson. He was looking Wells dead in the eyes as he said it.

Wells shrugged and then he nodded. "Yes, I am….I think….yes."

Thompson faced front again. His tongue came out and began to run over his bottom lip. He weighed it all up in his mind. He could very well get a serious bollocking for this, perhaps even a nice little suspension, that would be a nice conversation piece over dinner with Cindy. But then his mind went to the pictures of the little girl that was killed, and to the idea that her mother was still in the hospital, so distraught that she had to be sedated and taken off to the psychiatric ward. He wondered what it must have felt like to have your child killed right there in front of you and have a doctor tell you that there wasn't a damn thing they could do about it. Was it worth a bollocking? Was it worth a month-long holiday without pay? He certainly had enough savings put away for a rainy day, so…..

"Fuck it. You'll go far Johnny boy, you mark my words," he said. He turned the sirens on and hauled the car around in a full one-eighty and pointed it back in the direction of Corsica Road.

It took them just under ten minutes to get there. Thompson pulled the car into the side of the road a few doors down from the Richmond place. The police guard was still on the house, as was the yellow tape. The large number of reporters that had been hanging around earlier had largely dispersed. Now that Lottie Richmond was dead, and they had an 'official' cause, they had lost interest and gone on to hassle somebody else. There were two news crews still hanging around. One of them looked as if they were in the middle of filming. A smartly dressed young man with collar length hair was saying something into a microphone in front of the camera. Wells looked out of the car window at them just in time to see the cameraman alert the reporter to their presence.

"Watch out, here comes trouble," said Wells.

Thompson saw the reporter striding over, self-importantly with his camera crew in hot pursuit.

"No comment, routine inquiries," he said to Wells.

They got out of the car just as the reporter made his way over to them. "Kevin Tooms, Hemmington Local News. Can you give the people any indication of what went on here this morning?"

"No comment," said Wells, smartly.

"But, you had a little girl killed here this morning, and then just a few hours later a young woman, Katie Underwood was taken to hospital with a pretty nasty injury. That's two serious incidents on the same road just a few hours apart. Is there something that the police aren't telling us?"

Wells looked over at Thompson with a frown. Thompson walked around the front of the car and stood in front of Wells. "All we are doing is routine inquiries. The two incidents are unrelated. It's called a coincidence, Mr. Tooms. Now could you please fuck off and let us get on with our job."

Tooms winced and made a cutting motion with his fingers to the cameraman.

"Will that be on the six o'clock news, or the ten?" said Thompson with a smile.

"Ho ho, you're a riot, buddy," said Tooms. He retreated with the cameraman to the opposite side of the road.

"Right, come on, let's get this over with. Most people will probably be at work anyway, so it shouldn't take too long," said Thompson.

They knocked on the first two doors down from the Richmond's house. As they first suspected, there was no answer. They got down to the third house, which looked from the outside as if it had been abandoned years ago. The green paint on the door was dry and flaking and the letterbox was hanging on by one very loose looking screw. There was a whiff of decaying rubbish in the air as they stood in front of the dilapidated door.

"Christ. It smells like something died in there," said Wells. He rapped on the door with his closed fist. The door shook and bounced with the force of the knocks, causing the letterbox to finally give up the ghost and clatter to the floor.

"Shit," said Wells and bent down to pick up the piece of rusting metal. As he did so, the smell of decay became momentarily stronger. He looked up at the door and saw that he was eye-to-eye with the newly exposed letterbox hole. Something caught his eye. He couldn't quite make out what it was at first. It looked to him like someone had discarded a latex mask in amongst the piles of rubbish that were stacked inside in the door. After a moment, Wells' mind deciphered what he was seeing. The mask wasn't a mask at all, it was the face of a man lying in a twisted wreck on the floor. Wells shot up to his feet.

"I think that there's a body in there chief," he said to Thompson.

Thompson squatted down to the letterbox hole and screwed his eyes up to see inside. He popped back up again, his face contorted into a grimace.

"Let's get this door open," he said.

Both of them shouldered the door, Thompson at the top half and Wells at the bottom. The door let go without much of a fight and swung open, spilling Wells to the floor. Thompson stumbled but managed to stay on his feet. Wells scrambled back up to his feet sending wrinkled plastic bottles and squashed cans scattering in all directions. Thompson covered his nose and mouth with his sleeve for a moment. The smell from inside the house was so strong that Thompson was pretty sure you could have sliced and eaten it.

"What the hell happened to him?" said Wells, dusting himself down. The body of the man was contorted in a way that neither Wells or Thompson had ever seen before. He looked like he was kneeling in prayer facing the wall at the bottom of the stairs. His trousers were around his ankles and a humming chorus of flies was dancing around his unsavory end. His arms were splayed out sideways and his head was tipped backward at the most unnatural angle possible. Thompson knew what the cause of death was straight away, and he had a pretty good idea of how it happened.

"I think our friend here took a tumble down the stairs and snapped his neck clean in two," said Thompson.

"How long do you think he's been here?" said Wells.

Thompson squatted down in front of the body. The dead man's face looked like it was caught in one final and eternal scream. His eyes had been stuck open long enough for them to dry out and to take on a phony plastic-like appearance. The skin on his face had taken on a darkened and shriveled tone. The moisture had been taken out of it, probably, by Thompson's estimation, by a week of lying out there on the floor. He was about to pass the information onto Wells when his eye caught something else. There was a small trail of blood running from the corner of the body's mouth onto one of the many newspapers scattered all across the floor, along with endless bags of rubbish and empty takeaway cartons. He cautiously dabbed his finger into the small pool on the newspaper and, although it was mostly clotted, it was still malleable. Some of it got onto the tip of his finger and he smudged it across the newspaper. He stood up again, his tongue stuck into his cheek and a deep frown on his face.

"How long?" said Wells.

"From the look of his skin, a week. But look at the blood from his mouth, it's freshly spilled. It just doesn't add up," said Thompson.

Wells squatted down to look. He saw the blood and the smear from Thompson's finger. His eyes wandered across the body, looking for anything else that Thompson might have missed. Then his eyes caught onto something. On the outstretched right hand, on the first finger, he saw a raised pin-prick, not unlike the one that he had on his own hand.

"Chief, look at that," he said pointing to the hand. Thompson moved carefully around the body and took a look at the hand.

"Oh Christ, another bite?" said Thompson.

"I think so. Could that have been the cause of death?" said Wells.

"No," said Thompson, "The broken neck was the cause of death. He fell down the stairs. If I was to hazard a guess, I would say that he fell over his own trousers…." he trailed off, looking up the stairs and back down at the body. "Taking a shit? Did something scare him? He tries to get away…..and bang."

"And let me guess exactly what it was he was trying to get away from," said Wells, pointing at the bitten finger.

"I think we need to get out of here, seal the area off and call it in," said Thompson, standing back up.

Wells stood up, his knees popping as he did so. "I agree. This is one coincidence too many."

Thompson's eyes widened as a light bulb went on in his head. "That reporter, he said something about a girl being taken to the hospital. I think we should go and have a chat with her, see if she has a bite too."

"I think we should call this one in first," said Wells. He was unconsciously rubbing at his covered hand.

Thompson looked down at the body and then at Wells. "You're probably right. Ok, we'll call it in. But, I want to go and speak to that girl. I need to know if it *is* just a coincidence."

"Good enough," said Wells. They both headed for the broken door.

They were both glad to get out into the fresh air again after the stench of the putrid house they had just been in. Thompson looked up the road and saw the uniformed officer still standing outside of the Richmond's house.

"I have a better idea," said Thompson. "Let's get *them* to call it in."

Wells looked up the road and then nodded his approval. If they called it in then the first reply would be to come back to the station and start filling out the paperwork on the Lottie Richmond case. But they both knew that the case wasn't closed yet, no matter what the doctors or indeed the coroner said.

Thompson made his way over to the uniformed officer, and soon they were on their way back to the hospital.

The uniformed police called for backup. They needed a full team to come down, including forensics. Officer Gardner sighed after he had finished using the radio. His whole day was going to be spent standing outside of front doors. He thought it a fine waste of his training and skills but soothed himself with the knowledge that at least he wasn't going to get yelled at, spat on, or assaulted during his shift and he should at least be grateful for that. If nothing else, he could stand guard and add up the money he was making by simply doing nothing. He glanced inside the broken door just once to get a look at the body. He turned away from it, pulling the cracked door closed behind him. He had to resist a very strong urge to gag and retch, not only at the smell but the state of the body inside the house. His running buddy Officer Weston came with the yellow tape to put across the door. He too couldn't resist a quick look inside and his reaction was far more significant. He leaned over the edge of the pavement and vomited his breakfast into the grid below. The reporter that was milling around saw what was going on and got his camera crew to start recording again. He started to make his way across the road, microphone in hand before Weston intercepted him and sent him packing. Weston had a violent case of the hiccups after sending his breakfast into the sewers. Gardner couldn't help but laugh at the sound of Weston trying to bark orders to the reporter with his words being interrupted by loud, jolting hics.

As Gardner stood on guard outside the broken door, waiting for the backup team to arrive, the body of Boris Nelson began to twitch and shake, as if it had somehow begun to re-animate right there on the floor of his house. The rigor-mortis in his joints prevented him from moving from his final resting place, the lifeless, staring eyes still saw nothing, but his entire shell was buzzing and shaking, causing it to rock quickly from side to side as if it contained a malfunctioning clockwork. It continued for a few moments and then it was still again.

The skin on the left cheek of the dead body of Boris Nelson began to bulge. Little by little the bump grew bigger and more and more deformed. The dried-out skin began to split and tear until there was a hole no bigger than a penny broke open. Something small and black fell to the floor into the pool of drying blood. Eight legs uncurled from the small black body and began to whirl in the air. The spider managed to get itself onto its feet and it sat on the floor for a moment, as if it was trying to get its bearings before it made a move. It might have stayed there for longer but another small black body fell from the open hole, causing to scuttle out of the way. The open hole on Boris' cheek suddenly tore open wider and a steady stream of bodies began to patter onto the floor. As soon as they made contact, they ran for the dark areas of the room and hid away.

13

Perry was sat at Katie's bedside. He was thumbing through a copy of the Times newspaper, trying to engage himself in the reports to try and pass the time. Katie had come around after the operation for a few minutes. She had tried to speak, but the anesthetic had stunted her ability to string any words together. She was pumped full of morphine for now and he would have to wait until it started to wear off before he could have anything that resembled a conversation with her. He was desperate to know what the hell happened to her above anything else. How on earth had she managed to fall and smash her leg up so badly? At first, he thought that she must have fallen out of the shower, that she had slipped on the wet bathtub and gone right over backward. Plenty of times before she had nearly fallen getting out of it. He had heard her swear and crash into the towel rail that they had hung on the radiator many a time. Every time it had happened it had made him laugh right out loud. He would even tease her about it when she appeared at the bottom of the stairs dressed in her 'scruffs' as she called them which was usually a pair of grey jogging bottoms and a vest top. She would get him back for teasing her by shaking her red, and wet hair all over him, causing him to rise from his seat bellowing curses. One time she had done it and he had chased her into the kitchen, pinned her in the corner of the kitchen counters and started tickling her. She had shrieked and dug him in the ribs several times to try and get him to stop.

Perreeeeeee, stop it….. I'm….. I'm…..gonna pee myself, she had squealed through fits of laughter. He had stopped and wrapped his arms around her middle, preventing her from escaping.

Okay then, if I can't tickle you, then I'm going to have to EAT YOU UP, he had yelled playfully. He had buried his head into the smooth, sweet-smelling skin between her shoulder and her neck and begun to nibble gently with his teeth. Her knees had buckled and she had let out another breathless yell into his ear. But then her hands had gone around the back of him and gripped his denim-clad buttocks and pulled him in close. Her legs had lifted up and wrapped themselves around the top of his hips. He could feel her heat, the heat of her arousal and excitement. His mouth moved from her neck and onto her lips and the kissed, deeply and passionately, her tongue darting in and out of his mouth, inviting him to come and play.

Play they did, right there on the kitchen side. The memory of it was causing a stir in the trouser area right now, and then he looked over at her, lying on the bed, helpless and in pain. His insides ached, seeing her like this. His love for her, his deep unremitting love for her glowed inside him, bringing with it a horrible sadness and regret that he hadn't been there to take care of her when she had been hurt. His just hoped and prayed that she hadn't been lying on the floor like that for too long before he found her. The idea of her being there, afraid and alone was almost too much for him to bear.

He could make it up to her though, and that's exactly what he was going to do. He was going to take care of her until the metal was out of her body until she was free from the pain of it all until she could walk again. There was so much for him to sort out. He needed to take time off from work for a start, so he could be at her side for the first few weeks. He didn't really know if he would be any good as a nurse, but he was willing to have a bash at it. He was a damn proud man, and he always liked to turn his hand to anything that was put in front of him. He was always trying to please wherever he could. He knew all too well where his self-competitive edge had come from. He had shared a room with the reason for his main character trait for eleven years, his older brother John, he of the broken arm. John sure was the golden boy of the family. Perhaps it was something to do with the fact that he was the first born, and Perry himself had come along five years later, completely unplanned and unprepared for. It was as if his parents didn't have a clue as to what to do with a second child, almost as if it had unbalanced the perfect little world that they had made for themselves. For John, they had great and wonderful things planned, to do well at school, then onto college and then onto the finest university that they could get him into. They wanted him to be someone important, someone with standing, like a surgeon or even a politician, it didn't matter as long as it was a job with a *title*. Perry was always trying his hardest to compete, or even outdo John at every step of the way. But, no matter his efforts, he still couldn't break out of John's mighty shadow for love nor money, even when he did better at school than John, even when he had all of the opportunities that John couldn't aspire to, no matter how much coaching, no matter how many private tutors he had. In the end, he had become a lowly doctor, willing to serve his local community with his vast medical knowledge. A few years ago, John had come down from Cumbria where he was now living with an almost perfect looking wife by the name of Lesley. They had put off having children over and over again, and that day when he came to visit and they had spent an evening drinking themselves senseless in the Flying Horse pub, Perry had discovered why.

John had confessed his hatred for what their parents had put him through, trying to make him into something he was never going to be. It wasn't the fact that he didn't have the ability to do it, he just didn't want to become a trophy for his unshakable parents.

"I can't tell you how much seeing them again made me want to puke," he had confessed, slurring his words through the six pints of best bitter that was infesting his bloodstream. Perry was shocked, his own half-drunk pint forgotten in his hand.

"They still tell everyone that I'm a surgeon, even though they bloody well know that I'm nothing of the sort, and I never want to be either," said John and took another large gulp of his drink.

Perry had turned it over in his mind, trying to get it all to fit. It was hard to do it, it was like trying to cram a piece into a jigsaw that just didn't quite fit. John had gone along with everything in an almost sycophantic way, kissing arse and doing as he was told, and now here he was telling him the exact opposite had been going through his mind the whole time. Perry felt a pang of sympathy for him. He looked at him, staring down at the table in front of him, his bottom lip twitching and quivering as if he was about to burst into tears at any moment.

"Why don't you just tell them?" Perry had said.

"I have, but they don't listen. They just want something good to say to their rich arsehole friends. You know what they're like. That's why I don't ever want to have children. I don't ever want to fuck up a child like they *fucked me up.*"

His suddenly raised voice made heads turn and the mumble of conversation around the pub die down for a moment. John put his head in his hands and took a few shaky breaths.

Perry had brought him home and allowed him to crash on his couch. Katie hadn't objected, and she never would. Even though Perry had spent a large amount of time during their relationship telling her the story of the mighty John, she quite liked him when they finally met and found it easy to strike up a decent conversation with him. After that night, and after John's revelation, they had all got on even better. John made a visit every few months and he made sure that he stayed at Perry's house rather than stay with their parents.

Sitting here right now at the side of Katie's bed, running through his own personal history, over analysing everything that was going through his head, he knew that he had made the right choices in his life. He had managed to serve himself pretty well, and that any decision he made about Katie's care as she healed would also be the right ones too. So what if he had to have time off work, this was far more important, and if they didn't understand then fuck them, there was always other jobs for a skilled man like himself. He began to think of the possibilities of other career paths that he could take himself down. Perhaps he could be a doctor himself, or even a nurse, spending his working life caring for others. It was a pretty appealing prospect, and he was sure that he could do it.

He was snatched out of his daydream by Katie. She let out a long, moaning sigh from the comfort of her bed. He stood up out of his chair to see if she was waking up, but she had only turned her head to the side a little and gone back into her drug-induced sleep. Perry sat back down again, and let out a sigh himself. Christ knows how long he was going to be here. He would have got out his mobile phone and found a game to play, but the battery was already an hour dead. He folded up the newspaper in his hand and put it under the chair. It was one of those high-backed ones that he imagined old people sleeping in all day in a nursing home. It was amazingly comfortable for a piece of NHS furniture. He laid his head back, tucked his feet under the chair and closed his eyes. The warmth of the hospital was making him feel sleepy. The moment he set foot in a hospital he would start to yawn. Perhaps it was the never-ending warmth or the sight of all those beds that set him off, he didn't know. All he knew right now was that there was no better way to pass an hour or so than grabbing a nap. Everyone else in the ward was silent. He couldn't see if they were sleeping, or reading or doing something else peaceful because the curtains were still drawn all around them. He really didn't want to open them either, he just wanted to enjoy the silence for a little while.

He listened to the ambiance of the ward around him, the occasional footsteps, the rattling of trolleys or the soft purr of one of the phones. All of it was soothing, gently stroking his brain into a comforting doze.

He didn't know how long he had been floating just below the surface of consciousness when the clacking of shoes had pulled him back to the surface. He opened his eyes just in time to see the curtain drawn back to reveal a doctor and two well-dressed gentlemen standing just behind her.

"Who the hell are you guys?" said Perry. It was supposed to sound flippant, brazen, but his voice was thick with sleep and it came out as nothing more than a gravelly whisper. One of the men, the older looking one, stepped forwards and pulled some identification out of his pocket. Perry squinted at it and saw that the man was with the police.

"D.C.I. Gerald Thompson, D.C.I John Wells."

Perry tried to put it all together is his fogged mind. He could never get any decent brain activity on the go when he had just woken up. He was terrible in the mornings. He had once spent ten minutes looking for his mobile phone when it had been cupped in the safety of his own hand the whole time.

"Sorry, why are you here?"

Thompson looked around him. Most of the other patients around him were either asleep or were wearing earphones. He still didn't feel confident about talking near them in case one of them heard something.

"Any chance we could go somewhere a little more private?" said Thompson.

Perry frowned, a wall of defense was being quickly erected in his insides. The police? Why would the police want to talk to him? Did they think he did something to Katie?

Thompson must have picked up on it. "You're not in any trouble Mr?"

"Williams, Perry Williams," he answered automatically.

"Well, Mr. Williams…"

"Perry will do," he interrupted. He hated being called Mr. Williams with a passion.

"Perry," Thompson corrected, "We just need to ask you some questions about some of the goings-on this morning in your street."

"Well, I work the night shift," said Perry, looking over at Katie. "It's a good thing I do or I might not have found her."

"What happened?" said Thompson.

Perry pursed his mouth to speak, but then he also became aware of the fact that other people could possibly listen in. He knew he had nothing to hide, but he didn't like other people knowing his business. He stood up out of his chair. "Let's find that quiet room. I don't want to be too long, I want to be here when Katie wakes up."

"I'll keep an eye on her Mr….Perry, I'll come and get you if there's any change," said the unnamed doctor. Perry caught a glance at her name badge swinging from the hem of her dark blue top. It looked like it said, Wilton…or Wilson….he couldn't tell which from this distance. He nodded at her, "Thanks," he said.

The doctor led them to the corridor which led out of the ward and showed them into one of the consulting rooms. She left them to it, closing the door behind her.

"You were saying?" said Wells as they all chose a seat.

"Yeah…er…I found her on the bathroom floor when I got home from work. I thought she had fallen out of the shower," said Perry.

"Thought?" said Thompson.

"Yeah, but she already had her towel on. She only puts her towel on after she gets out. She never puts it on in the bathtub. She doesn't like the bottom of the towel to get wet off the bath y'see. It's cold when it touches her legs and she don't like it," said Perry.

"She had broken her leg pretty badly," said Thompson.

"Christ, yes. I never seen a break as bad as that before. There was a piece of bone sticking out. I nearly puked."

Thompson laughed convulsively. Perry frowned at him for a moment and then he joined in, leaning back in his chair and roaring his laughter. He felt some of the tension of this pretty lousy day lifting off him a little. Laughter felt good, even if it was a little inappropriate.

"I'm….sorry," said Thompson, mopping his eyes with his handkerchief.

Perry waved it off. "It's fine. If you don't laugh on a day like today, you'll go mad."

"That's the truth," said Thompson.

"Do you have any idea was caused her to have this accident?" said Wells, getting them back on topic.

Perry shook his head. "I have no idea. I was hoping that she could tell us when she wakes up."

There was a pregnant silence between them. Perry had an inkling that they were about to get to the point.

"Did you notice any unusual marks on her anywhere?" said Thompson.

Perry frowned, his bottom lip poked out in puzzlement. "What sort of marks?"

Thompson and Wells exchanged a look. It was subtle but Perry saw it. "Why don't you just knock off the bullshit and get to the point, then I might be able to help you," he said, a hint of irritation colouring his voice.

Thompson held up an apologetic hand, "I'm sorry, but what you have to understand is that what I'm about to tell you is a matter of utmost confidentiality. You mustn't breathe a word of it to anybody until we have all the facts. Is that okay with you?"

Perry shrugged, "Sure it is."

"Right. This morning, one of your neighbors Lilly Richmond?"

"Yeah, I know Lilly."

"Her daughter died this morning," said Thompson.

Perry felt a wash of shock blast over him. He knew Lilly alright, and he knew her lovely little girl. She had brought him a gift of Victoria sponge when he had first moved into the house. He had invited her and Lottie into the house to have a slice and a cup of tea with him whilst she told him all about the street he was moving into. He Liked Lilly. He liked the fact that she had done well for herself all on her own. He also liked the way that Lottie was a little bit rumbustious without being bad mannered and not one of those kids that hid behind their mother's legs all the time. Yes, he got on well with both of them. The idea that Lottie had died was a foul notion in his mind, a disgusting, horrible injustice on every level.

"What happened?" he spluttered.

"Anaphylactic shock from, what we think, is a bite," said Thompson.

"From what?" said Perry.

"We think….a spider."

Perry jerked in his chair. That cold shockwave washed over him again. "I can see why you want to keep this quiet. Does this have anything to do with…?"

"Newtown? We don't know. I really hope not. I don't want to start speculating until we know for sure," said Wells.

"Not long after Lottie Richmond died, we found the body of another resident. He lived at number eight….."

"Boris?"

"I don't know his name…."

"He lives in a shithole. He's a hoarder. The stink from his house when the wind is blowing in the wrong direction is ungodly," said Perry his top lip curled in disgust as he remembered the putrid wafts of Boris shit coming in through the windows.

"That's the guy," said Thompson.

"Boris Nelson, that's his name. Christ, we complained to the council about him over and over again. They said they were going to do something, but they haven't yet. He's dead?"

Thompson nodded. "Fell down his stairs, broke his neck clean in half. He had a bite on his hand, the same bite as Lottie Richmond."

Perry's hand went to his forehead and wiped off a slick of sweat that had beaded there. "God almighty. That's why you were asking about Katie? I haven't seen any bites on her, but then again, I wasn't looking for any. All I saw was that leg…." He trailed off, suddenly nauseous. He fought to keep it under control, his lips smacking and his throat working.

"Are you alright Perry?" said Thompson, concerned.

Perry held a hand up for a moment whilst he got himself under control again. "I'm fine," he croaked. He was about to ask what would happen to her if she had been bitten but they were interrupted by a rap on the door. Thompson stood up and went over to the door. He opened it just enough to stick his head out. Doctor Wilson was there and she looked to Thompson like she had seen a ghost.

14

Doctor Lydia Ochre had just arrived home. It had been a long drive back to Hemmington City. The traffic was unusually bad for the time of day which was mostly caused by enhancement works to the ring road on the outskirts of the city. She had the window open and the fans blowing cold air onto her the whole time she was driving but it didn't seem to slow the sweat that was pouring down her face.

It's a fever, you have a fever, her mind jabbered. It had been jabbering since she had left the hospital, telling her that she was being stupid for not saying anything and not getting some help whilst she still could. She reasoned to herself that the spider couldn't have done her any permanent damage, it wasn't big enough for a start. It was one tiny little bite on her wrist, that was all.

But it wasn't all, far from it. The pin holes in her wrist were swollen and angry. The itching on the skin around it was almost unbearable. She forced herself with all the will in her body not to scratch at it. If it was infected then she didn't want to risk spreading it around. She would disinfect it when she got home, and she would get some ice on it too. Then she was going on the internet to do her homework, just to see if it was possible that she was in any danger. If she was…..if she was….then she was going back to Layton General in an ambulance. That was her plan. If she wasn't in any danger, then she was going to dress the injury, dose herself up with painkillers and then get herself an early night. Hell yes, she would sleep it right off, and then she would get up the next morning as right as rain, no problem ma'am.

But there was this horrible sweat that she had on her right now. It just wouldn't stop. If anything, she was cold, her body was shivering in short convulsive waves. Then there was that horrible *aching* that dug deep into her joints. She wanted to sink into a red-hot bath full of bubbles. She began to imagine how it was going to feel, to sink into that wonderful, soothing water, feeling it enveloping her tired body. Oh, the ecstasy of it! Her skin began to tingle with anticipation. *Soon, oh so very soon* she told herself. The stationary traffic in front of her began to move again. She got the car in gear and set off. She felt a huge surge of relief that this time she made it through the temporary traffic lights and through the cone-lined road and passed the city limits. She could see the tower blocks rising up in the distance, that monstrosity of modern living that had become known as 'Suicide Towers' because of its legendary mortality rate. If you believed the urban legends, at least five people had ended their lives by hurling themselves off the roof of the building. Lydia knew that there had been at least one, a young man by the name of Richard Kane had gone hurtling passed her living room window whilst she was stood looking out over the city and contemplating the emotional and spiritual journey that she had been on in the last five years. She had been deep in thought, in almost a state of meditation when something large and dark and gone hurtling past the window heading downwards. She had jumped backward letting out a surprised yell, wondering what the hell she had just seen. Had it been a large bird that had flown into the side of the building? She didn't know. Perhaps she had imagined the whole thing, yes, that was more likely. She thought nothing more of it until she heard a chorus of sirens coming from below, and then it had been on the news. He apparently was trying to evade capture by the police for his little narcotic business when he had taken one giant leap for mankind on a permanent basis.

It took another ten minutes to get to the tower. She parked in her designated space, breathing a sigh of relief that nobody else had parked in her spot, which was what usually happened when she went on shift. She went to the outer door, pulled out her magnetic key and swiped it over the electronic lock. The door clacked open, allowing her to push her way inside. She called the lift and made her way up to her own little front door. There was a sweet, pungent smell of cannabis hanging in the air. There was something about that smell that comforted her. Perhaps it was the fact that the stoners were more likely to stay quiet and not roam the corridors and bellowing curses late at night like the alcoholics. Her clothes were wet with sweat and they felt horrible and clammy as they clung to her body. She let herself in, slammed the door behind her and turned the catch. She went straight into her bedroom where the duvet was still in the carelessly tangled jumble that she had left it in last night when she had got up for her shift. She stripped off all of her damp clothing, shivering despite the warmth inside the room. She grabbed her fluffy black dressing gown off the back of the door and wrapped it around herself. The feeling of the soft material against her clammy skin was absolutely divine after the sticky wetness of her sweated out clothing. She went through to the bathroom, jammed the plug into the hole and turned on the hot tap. She picked a bottle of her favorite lavender bubble bath and dribbled a cap full into the running water. The water didn't run hot enough to warrant turning the cold tap on which also meant that it took a little while for the bath to fill sufficiently. The smell of the bubble bath began to rise with the steam of the hot water. When it struck her nose, the feelings of anxiety began to ebb away. She would be fine, she would be just fine.

    She raised her hand up so she could have a look at the bite on her wrist. The skin around it was red and shiny with the swelling that had come up around it. The itching all around the site was incredible. Her hand came up in an automatic reaction to scratch at the injury. She managed to stop herself, even though the scratching would have felt so heavenly, almost orgasmic. She lowered her arm instead and went through to the living room to power up her laptop so she could do her research. The bath continued to fill as she perched on the edge of her sofa waiting for the computer to finish its boot sequence. If Lydia had looked down and to the right, into her bathroom sink, she would have seen a house spider sitting there. Granted, it wasn't easy to see it as it was spread-eagled over the plughole. It had stayed absolutely still when she was in the bathroom looking at the bite on her wrist, but the moment she went out of the door and into the living room it suddenly made its move, running up the side of the sink. It couldn't get a good grip on the porcelain and for a few moments, it looked as if it was running on the spot. It sat still for a moment, almost as if it was contemplating its next move and then it shot forwards again with incredible speed. Its legs skidded and slipped, but its forward momentum took it up to the ridge of the sink where it stayed for a moment, barely balancing on the rim. It moved again, this time slipping off the edge and spreading out its legs for the short descent. It landed on the lino-covered floor and ran around the back of the sink column. It sat there in the shadows, hiding, waiting. It had a job to do.

Lydia was searching through various pictures of spider bites, some of them were utterly horrendous to look at. Torn skin, yellow pus, and swollen appendages. Thankfully, none of them looked anything like the wound that she had on her wrist. She thought that she should spend a bit more time on it, research it properly, but the aching in her joints was crying out to be soaked in that beautiful lavender bath. She abandoned the laptop and went to the bathroom to check on the progress of the bath water. It wasn't as high as she wanted it to be, but there was enough for her to get in and let it finish filling up around her. She could lie back and turn the tap off with her toe, no problems there. She stripped off the dressing gown and dropped it to the floor, not caring that she would have to move it before she got out to avoid getting it wet. She pulled the bun out of her hair and fanned it out. Each strand felt like it was breathing a sigh of relief. It reached almost to the middle of her back and even though she was naturally jet black and she was two months shy of being thirty years old there was not a fleck of grey in there, not one. She put her hands on each side of the bath and stepped in. The water was halfway up her shins and the soothing heat as it touched her skin caused her to involuntarily urinate a little into the water. Ordinarily, she would have been disgusted to sit in the water after that, but today she just didn't care. She began to lower herself down and then stood right back up again. As she had begun to lower herself she'd felt her bitten wrist crackle. It sounded like someone was biting down on a generous mouthful of crisps. She thought that she felt it move out of place a little, dislocating itself slightly. She flexed it a little, and although it was sore and itchy as hell it felt as if it was working properly. She shrugged and placed her elbows on the sides of the bath instead to lower herself down. The water felt amazing, better than any massage, better than any lover, better than any meal. She felt as if she had entered the gates of paradise right there in her little tub. She leaned her head back and slid her body downwards until she was as flat as she could get.

Her hair was hanging over the back of the bath. The spider behind the sink column saw it.

It made its move.

It ran forwards, covering the small distance between the sink and the back of the bath in a matter of seconds. It charged up the smooth plastic panel and then it began to lose its footing on the smooth surface. It almost fell, but it put on an extra burst of speed, its flailing legs moving so quickly that they were almost a blur. It edged upwards, just a little, just enough to catch itself on the edge of Lydia's dangling hair. It scrambled into the tangled mess and rested for a few moments. Then it started to move again, this time more slowly. It picked its way through the mess of hair until it found a level surface to stand on. It had found the edge of the bath where Lydia's shoulder was resting right in front of it.

Lydia let the water run. It began to cover her belly. She decided to kick the tap off once it had covered the small mountains of her breasts. That would leave her enough room to top up when the water started to go cold on her. She closed her eyes, wondering if she would fall asleep or not. For the moment, she was happy just to smell the lavender rising up all around her and to listen to the trickling of water from the tap. She opened her eyes and was raising her foot to kick the tap off when she felt something tickling her left shoulder. She reached up with her right hand, thinking that it was just another loose strand of hair from the mess that was on her head and that she should probably give it a good washing whilst she was in here. Her hand arrived at her shoulder and she instantly felt something move. She felt something tickle the side of her neck and a moment later the feather-light ripple of movement went up to her face. She swiped at her cheek, causing the bath water to slosh over the side of the tub. Whatever was there moved upwards towards the top of her head.

She saw it.

For a split second, as it ran over her left eye, she saw it.

Spider.

Panic tore through her body. There was a spider on her head and the dirty bastard had just run right across her face. Her legs kicked convulsively as she tried to sit up, but the bubble bath that was diluted in the water had made the bottom of the bath as slick as a sheet of ice. She grabbed for the small rails that were on the inside edge of the bath so she could pull herself up. Her left hand found one first and she pulled as hard as she could to get her out of there.

There was another crunch from her wrist, louder this time, and there was pain. It was a horrible raw pain as if someone had poured salt into an open wound. It was closely followed by a feeling like something was tearing, ripping as easily as wet newspaper, and then her head hit the back of the bath again. For the moment, the spider was forgotten as confusion scrambled her mind. She looked at the bath rail that she had grabbed hold of. The world shook and wobbled in front of her eyes. Her mind couldn't process what she was seeing in front of her.

Her hand was still on the rail, but it was no longer attached to her arm. She stared at it for only a second, but time froze at that moment. She saw every detail, every little piece of what had happened to her. She saw her own hand, still hanging onto the rail. She saw the little scar on the back of the hand that she had gotten when she had been accidentally burned with an errant cigarette in her first experience in a nightclub a million years ago. She could see the nails, still mostly painted red but in desperate need of a top-up coating. The thumb ring, a gift from an admirer that she had gone out with a few times, but had never pursued because of his terrible halitosis. And then she saw the gaping wound where her arm used to be attached to it. She saw the green and red streaked discharge slopping from the flesh and plopping into the bath water and onto her naked leg. She saw her own arm which suddenly and violently ended just below the wrist, and more of that disgusting, stinking slime running down her skin, that terrible burning, itching sensation beginning to build underneath it. She saw the two knobs of bone, horribly white, sticking out the end of the injury as the skin began to peel away. The ends of the bones looked like they were made of plastic that had been melted by excess heat.

In that split second, she saw it all.

Her lungs went into spasm, pushing all the air out of her body and then they opened up, tearing in a huge breath to scream. That was when the spider made its move. It scuttled down her forehead, across her nose and as she was pulling in her breath to scream for her life, it dropped into her open mouth.

Lydia felt something rush down her throat and lodge itself in there. She tried to get the scream out, but she couldn't get any air to come out. She began to thrash around, trying to get herself upright so she could lean forwards to get her airway clear. The stump of her arm hit the hot water and pain unlike any other she had experienced so far in her lifetime, blasted up from it. It engulfed her, it made her body shake with terror and revulsion. The combination of panic and pain was just too much for her mind to cope with. It shut down and Doctor Lydia Ochre went to sleep.

Ten minutes later as the bath water began to run over the sides, its progress slowed by the overflow hole but not enough to stop the inevitable, the spider emerged out of Lydia's nose. She began to breathe again. This time in quick, shallow breaths. Her eyes popped open, but they saw nothing. The poison in her body began to go to work.

15.

Mary Benson arrived home three hours after Braden had abandoned them at the bowling alley. By this time Jax had gone from borderline hysteria to being sullen and quiet. For a child that normally would spend most of her time singing or play-acting for nobody, in particular, seeing her like this drove a stake of anger deep into Mary's soul. She wanted to get hold of Braden and slap him. Not punch, or stab or anything too extreme, she just wanted to slap him around the room, and ask, no, scream at him *what the hell are you thinking, what the fuck is wrong with you*, over and over again. They had to catch the bus home because Braden had taken the car. Jax had left her coat in there too and by the time they made it back through the front door, she had been shaking like a leaf in a high wind. Mary put the heating on and built a fire in the hearth. Jax put some cushions on the floor in front of the fire and positioned herself so that she could watch television. Mary offered her food, but she just shook her head. Anything that could take away Jax's appetite must have been pretty bad. In all fairness, Mary didn't feel like eating either. Her own appetite had been killed stone dead by the events of this morning. She sat on the sofa her eyes trained on the endless stream of meaningless jabber on the television. Her mind was working overtime, trying to work out where on earth she went from here. There was no way, no way on this earth that she could let Braden back into their lives, not after this. She felt so stupid, so idiotic for listening to his bullshit again. She had bought into it hook, line and sinker. Christ, she had even allowed herself to let down her guard enough to make love to him. Normally she wouldn't have let him near her, not just physically, but emotionally. She had known from the beginning that somewhere deep inside all of his bravadoes that there was a decent man, a decent and loving man who could give her all the emotional support and wellbeing that she could ever want. The problem had always been the job, the rush of the job was his drug, and he had now proven that he was willing to give up everything that ever meant something to him in order to keep at it, at that job, at that stupid fucking job.

    She felt tears sting her eyes, and she fought it back. She would be damned if she was going to lose it with her daughter in the room. She tried to put some practical thoughts to work in her mind to take her away from the burning feeling of anger and hurt that was sloshing around in her insides like a bad curry. He would have to move out. That would be the first thing. He would have to get his shit and get the hell out of her house. She would make sure that Jax was at school for that little episode. She didn't want to put her through any more hurt. Her life was going to carry on as normally as it could. She was pretty used to her dad not being around or being too damn busy to spend any time with her. Mary was pretty sure that Jax wouldn't want to spend any more time with him at all after this. That was something she would have to talk to her about somewhere down the line. Right now...

Practical, practical.

Divorce. That would be a good option. Might as well break the arm clean off then have a messy wound hanging around to start going septic. She was absolutely sure that she could get him on unreasonable behavior, especially once she had laid out the events of today. She would be granted a divorce in no time. That would get him out of her hair for good. Then he could go and chase all the stories that he wanted to without the burden of a wife to hold him back, and good fucking luck to him.

Practical, practical.

This was good. She was starting to feel a little more in control of everything. Control was good. Control meant that she could at least hang onto something whilst the whirlwind of change came through their lives. What else...

The house. She could get herself back into working full time, that wasn't a problem with her qualifications. She could find some way to work around Jax and her needs, of course, she could. She had managed before Braden had come along and she would manage again. She could get enough money together to buy out his interest in the house. She didn't think that he would have any bollocks to fight her. If she stood her ground and blasted him with enough legal guff to make his head spin, then he would give in. He didn't have time for legal shit, and she knew it. He would cave right in and then Jax would have a roof over her head without the upheaval of having to move. Mary was pretty sure that moving house would pretty much finish Jax off. No, she needed security right now and as much of it as Mary could give her. In her mind, she could almost see the dark tunnel that she was about to lead them down. But she also had just enough foresight to see that when they made it out of the other end that they would be a damn sight happier for it.

So, that was that. She had her plan and she was going to start with it tomorrow morning, or tonight, depending on when Braden had the nuts to show his face again. She was going to tell him to piss off and sleep somewhere else if he tried to get in the house. She got up out of her seat and went and locked the front door. She wondered if it would trigger an outburst from Jax, but she never even looked away from the television. She was lay on her side, a little bit like a dog who had come in from a cold garden to warm its cockles against that comforting heat. Mary went through to the kitchen. She needed a cup of coffee to try and get her head out of the clouds a little. As she was passing the dining room she caught sight of Braden's laptop sitting on the table. She paused for a moment. Something was whirring away in her mind. At first, she thought that she might have been thinking that it wasn't work that he was doing at all, but instead the idea that he was seeing another woman suddenly occurred to her. She never thought that he was the type, but as her mother had once told her, all men were 'that type.' She shook it off for a moment, telling herself that she was being ridiculous, that it just wasn't Braden's style. Then she thought to herself that it wouldn't do any harm to eliminate it from her line of inquiry. She went through to the kitchen and put the kettle on and returned to the dining room to power up the computer whilst she waited for the water to boil. She opened up the laptop and switched it on. It wasn't the most technologically advanced laptop in the world and it took a few moments before it finally booted up. To her dismay a password screen greeted her. She should have known. Braden didn't like the possibility of anyone messing up his work.

Well, that's that then, she thought and went through into the kitchen where the kettle was finishing its boil cycle. She dumped instant coffee into her favorite mug and poured the water on. She couldn't possibly know what the password was, could she? She mused over it for a moment and then tried to come up with some possibilities. Could it be their wedding anniversary? Could it be the day that they first met? Unlikely. Braden had a wonderful habit of forgetting things like that until the last minute. Every anniversary they had together had involved Braden leaping out of bed and telling her that he was going to make her breakfast in bed. She knew quite well that he was rushing out to go and grab something that could pass for a present. The fact that he always brought her a sausage and egg McMuffin for her breakfast and the fact that the spit on the envelope of her card where he had sealed it would still be wet gave the game away. She never said anything about it. In her mind, it was better that it was on the last minute then being subjected to the horrible possibility of indifference to the date that she kept burned on her mind forever and a day. She threw that one out of the window. If he couldn't remember the date on a day to day basis, then it was no good as a password. She milked and sugared her coffee and was about to go and shut the laptop down when something else occurred to her. He always remembered Jax's birthday. He had never been on the last minute with that. He would always be prepared with piles of gifts and birthday cake. A few times he had even organized a party or two for her and all of her friends. He had even gone to the trouble of decorating the house whilst she had been at school so he could spring the big surprise on her. He remembered that date alright. She went over to the computer and almost casually she punched Jax's date of birth into the computer. It paused for a moment and then the desktop popped up in front of her.

You see, you should have been a detective, she thought to herself as she sat down. She placed her cup of coffee on the table next to the laptop and pulled the chair up. She really didn't know where to start so she opened an internet window.

"Where to first?" she said to herself. Then she went for the internet history, thinking that Braden would have likely covered his tracks if he was up to no good. The list came up and she began to scroll through it. There were links to several news channels that she knew he liked to look at to see if his reports had made the front page. He had yet to get a front-page story, and that had bugged him for most of his career. He had got some good ones, there was no doubt about it and some of his stories had been incredibly well composed and written. The man had talent, and that fact was undeniable. She scrolled back up to the top again. She caught sight of the date of one of the news sights. It had been accessed today. Mary wondered for a moment how on earth he could have got on the computer at that time when he would have been at the bowling alley with her. Then she remembered that if he accessed the internet from his phone that it would show up on the computer so he could look at it again when he was home. She clicked on the entry and sipped coffee whilst the page loaded. The story of Lottie Richmond popped up and Mary read through it with a small sneer of horror growing on her face. Mary went back to the main page and saw that there was another story about the mutilated cat. She really didn't want to read any more about it but then she noticed that it had been found on the same road as the dead girl.

Another bloody sicko, she thought to herself and closed the window. That's what Braden was chasing? another sicko that prayed on animals and small children? Why would he go after something like that? Why was it so damn important to him? She didn't know and she was about to close the computer down. She was quickly losing interest in the whole thing. Then at the last moment, she decided to check his email account. Through sheer good luck, the computer had remembered his password so Braden could get into it quickly. The inbox was pretty sparse. There were some junk emails asking him if he wanted to get himself a nice solicitor so that he could rinse a load of banks and building societies for insurances that you didn't have to pay for and blah blah blah. There was one that caught her attention. It had been sent today and Braden must have picked it up from wherever he was right now. She clicked on it and the page filled with the message.

B.

Spiders found at Corsica Road. Not normal, but not 'them' either. Worth a look? Be careful bro...

S.E.

Mary sat in front of the screen just looking at that message. She read over it a dozen times. Surely, they must have been mistaken right? If there were spiders there, then the news would have been all over it, right? Not if it was a secret. Not if they were keeping it from the public to stop them from panicking.

Spiders found...

Something stirred inside her. It was a deep, swelling feeling of unease. She knew what Braden thought of the spiders that had invaded Newtown and very likely killed his father. He had been almost completely consumed by hatred for the man that had caused it. She couldn't remember the name without having to look it up. Not that it mattered. If Braden had any inkling that something like that was going to happen again he was going to be all over it. Of course, he was. He must have been harboring the deep-rooted need to somehow avenge his father's death. One night, not long after Newtown had gone up in flames, he had come home drunk, bellowing and shouting about how he was going to kill that fucker, the one who had set the virus-free. He was going to put his hands around his throat and kill him. He had woken Jax up that night and she wouldn't settle, no matter how much Mary comforted her. Braden had eventually passed out on the couch, and there he had stayed until the next morning. At some point whilst he was asleep he had pissed his pants, which confirmed to Mary that he had drunk way beyond his normal capacity.

Spiders found...

If there was any possibility of it happening again, then Braden wanted to be right in the thick of it. But they were killers. They killed people stone dead. If they were coming back and Braden was out there and not in his right mind, then they could kill him too.

"Shit," she said to herself and reached for her coffee. She was going to have to do something. She just couldn't sit by and let him get himself killed. No matter what was going to happen between them, she didn't want him dead. What could she do? Who could she talk to?

She focused back on the computer and went through Braden's contacts. One of them she knew straight away. Darren Masterson. Darren acted as a go-between for Braden and the news outlets all over the United Kingdom. He was the one that made sure that Braden kept on earning until he got his big break. She emailed him, telling him to phone her on her mobile as soon as possible and that Braden was in danger. Less than a minute after she had sent it she heard her mobile singing a merry tune in her handbag which was hung up on the hooks next to the front door. She scrambled out of her seat, banging her knee on the table as she did so. She hobbled through to the living room and dug the phone out of her bag. She hit the button and put the phone to her ear. Jax looked up at her momentarily and then went back to the television.

"Darren Masterson, is that Mary?" said the voice from the other end of the phone. Mary had never seen Darren in person but she guessed that he was overweight and in pretty poor health overall. He puffed and blew down the phone between talking. He sounded like a bull mastiff on heat. Mary went back through to the dining room and sat back down at the desk.

"Darren, hi, yes, it is. Have you heard from Braden at all today?"

"No, not a thing. Not heard from him for 'bout two weeks now. He's slipping in his old age. Has something happened to him?" said Masterson.

Snort, blow.

"He took off earlier today, said he had something he needed to do. Then I found an email on his computer. It was about the dead child, the one on Corsica Road," said Mary.

Masterson puffed and blew thoughtfully for a moment, "Oh yes, it's been all over the news. But the story is already broken, why would Braden go after that one?"

"The email said that they had found spiders at the site," said Mary. The puffing and blowing stopped for a moment.

"Spiders?" said Masterson in a slow and deliberate voice.

"Yes. It said it's not them, but they're not normal either. Darren, do you know what happened to Braden's father?"

Masterson took a big snort inward. "No, why?"

"He was killed in Newtown, either by those spiders or the bombs that went off. Braden has never been able to deal with it. If he has wind that those spiders are coming back then he will do anything to stop them, and I mean *anything,*" said Mary. There was a waver in her voice now. She took some deep breaths to try and calm herself.

"Right, listen to me, Mary. I'll get onto the police down there and I'll tell them that Braden has broken through the roadblock. If they find him down there then they will take him in, no questions asked. I don't suppose you know who the source of this information is do you?" said Masterson.

"No, It was just two initials, an S and an E."

The puffing and blowing stopped again as Masterson mulled it over. "Right, leave it with me, Mary. As soon as I hear that he is in the cells for the night then I will let you know. He's a good man and I want him safe too."

"Thank you," said Mary. The phone went dead in her ear. She felt like she was at a loss, what else could she do? She didn't know Masterson, could he be trusted? So many unanswered questions raced around her head. She decided to phone Braden herself, knowing quite well that he likely wouldn't answer, after all, he wouldn't want to talk to anyone that might actually talk him out of what he was attempting to do. She went through to the kitchen with the intention of making more coffee but was derailed by a knock on the front door. She marched towards it, thinking that it might have been Braden. She was ready to tear a strip off him whether Jax was in earshot or not. She opened the door and Trent from next door was standing there. The smile that was painted across his face dimmed when he saw Mary. He picked up on her vibe straight away.

"What has he done now?" said Trent.

Mary opened her mouth to answer and burst into tears. She stepped forwards and allowed herself to be wrapped up in Trent's strong arms. He carried her into the house and snicked the front door closed behind them. He stood with her for a moment, letting her get it out of her system. Eventually, she loosened her grip and stood back a little.

"Sorry," she said, wiping tears off her face. She took a few steps backward and looked over at Jax. She was still on the floor with her back to her. She was pretty certain that she had gone to sleep, otherwise, she would have been right at the front door with her, wondering who it was. It was a slim opportunity, but it was all she needed right now.

"Come on," she said to Trent and began to lead him upstairs. It wasn't the ideal solution, but it had kept her going for the last year or so. The moment that she felt him pushing into her, hard and erect, she began to feel a little bit better about things.

16.

"Where is she?" Perry growled through his gritted teeth. He had gone back to the ward where Katie had been sleeping and he had found the cubicle empty. The bed had been taken away leaving the huge empty space like a gum after a tooth extraction.

Doctor Wilson had tried to talk to Thompson and Wells outside the door of the room, but Perry had stuck his head out and heard everything that she had said. Katie had a bite on her finger and they were going to isolate her whilst they treated it. Perry had bolted from the room and gone straight back into the ward. He would be damned if they were going to take her off to isolation. He would lie down in front of the bed if he had to. But he was too late. Katie was already gone.

"We need to make sure…." began Wilson, but Perry cut her off.

"You tell me where the *fuck* she is right now," he yelled. The other patients on the ward began to pay attention, craning their heads around to watch the circus that was threatening to develop right in front of them.

"You need to calm yourself Perry. I won't take you anywhere, anytime if you shout at me like that. In fact, the only thing I will do is have security escort you from the building. I know you are worried, but she is going to be fine, and I don't think you are any good to her like this," said Wilson. Her voice was calm and steady, almost soothing. Thompson had an idea that she had been through plenty of moments like this in her illustrious career. She handled it like a pro, and he was impressed.

Perry closed his eyes for a moment and took some deep breaths. His bunched-up shoulders and his closed fists began to relax. He was coming back down to earth, at least for now. His eyes opened again. "I'm sorry, I'm just…..y'know, it's been a tough day."

Wilson smiled at him, "I know it has, but we are going to make her better, I promise you. She's tougher than you think."

Perry nodded, "Yeah, she's pretty stubborn too," he said and they both chuckled.

"Follow me," said Wilson and she lead Perry out of the ward. They went back to the main corridor and walked almost to the other end of the building. Thompson and Wells followed behind them, neither of them speaking, each one lost in their own thoughts. Both of them were thinking pretty much the same thing, that they were glad that it wasn't one of their loved ones in isolation.

They turned right towards a door that had a mechanical number lock on it. Wilson punched the buttons and turned the catch. The door opened up and she led them all inside. They walked down another corridor that had a darker, more sinister look about it than the rest of the hospital. It didn't take Thompson long to realise that it was because there was no natural light in there. No windows meant no infections could possibly escape. The very idea sent a shiver of fear down his back.

Wilson opened a door on the left-hand side and went inside. They found themselves in another ward. The layout was somewhat different to the ward that Katie had been on before. The ward was behind two large windows with a set of double doors in the middle. There looked to be another mechanical number lock on the double doors. Katie was in the bed nearest to the left-hand window. Perry said her name and pressed his hands against the glass. She was still mercifully asleep, completely unaware of anything that was happening around her.

"She has a bite on her finger," said Wilson.

"Will she be alright?" said Perry.

"Well, she's not allergic, I can tell you that for sure. If she was, she would have already had a reaction to it. She is stable, for someone that has just had a major trauma and an operation," said Wilson.

A look of mild relief came over Perry's face. Wilson saw it and she pounced.

"Why don't you go home and get some of her things together? She is going to need some of her own stuff around her to make her feel more relaxed. She won't be awake for a good while yet, given the number of painkillers she has had. You have plenty of time to make the trip and get back here."

Perry stiffened a little.

"I'll be here looking after her. I promise she won't wake up whilst you are gone," said Wilson. She offered him a warm smile. Perry's shoulders relaxed again.

"Okay. I could do with cleaning up the bathroom too. It was a mess when I left it. I'll bring her phone and her tablet, give her something to do," said Perry.

"Bring plenty of clothes too," said Wilson. Perry nodded and Wilson led him out of the ward.

Thompson and Wells were alone for a moment. They both looked at the sleeping girl through the glass.

"How come I'm not stuck in there too?" said Wells.

Thompson shrugged, "She treated it, so I'm guessing you're in the clear. Anyway, don't give me ideas."

"You could stick me in there and do all of that paperwork your fucking self," said Wells.

"I'll get Roberts bitten too, then he can join you," said Thompson.

They both chuckled and then fell to a momentary silence again.

"Are we going to call it in?" said Wells.

Thompson sighed, "Yes, I think we are. There's not much more we can do here. We need to pass this one over to the big boys. We have all the evidence we need. Case closed."

The door behind then clicked open and Wilson came back inside. Thompson turned to face her.

"We are going to be on our way, would you…."

"Make sure I call you if anything changes? Yes, of course, I will. I'll also call when she gets better," said Wilson.

Thompson smiled, "Thanks, I like to have a little closure on everything."

They headed for the door and Wilson let them out. They began to make their way down the long corridor of the main building and towards the exit.

"Do you think she is going to make it?" said Wells.

Thompson clapped him on the back. "Why wouldn't she? I think this one had been wrapped up before it could get out of hand," he said.

They went out of the building, tossing up an idea or two about what they were going to eat once they had passed this one over.

17.

Braden had parked the car on Helmsworth Drive. It was a little unassuming cul-de-sac about four streets away from Corsica Road. He did have an idea that he might park up at the leisure center at the other side of the woodland and sneak through the woods to see if he could find anything out that way, but the email that he had read had put him off the idea. He was unarmed and unprepared to face anything that might threaten his life. He couldn't talk his way out of trouble if he came face to face with a spider, no way on earth.

Since the Newtown incident, he had spent many weeks trying to get as much information about the spiders as he could lay his hands on. A lot of the stuff on the internet had been speculation and the only real evidence he could get was from the many camera phone videos that had been taken at the time of the Wythenshawe hospital deaths and some footage from the news helicopters that had attempted to follow the course of the spider swarm as it made its way over to

Newtown. Braden couldn't help but think that if the government and the army had acted a little quicker, then his father could very likely have had enough time to escape the onslaught that caught the townsfolk sleeping. Still, there was nothing that could be done about that now. All he needed today was any kind of proof that they could be making a comeback. He wasn't going to find that out just by knocking on doors, he needed to see the garden where Lottie Richmond had died. He wanted to get the story out to the masses so that another Newtown would never happen. Only then he could put it all to rest and go and try to live a normal life with his wife and his daughter. He had to keep pushing them to the back of his mind. Every time he thought about the way he had abandoned them in the bowling alley he felt a horrible crawling disgust in his insides. He was disgusted in himself, in how he had acted. Why couldn't he just have been honest about the whole thing right from the moment it had all kicked off. Then at least he might have had a chance to explain it to Mary. She might not have understood and he was pretty sure that she would have sent him packing anyway, but at least he could have tried. There was no point in battering himself over the head about it now, he had already torn off the band-aid in the most painful way possible, it was better to just let it bleed out.

He got out of the car, locked it up and then began walking. He had a route plotted out in his head that would take him to the main road. There were a few little side alleys that led right onto Corsica Road. Hopefully, there would be still enough cars parked on the road for him to hide behind. He hoped that the Richmond house would be easy to find. Perhaps there would still be police there, or even worse, a news crew. He would have to be smart about finding a way in, but he comforted himself by thinking that he would cross that bridge when he came to it. His phone had plenty of memory in it for him to take videos of anything that might be newsworthy. There was enough signal for him to upload all the evidence that he needed to back up his story. He couldn't just go off one email, he had to get some evidence for himself. Every time there was an incident, someone would claim that it was the work of the spiders. Christ, he had lost count of how many claims there had been and every one of them was false. This time, however, his source was just about as reliable as it came, not that he could reveal it, because if he did then they would shut him up, probably permanently. If this did turn out to be a front-pager then his source would want a nice big bite of the pie. But all that could be negotiated later.

He was just turning onto the main road and it wouldn't be long before he found one of the alleyways to sneak down. He was pretty certain that there wouldn't be anyone guarding them, in fact, he was pretty sure that the police didn't even know that they were there. He knew all about them. He had been here before around three years ago, after a young man by the name of Neville Walter had hung himself in his bedroom after he had spent months and months being bullied online by a large number of his so-called school friends. Braden had been chased away by the boy's uncle, who had come after him brandishing a large cricket bat. Braden had been all but convinced that the uncle would make good on his promise to cave Braden's fucking head in if had caught him. That was one of the rare occasions where Braden couldn't talk his way out of trouble, or talk his way into someone sharing their story. Braden hadn't bothered pursuing that one anymore. His story about the dangers of cyberbullying had run without the input of the family. He had taken refuge from the bat-swinging uncle down one of the alleyways and had breathed a sigh of relief that they had led through to the main road. There was much less chance of him sustaining a malicious head injury if there were witnesses. The uncle had given up the chase once Braden had made it to the main road, which probably had nothing to do with the number of witnesses but more to do with the fact that he was terribly out of shape.

Braden saw one of them coming up on the right-hand side. He decided to walk right past it at first, just to double check that it wasn't sealed off or being guarded. He slowed his pace as he approached the small gap in the houses and whipped his head to the right as he was upon it. He saw straight through to Corsica Road. There wasn't a policeman in sight. He carried on past, stopped and pretended to tie his shoe. There was a fair amount of traffic bustling up and down the main road and he didn't want to look too conspicuous. A horn blared, making him jump. He nearly lost his balance and went sprawling backward onto the pavement. Falling on his arse would have been a really good way to look inconspicuous. He swore under his breath, stood up and nipped down the alleyway. As he got nearer to the other side, he could see that there were quite a few cars still dotted about, enough for him to progress onto the street without being seen. He pressed his back against the wall and peeped around the corner. He was towards the bottom end of the street near to where the road joined the main street in a sharp left-hand turn. There was a roadblock across the top of the road. No police there.

Good.

There was one standing outside a house further down and Braden saw the unmistakable yellow police tape across it. It was going to be tricky, and he knew that he would have to try and get around to the back of the houses. Hopefully, there would be an alleyway somewhere up the street. He was going to have to chance it. There was no turning back now. Another officer was busy talking to a news crew that was, by the looks of things, trying to set themselves up. One of them had a deckchair out on the pavement.

That's got to be Tooms. He of the aching feet, he thought. He and Tooms had once come to blows over an exclusive. Braden had easily lost that little exchange and he had carried a grudge against Tooms ever since.

He took some deep breaths to try and slow down his racing heartbeat. He had to play it cool. If he was running too fast, then he was apt to make a mistake. If he made a mistake, then he would end up getting caught and then this whole damn thing would have been for nothing. He could just see himself going back to Mary and explaining to her that he had just fucked her and their daughter over for absolutely nothing. He breathed again, closing his eyes as he did so. There was a real chance that he would find nothing, he knew that but he still had to try damn it, he still had to try. He knew that everyone at some point in their life statistically would have their day in the sun, it was just that he also believed that people who tried harder would enjoy more sunny days than others. He felt the constant *boom-boom* of his heartbeat beginning to slow down in his ears. It was time for him to move.

He looked around the corner again and planned his move. There were two cars parked end-to-end in pretty close proximity to each other. He needed to go and duck down between them first. There was another lone car a little bit further up the road on the other side that would shield him from the policeman in front of the house. He would have to wait there and plan his next move from that point. It was good enough. It would work. He peered around the corner again. The officer showed no sign that he had seen Braden. He suddenly bolted from his hiding place and hot-footed it to the safety of the two cars. He ducked down and then slowly lifted himself up so that he could see the house. Two doors down from it was, what looked like, an alleyway.

Bingo.

Braden ducked down again. He went on all fours and stuck his head out from the edge of the car bumper.

Everything is just fine. GO!

He sprang up again and ran for the next car. He dropped down again, badly out of breath. The fear of being caught was working against him. It was flooding his body with adrenaline which kept him fast, but it was sucking the wind right out of him. He was ducked down at the side of a battered Seat Ibiza. He had caught sight of the inside of the car that was decorated with more pink things than he had ever seen in his life. The seats and the wheel were covered in some sort of pink coverings and there were two fluffy pink dice hanging from the rear-view mirror. He wondered how they had so much money to decorate the inside of the car with such awful shit and yet they couldn't afford a decent car instead. He laughed to himself and found himself being in danger of being unable to stop. That would have just been the last straw, being caught because he was sitting here laughing like a loon. He could sell that story, no problem. *Laughing lunatic found on death street*. The thought made him want to laugh even more.

I'm losing it, I'm just about fucking losing it, he thought.

He bit down on the inside of his cheek. The pain was fresh and scalding and he began to taste the coppery warmth of his own blood on his tongue. The laughter that had been bubbling up inside of him subsided. He felt his focus coming back. He loosened up on his cheek and then ran for the next car. This one would take him one car away from being right opposite that alleyway and into the clear. He was nearly there. He felt a pulse of excitement roar through his innards, making him want to laugh out loud. He gnawed the cheek again, bringing the pain that shut those ideas down. He was almost at the car and he suddenly lost his footing. He began to stagger forwards, wheeling his arms to try and get his balance. He managed to pull some of it back, but it didn't stop him from crashing into the car hard enough for the door panel to cave in a little. His head struck the side window hard enough for him to see stars. He thought that he had got away with it, that his clumsiness hadn't tripped him up this time when the cars inbuilt alarm started to go off. The high whistling tone rose and fell causing Braden to put his hands over his ears. The lights on the side of the car began to flash on and off.

"Shit," said Braden. The game was up. The police were going to come down the street to see what the hell was going on. He was caught. The whole thing was going down the shitpan right now. The only thing he was going to get from running out on his wife and daughter was a night in the fucking cells. Unless....unless.

The policeman on the door was yelling for his partner. His eyes were off the car just for a moment. Braden sprang forwards to the nearest house and pressed the door handle down. Mercifully the door was unlocked and he piled himself inside. He closed the door behind him and sat with his back against it breathing hard. He reached his hand up to the knot that was growing on his head. It came away clean, he hadn't cut it open which was a good thing. He closed his eyes, breathing slowly again, hoping that the occupants of the house didn't find him and turf him straight back out onto the street for the police to deal with. He would try and talk to them, he would sell them a nice ol' bag of Braden Benson bullshit, and hopefully, they would let him stay. Perhaps if the bullshit was a high enough grade then they would give him a cup of tea and a biscuit whilst he picked through their brains to try and get more evidence for his story. He tensed up as he heard footsteps outside. It was soon followed by muffled voices. Braden couldn't make out what they were saying. The PVC door was too well insulated to let much in the way of sound through. He began to pray to himself that they wouldn't try the front door.

Please....please...please...

The car alarm stopped and soon the voices and footsteps began to move away. Braden let out a long and shaky breath. He slowly got to his feet and saw a letter on the little table just inside the door. He picked it up and squinted at the name.

Jenny Roberts.

The name escaped him for a moment until he realised that this was the house of the mutilated cat. On the wall just to the left of him was a framed picture. It was one of those nauseating frames that was crafted into a word. Mary had tried to convince him to get one of them once upon a time. He had refused, telling her that they were tacky. Looking at this one, he wasn't inclined to change his mind any time soon. The letters of the frame spelled out the word *'love.'* Right in the middle of the 'O' was a picture of Jenny Roberts. She was beaming, showing her big horsey teeth. Next to her was a man who looked like he had been smoking too much dope. His half-lidded eyes and his gormless expression gave the game away. Jenny was holding up a ginger and white cat that looked as if it took no enjoyment out of having its picture taken. The cat looked mean and pissed off. This was the house where that poor little bugger had met his fate. Perhaps he could ask a question or two here before he moved on to the Richmond's place.

He guessed that it wasn't going to be that simple. After all, nobody had come to challenge him for coming into their house. Perhaps they had gone out this morning and forgotten to lock up. Perhaps they had left to get away from all the hassle that was going on at the top of the street and had forgotten in their hurry to leave. But Braden began to get the sense that something wasn't right in this house, something wasn't right at all. He couldn't quite explain what it was that was making him feel like that. The hair on the back of his neck felt like it was standing to attention. A shudder wracked through his body turning his skin into goose pimples. He felt the strongest urge to just get up and go right back out of the door again. He even toyed with the idea of throwing himself on the mercy of the police, anything to get him the hell out of here. He...

He caught sight of something in front of him. From where he was sitting, he could see right through into the kitchen. From the looks of it, there had been some serious money spent in there. The set up looked like it was almost brand new. The floor was covered in tiles that could only have been a few weeks, perhaps a month or two old. They weren't showing any signs of any wear or tear like his own kitchen at home which looked like they had been shitting on it for three hours every day. Some of the floor was wet. The sunlight coming in from the windows was highlighting the large puddle on the floor. At first, Braden thought it was just water, but as he stood up and took a step forwards. There was something else in there too. It looked like a pile of clothes that were somehow propped up against the cupboard under the sink. The bright sunlight streaming in from the back windows made it difficult for Braden to make it out clearly. He took another couple of cautious steps towards the kitchen and then he saw something out of the corner of his eye. To his right-hand side was a doorway which led into a living room. There was a sofa against the back wall and an armchair jutting at a right angle from the edge of it. Braden looked at the floor and saw the pink jumper that had caught his eye. At first, he thought there was another pile of clothes on the floor and then his mind finally allowed him to recognize that he was looking at a dead body. He clapped his hands over his mouth and felt his stomach clench into a tight knot. for a moment, he thought he was going to vomit, but he managed to stop the bubble of acidic tasting bile from getting any further than his throat. The body on the floor was barely recognizable as a human being. The body was Jenny Roberts. He could tell by the section of her face that still remained. The left side of it looked like it had been burned away. The bone of the girl's skull was an open, bloody hole. Braden could see right into the girl's mouth and brain cavity. He could see the large teeth, the same goomers that he had seen in the photograph in the hallway. They were unmistakable. Whatever was left of her brain was slowly dripping out of the hole and onto the polished wood floor below. Her eye was sitting in the middle of the pool of pulp, bright blue and glazed over. One of her legs was jutting out at an unnatural angle and the other one was missing below the knee. Every wound on the body gave Braden the impression that it had been gnawed, eaten by something. He turned away from the scene. He was breathing hard, feeling like he was going to pass out at any moment. He bit down on his already wounded inside cheek, bringing fresh and sobering pain through his head. The faintness began to recede and he started his slow breathing. In the back of his mind, he knew that the pile of clothing he saw in the kitchen was also a dead body and one that was probably in a similar state to the one he had already encountered. He pulled his phone out of his pocket. He had to get a picture of the body. He had to go and report it to the police, and then he had to get the picture to Darren Masterson. Braden knew that something inhuman had inflicted those terrible injuries. He had his suspicions on what it was

   (spiders)

but he didn't have enough evidence to prove it. His only real hope of that was to actually find one of them.

You could be wrong, you could have all of this so wrong, he thought. He wanted to be wrong, he wanted so badly to be wrong. Either way, he would have a story that would be worthy of the front page. Perhaps whoever or whatever had done this had done the same to Lottie Richmond. He turned on the camera, quickly pointed it at the body and hit the button. The phone flashed and he stepped past the living room door so he wouldn't have to look at it again. He still had another body to deal with in the kitchen, but he needed to get the wheels in motion first. He tapped a few buttons and then he was sending the picture to Masterson. Braden started to psyche himself up to go and look at the body in the kitchen. He decided that he was just going to get as close as he could and get a quick snap of it without looking directly at it. His stomach had always been a little weak. He liked a good horror film as much as the next man, but the sight of real blood and guts was always a little too much for him to take. He took a few more deep breaths and then he crept towards the kitchen. The smell coming from the kitchen reminded Braden of the time that the drains had once started backing up during a pretty violent rainstorm a few days after Newtown had gone up. Despite his deep breaths and mental preparation, his heartbeat was still hammering away ten to the dozen. His phone suddenly rang in his hand. He let out a reflexive yell and he nearly dropped the damn thing. He looked at the screen and saw that it was Masterson. He punched the button and held it to his ear with a hand that was shaking badly.

"Darren, I can't talk right now, I've.."

"Are you still in the house?" said Masterson, cutting him off. He was puffing and blowing almost in a frenzy.

"Yes, there's anoth.."

"Braden, get the fuck out of there now. *Now goddammit,*" roared Masterson.

"I just need to get one more picture...."

"Forget it Braden, get the hell out of there, that picture that you sent me....the spiders Braden, the spiders..."

"What the hell are you talking about?" said Braden. Masterson was really beginning to freak him out now. His feet were beginning to twitch as if they wanted to rebel against the rest of him and start running all by themselves.

"*The fucking spiders in the picture, in the corner of the room. Now get the hell out of there, get out now,*" screamed Masterson.

Braden's breath caught in his throat. It wasn't possible, it just wasn't possible. He cut

Masterson off and opened the folder containing the pictures. The picture he had taken of the body popped up in front of him. The picture was at a slight angle. The bottom half of the dead body was missing from the picture, but the skirting around the top of the wall where it met the ceiling was visible. Right there in the corner was a collection of black spiders. The skin on the backs of the spiders had caught the light coming in from the living room window. It looked as if they had been coated with a glossy black paint. Braden had seen the footage of the spiders from Newtown. They had been ugly, mutated parodies of their former selves. These spiders were something different. They looked almost normal. Now he knew what that email was talking about. This was something new, something utterly terrifying. Braden felt his bladder let go in a hot gush. It warmed his inner thighs and then went as cold as his insides. They were in here with him and they had killed the occupants of the house and eaten parts of them away. How long had they been here? A week? A month? He didn't want to know. The front door was less than five feet away, but to get to it he had to go past the living room again. He closed the picture and returned the phone to his pocket. Whatever happened now, he had got the scoop that he was, in turn, hoping for and hoping he would never see for the rest of his life. He heard something in the living room. It sounded like a steady patter of water dripping down from the ceiling, but he knew that it was them. They knew he was here. The sound broke his paralysis. They might have just decided that they wanted Braden Benson for pudding. He ran, his feet slipping in the steaming rank of his own piss. He nearly lost his footing, but he was so determined to get the hell out of there that he managed to hold his balance. As he bolted past the living room and he couldn't help but glance into the doorway. The spiders were on the move. they had already made it to the arm of the chair and were making their way, like a black scuttling carpet onto the dilapidated corpse of Jenny Roberts. He roared in panic and stone-cold terror. He reached for the door handle and tore the door open into his own knee. Still bellowing like a madman, he got out of the door, turned around and saw with horror that the spiders were tearing across the hall floor towards him. He scrambled the door shut, trapping two of them under the door sill.

Their legs twitched and shook, firing random commands as the life was crushed out of them.

"Oi, what the hell are you playing at?" said Officer Weston. He saw Braden bolting out of the door and he was making his way over to Braden.

Braden took off up the street as fast as he could. Weston was going to give chase, but he had far more important things to think about and he couldn't leave the scene of a crime anyway. He watched Braden go and shrugged his shoulders. Some people acted nuts just for the sheer hell of it.

Braden charged away. His wet legs felt like they were beginning to freeze as the wind hit them. His chest felt like it was going to burst. He couldn't get enough air into his lungs, such was his panic and effort to get away. He ran blindly down the alleyway and stopped only when he had got back onto the main street.

All he could think about was Mary and Jax. His beautiful Mary and Jax. They were going to die. They were all going to die.

18.

Thompson had just closed the door of his car when his phone began to buzz in his pocket. He snatched it out and answered it without bothering to check who was calling.

"Thompson, what the fuck is going on?" bellowed Roberts down the earpiece. Thompson winced at his own foolishness. If he had looked at the screen properly, he would have ignored it. It was hard enough to get a word in edgeways when you were standing right in front of Roberts, it was damn near impossible over the phone.

"I have reports of another death on Corsica Road and a journalist asking me for a statement on a girl that was injured on the same street. What the fuck are you trying to do to me? Do you not think I should have been informed before everyone else? Do I have to be the last person to know *everything* that's going on in my department?"

He paused for breath and Thompson pounced. "We are on our way in right now. This is a more serious situation than we first thought."

"Then why didn't you call it in sooner?" said Roberts. It sounded like he was gritting his teeth hard as he was speaking. When Roberts was in this kind of mood, there was no telling what would happen. Just after his promotion, Roberts had once thrown Thompson against a door for filing his reports an hour later than he had asked for. Thompson could still point to the places that were left angry and bruised by Roberts' actions. He had almost filed a complaint, but he had been talked out of it, and Roberts had been a lot nicer to him for a little while after.

"We weren't in possession of all the facts. What use would it have been to come back with half a story?" said Thompson. He was doing his level best to keep the tone of his voice non-confrontational. He didn't want to cause any more trouble for them.

There was a momentary silence at the other end of the phone. Thompson was sure that he could almost hear the cogs in Roberts' mind turning over.

"Just get back here as soon as possible," he growled down the phone and then he hung up.

Thompson let out a long breath and returned the phone to his pocket. He started the car up.

"I'm guessing that we are in trouble?" said Wells.

"No more than usual," said Thompson. He put the car into gear and began negotiating the route back out onto the main road.

"I'll let you do the talking," said Wells. He was trying to be funny, but the joke fell to the floor and died bloodlessly there.

They stayed silent for the rest of the drive back to the station. Wells rubbed at his bitten hand. It had begun to itch again, not in the same maddening way it had done before, but enough to make him want to gnaw at it. He rubbed at the dressing, trying to get a little relief, but it did no good. He flexed his fingers, stretching them out as much as he could. The bones around his knuckles crackled, making him wince. He couldn't stand it when anyone popped their knuckles, the very sound of it turned him green. He returned his hand to his lap and left well enough alone.

Thompson pulled his car into his designated space and turned the engine off. He turned to look at Wells.

"Listen, I'll take the heat for this one ok? No sense in us both getting into trouble," he said.

"Oh no you don't," said Wells. "You keep trying to pull this one on me and it doesn't wash. We're partners. Any shit you walk in, I walk in it too."

Thompson opened his mouth to protest.

"I won't hear another word about it," said Wells cutting him off. He got out of the car before Thompson could say anything.

They buzzed themselves back into the building and headed for the staircase. They made it to the second floor and went in through the heavy fire door. The buzz of activity felt like it simmered down a little as they walked in. Thompson suspected that the gossip chain had been active in the last few hours. News of their impending dressing-down must have reached the ears of pretty much everyone in the department. Thompson would have felt more annoyed about it had he not joined in with the gossip chain on a regular basis. He supposed that he had to take his turn being on the wrong end of it a few times just to balance the whole thing out. Roberts saw them coming. He raised a hand in the air, snapped his fingers and then pointed down.

You, here, now! said the gesture.

Thompson let out a long sigh, puffing out his cheeks and trying to keep the nub of irritation at this ridiculous man down to an acceptable level. He had a pretty good idea that he was in some deep water, and he needed to swim rather than allow his head to be pushed under.

They went into Roberts' office and shut the door behind them. Roberts was sat behind his desk, his hands placed on the top of the oak as if he was about to recite poetry, or give a rousing speech.

"Explain yourselves," said Roberts.

"What do you need to know?" said Thompson in his usual, overly calm voice. It was a voice that he saved just for Roberts, just to needle him as much as he could without raising his voice.

"Don't play games with me," said Roberts. He leaned back in his reclining office chair and folded his arms across his chest. His chair creaked in protest at Roberts shifting his considerable weight backward.

"Games? We aren't playing games," said Thompson. He looked over at Wells, "Are we playing games?"

Wells shook his head. He said nothing. He was beginning to break out in a sweat. The office suddenly felt very warm to him all of a sudden.

Roberts lowered his head for a moment. Thompson knew he was collecting his temper. A glow of red was beginning to creep out of Roberts' collar.

"We investigated the scene of Lottie Richmond's death and there was an incident," said Thompson.

Roberts' head came up again.

"We found this," said Thompson. He rooted in his pocket and drew out the crumpled evidence bag that he had put the dead spider in. He flopped it onto Robert's desk. Roberts picked it up and slowly eyed the contents. The plastic bag rustled under his fingers.

"A spider?" said Roberts.

"Yes sir," said Thompson.

Roberts frowned at him, almost comically. "Why on earth have you brought me a dead spider?"

"I believe that is what killed Lottie Richmond, and one of them attacked Wells, bit him right on his hand."

Roberts looked at Wells and then back at Thompson. "Please tell me you have evidence to support what you are saying."

"There was a bite, just like the one that Wells has, on the body of Lottie Richmond. We also found a body in number ten Corsica Road, he too had a bite. There was also an accident involving another one of the neighbors this morning. A young girl by the name of Katie Underwood broke her leg pretty badly after she fell out of her shower. We think she was trying to get away from something. She had exactly the same bite on one of her fingers. Of course, we don't know for sure how it happened, and we won't know until she wakes up from her operation to piece her leg back together."

Roberts was looking at him the whole time he was speaking. The telling off he had planned for Thompson was now all but forgotten.

"Are you sure about all of this Thompson? Are you really sure?" said Roberts.

"I'm as sure as I can be with the evidence I have," said Thompson.

Roberts leaned back in his chair making it creak even more. He looped his hands behind his head and looked up at the ceiling. Thompson wondered to himself if Roberts had ever trained to be an actor of some sort. Every gesture he made was over-blown theatre.

"I'm going to have to take this to the big boys Thompson. They are going want to know where I got my information. I need you to write me a detailed report as soon as you can," said Roberts.

"Of course," said Thompson.

Roberts turned his attention to Wells. "Are you alright?" he said. The colour had drained from Wells' face. His lips had taken on a slightly bluish hue.

"My hand…." said Wells. He was cradling the bitten hand across his other forearm. Thompson looked over at him and he saw the distress on Wells' face.

"What's wrong?" said Thompson.

"…..hurts," mumble Wells. His voice sounded like it was becoming more distant, less coherent. He was fading into unconsciousness.

"Show me," said Thompson and he took hold of the injured hand. He lifted it up off Wells' forearm so he could try and take the dressing off to look at the bite. Wells' hand felt as though it was filled with air like there was nothing inside it. The skin felt cold and dead beneath Thompson's fingers. He took hold of the edge of the dressing, ready to start taking it off just as Wells slipped into a dead faint. He rolled sideways off his chair and descended gracefully to the floor. As he went, Thompson reflexively gripped his hand in an effort to stop him falling. Wells' hand crunched and crackled under Thompson's grip. He looked down and saw that Wells' hand and a long section of his forearm was hanging from his own closed fist. The fingers that he had clamped down on had collapsed into a stomach-churning mess of red, chunky flesh. Pieces of skin from the collapsed fingers sat on top of the sludge, pale white like the skin on a blister. Thompson leaped out of his chair, letting out a high-pitched yell. He shook the severed appendage off his hand, sending pieces of red sludge flying in all directions. It slopped onto the floor and began to dissolve into a foul-smelling green slime. The skin on Wells' severed arm began to break apart until all of its structure was gone. Smoke began to rise up off the carpeted floor all around the severed limb.

"Jesus fucking Christ...." bellowed Roberts. He scrambled around his desk, pulled the door open and began yelling for someone to call an ambulance. Some of the smoke caught Thompson. His throat immediately felt like it was trying to close up on him. Whatever that green shit was, it was burning the carpet away. The fumes coming from it were poisonous, he was sure of it. Roberts was turning around to come back into the room.

"Get out of here, quick," said Thompson. His voice was gravelly and horse from the effect of the fumes. Roberts stared at him for a moment, and then the stench of the burning floor hit him. He put his hand over his mouth and nose and stepped back out of the door again. Thompson moved around the prone body of Wells and into the doorway. He squatted down near Wells' head, hooked his hands under Wells' armpits and started to drag him towards the door. He tried as best as he could not to look at the arm that was now missing just below his elbow and the putrid slime that was oozing out of it. He turned his head to where the air was a little fresher and he took a gasping breath. He held the air in his lungs and pulled Wells with all the strength that he had. He began to move backward out of the door of the office.

"Leave him, *leave him in there*. There's nothing you can do for him," yelled Roberts.

Thompson felt his temper flare. He couldn't believe the words that were coming out of Roberts' mouth. He wasn't going to leave his partner, his friend to die.

"Get out of the fucking way, or I'll throw you in there myself," he shouted at Roberts.

Roberts moved away, shocked by the suddenness with which Thompson had shouted. Thompson gave Wells three more good pulls and he had him clear of the door. Roberts banged it shut, causing the glass to vibrate. The room quickly became engulfed. Roberts' desk became obscured by the grey fog that was rising up off the floor. Everyone in the department had abandoned their desks and were stood watching the grotesque scene that was unfolding in front of them.

"Someone call an ambulance *now*," roared Thompson. A moment later the fire alarms began to screech and howl all around them. The assembled hoard began to make for the exits. Thompson could have cheerfully shaken each and every one of them. One person stayed behind, she had her desk phone in her hand and she was yelling for the ambulance.

"Thank you," Thompson called over and she nodded at him to show that she had heard. He looked around again to tell Roberts to get something to put under Wells' head, but he had already gone.

"Fucking arsehole," Thompson whispered to himself. He looked down at Wells. His eyes were opening, but they were rolling over white. He was in a bad way. Thompson felt momentarily helpless. He didn't know what to do for the best. He looked down at the stump of his arm. There was no blood that he could see, just that horrible green stuff slowly trailing out of it. He didn't know if he should tie it off, or whether he would just end up making things worse. His thoughts were interrupted by the woman that had been on the phone coming over to him. She snatched coats off the hooks and balled them up to make a pillow for Wells.

"Ambulance is on its way. Three minutes. They have one two streets away," she said.

"Thank God for that," said Thompson. He hooked his hands behind Wells' head and lifted it so that the woman could stuff her makeshift pillow underneath. Thompson looked up at her face and he caught her eye. He had seen her around the station for as long as he could remember, but he could never recall a single time that he had ever engaged in conversation with her. The irony of her being his saving grace now was not lost on him. In retrospect, he wished that he had made the time just to at least say hello, just once, so he could feel less of an arsehole right now.

"Harriet Smithy," she said, picking up on his vibe.

"Thanks for sticking around Harriet," he said. It was the best he could come up with.

"No problem. I'm going to go downstairs and look out for that ambulance. Do you need anything else?" said Harriet.

Thompson looked down at the prone body of Wells. He wasn't going anywhere, he was still out cold. He looked up at Harriet and shook his head. She pointed at the oozing stump of Wells' arm.

"I would stay away from that if I were you," she said and then she was gone, leaving the two of them alone.

Thompson sat down on the floor on the right side of Wells. The howling of the fire alarms normally irritated the shit out of him. Every Friday morning the damn things would be tested, and every Friday morning, almost without fail, he would forget that they got tested. They would erupt into life for five seconds, causing him to swear and place his hands over his ears until that godforsaken shrieking had stopped. But today the shrieking floated over his head as if it was coming from a long distance away. The pain in his ears from the noise paled into insignificance with what had happened since he had arrived at work today. It was going to be tough to keep this out of the press. It was going to be equally tough to talk to Wells' family about what had happened to him. One thing he did know for sure was that it was very likely that he was going to end up in that isolation ward along with that poor unfortunate girl who was already in there. Everything was just such a fucking mess, and he had a horrible crawling fear in his guts that things were going to get a whole hell of a lot worse before they got better.

He looked down at his partner. He jumped a little when he realised that Wells had opened his eyes and he was looking at him. A smile broke over Wells' face that sent a cold snap right down Thompson's spine. It was like looking at a corpse grinning.

"You OK chief?" he said.

"Been better," Wells croaked. He started to move as if he was trying to get up off the floor. Thompson pressed his hands onto his shoulders to keep him still.

"Take it, easy old buddy, help is on the way. Try not to move," he said.

Wells stopped moving and relaxed his body again. A frown furrowed across his face. "….feel funny," he said. Thompson could barely hear him over the howling fire alarms.

Wells suddenly reached out with his remaining hand and gripped Thompson's collar he pulled him down with amazing strength.

"I'm…..infected," he growled in Thompson's face. A waft of foul smelling breath hit Thompson's nostrils. He would have recoiled away from it, but Wells' grip was firm.

"I….can….feel….it," grunted Wells.

"Wh…what can you feel?" said Thompson. He was suddenly scared. He wanted to be as far away from this Wells shaped thing on the floor as he could possibly get.

"E…..e…..everything…..c…c…ch..ch…changes," grunted Wells. His mouth opened wider and wider until the skin around his mouth was stretched as far as it could. Wells began to scream. It started softly at first and then it rose in pitch and volume until it was louder than the fire alarms. Thompson fought to get away from his grip, pulling at Wells' hand, feeling his shirt giving out under the arms in his efforts to free himself. He could feel his own scream beginning to build inside his chest, he was going to scream until his voice became horse, he was going to scream until his sanity cracked right down the middle and spilled out of his ears. He was going to scream himself to death, until his heart froze still in his chest and dropped him to the floor, his blood halting dead in its tracks as it ran through his veins. By Christ, he was going to scream.

But Wells dropped back to the floor, his mouth and his eyes closing, his grip on Thompson's collar relaxing, spilling him to the floor. Thompson scrambled away and got to his feet, his heart thundering in his chest and his breath coming in short snaps. He looked down at Wells, ready to run. But Wells was out, and he looked just like his old self again.

The door at the far end of the office burst open, and Harriet came through closely followed by two paramedics and three firefighters. A moment later the fire alarms fell silent.

Thompson stepped backward until his back struck the wall. The room had suddenly become deadly silent. Even with the loud voices of all the new people in the room, everything was silent. Thompson went for the door. He needed to get out of here. He needed some air, and something to bring him back into the realms of normality.

He went out to the car park where the rest of the building's staff were assembled. Some of them came over to him, trying to ask him questions, but it felt like their voices were coming from inside a bubble, far away and muted. He stood for a moment, not responding, not saying a word.

He caught sight of Roberts and strode over to him. Roberts cowered a little as if he expected Thompson to lay him out right in front of everyone. Thompson saw that Roberts still had the evidence bag in his hand with the dead spider inside. Thompson pointed at the bag.

"Get that to whoever deals with these things. Don't wait, get it done," he said. Then he moved away. He headed back to his car. Right now, he needed to drive. He needed to get away from here. He needed to clear his head so that he knew what his next move would be.

19.

Doctor Wilson put the mask over her nose and mouth in readiness to go and tend to her patient. Her shift was two hours beyond the finish line and she should have been at home, lying on the couch and snoring away with the television blaring in the background. But such was the way things were in her line of work, there was nobody available to cover her, especially as the isolation ward was now active for the first time in her tenure at the hospital. They were all trained on how to use it, but most of the training had fallen by the wayside, simply because it had rarely been put into practice. By all accounts, she had been incredibly lucky that she had never even witnessed anything that even came close to an outbreak, not even a scare. Lucky yes, but prepared, no.

She looked in through the large window at her patient. The young girl Katie was slowly writhing in, what looked to be, pain. The slow drip of morphine that had been pumped slowly into her over the last few hours had obviously run out. Wilson needed to get her on another strong painkiller before she woke up fully, otherwise, it was sure as hell going to get noisy in there. She also needed to explain to the girl exactly where she was and how she had ended up there.

Wilson was all kitted up. She had pulled staff nurse Renfrew off his normal duties to keep an eye on her from the other side of the door. She had warned him to get kitted out just in case she needed him to come in and assist. Bite or no bite, that girl had just undergone major surgery and any movement this soon afterward could have caused her more damage and certainly a hell of a lot more pain.

"Are you ready?" she said to Renfrew.

"Ready as I'll ever be," he replied in his thick Scottish accent.

"You see me wave, you get in there ok?"

"*Gaw tit,*" said Renfrew and covered his nose and mouth with his mask.

Wilson nodded at him and then reversed through the double doors, pulling her trolley of equipment along with her. The doors swung behind her and latched shut. There was a strange silence in the room as if the walls were absorbing every sound. Katie was moaning and whimpering. Her eyes were flickering open and allowing a steady stream of tears to run down the sides of her face and onto her ears.

"It ok, don't worry. You're in the hospital, but everything is going to be fine," soothed Wilson.

Katie's eyes looked like they were grasping a little focus at the sound of Wilson's voice. The wandering eyes found Wilson's face. Katie's writhing and moaning stopped as her eyes locked on to the doctor in front of her.

"....hurts," Katie rasped, "Leg....hurts..."

Wilson leaned in and stroked her arm. "I know it does sweetie, I'm going to try and make you more comfortable and then we can talk," she said.

Katie gave her a weak nod and a fresh splash of tears ran down the sides of her face. Wilson's heart ached for her a little. She didn't often get pangs of emotion, she was normally in 'work mode' where emotion did not belong. Emotion would get in the way of important off-the-cuff decisions that she had to make to save lives. But, with Katie, something about her young face, her helpless look made her heart go out to her. She set about preparing a generous hit of painkillers into a syringe. She took it over to Katie.

"Gonna make you feel a little better now ok?" she said.

Katie nodded again and Wilson jabbed her upper arm with the painkiller. "Right, just give it a minute to work and then we'll have a little chat."

Wilson set to work taking Katie's blood pressure and checking her heart rate. She finished off by taking her temperature which was a few degrees above normal. She carefully checked the bite on her finger. It was horribly swollen and a steady stream of pink and green pus was running from the wound and dripping onto the bed. She would deal with it, but she needed to make sure she was comfortable first. Katie's writhing was slowing down and her breathing rate was falling into a more natural rhythm. Wilson pushed the trolley out of the way and pulled a chair up next to Katie. Katie turned her head towards Wilson.

"Why are you wearing a mask?" said Katie.

Wilson hesitated a moment and then she pulled it clear of her nose and mouth. "Just a precaution. I don't want you getting any infections," said Wilson. There was no point in alarming her just yet, not until she knew exactly what she was dealing with.

"Can you remember what happened?" said Wilson.

Katie frowned for a moment. Wilson could almost see the cogs turning in her head through the pain killing fog. "I fell…..I was in the shower….something…"

Her eyes closed again and her voice trailed off. Wilson gave her a gentle shake. Her head turned toward Wilson and she opened her eyes again. She offered Wilson another smile and then her face dissolved into a look of utter terror.

"Spider…..a spider," she said, her voice cracking and cutting out. "I feel so silly….I tried to kill a spider and I fell."

She tried to sit up but Wilson carefully placed her hands on Katie's shoulders, holding her down on the bed.

"Be careful, you have to keep as still as you can. You've had surgery on your leg," said Wilson.

Katie swallowed hard and wrinkled her face up again. "….thirsty," she croaked.

Wilson poured water into a plastic cup and pushed the lid on. She poked a straw through the lid and guided it to Katie's mouth. She took a few long sucks on the straw and then began to cough sending water spraying out of her mouth and dribbling out of her nose. Wilson took the cup away and wiped Katie's mouth as her coughing fit came to an end.

"That'll teach you. Take it slowly," said Wilson.

Katie shifted over a little, her face contorting into a look of pain. She settled again and let out a long sigh.

"So, tell me about this spider," said Wilson, trying to start up the conversation again.

"Spider….yes. It was on the shower head. It….fell into the bath, I was trying to get away from it. I tried to kill it, but I fell. My leg….my leg…"

"You broke your leg, yes you did. We fixed it up. It's got a nice little metal stabiliser holding it all together," said Wilson.

Katie gently reached down to her leg and she felt the metal sticking out of her leg. Wilson carefully moved her hand away.

"It has a drain in it at the moment, so try not to touch it," said Wilson.

"Where's Perry?" said Katie.

"He has gone back home to get your things. You're going to be here for a little while until you can get about again. He was the one that found you," said Wilson.

Katie closed her eyes and smiled. "My hero," she said.

Wilson laughed, the first genuine laugh she had done since those policemen had visited her. She took that light-hearted moment to address the elephant in the room.

"You have something on your finger, I'm not sure what it is, but I think it might be infected. I need to take care of it."

Katie raised the hand and looked at her finger. She pulled a disgusted face and lowered the hand again. "That's fine," she mumbled.

Wilson stood up ready to go and pull her trolley over so she could start on the bite. She wheeled it over to the side of Katie and pulled a chair up so that she could get comfortable. The dribbling finger was now hanging off the side of the bed. Katie coughed again, loud and abruptly. As she did so, the infected finger fell right off her hand and slopped to the floor below. It sat on the floor, looking like a pink slug sitting in its own slimy trail. Wilson sucked in a breath. If Katie had heard her or felt the finger go, she wasn't letting on. Wilson was interrupted by a tapping on the glass behind her. She turned around and saw Renfrew beckoning her over. She told Katie she would be back in a moment and she made her way through the doors to where Renfrew was waiting.

"What is it?"

Renfrew pulled down his mask. "There's another one coming in," he said.

Wilson was mystified, "Another one?"

"Another bite victim. He's on his way in now."

Wilson felt her stomach drop, "Oh shit, that's all we need. You need to contact the CR and tell him we need more staff here, got it?"

Renfrew nodded and headed for the door, but he was cut off by the arrival of their new patient, banging through the main doors. Wilson looked down at the man on the trolley and her mouth fell open. It was the man from the police, the one she had treated for the bite. She saw with increasing horror that one of his arms was missing. It had a mucky looking dressing on it, but nothing in the way of a tourniquet, which she would have expected with a missing limb. She looked down at the remaining hand and saw that it was clean. It had no bite and no dressing that she had applied earlier. Her mind flashed to the finger of Katie Underwood dropping off like an old scab, and she put two and two together to make the most horrendous four of her life. The bites were highly infectious.

The next few hours were going to be the most challenging of her career so far, of that she had no doubt.

20.

    P.C Gardner was contemplating what he was going to do once the backup team and forensics had arrived. His primary concern was getting something to eat. It seemed like a long time since he had been eating his breakfast, and the events of the day had meant that he had missed his lunch. Even though he was supposed to have been relieved from duty five hours ago, it hadn't happened. He had asked and asked for a replacement time and time again but nothing had happened, and now nobody at the station was even answering him. Perhaps he would phone in sick tomorrow and see how they would deal with that. The reality of it would be that he would have to subject himself to a return to work meeting and have to justify his absence to someone who he really had no time for. The bottom line was, he would show up, he knew he would. Days like today were in the minority. It wasn't often he had been involved with such a high-profile case, one that had attracted the press. At the start of the day the press had been buzzing around like wasps around a bowl of sugar. Now there was only one news crew left. They were hanging around at the top of the road near their van. The mostly sunny day had given them the opportunity to get out a few folding chairs and sit out on the pavement. Their journalist had been sitting there in his shirt and tie, smoking cigarette after cigarette and keeping an eye on what was going on. He hadn't tried to approach Gardner since Weston had sent him packing from the door that he had been guarding. Weston was still outside the door of Lottie Richmond, still waiting for an update and a relief officer just as he was.

Gardner lifted himself up on his toes and felt his ankles pop. His legs were as stiff as boards. He almost envied the journalist and his comfy chair, almost. His personal opinion of journalists wasn't favourable at all. Take this one for instance. He was trying to make a living out of the death of a baby. The more primeval part of him wanted to go right over that road to him and punch him right in his stupid, grinning face. He would steal his fucking chair too, just for good measure.

But he couldn't. It wouldn't be allowed, he would get into trouble and he would be disciplined. He couldn't, however, get into trouble for fantasising about it, and it helped him to pass the time.

He looked up the road at Weston, saw that he was looking in his direction and flipped him off. Weston turned around and wiggled his arse at him. The reporter across the road straightened up in his chair, probably wanting to catch some footage of them goofing around at a crime scene. Gardner resisted the urge to carry on the banter and put his hands behind his back again. The reporter relaxed in his chair again and lit another cigarette. Gardner decided to keep an eye on him to see if he would pitch his cigarette end into the gutter just on the off-chance that he decided to go and book him for littering. Anything to break up the monotony.

Something moved in the corner of his eye and he turned his head towards the top of the street. The forensics van was on its way towards them along with two more police cars. Gardner almost felt his feet breathing a sigh of relief inside his polished black shoes, just knowing that very soon they were going to be comfortably tucked under the table of the café less than half a mile from here. He could taste that first sip of coffee and that wonderful first bite of the sausage and egg bap that was in his near future. His mouth began to water at the prospect of it. He glanced up at Weston again and gave him the thumbs up. Weston returned the gesture, and Gardner knew he wouldn't be in that café alone.

The van pulled up right in front of Gardner and the police cars stopped behind it. The uniforms got out first. Two of them came over to Gardner and two went over to Weston. Gardner recognised the faces immediately. W.P.C. Louise Booth and P.C. Harry Turner. They were usually on the opposite shift to him and Weston.

"Where in the blue hell have you been?" said Gardner.

"Sorry Gardy, We have had three shoplifters and a pretty lively domestic to deal with. They would have sent you, but the Chief said that you would be better served standing here doing absolutely nothing because that's what you do best," said Booth. She had an excellent line in sarcasm, but her delivery of it was priceless.

Gardner clutched at his sides comically. "Ooh, ooooh, Jesus, my sides have just split," he crowed, probably a little too loud.

"So, you got a body?" said Turner.

"Yeah, it's pretty nasty in there. The guy was one of those hoarders, never threw anything away. The smell is horrendous," said Gardner flapping his hand under his nose to accentuate the point.

"Well, we're here now, so you and your boyfriend can get out of here," said Booth.

"Fantastic, I can take him home and grease him up," said Gardner. He left them laughing and made his way up the road. Weston met him halfway.

"What's the deal with that place?" said Gardner pointing at the Richmond place.

"It's forensics job now. But the death was anaphylaxis, open and shut. Christ knows what they are looking for." said Weston.

"Shall we go and eat?" said Gardner. His stomach rumbled, as if it knew it was about to be nurtured.

"I thought you would never ask," said Weston. They headed off to their patrol car, glad to be leaving the events of Corsica Road behind.

The forensic team was unloading their kit from the van, including the marquee that they were going to set up at the front door to stop any prying eyes from seeing what was going on.

"Shall we take a look?" said Turner. The expression on his face told Booth that he was less than keen to do so.

"I'll do it unless you want your first corpse to be something prettier," said Booth.

Turner shrugged. "I suppose I have to do it sometime," he said, still with a look of apprehension on his face.

Booth gave him a nod. She felt a little bad for him, but she knew very well that if he didn't pop his dead body cherry here then it could possibly happen with something far worse. Her own first experience with a body that wasn't on a photograph had been a road traffic accident out on the M6 that cut around the edge of Hemmington. Two cars had clipped each other, trying to race. One of the cars, a Ford Focus had been thrown to the left, sending it off the hard shoulder and into a tree.

It had been pretty obvious when she had arrived on the scene with her then partner Sergeant Pearson, that the driver of the Focus was young, stoned out of his mind and hadn't been wearing a seatbelt. The smell of cannabis had hung around the wreckage in a pungent fog. The driver of the car had gone through the windscreen and collided headfirst into the trunk of the unfortunate tree that happened to have been growing in the wrong place at the wrong time. The collision between the wood and the cranium of the young driver, who was projected out of the car at nearly eighty miles-per-hour had been a no contest. Gore, chunks of broken skull and soft meaty pieces of brain were spread all around the trunk of the tree and the grass behind it. The spine of the driver had been snapped clean in half, and the remains of the body were folded up like a cheap accordion on the twisted and bent metal of the car bonnet. Booth had taken one look at the carnage and thrown her pasta salad that she had for lunch up onto the surface of the hard shoulder. The other car, a very ancient looking Honda Civic was two hundred yards up the road and facing the wrong way. The driver of that car managed to get out without a mark on him, although he would later be up in court for causing death by dangerous driving.

Booth wondered to herself if Turner was going to throw up. She had apologised to Pearson at the time for having such a weak constitution, but he had waved it off, telling her that *everyone* throws up at the sight of their first body. She had asked him if he had thrown up, to which he replied that he never threw up, ever.

"Ready?" said Booth, placing her hand on the broken door.

Turner gritted his teeth and offered her a nod. The reality was that he was never going to be ready, even if he waited until his retirement day.

Booth gave the door a push. It ground across the rubbish that seemed to be ingrained into the floor below it. The smell from inside the place was a wall of festering stink. Turner tried his best to suppress a retch. Booth wrapped her sleeve across her nose and turned away from it for a moment.

"Christ almighty. That's rank," she said.

She fumbled in her top pocket and brought out a small torch. She clicked it on with her thumb and waved it around the hallway in front of her. She took a step forward and waved the torch all around the floor. Turner followed, expecting Booth to keep moving, but she stopped just inside the doorway and he bumped into her.

"Shit," said Booth.

"What is it?" mumbled Turner from behind her.

"I thought this body was supposed to be fresh," she said and shone the torch at the floor again.

Turner came out from behind her and took a look for himself. Under the spotlight, he could see a man's clothing spread out over the floor, but there was no flesh and skin there, only yellowing bones and a pool of something that looked like link sausages.

"Someone is shitting us, Booth," said Turner.

Booth didn't hear him, she was moving forwards towards the body. There was no way in her mind that it could have been anything other than an old corpse, one that had been in here undiscovered for months. Perhaps they had just misunderstood what they had been told. Perhaps they had got it wrong. Her hand went to her radio to call it in and double check.

"Booth, let's get out of here, I don't like this," said Turner.

"Alright, but I'm going to find out who…." She broke off. There was movement out of the corner of her eye. As she turned around to leave the torchlight waved across the filthy room. Something moved, she was certain of it. She moved the torch again, scanning the hallway and the doorway to the living room.

Nothing.

She moved the beam upwards towards the ceiling. Her heart felt like it stopped dead in her chest, and then it gave a huge lurching beat as the adrenaline began to course through her entire body.

"Fuck me," she croaked from her tightening throat.

Turner looked up at the beam. He was barely able to register what he was seeing. It looked to him as if the whole ceiling and the top sections of the wall were alive, a black seething mass of movement. Booth began to back away.

"Out Turner, get out…." She was saying, but he couldn't move. He was transfixed on the rustling hoard of darkness that was above their heads. As he looked on a large clump of them came loose and fell to the floor. Booth's torch followed them and they both saw with increasing horror as the chunk of blackness untangled itself.

"Spiders," said Booth. "Spiders…get out of here *now,"* she shrieked.

Turner staggered backward. His feet hit the step and he stumbled back into the street. Booth came storming out after him. She crashed into Turner and nearly knocked him right off his feet.

Tooms, the reporter across the road saw the two police officers come barging out of the house. He was already out of his chair the moment he heard shouting from inside.

"Bobbo, get the camera rolling," he shouted. He began to cross the road towards the two officers.

"Close the door," bellowed Turner.

Booth took a step inside to try and grab the splintered and ragged door. But the movement and the darkness that was on the ceiling was now raining down onto the floor. The spiders untangled themselves from each other and came down the hallway with incredible speed.

"….too late, get away," she shrieked.

They both took off for the other side of the road, almost wiping out Tooms and his cameraman. "Stay back," she yelled at him.

They made it to the other side of the road and turned back to look at the house. The spiders were starting to emerge. The walls surrounding the door were already turning dark. They headed upwards and sideways, covering the ruined house with their small black bodies.

"What the *fuck*," said Tooms. "Bobbo, are you getting this?" he shouted.

"I'm getting it, boss, I'm getting it," said Bobbo in a strangled voice.

Booth was already on her radio calling it in. She knew the protocol, just like anybody else.

Unusual Activity.

She yelled down her radio, trying to get somebody to get off their backside and answer her. She was too busy to see Tooms making his way across the road again.

"Come on Bobbo, let's get a closer look. This is news, my friend," he said, a smile breaking out over his face.

Tooms jogged across the road and veered off to the left of the spider encrusted house. Bobbo came with him, making sure that he was behind Tooms every step of the way.

"Are you getting this?" said Tooms.

Bobbo nodded. He focused the lens on the mass of tiny bodies crawling all over the bricks.

"On me, on me," said Tooms. He rolled his finger to tell Bobbo that he was going to record a report.

"Hang on, let me pick one of them up," he said. He put his cupped hand into the mass of spiders. "Y'see, they don't bite…" he said, a big shit-eating grin breaking out over his face.

A moment later the grin was gone. Tooms drew his hand out of the spiders and began to shake it as if he had touched something hot. Bobbo could see the spiders running up the arm of his sports coat, crawling across his chest. Tooms began to curse and yell. He whirled around beating at his own skin. His curses began to disintegrate into yells of pain and anguish. He fell to the floor in the middle of the road and began to roll. His screams became illegible, high and gobbling. Bobbo felt something beginning to needle his ankles as if he was being given half a dozen blood tests all at the same time. He began to involuntarily stamp his feet, to try and get the pains to stop. He abandoned his viewfinder for a moment to look down and see what was causing the problem, and he saw dozens of spiders crawling over his shoes, up his ankles and disappearing under the material of his trouser leg. He dropped the camera which struck the pavement like a bomb. Pieces of broken glass and plastic flew in all directions. The spiders swarmed over it, covering it in a myriad of scuttling legs and black hairy bodies.

Bobbo ran for the other side of the road, jumping up and down as he tried to run. The skin on his legs began to burn, a deep intolerable pain that felt as if his flesh had been set on fire. He fell down, roaring at the police officers for help. But they were busy. They were busy running in the other direction.

"We need everything down here, there are spiders everywhere, and I think they are venomous. Send everything you have," yelled Booth into her radio.

By the time they had got to the bottom of the street, Boris' house was covered from floor to ceiling, from roof to pavement in spiders.

21.

Probably the best thing about Ken Rogers' job as the maintenance man of Suicide Towers was his little hideaway, or as he liked to call it, his office. It was actually a small room situated around the back of the base of the tower that was supposed to be a storeroom for all his tools and equipment. When he had started the job just after the tower had been finished, and the residents began to move in one by one, he had found himself in and out of the equipment room, grabbing the right things to fix a leaking tap, or a door that wouldn't quite close properly and all of those other little quirks that you always tended to get on a new building. During the colder months of the year, he used to stall going to the next job simply because the boiler in the room gave it an ambiance that was good enough to fall asleep in. He had mulled an idea over one evening after he had sunk a few beers in front of the football and he had returned the next day carrying an old office chair that he kept in his kitchen. He normally sat on the chair when he was supposed to be doing the washing up, or some other task that his wife Sandra had sent him in there to do. He had reasoned to himself that the chair could be put to much better use in the equipment room of the towers so that he could have himself a nice sit down and perhaps enjoy some tea from his long silver flask which looked to him like some sort of space-age sex toy. Perhaps he could even lean back in the chair, have himself a smoke and then catch a little nap whilst he was in between jobs, the rumble, and warmth of the boiler acting like an industrial lullaby to send him on his way. It had turned out to be one of the finest ideas that he had ever had in his whole miserable life. That chair had changed his working day from an endless grind to a little hard graft and a whole lot of lounging. It had altered the entire balance of his day-to-day life by making it far more appealing to be at work than it was at home. Just to be able to spend so much time without getting a flea in his ear from Sandra every two minutes was an absolute blessing. He also knew that if they had a falling out then he could come right back to his little haven and stay there until the storm had blown over. It was the perfect companion on every level. He began to stash other things in the little room, a bag of snack foods and cans of cola so he didn't have to waste valuable lounging time going to the shop. All-in-all, he had himself a nice little set up in his 'office.'

It had been a quiet day for Ken so far, and by quiet, it meant that nothing had happened that he needed to fix or take care of. His day before he had set off for work had been anything but quiet. Sandra had been in fine voice since the moment he had opened his eyes. She usually started kicking off if he snoozed his alarm and decided on another ten minutes sleep. She was such an unbelievable stickler for keeping things happening right on time. Ken had worked out a long time ago, that if things didn't go exactly as Sandra had planned then the whole entire day was fucked, at least in her mind. His blasé attitude to just about everything really got on her goat. This morning he had double-snoozed which had sent her into overdrive. She had stormed into the room, still wet from the shower and torn the duvet off the bed, roaring at the top of her voice to inform him what a lazy shit he was (as if he didn't already know.)

He had rolled off the naked bed, got himself dressed and walked straight out of the house without even bothering to brush his teeth. Sandra had continued her verbal assault on him even after he had closed the front door behind him. He started walking, still with his teeth gritted and his fists opening and clenching until he had reached the end of his street. By the time he was halfway to the tower, which poked up from the landscape like a green-striped phallus, he was beginning to feel a whole lot better. He began to enjoy the Indian summer which gave the normally cold air a soothing warm glow. He felt the generally shitty start to the day beginning to ebb away. Soon he would be in the comfort of his office and the rest of the day could just about go to hell as far as he was concerned. He even called in at the coffee house which was on the corner of Lancaster Road, about half a mile from the tower, and got himself a nice big cup of black tea. By the time he got to the office, it would be just about hitting the right temperature for drinking. He was going to set everything straight, and perhaps even contemplate what he was going to do about the thorn in his arse that was called Sandra.

He had drunk the tea and took an hour or so to go through the newspaper just to kick things off, then he had spent half-an-hour in quiet contemplation of how he could get away from Sandra, or perhaps alter things so that she wasn't such an incorrigible pain in the arse. He thought of drugging her somehow, perhaps with a healthy dose of cocaine or something else to give her a kick. Maybe he could give her so much that she would drop dead, giving him the freedom of his own home to behave however he pleased. He stretched out in his chair and stacked his feet on the pile of old newspapers that he had collected and made into a footrest. Waves of tiredness were washing over him. He needed to recharge the old batteries before he could do anything else.

He managed to sleep well into the afternoon before the buzzing and twinkling of his mobile phone snapped him out of his slumber. He scrambled the phone out of his trouser pocket, his cloudy mind unable to tell him exactly where he was, or what he was doing. He got the phone in his hand. He hit the answer button and held it to his ear. A post-sleep headache was pulsing and snarling around his temples.

"Kenny got an urgent for you."

It was Tillart, that scrawny office-boy puke from the association office. Ken really had nothing against him, it just stuck in his throat that someone so much younger than him could order him around like his own personal pet. He fumbled his notepad and pen off his counter at the side of his chair.

"Go ahead," he mumbled.

"Got a water leak. It's coming in through the ceiling of apartment 332. The leak could be coming from the flat above, ok?"

Ken scribbled it down in his barely legible handwriting. He got the basics – *leak 332 flat above.*

He hung up the phone without making niceties with Tillart and got his head together. He had to get the main water supply shut off first. It was quicker and easier. He scooped up his toolbox and pushed his way out of the office.

He let himself into the main building and headed left to the utility room. He opened the door with his key and yanked it open. The door gave off a rusty squeal as it came open. Ken made a mental note to bring the oil along next time to give the hinges a good going over. He went inside and found the mains water valve.

He grabbed the handle and pushed it anticlockwise. He heard the rush of water going through the pipes getting choked off. The mains electricity box was the only noise left in the room. The insectile buzz sounded very loud inside the small room without the hiss of the water running through the pipes.

Ken went out of the room, pulling the door shut behind him. He got in the lift and headed up to the twelfth floor where the complaint had come from. He went to 332 and found a scrawny old man standing outside the door his thin, pale arms folded across his chest in a gesture of utter annoyance. He saw Ken coming and began to shout, his arms flapping wildly in the air.

"Stupid nigger bitch. In and out all hours of the night, now this. As soon as she fucks off back to her own country, the better."

Ken strode passed him. He felt a strong urge to give the old bastard an elbow to the ribs to see if that would change his views on Mr. Working Class Whitey. He chose to ignore him and went into the flat to see what was going on. He could hear the water dripping in the hallway and the kitchen of the flat. It wasn't a small amount of water either. The floor was soaking and the walls were painted with clean streaks through the nicotine stains. The ceiling was bulging, carrying the weight of leaking water within it. By turning the mains off he was pretty sure that the problem, at least for now, wasn't going to get any worse. He made his way out of the flat again, ignoring the ranting of the old bastard that lived there and he made his way to the stairs. He went up a flight and came through the fire door. He made his way to the end of the corridor and to the flat, number 432, that he reckoned was the source of the problem. He rapped on the door, purely out of habit. He had a pretty good idea that if the occupant was home that they would have reported the leak themselves. He went straight to his toolbox and took out his large roll of master keys. He flicked through them until he found the matching key and he unlocked the door.

"I'm coming in," he bellowed, again simply out of compliance with the normal protocol. He pushed the door open and wasn't surprised to find that the flat was empty. He could hear water splashing onto the floor somewhere off to the left. The living room he was standing in was almost anally tidy. Every piece of furniture looked like it had cost a pretty penny. Whoever it was that lived here, she had kitted herself out pretty well. He momentarily imagined asking her out for a drink, to try and compensate her for the water damage that had happened. Perhaps he could get her drunk enough to bring him back here on a more sociable basis. If he didn't get anywhere with her, he could fuck her couch, such was the quality of it.

He walked around the living room for a moment, admiring all of the expensive looking knick-knacks that she had collected. She had a hell of a nice television too. It wasn't overly large, but it was one of those new fancy ones with a curved screen that he personally had his eye on for a while now. He squatted down to look at the curvature on the screen, wondering just how much the picture quality on it would be so much better than the tiny, cheap little thing he had at home. As he was looking at the screen he heard a noise behind him. At the same time, he saw movement on the screen, as if someone had come in the room behind him. He initially suspected that the old bastard from downstairs had followed him up so he could come and put the boot in a little more. He stood up and turned around, ready to give the old fucker a piece of his mind.

What he saw killed the words dead in his mouth. He felt his bladder give way in a rush of warmth that cascaded down his legs.

There was a spider coming through from the hallway that led to the bathroom. It was a spider that was as big as a horse. It came through the hallway and stood at the other end of the living room. Ken only looked at it for a moment, but at that moment, he saw everything. The huge thick legs that had tufts of spiky hair covering them, the pulsating abdomen...and then there was the human face, the naked and hairy female human body. He saw the tattoo that it had just above its right breast, and the few remaining teeth that were still left in its mouth. Ken stumbled backward against the window, pressing his back against it. He began to move sideways, hoping that he could get to the short hallway that led to the front door so he could bolt out of there. His breath was coming in shallow hitches, his chest hurting from the effort of pulling in so many short breaths in such a short space of time. The spider-thing suddenly charged at him, battering furniture out of the way as it advanced. He wanted to run for it, but his legs and feet were frozen to the floor, the paralysing fear tearing through his body. The spider bore down on him, its fangs sprouting from the upper gums where the teeth were missing. He brought up his arms, trying to defend himself from the onslaught, but it was to no avail. He felt the front legs encircling his body. He felt them tighten, his ribs resisting at first and then splintering with an ear-splitting crackle. His last breath was forced from his deflating lungs, sending out a strangled bray and a jet of bright red blood spraying from his mouth. The fangs came down and punctured his carotid artery. He was lifted from the floor, his urine soaked legs twitching and shaking as the last of his life force left his body. The spider suckled the blood from Ken's body, drinking it down as if it was a quick shot of whiskey being knocked back by a Friday night drunk. Ken's skin began to wrinkle and shrivel, taking on an appearance that made it look like damp cardboard. The spider finished its meal and dropped Ken's ramshackle body to the floor where it folded up in a battered heap.

The spider slowly made its way back to the dark hallway where it had been hiding. It sat in the dark, waiting for its next victim to arrive. It had to rest, it had to preserve the meal it had just taken. It watched the hallway with the eyes that had once belonged to Doctor Ochre. Somewhere in its mind, it could still remember her, still, remember fragments of the life that she had led. But all of it was clouded with a new incentive, a new mission parameter.

Wait.

Wait for them.

22.

Thompson had returned to the hospital a full hour after Wells had been taken in. His gut instinct had been just to go home, pack up a supply of clothing for him and Cindy and head for the coast. He had never been one to want everything to just blow over without him involved, but seeing Wells in such a bad way had allowed that feeling to break through that hardened wall that he had built around his emotional state during all of his years of doing the job. It had been through a sheer force of willpower that he had headed for the hospital. He probably should have stayed behind to help get the station up and running again, but to hell with all of that. Roberts could take charge of that little cleanup. He needed to earn his fucking pay doing something other than shouting, bawling and overacting his way to home time.

He went into the hospital and asked the receptionist where he could find Wells. She punched a few buttons on her computer keyboard and then asked him to take a seat for a moment. Thompson found an empty chair next to the left-hand wall. The chair next to him was occupied by, what looked to Thompson, like a homeless man. His clothing was faded and threadbare around the edges. A thatch of thick and matted hair jutted out from under a black beanie hat. His considerable beard had the same consistency of his hair. The moment Thompson sat down the man looked him up and down.

"'ere, you got a quid for a starving genius?" said the man.

Thompson looked at him curiously. The tramp smiled, showing the few remaining tombstones of his teeth.

"Genius eh?" said Thompson.

The tramp saluted him. "Aye laddie, smartest brain in the entire northern hemisphere," he said tapping his head with a finger.

"Tell me then, how come you don't have any money if you're such a genius?" said Thompson.

The bellowed fresh laughter into Thompson's tired face. "That's a fine question, my friend. Let me put it to you this way; Could you compare the quality of life that you have with the quality of mine?"

"I don't follow you," said Thompson.

"This morning, I was over in the fine city of Hemmington, trying to get together enough brass for a morning cup of tea. I had made it up to three pounds and twenty-two pence, and I decided to delay my morning refreshment to see if I could gather enough funds for a chocolate croissant to go with my morning tea. Do y'know what happened then?"

Thompson shook his head. He was honestly fascinated by this strange man.

"Well, a young fella in a nice suit comes up to me, hands me a tray with a great big frothy coffee and a full English in a little plastic tray. I goes to shake his hand to thank him and he has a twenty-pound note curled up in his hand. Yessir, he wished me God's speed and he went on his way."

"That was lucky," said Thompson.

The tramp wheezed again, "Nothin' to do with luck Chief. The natural instinct of every human being, if you strip away all the bullshit that they surround themselves with, is to help their fellow man. I have lived this life of mine for over thirty years, bin to pretty much every town and city in the country. I used some of that twenty pounds to jump on a bus to this fine town. Might stay a while too."

"How does it all make you a genius?" said Thompson. He had a smile on his face, he couldn't help it.

"I don't have no mortgage to worry about, no housework to do, no taxes to pay. I don't have to worry about needing somewhere to sleep at night. God's green grass is my mattress and the sky is my blanket. Wish it was heated during the winter mind." He roared again and slapped his own leg.

"That's one way of looking at it," said Thompson.

"It's the only way of looking at it chief. We only get so long on this earth my friend, you have to make the most of it, whatever your lot in life is. Mine ain't as prosperous as most, but I'm doing everything I can to make the best of it, after all, it's the only life I got."

There was silence between them for a moment. Thompson decided that this guy was absolutely right, he was a genius. He had made everything bad that was going on in his life right now seem like a minor inconvenience. He really had no idea of how lucky he was. He dug into his pocket, fished out his wallet and took all the notes out of it. He wasn't sure how much there was in there, he guessed it was around fifty pounds or so. He held it out to the tramp.

"Here, go have yourself more adventures. Take a look at Layton Valley if you get a chance. Beautiful spot," said Thompson.

The tramp took hold of the money, his smile growing visibly under his beard. "God bless you, my friend. Whenever you feel life is getting a little hard, just remember, do the best you can with what you got, you feel me?"

"Yeah, I feel you," said Thompson he offered his hand, "Pleased to meet you Mr?"

"Robert Green, at your service." He shook Thompson's hand. "So, what has brought you to this lovely establishment? Less'un you know somebody that's giving birth, I'm hazarding a guess that it ain't good news."

Thompson shook his head. "My friend…..work partner, he lost half his arm."

Robert offered him that smile again. "Did he get in an accident?"

"No, he was bitten…," said Thompson and then he bit his tongue. He had almost let the cat out of the bag right there.

"Bitten? What kind of creature could bite off'un a man's arm in such a fashion? I don't see no lions nor crocodiles around these parts," said Robert.

"No, no there isn't. I think it must have got infected," said Thompson. He wished he had kept his mouth shut. The receptionist was coming over to him which meant that he was going to buy himself a way out of this alleyway he was stuck in.

"Mr. Thompson?"

"Yes," he said standing up.

"This way please."

He turned to Robert and offered his hand. Robert shook.

"Good talking to you my friend," said Thompson.

"Hope your friend is feeling better soon," said Robert. "And thanks for the cash, stranger. You heed my words, you do the best with what you got and you will never go wrong."

"Layton Valley, you should check it out. Perhaps sooner rather than later," said Thompson.

"I'll do that Mr. Thompson, sir. Perhaps I'll set up home there for a while."

Thompson turned and followed the receptionist out of the waiting area on Roberts laughter.

It was a long walk through the hospital to the isolation ward. It was long enough for Thompson to wonder what he was going to find when he got there. He and Wells had been through the mill together throughout the years that they had been put together as a partnership. They had put behind bars some of the vilest, despicable pieces of human waste that the country had ever seen, and at the end of each case, they didn't sit on their laurels, they didn't pat themselves on the back, they just got on with the job. He wanted to honour their partnership right now by just getting on with the job right now. He needed to make sure Wells was alright and then he needed to make sure that Roberts was going to take his thumb out of his arse and get this situation under control. He didn't want anyone else coming into this hospital in the same condition as Wells, not on his watch.

They were three-quarters of the way down the corridor when the first of the screams came echoing down the walls.

Thompson instinctively broke into a run. He charged for the door and he was about to try and shoulder charge the lock when it popped open. Doctor Wilson came staggering out of the door and slammed it behind her. The front of her uniform was splattered with gore. Blood was streaked across her chest and halfway up her face. Some of it was still running down her clothing and dripping onto the floor. Wilson frantically turned the lock with hands that was shaking badly. A moment later something crashed into the doors from the other side, something big and heavy. That ear-splitting shriek blasted out from inside the ward.

"Need guns….." rasped Wilson.

"What? What are you talking about?" said Thompson.

"We need someone with a gun, right now…" she shrieked. The door banged again as if to highlight the point.

"What is it?" said Thompson.

"Katie….it was Katie…she killed Renfrew…she….she…"

The door crashed again, this time it looked as if the right-hand door buckled a little.

"We have to evacuate…..get the army in here….." cried Wilson. Thompson was looking at her dumbfounded. Wilson grabbed him by his shirt and shook him. *"Do something"* she roared in his face.

Thompson grabbed his radio and began to call for assistance.

The door banged again. The top of the right-side door bent forwards a little, just enough for a small hole to open up. Wilson grabbed Thompson.

"Let's get out of here," she yelled.

Through the gap in the door, something began to poke its way through. Thompson couldn't make it out, his mind wouldn't unscramble the image he was seeing. It looked like there was a huge, misshapen spider leg poking through the hole. Then Wilson was pulling him down the corridor. He turned his head forward so he didn't fall. They passed one of the fire alarm buttons that was littered all through the hospital. Wilson balled up a fist and punched the glass as hard as she could. The fire alarm began to wail all around the building.

"What the hell happened in there? Where's Wells?" roared Thompson.

"They changed, they both changed. They turned into...." She broke off, scrambled her phone out of her pocket and showed Thompson a picture that she had snapped.

When Thompson saw the picture, he couldn't believe it, he wouldn't believe it and then the door of the isolation ward was broken right off its hinges. The creature that had once been Katie Underwood began to emerge from the broken hole. When he saw it, Thompson began to understand.

Wilson pulled at Thompson's sleeve. "Run," she screamed.

They charged down the corridor, turning a sharp right towards the main body of the hospital. Thompson could hear the tapping and skittering of the spider-like legs of the beast as it chased them. Any moment now he would feel the weight of it crashing down on him, pinning him to the floor to do god knows what to him. They reached the lift and Wilson began pounding the button. By sheer good luck, the lift was on their floor and the door slid open. They both got inside and Wilson hammered the button for the ground floor. Thompson looked up the corridor that they had just run down and he saw the creature scuttling towards them. The six extra legs that Katie had grown were clumsy, awkward even, but they still managed to propel her down the corridor and towards them with alarming speed. The two front legs which were by far the most dexterous looked to Thompson like they had grown out of the pulped remains of her own arms. Katie's distorted features saw the lift door closing on Thompson and Wilson and it let out a screech of frustration. It put on an extra burst of speed, but it was too late. As the lift door closed, the Katie thing crashed into it and let out another yell. It was just that little bit too slow. The new legs that it had grown were taking some getting used to. It began to make its way back to the isolation ward. The Wells thing was still trying to stand when she had left to go after Wilson and Thompson. She was halfway back to the ward when the Wells thing came scuttling around the corner. It stopped to look at her for a moment and then it charged down the corridor. It stopped only when they were face to face. They knew both of them knew what they had to do next. Something deep inside of them was telling them what the next phase was. They started to move again. But they were in no hurry. They had all the time in the world.

    After all, their day was about to begin.

23.

Perry Williams had fallen asleep on his couch around ten minutes after returning to his home. It was the curse of the night shift that his body clock was set to sleep mode even after everything that had happened today. When he had arrived home, he saw that there was a policeman now standing in front of the door at Boris' place. God only knew what was going there. Perhaps they had found Boris dead, rotted down to nothing more than a few scraps of flesh and bones. It wouldn't have surprised him. Little did he know just how accurate that his perception was.

It was his intention to head straight upstairs and pack everything that he thought Katie would need into her purple rucksack. It wasn't big enough to fit everything in, but it certainly would have done her just for now, at least until he knew exactly how long she was going to be in the hospital. The moment he had walked in through the door and found himself amongst familiar surroundings, a huge wave of tiredness crashed over him like a wave in a high wind. He thought that it would be fine if he just sat down for a moment and gathered himself. Perhaps he could shut his eyes for five minutes whilst he got his head together again.

A few moments later he began to snore. He didn't wake up again until someone began to bang on the front door. Such was the suddenness and the violence with which they knocked that he jumped straight up off the couch. He stood there for a moment, his head still swimming with sleep and his senses unable to process what had snatched him from his slumber in such a violent way. The banging on the door came again, and he stumbled through the room and into the hallway. Again, the banging. Christ, did they have to knock so loud?

"I'm *coming*" he roared. He gripped the handle and pulled the door open.

"You have to evacuate, right now." said the woman at the door. It took a moment for Perry not only to register what she had said but the fact that the woman looked like she was dressed in army gear.

"But, I just got back…I…"

The woman caught hold of his shirt. "You have to evacuate now, the whole street is going up," she bellowed into his sleep puffy face.

Without another word, she dragged him out of his house. He fought her at first and then, as he made it out onto the street, he saw the flames. All of the houses up the street were burning. Flames rose up into the air, sending a column of smoke up into the early evening sky. He saw two more army men standing in the street, and it looked to him like they were wearing flamethrowers. Was that even possible? Why would they be torching the street?

He was manhandled to the opposite side of the road and he lost his footing on the curb and spilled to the floor. He looked back at the burning homes, the horror of his own dwelling catching fire began to rise up in him. Then he saw something else, something starting to cover the outer skin of his house and the ones next to it. He saw the darkness creeping into his own front door, coating the white walls of his hallway. Whatever it was, it was alive and moving. It began to spread across the road towards him. It was only then that his eyes began to focus properly. The adrenaline pumping through his body pushed the last of the sleep from his brain, making it clear again. The darkness coming towards him and consuming his house was made up of spiders. Hundreds, thousands of them, all scuttling across the road towards him. He was about to scramble to his feet when he was yanked up by his collar.

"Run, *get out of here*." The woman shrieked in his ear.

He took off down towards the far end of the road, as fast as his legs could carry him. Behind him, he heard the woman who had pulled him out of his home begin to scream. He looked back and saw her being consumed by the creeping carpet of spiders. He saw her eyes, bugging out with terror and pain, and her open mouth, fixed in that final scream, and then….

Whhooooshhhh…..

One of the soldiers turned his flamethrower on her. She was engulfed in the fire. Perry saw her burning body fall to the ground, thrashing and flailing in the ball of flames. The spiders that had clung to her body were turned into pieces of ash almost instantaneously. The rest of them began to run away from the heat and up the road to where Perry was standing. He turned and ran as hard as he could. He heard the *whoosh* of the flamethrowers again and again and he could swear that he could feel the heat from them at his back.

He got clear of the street and onto the main Hemmington Road. He headed south, running as much as he could. He slowed to a fast walk, heaving air into his lungs. He bent over double for a moment, trying to gather himself, trying to get through his head what he had just witnessed. He had to get to the hospital, just to talk to Katie, to tell her what had happened. He stood up straight again and started to walk. The hospital was only ten minutes down the road. He would be there soon, he reassured himself. Then he could try and make sense of what had just gone on.

His hands patted his pockets, looking for his mobile phone, but then he realised that he had taken it out and put it on the arm of the sofa as he always did when he was planning to have a few quiet moments on the sofa. He cursed himself for his mistake, swearing out loud and patting his pockets again in case the phone had magically been transported. Surely there would still be people at the hospital, he prayed that there would be people at the hospital, just to break him out of the weird feeling of disassociation that he felt from seeing his street overrun by spiders.

He started forward again, going at a steady jog instead of the all-out pelt he had run at before. He reached the point in the road where it bent sharply to the left. This was known as scrap corner due to the excessive amount of crashes that had occurred on this bend by boy racers and other foolish drivers who took it too sharply. The road had been temporarily jammed up with traffic in both directions on more than one occasion whilst the twisted remains of another vehicle were lifted from the scene. The local council had been inundated with complaints about it for, what seemed like an endless run of months and years. The only action they had taken so far was to erect signs on both ends of the corner advising motorists to take it easy on the bend. The signs had pretty much no impact on the number of written-off cars that had resulted from the bend, and so the complaints went on.

Perry came around the bend and the hospital building loomed ahead of him. A roadblock had been put up cutting off the right-hand turn to the hospital. It wasn't a police roadblock either, it was the army again. Two high-sided army vehicles stood behind the metal barriers, almost fully blocking the view of the road ahead. Two soldiers, armed with rifles stood at either side of the blockade. Perry froze to the spot, wondering if he should retreat and try and find another way around. But before he could decide, one of the soldiers shouted over to him.

"Oi, come over here."

Perry paused for a moment and then began to walk slowly forwards. His body was coiled like a spring, ready to dive for cover if they tried to shoot at him. However, the soldiers kept their guns down and allowed him to approach.

"Where have you come from sir?" said the soldier. His cool blue eyes stood out from under his helmet like piss holes in the snow.

"Corsica Road. I was told to run. They had flamethrowers…..there were spiders everywhere. What's going on?" spluttered Perry.

"Can't say for sure just yet. We have been told it's a terrorist incident."

Perry frowned. None of it made any sense to him. "Terrorists? That doesn't…"

"That's all we are prepared to say at the moment, sir. You need to clear the area," said the soldier in his robotic voice.

"I have to get to the hospital, my girlfriend is…."

"The hospital has been evacuated. She will have been moved over to Hemmington. I would suggest that…."

The soldier didn't finish his sentence. From behind the roadblock, there was an almighty crash. Glass came flying over the roadblock causing the soldiers and Perry to shield their eyes. A moment later there was a chorus of shouting and rapid gunfire. The two soldiers jumped over the barrier, drawing their guns and vanished between the vehicles. The gunfire lasted for less than a minute. Through the popping of bullets, Perry could hear screams of agony and a sound of something splattering across the floor. Perry felt the ground underneath him shake as if something heavy was treading on the floor nearby. Alarms from the cars lined up in the car parks began to howl and wail. The ground shook again and again. More screams of pain rang out, echoing around the street. Again and again, the screams rang out until the gunfire and the bellows of anguish were gone.

All that remained was the vibrating of the ground and the ringing of the alarms from cars being shaken by the turbulence. Perry was frozen to the spot for a moment, wondering if he should just run for it, but his curiosity was too great. He made his way around the roadblock and ducked down behind the front of one of the vehicles. He waited for a moment, breathing hard, his heart a steady beating drum in his ears. He forced himself to rise up slowly so that he could look over the front of the van and see what had happened near the hospital. As the view opened up before him the horror that was already pulsing through his body stepped up a notch. The bodies of the soldiers were strewn all over the road leading up to the front of the hospital. Most of them had been torn apart, as easily as one might tear paper. Blood, intestines and severed limbs littered the floor, some of them still twitching with the convulsions of their sudden death. Perry wanted to stop looking at it, just close his eyes and hope that it was all just an illusion, but he couldn't. He couldn't tear his eyes away from it. He was utterly transfixed by the carnage that had happened in such a short space of time.

He caught sight of something moving out of the corner of his eye. He snapped his head towards it. When he saw it when he saw the thing that had caused all of that carnage, his vision began to swim and his legs threatened to buckle beneath him. If he hadn't been hanging on to the vehicle he would have crumpled to the floor.

The monster in front of him was almost beyond description. It was the legs that he saw first, those long insect-like legs that were growing out of its body. The surface of the skin was shining and wet, as if they were still new, not hardened to the outside atmosphere yet. They were holding the body of the abomination off the floor. It was swaying slightly as if there was a stiff breeze blowing. The body was still mostly human. It was bloated and bruised all over from its head right down to its dangling feet. The bottom half of its face was missing, from the nose down. It looked as if it had been torn right off in a horrible accident. In the shredded and bloody ruin, two large fangs were curling downwards, fangs that were big enough to tear a human body apart. The creature lumbered over to where Perry was hiding. He was utterly powerless to do anything about it. His legs felt totally numb, barely able to support his weight. All he could do was stare at the monster in front of him. His eyes flicked all around its body, finally coming to rest on its eyes, those green eyes, that looked to him like they almost carried the sparkle of the stars from heaven itself.

And that was when he realised. He realised who was standing in front of him. The muscles in his legs began to work again. He pulled himself up and walked around the edge of the truck. Now there was nothing between them but the clean fresh air of the oncoming night. The monster took a couple of steps backward. He saw her. He saw the metal rod, attached to the human leg that had been broken on the floor of their bathroom this morning. He saw the red hair, matted with human blood but the glow and the styling of it still intact. Then he looked at the eyes again. The eyes that he had seen lit up with life and her love for him, every time he had learned in for a kiss, every time he had held her in his arms and told her that everything would be just fine as long as they had each other.

This monster, whatever it was, it was her. It was his Katie, and deep within his jackhammering heart, he knew she was still in there somewhere.

"It's me," he yelled up at her. "Don't you remember? It's me, Perry."

The monster didn't move. It stood its ground.

"You are Katie Underwood. My Katie. You must remember, you must."

The monster didn't move. Those eyes were fixed on Perry. He thought although it might have been his imagination that a frown had creased its forehead. Its mind must have been working it over.

Perry took a step closer to the monster. "Come on, *think*," he yelled. The monster recoiled a little.

Just for a moment, Perry saw that frown on its face begin to smooth out. He felt a huge surge of elation. He was getting through to her. He knew it. He began to step slowly forwards towards her, trying to see the human behind the horrific mutation. His heart ached for her. He so desperately wanted her to be cured, to be restored to her former glory. He had agonised over looking after her whilst she recovered from her broken leg, and now he wanted to take care of her more than ever. The monster stood its ground for a moment, looking down at him. Those eyes sparkled, just for a second. Perry saw it, and he knew that she knew who he was. Those memories of their life together were still deep within her contorted brain.

But then something roared above them, a piercing, shrieking roar that echoed all around the complex. Perry looked up and saw another monster attached to the side of the building. It was scuttling towards the ground with frightening speed. The Katie monster turned towards it, saw it coming and then uttered her own scream. Perry clapped his hands over his ears to try and drown out the deafening noise. The shriek stopped when the other monster reached the ground and ran over to Katie. The new monster looked down at Perry, its one remaining eye burning a hole right through him.

"No…." was all he had time to get out and then the monster was upon him. It pinned him down with one of its legs and then the huge fangs were clamping down on the front of his neck. Perry beat at the leg holding him down, punching it as hard as he could. He tried to draw in another breath to shout for Katie to help him but the fangs clipped together, neatly snipping through the skin, the flesh, the tendons, and the bone, severing his head from his body. In his last waking moment, Perry felt the large arteries in his neck let go in a warm gout and then he knew no more. His head rolled three feet from the rest of his body with a fountain of gore following it, coating the grey concrete surface in a deep red colour.

Inside the mind of the Katie monster, there was a momentary conflict, a fleeting need to feel something for the man that had just been torn apart. It wanted to scream out, to stop it from happening. Just for a moment, it felt human again, and then it was gone. Back to the primary urge that was infesting its psyche. It had to survive, they all had to survive. It could feel them within its consciousness, every single one of them, hiding away, waiting for the moment. The first ones had only been the scouts, the ones who were going to set the whole thing in motion. They had done their job admirably. It felt the change deep within its guts. It was time to bring the army in. It was time for the next phase of their survival, and the only way they were going to survive was to dominate, to take over. It had already survived an attempt to stop it once, and this time it would not fail.

The Katie monster grasped onto that feeling that it had deep down inside and then it opened its mouth once again. It began to emit a clicking noise, so loud and so deep that it vibrated through its body. The Wells thing began to make the same sound, perfectly in sync it amplified it to the point where it was echoing around the town.

A few moments later the ground beneath them began to shake.

24.

Braden didn't know how long he had sat in the car. The moment that he had sent in that picture, the thrill of the chase had ebbed away. He had got the story, got the proof he needed and now it was done. Did he feel fulfilled because of it? Not even a tiny bit. The echoes of Jax's crying were still bowling around his mind. He supposed that a heroin addict would feel the same after falling from grace when they had promised over and over again that it was all over. He was feeling the entire career that he had spent twenty years building fading away. The love of it had curdled in his insides and left him feeling empty. It was over. Whatever he did from this day forwards would have nothing to do with journalism ever again. All he had left was the sliver of hope that Mary would allow him to speak to her again, allow her to listen to what had happened. He wanted her to understand his motivation and to forgive him again. Without her, without his daughter and without his career what was he? Who was he? He was just another soul cast into the darkness of uncertainty. He wanted to cry, just put his head into his hands and cry for the man that he had just lost, but he couldn't.

There was no emotional hit there, just a big empty space deep inside of him. He wondered what he should do right now. He wondered if it was a good idea to even go home or should he just hit the pedal and keep going until he ran out of road and options. Would anyone even care if he vanished? He sat like that for three hours, just trying to get to grips with where he would go from here.

He was jolted out of his thoughts. The car felt like it was vibrating. The engine wasn't even on so it couldn't have been that. He opened the door and stepped out onto the pavement. It was the floor that felt like it was humming under his feet. As he stood there, his hands out in front of him trying to feel the vibration it suddenly got stronger and more violent. He swung his head around trying to see if there was anything obvious causing it. He saw a column of thick black smoke rising up from the direction of Corsica Road. He could hear that mysterious sound, almost like a Geiger counter but ten octaves lower. Birds were blasting out of the surrounding trees and taking to the air. The huge volume of them was almost enough to block out the sun. The sounds of their collective chirping almost made

Braden want to clap his hands over his ears. The windows of the houses in the cul-de-sac where he was parked began to split and crack. Tiles began to come loose from the roofs and crash to the floor. One of them struck the floor a few inches from where Braden was stood.

Earthquake, he thought.

He bolted back into the car and cranked the engine. He slammed the car into drive and hit the pedal hard. He screeched out of the cul-de-sac and headed for the main road which would take him towards home. As he drove down the road he could see people coming out of their homes and looking around them as if they could find a solution to what was going on in the air around them. Through his open window, he could hear car horns blaring and the sounds of metal bashing and squealing. The car weaved and wobbled on the shaking ground and Braden wrestled with the wheel. He brought the car to a halt near to the junction of North Road which would have taken him home. The junction was almost completely blocked by overturned and smashed cars. Screams of pain and anguish filled the air over the smashing of cars hitting cars. Some had run off the road and collided with lamp posts and pedestrians. One had managed to plow straight into the front window of one of the many pound shops that made up North Road. The entire shop front had been pushed inwards by the force of the impact. The pavement under the car was awash with human blood and broken bodies. Braden fell out of his car and tried to start running. The thrumming of the ground underneath him made it almost impossible to keep his balance. Trying to run was only making it worse. He knew he had to get away from the main road and try to get back home on a back route of some sort. He knew that near the top end of North Road was an entrance to the Layton Canal. He was pretty sure if he walked along there that he could get off again at the bottom end of Layton town. Then it would only be a half-hour walk home. It would take him longer than if he stuck to the road, but the carnage that was unfolding in front of him meant that it would have been too dangerous to stay on the main routes for very long. He would have to traverse the Hemmington Road, and he wasn't sure just how far he would get before he was cut down by a swerving car. But he had no choice. Standing here, feeling the earth beneath him shaking and stirring, causing his calf muscles to bunch up to keep his balance, he knew he couldn't just stand here and wait to see if it passed. A loud bang came from behind him. He turned around and saw with horror that some of the road he was standing on was beginning to crack. That got him moving. He weaved around the wreckage of cars that was beginning to block up the road. Car alarms and burglar alarms were buzzing and whining their self-important tones to nobody. The noise was almost carried away by the noise of the birds still flying for their lives in the sky above. Braden moved around two cars that had hit each other head-on. One of the drivers had gone through the windscreen and was lying on the twisted metal of the bonnet. One of the peaks of bent metal had torn off most of the right side of his face. Blood was coating the light blue paint in a deep red torrent. The young man was groaning softly through the remains of his smashed teeth.

Clunk, click, every trip, shit for brains, Braden thought to himself as he passed by. The driver of the other car looked like she was asleep behind the wheel. The airbag had deployed and hung down limply from the collapsed steering wheel. Braden kept on moving, dodging through the trashed cars and panicking hordes of people that seemed to emerge out of all directions. One of them was a bald man in a suit. He was carrying a clipboard and running around in a circle. He was screaming at the top of his voice for someone to switch it off, switch it off, switch it the *fuck* off. The ripples running through the floor were getting stronger and more violent, making it even harder for Braden to stay on his feet. He had to lean on some of the wrecked cars and the long fence that ran alongside the edge of the pavement. He could see the canal path through the metal railings and he knew that he was nearly there. The canal barges that were moored by the side of the water were rocking back and forth and crashing into each other like a giant, bizarre Newton's cradle. There was bellowing and shouting coming from the boat owners that were aboard. Even over the chaos on the main road, Braden could hear then yelling at each other. He had a pretty good idea that they had no idea what was going on. He forged ahead. The entrance to the canal was just up ahead. He tried to run again but the waves of motion beneath his feet made it too risky. A car suddenly whisked past right in front of him and smashed into the metal fence. The fence held its ground for a moment and then it creaked backward and gave way. The car went with it, its rear end lifting up off the ground. It flipped onto its roof and slid down the sharp embankment down to the canal. It collided with one of the barges with a loud and impersonal bang. It rested against the boat for a moment and slowly pushed it towards the middle of the canal. The car slipped into the water taking it and its occupant down into a watery grave. Braden pushed on, trying to kick the idea of drowning in that way out of his mind. A big part of him wanted to try and help, but he was all too aware of what would happen if another car came crashing down on top of him. He had to keep moving. It was the only way he was going to get back to Mary and Jax and get them the hell out of here whilst he still could. He went through the metal kissing gate and scrambled and fell down the dirt path down to the edge of the canal. The water was being slammed onto the edges of the walkway, flooding them. Braden stopped in his tracks. There was no way he was going to be able to walk up the pathway, he would be swept into the water, such was the force of the waves crashing over the sides of it. The barges were also being slammed against the edges, breaking them open and letting water flood into the open wounds inflicted upon them. Braden sat down, not knowing what to do. He thought about going back up to the road, but it was just as likely that he would be wiped out by a car or falling masonry from all of the buildings up there. He was trapped, right here on the edges of the canal. He pulled his knees up and wrapped his arms around them. He was starting to count the blessings he had been given in his life. He was residing himself to his fate at the edge of this canal when he heard and felt something pop deep beneath the earth. Then there was a new sound. It sounded like a rushing of water. Braden saw the waves that were crashing against the edge of the canal were suddenly being pulled towards where he was sat. He braced himself, not knowing what was going on, then he saw that the water was being pulled downstream. The barges all began to get dragged along in the same direction. Some of them began to jackknife until they reached the end of their mooring ropes. The ropes held them for a little while, making the barges look like big ugly kites stuck in the middle of the canal. Then the rush of water in that direction intensified. Somewhere under the bed of the canal, a massive hole had opened up and the water was pouring down the breach in the canal bed. Braden saw his chance and took off up the path, staying as far from the water's edge as he could. He fell often, the shaking of the ground taking his legs out from under him. More and more boats went crashing past him, flipping around and battering against the concrete edges of the canal. Some of them were manned, with people starting up engines that were barely equipped to deal with the force of the new current that the canal had developed. About a mile up the path, Braden, battered and muddy began to believe, just a little, that he might make it back to Mary and Jax alive, perhaps not in one piece, but alive nonetheless.

25.

Thompson was just pulling his car into his driveway when the earthquake began to happen.

After the day he endured so far, nothing at all on this earth and beyond it had the capacity to surprise him. When he felt the ground begin to move under his feet, he almost rolled his eyes and sighed. He bolted from the car ran up the steps towards the front door. The shaking of the ground was enough to make him stagger and to grip the handrail a little tighter, but not quite enough to take him off his feet. As he got to the front door, it was torn open by Cindy. Her eyes were bulging with fear, and she grabbed hold of him.

"Gerald, what's happening? The television is talking about terrorists. Are you hurt?" she sobbed in his ear.

"I'm fine, don't worry. We need to get out of here, get as far away from town as we can."

Cindy pulled away from him and looked him in the eyes. She saw something that she wasn't used to seeing in them. It was fear. He was actually scared, and Gerald Thompson didn't do scared, at least not in the time that they had been together.

"Gerald, you're freaking me out, what's *happening*," she shrieked.

"I don't have time to explain right now, we need to get moving. I'll explain everything to you when we are on the road, OK?"

"'k," she said in a weak voice.

The ground beneath them suddenly lurched, snapping them into action. Cindy bolted back inside the house. Thompson followed her. He left the door open so they could get back out quickly if they needed to. There was a big ugly crack in the living room ceiling. Dust and pieces of plaster were raining down on the wooden floors.

"I need to get my medications," said Cindy and she went into the kitchen to get them out of the bottom drawer. He followed her, went into the cupboard and grabbed a bag to put them in.

"Here," he said, standing next to her and holding the bag open. She threw the boxes in and slammed the drawer shut.

"Right, anything else we need we can pick up along the way. We should…"

The ground lurched again, almost throwing them both off their feet. Thompson grabbed hold of Cindy to stop her from falling, wrapping his arm around her waist to steady her. The shaking of the ground stopped for a few moments. Outside, alarms from cars and houses were shrieking and howling across the town, cutting through the sudden silence that had fallen.

But then there was another sound, a creaking hooting noise. Thompson had heard that sound before, he was sure about it. He groped around in his memories for a moment and then it came to him. It was the same noise that the water pipes had made when they had first moved into their house in Newtown all those years ago. But this noise sounded like it was coming from the kitchen cupboard under the sink.

"Gerald?"

He went over to the sink and carefully tipped his head over the edge. The washing up bowl was in the way, so he snatched it out of the sink and threw it on the side.

"Oh, dear god," he said.

There was something coming up the plug hole. It took a second for him to work out what it was, and then he realised. The small holes around the plug had turned black. Dozens of thin black legs were poking up out of the holes, feeling around, trying to get a grip. Then a black body popped through, and then another, then another and soon it was a torrent. The sink was beginning to fill up with spiders, hundreds of them. They couldn't make it up the sides of the sink, it was far too slippery for them, but soon, just in their sheer numbers, they would reach the top, and then the house would be full of them.

"Come on," roared Thompson. He grabbed Cindy who was clutching the bag of medications to her chest. They managed to get out of the kitchen just as the first of the spiders managed to get to the top of the sink. He pulled her through the living room, heading for the open door, but something caught his eye, something above them. He looked up and he stopped dead in his tracks. The spiders were beginning to swarm out of the crack in the ceiling above them. They started to patter onto the floor below and run towards them.

"Upstairs, come on," he yelled.

"But, we'll be trapped up there," wailed Cindy.

"We can climb out the bedroom window onto the garage roof, we can get to the car that way," he said.

Just as he finished his sentence, a spider dropped onto Cindy's shoulder. Without thinking, he hit out at it, knocking it to the floor. Cindy squealed and ran for the stairs, the spider in hot pursuit. Thompson followed her, bringing his shoe down on the spider, popping it with his weight. They headed up the stairs, rounding the corner and finishing the ascent to the top.

"Bedroom. We can at least shut the door, slow them down a little," said Thompson. Cindy made it to the top and thundered across the landing. Thompson caught his foot on the last riser and spilled to the floor. He rolled over on his side ready to get to his feet again and he caught sight of the bathroom through the open door. Water was spilling out of the toilet, running down the sides of the bowl and pooling on the floor. At first, the water was clear and then drowned spiders began to appear in the clear water, just a few at first and then in a steady stream. After a moment the water slowed to a trickle and live spiders began to push their way out from under the lid. They were slowed down by the water on the floor, where they floated helplessly, their legs flailing for a foothold so they could run towards Thompson. He scrambled to his feet and ran for the bedroom. The dreadful realisation that he had forgotten about the en-suite bathroom, suddenly at the forefront of his mind. He ran into the bedroom and slammed the door behind him.

"Block the bottom of the door, use the pillows and then put something heavy on top of them, they won't be able to get in. We don't have a lot of time," he said.

Cindy set to work, and Thompson went to the door of the en-suite. He poked his head into the little room so he could grab the door handle. The toilet seat was up and he could see the water level in the bowl rising quickly. They were coming. He pulled the door shut.

He estimated that they had around two minutes before the spiders got in here. He had to move fast. He looked out of the window and saw the roof of the garage. It was too far over to the right-hand side for them to be able to climb out of the opening. He had to break the glass. He pulled his police baton from the side of his belt, flicked it open and slammed it against the glass. It was tough glass, fancy double gazed stuff that was designed to be more secure. However, it was no match for a scared D.C.I. The glass didn't just break, it exploded, sending shards of glass outwards and onto the car below. Cindy let out a reflexive shriek.

The edges of the window were still full of jagged pieces of the broken glass. He ran the metal baton around the edges, clearing as much of it as he could. Another scream from Cindy made him turn his head. She was backing away from the door and towards him. The spiders were squeezing their way around the thin cracks of the door and were spreading out, turning the wall around the frame into a mass of wriggling black bodies.

"Come on," he roared and pulled her towards the broken window. He positioned her in front of him.

"Get out there," he yelled.

She hesitated for a moment. Thompson looked over his shoulder. The swarm of spiders was turning the ceiling, the walls and the floor into a blackened creeping death. The darkness and flailing legs were less than two inches from where he was standing. They had run out of time and options. Thompson ran for the window with as much might as he could muster. He grabbed Cindy around her middle and pulled both of them through the open space, pushing with his legs as hard as he could to get them clear. As they fell from the window, he instinctively pulled Cindy on top of him to cushion her fall. For a brief moment, as they flew through the air, he was convinced that they were going to miss the roof and go sailing right down onto the car. Then, a bare second later his back connected with the roof of the garage. In his haste, he had misguided the jump, mercifully not as badly as he had thought, but he landed right on the edge of the roof, the hard wooden beam connecting with his spine. That, combined with the weight of Cindy landing on top of him, knocked every single piece of air out of his lungs. For a moment, he couldn't breathe at all. He lay there under his wife, his face turning an ugly shade of purple. He thought that he would never breathe again and that these were his final moments, lying here on the garage roof with an army of spiders taking over his house. What a way for the mighty Gerald Thompson to sing his swan song. Then his lungs unlocked, and he tore a breath into his lungs. He began to breathe hard and fast, trying to get the spots that had appeared in front of his eyes to clear. His back was in utter agony, a pain that bled into his ribcage and squeezed all of the muscles around it. But, he was alive, and that was good enough for now. Cindy rolled off him, helping him to catch his breath a little better. He was hurt, but he was going to be just fine. He looked up at the window they had just come out of. The spiders were beginning to swarm out of the window. He looked to his right and he saw the roof of the car just below them. He rolled over and got to his feet as best he could. Cindy was already on her knees.

"You 'k?" he squeezed out of his wounded lungs.

She said nothing, only nodded her answer.

"Come on, we have to move," he said. He pulled her to the edge of the roof. She stepped off and onto the roof of the car. She was wearing her favorite trainers, the ones that she liked to doss around the house in, they were perfect for standing on the slippery roof of the car. She stood on it for a moment, wheeling her arms for balance and then she climbed down. She pulled the passenger door open and got in just as Thompson was making his own descent onto the roof. His work shoes had no grip on them at all, and the moment he transferred his full weight to the roof of the car his feet went out from under him. He fell backward onto the roof of the car, his lungs and back exploding in a fresh hit of pain. But, he didn't have time to contemplate his situation, he was sliding backward off the back of the car. He scrambled for something to grip on to, but there was nothing. He fell to the hard ground below, headfirst. It was only the fact that he got his arms up in time to protect his fall that stopped him from smashing his head onto the unforgiving concrete of the driveway. His right forearm took the weight of the fall and then he rolled into a sitting position on the floor. He got to his feet as fast as the pain in his body would allow and he stumbled for the car door. He reached for it with his freshly wounded arm and as he pulled the handle a bolt of sickening agony ran up to his shoulder. He gritted his teeth against the pain and he got into the car, slamming the door shut. He fumbled the keys out of his pocket and stuck them into the ignition.

"Gerald, hurry up," shrieked Cindy.

There was a pattering noise on the metal of the car. It sounded like spots of heavy rain landing on the metal, but they both knew it wasn't raining. It was the sound of the spiders falling from the broken window.

Thompson gunned the engine and slammed the car into reverse. He hit the pedals and the car screeched backward off the driveway. Pain was roaring out of Thompson's arm as he turned the wheel, but he would deal with that later. Right now he had to get Cindy to safety, and that was all that mattered. He shifted the gear and prepared to take off down the street. He saw the front of the house, the spiders falling from the window onto the roof where they had been a few moments ago, and the open front door with the darkness creeping out of it in all directions, and he wondered, just how far this went.

He hit the pedal again and the car jerked forwards, tearing them away from this horrendous scene.

They were alive. They had made it and at least for now, they were safe and that was all that mattered.

26.

Braden ran the rest of the way home as best he could. The ground had been rumbling and shaking the whole time he had been running, threatening to knock him off his feet at any moment. He arrived at his front door six minutes before the ground under Layton began to open up. He was blissfully unaware that it was going to happen and his mind was focused on getting Mary and Jax to safety. He came through the door shouting their names over and over again. For a moment, there was no reply and he thought that they had either already left or had never got back home, to begin with. Then Mary came through from the kitchen. He began to apologize and to try an explain what was going on, but Mary walked right up to him and unloaded a slap across his cheek. It shut him right up straight away.

"That's for walking out on me and your daughter," she said in a low, trembling voice.

The ground shook again, this time even harder than it had done before. Books fell off the shelves and lots of Mary's cut glass ornaments juggled and fell over.

"We have to get out of here, now!" said Braden. He looked around the room, "Where's Jax?"

"Under the kitchen table. I thought that was what you were supposed to do when there was an earthquake," said Mary.

"It's not an earthquake. We need to get out of here," said Braden.

"If it's not an earthquake then what is it, Braden?"

"I'll fill you in when we are on our way. Get Jax and let's go."

Mary went and got Jax from under the table. Despite her hatred for her father for him running out on them, she ran straight to him and clamped her arms around his middle. Braden hustled them outside carefully. The ground was still bucking and shaking beneath them.

"Where's the car?" said Mary.

Its stuck on the Hemmington Road, the whole road was jammed up with crashes.

"What do we do now?" wailed Jax.

"Come on, get in," said A voice from behind them. It was Trent, fresh from his encounter with Mary. He had only left the house six minutes before the ground had started to tremble. He was holding the back door of his land rover open. Braden grabbed Mary and Jax by the hand and led them to the open door.

"Thanks," said Braden.

"S'okay, you can help navigate," he said. Braden went to the passenger side and jumped in. Trent got the engine purring and he tore off the driveway. The land rover coped with the bumps and the shakes from the road beneath them. It ate up the cracking road in front of them.

"You need to stay off the main roads. Too many accidents and people running around like headless chickens. Can this thing go off-road?"

"You bet it can. I go off-roading every weekend with this baby," bellowed Trent.

"Head for the Valley, we need to be as far away from a populated area as we can," said Braden.

"Right you are," said Trent. He had a large tablet computer stuck to his dashboard. From what Braden could see, it had a full satellite view of everything around them. Trent's eyes danced over the screen and then went back to the road in front of them. He hurled the wheel over to the right and the car snatched its way down Hawthorn Lane, a back road that ran almost parallel to the main road towards Layton Valley. Mary placed her hand on Jax's chest to help keep her in her seat. Her free hand was clamped to the handle that was just above the door to her left.

"It's a dead end down here," said Braden.

"Only if you want to stay on the roads it is," said Trent. He hit the gas harder causing the powerful engine to roar and the car to pick up the pace even more. The ground suddenly shook hard, causing the back end of the car to begin see-sawing. Trent pulled a handle just below the gear shift and the car picked up the traction again, running back on the bucking road smoothly. The backs of the houses that they were speeding past were beginning to crack and break apart. Tiles from the roof began to crash down into the road all around them. One of them struck the bonnet of the car with an almighty bang. Braden, Mary, and Jax all flinched and yelled out, but Trent took it in his stride, he didn't even blink. Braden looked into the side mirror on the door at the road behind him. The vibrations of the car and the shaking ground made it difficult to see, but it looked to Braden like the road was caving in behind them. He stared at it, trying to make sense of the image he was seeing, thinking to himself that it must be an illusion and then he saw the houses that had been breaking and splitting as they had gone past them falling inwards towards the road, but vanishing into an unseen blackness.

"Trent...."

"I know."

"I mean it man, step on it."

"I know..." said Trent. He floored the pedal and the car built up even more speed.

"Hold tight everyone, it might get a little bumpy," yelled Trent over the roar of the engine. The end of the road was coming up. It was lined with a long hedgerow and what looked like a chain-link fence behind it. Braden knew that beyond that hedge was the rugby field. If they could get to the rugby field and his car was as good as he claimed that it was then they could, just maybe, make it out of here in one piece. The car surged forwards towards the hedgerow and a moment later it tore through both the greenery and the chain-link fence behind it. a burst of sparks flew up from underneath the front of the car and Braden thought for a moment that they had done some damage, but it showed no signs of slowing down. It bumped up and down as it ran the paving slabs that surrounded the perimeter of the rugby club and field. Then everything became a whole lot calmer. They were running across the grass of the rugby field. The far end of the field carried on to the Bollin Way which was an open pathway that leads straight through Layton Valley. The pathway was designed to be used on foot, but it was just about wide enough for the car, or at least that's what was going through Trent's mind as he rushed the car onto the field. There was a helicopter up in the air, still low enough for them to be able to see that it was an army issue helicopter. On the car-park to the left, there was a large police van parked at an angle. Braden couldn't tell for sure, but he thought that there was someone standing near it. He was suddenly distracted by another series of huge bumps from the ground below them. It was enough to lift the wheels of the car up from the ground as if they were running over a series of small ramps. The rugby club building that they were passing on the left-hand side began to cave in. Just like Braden had seen in the mirror on his door a moment earlier, the rugby club was vanishing into the floor. The houses that ran across the back of the club folded in on themselves. The sound of breaking glass and cracking masonry was audible even over the roar of the car's engine. The line of destruction was building its way towards the field and Trent nudged the car over to the right-hand side of the field. He would have to run it back over to the left to get on the Bollin Way at the last moment. He just hoped and prayed that the hole that was apparently opening up below them wouldn't stretch as far as the pathway. Everything seemed to suddenly go very quiet. The air outside of the car seemed to be completely silent, an eerie silence that felt like it was creeping inside the car and enveloping them all in its cloak of cold fear.

"Oh no...." said Mary from behind Braden. She was looking out of her window and she could see the huge hole that had opened up in the ground. The most horrifying thing that she could see was the fact that there was no skyline anymore, no church spire from the middle of the town, no trees, nothing at all. It was as if Layton had been swallowed by the earth. Trent had taken his foot off the gas and the car had slowed down to a coast. He was looking at the scene, his mouth open in disbelief.

Then the blackness began to flood out from the hole in the ground. Braden saw the long spindly legs beginning to appear over the edges of the hole. His whole body felt frozen for a moment and then it felt like it was losing all of its strength all at the same time. These weren't just the poisonous house spiders he had seen on Corsica Road, some of these spiders climbing out of the earth were the size of a horse. The smaller ones crawled all over them, making their outer skin look like it was alive and rippling. It was a vision of hell itself, rising from the hole in the ground that had once been Layton.

"Spiders.....spiders......*spiders...SPIDERS..*" His voice rose until he was unable to produce anymore sound. Trent saw them spreading out from the hole and heading in their direction. He snapped out of his momentary trance and hammered the accelerator down to the floor. The wheels of the car spun a little and then found their traction again. Trent began to turn them in the direction of Bollin Way. It was going to be a boot race between them and the spiders to see who got there first. Damn it, it was going to be a close call. The car narrowed the distance quickly, but the spiders had a head start on him. A cluster of them reached the edge of the path and then turned into the direction of the car and began to scuttle towards it. Jax screamed her high-pitched whistling scream from the back seat. Mary pulled her in and buried her head into her chest.

"Don't look at them. We'll make it honey, we'll be just fine, I promise," said Mary. Looking at those huge spiders made her feel physically sick to her stomach. She didn't know if they were going to be alright at all, in fact, she was willing to bet heavily against it.

The car and the spiders hit head-on. The spiders were pretty hard-wearing, but they were no match for the sheer power and weight of Trent's car. Most of them were sent up into the air, twisting and turning as they went. Some of them were smashed against the grill at the front of the car, some of them breaking open and splashing a grotesque combination of blood and mashed guts up onto the bonnet and the windscreen of the car. The car slowed a little at the point of impact, but Trent got it back up to full speed quickly. A spider managed to find some traction on the passenger side of the car. The combination of its body and its leg span covered the entire window on Braden's side. He pulled away from it, almost lying down in Trent's lap. Trent elbowed him away.

"They can't get in here, this thing is water-tight," he said.

Braden straightened up in his seat, trying not to look at the spider. It was being pulled across the window by the sheer force of the wind. It suddenly lost its grip and was sent flying backward. Mary caught sight of it as it went past and let out a small yelp of terror. Braden looked into the mirror again. The spiders were still giving chase down the narrowing pathway. It looked like they were managing to leave them behind just a little at a time. If Trent kept the speed up, then he would be able to outrun them. The pathway was getting narrower as they forged ahead. The tall hedges that lined either side of the path were beginning to scratch and claw along the sides of the car, sending a trail of leaves and broken sticks in their wake.

"It'll open up soon," yelled Trent. He could see Braden holding onto the edge of his seat for dear life, his knuckles turning white as he clung on.

The scratching of the bushes on the sides of the car hit a crescendo. For a moment, it felt to Braden that at any moment, a large branch would come crashing through the window and impale either him or Trent and that would be the end of the whole sorry mess. Instead, the crashing of branches died away and the car picked up the pace even more. Braden saw that Trent had been absolutely right, the pathway had opened up in front of them. The man-made gravely path had given way to a slightly muddy trail that was flanked on both sides by overgrown grass the stretched out on either side.

"This leads all the way through to the Valley road. It's a pretty straight run, nice and easy," said Trent.

Braden checked the mirror again. He could still see the spiders coming out of the narrow pathway onto the wide-open space that they were now driving on. They were scattering in all directions rather than making a direct line for them. They were leaving them behind and if they kept going at the rate they were going at then they would be far enough away to relax a little and perhaps put a plan together. Braden didn't want to even entertain the idea of stopping and discussing a strategy until they were somewhere where they could see them coming. He sat back into his seat and forced himself to take it easy a little. He was physically spent and his emotional state wasn't too far behind it. He needed to regroup a little in the space of his own mind. So much had happened in such a short space of time. His thoughts momentarily turned to his last payday, but then he realized that if this spider problem was more widespread than just Layton, then all the money in the world wouldn't mean anything at all. Braden rationalized it by thinking how lucky he was to even be alive right now. That had to count for more than any payday. It was the last remnants of his competitive nature twitching away in his guts. He looked over his shoulder and saw Mary curled up on the back seat with Jax and he knew that if he hadn't had walked out on them to chase the story then they would likely not have even been here right now. He would have never seen the spiders in the house, he would never have made a run for it when he had the opportunity, he would have been just like everybody else. It was almost a certainty that if he had seen the photograph out of context on the internet that he wouldn't have believed that it was real. In a roundabout way, he had saved his family and himself by walking out on them. Mary offered him a weak smile. She looked like she had been through the wringer.

"We'll be alright, I promise," he said. "If we can get away from populated areas I'm sure we will be fine."

Mary said nothing, she just nodded. She was gnawing the inside of her cheek, which usually meant that she didn't believe a word he was saying. It was her way of not saying something that she might regret. Given the situation that they were in it showed a hell of a lot of self-control.

The car rolled on. The path was heading upwards which made the engine work harder. The four-wheel drive never missed a beat, even when the ground underneath them became softer and more uneven as they made altitude.

"Have a play with the radio see what you can find," said Trent.

"How about some nice soothing music for us all," said Braden.

Trent smiled and he looked at Braden for a moment. "Now, wouldn't that be nice. I mean the other radio, the one in the glove compartment."

Braden hooked his hand under the glove compartment handle and pulled it open. It dropped down revealing a very high tech looking CB radio.

"What the hell do you do for a living?" said Braden.

"Well, I could tell you, but I would have to kill you," said Trent.

Braden held his hands up, "I'll just mind my business."

"Don't worry, I'm kidding. I'm a park ranger," said Trent.

Braden was struck dumb for a moment as he processed the information.

"Nobody knows the countryside around here as well as I do," said Trent.

"That's why you have a decent car and all this equipment," said Braden.

"Correct," said Trent. "Now, why don't you have a go of that radio, see what you can find. If there is a military or police presence around here, then we will pick it up."

Braden lent forwards and picked up the small headset and put it on his head. He instantly felt somehow more powerful and important just by doing so. He turned the volume dial which clicked the rig on. Lights flickered and ticked and the radio burst into life in his ear. There was nothing but static so he turned the tuning dial slowly listening out for anything that sounded like a voice.

Trent turned briefly to Mary. "If you drop the little compartment between the seat, there are chocolate bars and drinks if you want them. Please help yourself, I have plenty of them."

"Thank you," said Mary.

"No worries, make yourselves at home."

Mary reached over and squeezed Trent's shoulder. Braden didn't even see it, he was too busy playing with his new toy.

27.

Cindy had fallen asleep. Her head was slumped to one side and a trail of drool was making its way slowly out of the corner of her mouth and down onto the front of her pale blue top. Thompson looked out of the windows, trying to get his bearings for a moment. As his head cleared after the mayhem that they had just been through he began to evaluate, just like a good Mr. Policeman should.

The Spiders.....

Christ, all those spiders coming out of the drains, out of the toilet for god's sake. Each one of them looking almost identical. How many were there? Hundreds, thousands, more than he could count. They were the ones that had bitten Wells and turned him into something else....something truly monstrous.

The silence surrounding the car was deafening, painful almost. They were parked up right at the top end of Layton Valley, right on the viewing point that brought so many tourists in throughout the year. It wasn't unusual to find groups of back-packers and ramblers scattered around on the grass or sat on the benches that overlooked the site that was once called Newtown and the city of Hemmington. It was also a good site for the local teenage population, new driving licenses in hand and struck down with terrible cases of lovesickness to park up their rust-bucket cars and give in to their raging hormones, long after the sun had gone down and the last of the ramblers had departed. He had a momentary lust for the times that he had done such a thing, how new and exciting everything was in those days of innocence. Everything to him felt so numb right now as if everything he had once believed had all turned into dust in the space of one day. It had all started with another case to solve and it had ended with his partner as good as dead and he and his wife uprooted out of their home that had been overrun with those horrible things. He wondered what they would do now, where would they go? What the hell had happened to the rest of Layton and everyone who lived there. He turned the key in the ignition just enough to put the power on and he thumbed the radio button to turn it on. He tapped the button to tune it in and he watched the numbers roll around until they stopped. The speakers suddenly burst into life, a little louder than he expected.

"……attack has originated from. All we know at the moment is that there are casualties filling the A+E departments all over the area. Layton Hospital has been the worst affected area.

But, do you have any idea of what actually happened? Was it a bomb? A chemical attack? The public need to know.

I can't make any specific comment on the type of attack at the moment, not until we know for sure. As I say, all we know is that the police and the army are dealing with a major incident in the town of Layton. Residents who have managed to escape the attack should head over to Hemmington where there are rescue stations that have been set up. Residents of Hemmington can be assured that there is no immediate threat to the city and that the attack has been contained to Layton town. That's all I can tell you right now, and when I have more information we will be sure to let the public know…..

Can you comment on why all video streaming services and all social media apps have all crashed at exactly the same time? Is there a link to the attack in Layton?

I can't comment on specifics, I have given you as much information as I have available to me at the moment. When I know more then you will be given a statement."

Thompson listened to the interview for a few moments longer. He was starting to get that feeling in his guts, the same feeling he had just before they had moved house, that same feeling when he saw through the face of a man protesting his innocence.

"What shall we do?" said Cindy suddenly, making him jump. He hadn't even realised that she was awake.

"I think we need to get out of here. I have a feeling that it won't be safe up here for much longer," he said.

"Are we going to Hemmington?" she said.

Thompson thought it over for a moment. He gently pulled up his sleeve and had a look at his arm that he had hurt in the fall out of his bedroom window. He could move it, but it hurt like a bastard and it was turning an ugly shade of purple. It needed looking at. If they took off for the coast and he ended up with gangrene then he would be in a world of shit.

"Yes, I think we should go and check it out, see if anyone else made it," he said.

"I could murder a coffee," said Cindy and then she laughed weakly.

"Coffee it is then my dear, coffee it is."

From where they had been parked, there were only two ways to get into Hemmington and one of them involved going back through Layton. Thompson took the latter option which took them east on the Valley road. It was a long way around that brought them into the city directly via the bypass. He figured that they should be there within the hour and then they could relax a little and let everyone else take charge. At least, that was his intention. He knew quite well that he would be offering up his years and years of service and experience to help out wherever he could. He also knew about the air raid tunnels that ran beneath the city that had kept the city's residents safe during the blitz. It was nothing more than a tourist attraction now, a nice little piece of living history. He doubted that they would protect anyone from anything these days. Still, it was good to have in the back of his mind…..just in case…..just in case.

Ordinarily, he would have enjoyed the drive through to Hemmington This was some of the most incredible scenery in the local area. But his mind was so preoccupied that he couldn't take any enjoyment from the majestic views that were opening up in front of him. His guts were still uneasy, very uneasy. They had a plan, it made the most sense and yet there it was still crawling around inside him. The closer they got to Hemmington, the more the feeling stirred within him.

He tried to shake it off. They couldn't just run for the coast, could they? Or could they…. Perhaps he was wrong this time. Perhaps his instincts had finally gotten out of whack. After all, he didn't have any hunches about what happened to their home. He mulled it over in his mind as they began to descend towards the city. He decided to assess the situation when they got there, and if things didn't feel any better, they would leave, go for the coast, have a nice cold pint and wait for it all to blow over.

His insides settled a little as if they were agreeing with his idea, but the nub of his discontent wouldn't quite go away fully. He pushed on, taking the car down the winding road and onto the A74 bypass road. They managed to get half a mile up the bypass before they hit two solid lanes of stationary traffic. They were perhaps two miles from the city limits.

"Jesus. How long do you think this is going to take?" said Cindy.

Thompson scanned the cars in front and the one in the lane next to him. He saw that they all had something in common, none of them had drivers.

"I think we have to walk from here," said Thompson. Cindy's face fell.

He shut the car down and they got out onto the tarmac. It felt decidedly odd to be standing in the middle of the bypass road. It almost felt like they were in no man's land, a ghost town. The bypass had been turned into the world's biggest car park. He looked around to see if there were any more cars coming, he didn't see any. He checked his watch and was dismayed to find that the glass had a large crack across it. The watch was still working and he could just about make out that it was just past seven in the morning. His whole concept of time had been utterly distorted, he felt as if he should be raiding the sandwiches for lunch. He stretched, raising his arms above his head. His back and his ribs cracked painfully. He had banged them up pretty good but he was sure that there was nothing broken. He was certainly getting too old for this shit.

"Shall we?" he said to Cindy. She nodded without saying anything and they set off. Thompson pushed the button on the car to lock it, purely out of habit. It wasn't going anywhere and at least he would know where it was if they needed to leave. They walked forwards, weaving around the cars. Some of them hadn't been parked straight, probably having to pull to a stop in a hurry to prevent them from hitting the stationary car in front. They walked and weaved for around ten minutes and Thompson had to stop. His ribs were aching murderously and he needed to rest for a little while. The city was unfolding in front of them through the early morning mist. Thompson looked back to see if there were any more vehicles joining the stationary conga back down the road. They could see both ways because the road was almost perfectly straight in both directions.

"Are you ok? We should walk down the other side of the road, there are no cars there," said Cindy.

"Better not. I think that road is probably still in use. Could be dangerous. I'm ok, I just need to...." He broke off and looked back down the road again. He could hear the roar of an engine, a diesel engine somewhere. Then he saw the lorry heading for the end of the tailback. He thought that it was going to slow down and pull up at the end of the line. He was going to suggest waiting for the driver to catch up to them. Perhaps he had come from another town, somewhere else that was a safe house for them, somewhere that could put to rest that crawling in his guts. He stood up straight, ready to wave at them when they finally got close enough. Then his sliver of hope turned to horror. The lorry kept on going, roaring towards the parked cars at full pelt. He could quite tell how fast it was going, but it was going to be a no contest. The lorry collided with the cars at the back of the queue. The hollow bang, followed by the shrieking of metal echoed around the road. A moment later the lorry exploded in a ball of flames that roared upwards into the sky. Cindy screamed and went down to the floor. Thompson shielded his face with his arm. He could feel the searing heat from the explosion even though they were a safe distance from it. It was followed by smaller bangs as the fuel tanks on some of the parked cars ignited.

"We need to get moving, quicker. Let's get to the other side of the road, just like you said."

"But, I thought you said it was dangerous," said Cindy.

"It is, but I'm pretty sure that lorry was trying to get away from something. You wouldn't crash like that unless you were in a blind panic."

The reality of the situation hit home. Thompson saw Cindy's face drop in fear. "Oh no, you don't think..." she said.

"Yes, I do. We have to get to the city as fast as possible," he said. He grabbed Cindy by the hand and started to squeeze past the parked cars towards the central reservation. He climbed over the barrier first and then helped Cindy over. He frantically looked up and down the road, checking for moving vehicles.

"Right, let's get to the hard shoulder, then if something comes we can at least get on the grass. There isn't much of it, but at least it's a chance," said Thompson.

Cindy nodded her agreement, a tear spilled from her eye and rolled down her cheek. He wiped it away with his thumb and them, the light gust of wind brushing his ears and then there was…. Then there was….

What was it?

He could only describe it as a rustling sound like something was moving around in the grass next to the road. He swung his head around to get a better listen. It wasn't coming from the grass…. Where the hell was it coming from?

He turned around and looked back down the road. A thick column of black smoke was rising up into the sky from the crash. It was partially obstructing the view of the road behind him as it stretched off into the middle distance and then bent to the left and out of view. The hills of the Layton Valley road poked up on the horizon. But there was something….something not right about what he was seeing. He blinked his eyes a couple of times and then squinted, trying to get it into focus. He was certain that his eyes were getting worse. He had turned down an eye test on the last three occasions and now he was beginning to regret it. The hills were shimmering as if a heat haze was rising up in front of them, but there wasn't enough heat in the atmosphere to create one. There was something more about those hills, and again, he couldn't tell if his eyes were playing tricks on him, but the lush green that was usually associated with them had turned into a dark grey. If a cloud had been casting a shadow over them, then he wouldn't have thought twice about it, but the sky above them and above the hills was almost perfectly clear and the deepest blue he had ever seen.

And then he saw the shadow that was encasing the hills start to creep around the bend of the road in the distance. He saw the rippling effect slowly build up until the whole of the road was shimmering and shifting. Then he realised what was happening, then he realised….

He turned away and started to run, his aches and pains from the garage roof exploded, threatening to take his wind away. Cindy was a few hundred yards in front of him, she hadn't even realised that he had stopped.

"*Run*" he screamed with all the force in his body.

Cindy turned and saw him running towards her, she saw the terror on his face and then she saw what was making its way down the road towards them. She froze to the spot, her mouth gibbering silently at the black wave of horror coming towards them.

"*They're coming,*" roared Thompson. He caught up to Cindy and grabbed her. She let out a terrified yell and then her legs began to pump, her soft and comfortably sprung trainers pounding the road. She started gaining ground, leaving Thompson lagging behind. He was already badly out of breath and running out of steam quickly. His injuries were just too much for him to keep going. He gritted his teeth hard and put on another burst of speed.

I'm not going to make it…..I'm not going to make it, his mind jabbered.

He cast a look over his shoulder. He saw that the spiders had made it as far as the crashed lorry. They didn't even try and avoid the fire, they simply swarmed over it, the hundreds, thousands, *millions* of bodies catching fire as they scuttled into it. They started to break through, turning the parked cars into a living, black shapeless mass. The road on Thompson's side was becoming a carpet of charging spiders. He saw that behind the initial charge that there was a tidal wave of black heading towards them. It was probably only six feet high, but to Thompson, it looked like a wall of hell flowing towards them. The blackness spilled out over the sides of the road, covering the grass, enveloping the trees. Death was heading right for them.

He turned back to the front, letting out a guttural roar. He managed one more burst of speed, setting his ribs and his lungs on fire as he did so. He squeezed his eyes closed for a moment, desperate to survive, desperate to go on just one more day, losing the hope that it would actually happen.

Then there was another noise, in front and above. A fluttering, a whirring…. He popped his eyes open and saw the helicopter tear across the sky above them. It flew over their heads from in front of them and then took a sharp right turn. A moment later it flew over them again and dropped down smoothly onto the road ahead of them. Someone was leaning out of the chopper, waving to them beckoning them in. Thompson could see the young soldier's mouth working. He was yelling something to them.

Come on.

Cindy made it first and the soldier whipped her with ease into the chopper. The soldier began waving at Thompson, telling him to move faster. He was closing the distance, but much too slowly. The soldier suddenly reached inside the cab and brought out a rifle. For a moment, Thompson thought that he was going to shoot him down. As the soldier fired, Thompson brought his arms up across his face, bracing himself for those metal tipped slugs to hit home, but none of them did. He realised that the soldier was firing at the incoming swarm to try and buy him some vital seconds.

Thompson made it to the bird. Another soldier popped out from the open back of the chopper and pulled Thompson up. The chopper started to lift up off the floor before he had even got both of his feet inside. He slammed backward into the seat and scrambled to get his seatbelt on. For a few moments, he couldn't get any air into his lungs. He thought that having escaped that now he was going to roll over and die right here in this helicopter. He looked out of the open door and he saw the carpet of spiders all over the road where he was stood a moment ago. They moved with frightening speed, taking over the tarmac like a spreading pool of dark water. The chopper turned and began to head towards the city, cutting through the air with ease.

Thompson turned towards Cindy. She was turned towards him, a look of anguish spread across her face. He was just reaching out to grab hold of her hand when he saw it. He saw the spider running up the pale blue of her jeans leg. He let out a guttural yell and brought his open hand down on it. The spider was crushed beneath his hand. He slapped the broken carcass off her and onto the floor of the helicopter. The chopper made a sudden sharp right turn, sending the crushed body out of the open side. Thompson wiped his hand on his trousers, getting the pieces of broken legs and guts off his skin. He didn't know if Cindy yelled out, it was far too noisy inside the chopper to hear much of anything. He also knew that the soldier was too busy speaking into his headset to notice what had happened.

As Thompson's hand had come down on the spider, its fangs had punched through the denim and into the soft skin of Cindy's leg, but because of Thompson's heavy-handedness, she hadn't even realised that she had been bitten.

The helicopter flew on towards Hemmington city and the mass swarm of spiders was not far behind it.

The Plague of the Whisperer

"The hands of time can only move forward. Your fate is incoming, whether you like it or not."

1.

Doctor Michael Briggs snapped fully awake, as he usually did these days. It was a very rare occasion where he awoke from sleep in a relaxed and easy fashion. It had become as much a part of his life as eating or breathing. The only difference these days was that the slick of sweat that used to paint his skin was vastly reduced. Sure, the nightmares were still the same, with a little variation here and there, such as a change of location, or a different person becoming the monster he had encountered in the long-dead village of Newtown. He had become accustomed to them. He had integrated them into his daily routine in a similar fashion to a battered child incorporating their daily bouts of abuse into the list of chores for the day. It was just the way it was, and there was no way of changing it. If he had caused a fuss and been jabbed in the rear end with a needle full of sedatives then the nightmares would take a little longer to get going. Even though the cloud of drugs, they would still be there. Sometimes they would add some strange anomalies to the dreams. Perhaps he would be floating above the ground, unable to swim away from the horror chasing him instead of the usual sticky-feet problem that would get him every time.

He checked the time and found with some disgust that it was just after ten. He had been asleep for a whole hour. It was pitch black outside the tiny windows, and the honking of the regular gang of geese off in the distance was still at a dull quack, rather than the full chorus that usually greeted the dawn. He lay down for a moment, just to see if the possibility of continuing his sleep was going to be fruitful. However, his sandy-dry throat and the adrenaline hit that bolted through his body when he had awoken had made it a pretty quick ruling, he was done for the night. The regular evening medications that gave him the ability to fall asleep pretty easily, which included a generous hit of an anti-psychotic drug Lobopine, had all but worn off. The usual haziness was still there, and the desperate need for a decent cup of tea, or if the occasion warranted it, a decent cup of coffee.

He got up off his bed and pulled on his loose jogging trousers over his shorts and put on a vest top. He found his threadbare slippers and wiggled his feet into them. He stretched, relishing the feeling of his bones clicking and popping themselves back into place again. He exhaled and bent himself over and tried to touch his toes. It wasn't long ago that he could actually pinch his own toes from this position, but age and sleeping on a crappy bunk for so many years had stiffened him up. He let out his breath and tried to reach for his toes again. He felt his spine crackle and then he brought himself slowly back up to a standing position.

He heard footsteps on the corridor outside his door. There was a rattling of keys and then the thin blind on his door clacked open. It was one of the nurses doing their two-hourly checks. The disembodied eyes peering through the window flicked around the room and then locked on him.

"You okay Mike?" said the male voice. It sounded like Nurse Peter Decker. Peter was generally one of the good guys, but his brick-shithouse build made him a guy not to be messed with. Briggs had found out, during one of their many late-night conversations that Decker had once been a bouncer. He had joked with Briggs that nursing wasn't actually much stroked the side of her face for a moment. "It will be fine. We will be fine, I promise you," he said.

She only nodded again and offered him a weak smile. It was all she had at the moment, so it would have to do.

They crossed the road and got onto the faded red of the hard shoulder. They started to walk forwards towards the city. Thompson's back and ribs were throbbing steadily in time to his beating heart. The pain in his wrist was like a bad tooth that was ready for extraction. He gritted his teeth and pushed on, putting on foot in front of the other. Cindy walked in front of him. She was still sniffing and wiping tears from her face as she walked. Thompson knew it wasn't too far to the city, but right now it felt like it was a hundred miles away. Everything around him felt like it was unreal like it was all part of a dream. Seeing the road beneath his feet only added to the growing sense of unrest within him. He could hear the fire burning from the wreckage of the lorry on the road behind different except that he got some weekends off.

"Yeah, I'm fine," said Briggs.

"Need something to help you sleep?"

Briggs shook his head. "No….thanks. Mind if I go and watch television?"

"Not at all, you go right ahead," said Decker. The blind clicked up again and Briggs heard Decker walk on to the next room to carry on his checks.

Briggs grabbed his cigarettes and tucked them into his pocket. He opened the door and stepped out into the corridor. The lights always seemed to be far too bright, no matter what time of day it was. There were no dark corners to be found here, none at all.

He walked the length of the corridor and into the small kitchen. He snapped the kettle on and found a plastic cup sitting on the edge of the sink. He rinsed it out and dumped a teabag in along with two sugars. He had never taken sugar before he had come onto this ward, but the quality of the tea was so bland that he needed the sugar just to give it a little flavor. He added the boiled water and left it to brew for a few moments, not that it would make any difference. Getting any flavor out of the cheap-ass teabags was like drawing blood from a stone. He grabbed a spoon and squished the teabag around and then dropped in a splash of milk. He left the kitchen and went through into the lounge area. He was expecting to see some of the other inmates dotted around, not many of them slept well, but he was surprised to find that the room was empty. He went over the wall-mounted television, reached around the back of it and switched it on. It was set to the news channel by default at this time of night, there was nothing else on that was worth watching. He settled down in the armchair directly in front of the screen and set his cup of tea down on the table next to him.

The screen lit up in front of him. There was a business report going on. How utterly dull, even considering the hour. He would have rather watched the endless teleshopping that was on all the other channels than watch this rubbish. He picked up his tea and took a precautionary sip. Foul-tasting, check. Too hot, check. He set it back down again. His lungs itched for a smoke. He supposed he could persuade one of the nurses to let him into the outdoor smoking area, even though they usually didn't allow it. But, he had been very well behaved over the last year. He hadn't had any trouble since he had words with Doctor Low. That had been the last time he had seen the good Doctor. Their little exchange had led to him being sedated for a week-long period whilst they dealt with his supposed psychotic episode. He knew what the truth of it was, he just hadn't told Low what he wanted to hear, and he never would. He had the power of stubbornness and the truth on his side. He would be vindicated, he knew it only too well. It was all he had to keep him going, and it was more than enough fuel. He had been going for five years now and he still had plenty of that fuel left in the tank.

He got up and went out of the lounge towards the nurse's station. He met Decker, who was finishing his round and heading towards the station.

"Any chance I could go out for a smoke?" said Briggs.

Decker mulled it over for a moment, his face contorting like a bad character actor trying to remember his lines. "Well, you know the rules Mike, but I think I could make an exception in your case," he said. He jangled his large bunch of keys and found the one for the back door. He led Briggs to the door and let him out. He dug into his pocket and handed Briggs his lighter.

"Make sure I get it back when you're done," said Decker.

Briggs gave him a thumbs up and Decker left him to it. He fished a cigarette out of his pack and stuck into the corner of his mouth. He snapped alight to it with Decker's slim gold zippo and dragged deeply. The itch in his lungs began to abate a little and he dragged deeply again. He plumed out smoke into the still, cool night and took pleasure in the feeling of the nicotine rushing through his system. He didn't think that there was a finer feeling in all of the world, other than a cold frothy pint of ice-cold beer, or the feeling of a good woman next to you in your bed. The other two were as far out of his reach right now as they possibly could be, so he made the best of what he had right now. He had another drag, wonderful. He wondered about how many cigarettes were being enjoyed in such a fashion all over the world, pondering whether or not anyone else was taking as much pleasure from one as he was, he doubted it very much. He walked down the small path that led to the tiny garden area. Usually, during the ten-minute breaks that occurred every two hours during the day, the place would have been full of other inmates sitting around in various states of dress. He went to the far-right bench, the one that was usually reserved for 'The Don,' and he sat himself down. The Don was a hard person to try and figure out. He seemed to have it permanently stuck in his mind that he was some sort of crime boss. The only crime he could ever commit in this place was bringing in the odd bag of M&Ms after he had come back from his allotted free time, where he was allowed to leave the hospital on the trust that he would come back after two hours. Briggs had heard a rumour that everything he came back with, he had in fact stolen from the supermarket that was just outside the hospital grounds. He would usually have fed this information to the nurses in exchange for better treatment, but he didn't think that ratting on The Don would do him any favors. Besides, The Don was a good man to have on his side. His reputation as a man with 'connections' was wholeheartedly bought into by most of the other inmates, giving them a little bit of fear of him. Briggs didn't buy a word of it. He reasoned that if he was so well connected that he would have been gone from the hospital a long time ago. Briggs had still placated him with regular supplies of cigarettes whenever he ran short. The Don always offered him a nod whenever he was out in the garden sitting in his usual spot. About six months ago, the word came around the wards that The Don's real name was Neville Jones. A twitchy and hypomanic young man by the name of Rebel Wilton had called it him to his face. The Don sure as hell didn't take too kindly to his hard-man image being sullied in such a fashion and he had punched Rebel, just once, right in the side of his jaw. Some of Rebel's teeth flew out of his mouth and clattered off the nearby wall before coming to a bloody rest in the middle of the floor. Rebel went down like a sack of shit and ended up impaling one of his own teeth into his left buttock. The Don had been put to sleep for a few days after that incident, but he never missed a beat. He actually had more swagger about him having dished out a one-punch beating. Rebel Wilton wasn't seen again on the ward.

But, that was the nature of the daily grind in the Tulip Suite. They came and went with such regularity that Briggs never really knew any of them. He was the only mainstay, part of the furniture, a regular. Even the staff had turned over three times since he had first arrived. They normally didn't stay for more than a year, such was the daily grind of dealing with the mentally infirm, and the long shifts that they all seemed to work. He had seen it all.

He took his last drag and then pitched his dog-end into the grass. He toyed with the idea of having another, but his head was pretty light as it was. He made his way back inside, went to the nurse's station to hand Decker his lighter back and then went into the lounge again. He took his seat and picked up his cup of tea. It was just at the optimal temperature for drinking. He took a swig and turned his eyes to the television screen.

There was a breaking news story unfolding on the screen in front of him. The suited newsreader looked as though he had suddenly been thrust into something that he was very ill prepared for. Even under the powder that was dashed over his skin before he went on the air, a visible sweat was breaking out. Briggs got up from his seat and hiked the volume up.

'....getting reports of two terrorist attacks in the town of Layton. Armed police have been called to Layton General Hospital to deal with an incident of unknown nature at this time. The other incident is on Corsica Road which is just near the main Hemmington Road that runs through the center of the town. There is apparently a major fire happening too. The reports we are getting are that these two incidents are linked. We have no further information at the moment, but we will bring you more updates when we have them.'

Briggs watched the screen and listened carefully, his cup of tea forgotten in his hand. A small fizz of something began to build up in his insides. It took a few moments for him to work out what it was that was bubbling up in his innards.

Hope.

As awful as it was to see something terrible happening to people out there in the wider world, he couldn't help but feel ignited by it. There had been other incidents before, and he had felt that buzz of hope, only for it to come to nothing. But still, it was there.

Hope.

It was that terrible blinding hope that all he had been saying for all these years was about to come to pass. He had hope that his virus, his creation that had been unleashed on the world to try and heal it, that had turned into something so monstrous that nobody could have stopped it, had finally risen from its fiery grave again and would put him back in the drivers' seat once again. It was too beautiful a fantasy to resist.

He would know soon enough. If it was what he thought it was, then something would happen, and it would happen soon.

He decided that another cigarette would be a good idea after all. He drained his cup, grimaced and went to find Decker to let him out again.

2.

"There's someone here to see you," said Decker.

Briggs had been napping in his chair, leaning back as far as he could, his legs crossed and his arms folded across his chest. He hadn't even been aware that he had gone to sleep. He checked his wrist to look at the time and then he realised that he hadn't put his watch on when he had gone walkabout in the middle of the night. He squinted at the television and saw that it was just past midnight

"I have to take you through right now," said Decker.

"Wha?....." muttered Briggs, his mind still fragmented from his nap.

Decker bent down so he was in Briggs' ear. "Doctor Low is here to see you."

Briggs' mind came back into focus, fast. The last time he had seen Low he had ended up slapping him right out of his chair. What on earth could he want with him now? More to the point, why was he here in the middle of the night?

And then he looked at the television again, still they were reporting terrorist attacks, still, they had no actual coverage. The adrenaline sparked in his body. He got up out of his chair, straightened himself out and clapped Decker on the shoulder.

"Lead the way," he said.

Decker led him through to room three, tapped on the door with his knuckle and then opened it up. He held it open to let Briggs in and then left the room, closing the door behind him.

Briggs looked at the man sat in the corner of the room. This guy had been the bane of his life for the last five years. This guy had tried to get him to change his story to fit what the world's media and the government that he had been employed to serve had labeled him. Five years of digging his heels and sticking to his guns. He knew that one day the truth would set him free, he knew it deep in his heart.

There was something different about Low's demeanor this time. He wasn't grinning and peering over his glasses in that condescending manner that he usually did. It usually sent the message that they were about to get on the same old merry-go-round again until one of them ended up walking out of the room. It was usually Briggs that did the walking, soon to be followed by a needle full of sedatives, whether he had done anything to deserve it or not. Briggs went and sat down on the seat directly opposite Low. He also mentally noted that Low wasn't carrying the weighty file that contained everything in Briggs' history, including every single conversation that they had been through. No, this time he was simply sitting in his chair, his arms folded and with an unreadable expression on his face.

"Well?" said Briggs, waiting for the bullshit to start.

"I have some people on their way that want to talk to you Mike," said Low. He looked as though he had been given a turd to eat and no matter how bad the taste of it was, he wasn't allowed to spit it out.

"Is that so? What makes you think that I want to talk to them?" said Briggs.

Low shook his head slowly. "I don't think you are in a position to play games."

Briggs laughed bitterly. "I am in no position to do anything other than watch television, eat terrible food and smoke enough cigarettes to make me throw up. It's all I've had to do for the last five years. In fact, I'm starting to rather enjoy it."

"These people that want to talk to you are in a very prominent position," said Low, picking his words carefully. "They could hold the key to you getting out of here and out of my hair, which I can tell you would be an absolute mercy. I would advise you to comply." His voice was monotone as if he was reading from a script.

"I don't have to do anything of the sort. You forget Mr. Low, that I have absolutely nothing left to lose. I….."

Briggs was interrupted by the door opening behind him. He turned around to see Decker holding the door open and two men dressed in suits and ties that probably didn't leave much change from a grand came inside. Low looked up at the men and shrank back in his seat a little.

"Out," one of them yelled and Doctor Low leaped out of his seat and went out of the door. The two men grabbed a chair each and positioned them in front of Briggs.

"Who the hell are you guys? Are you the secret service? MI5? Spies in the house of love?" said Briggs.

Neither of them looked impressed with Briggs' attempt at humor.

"Doctor Michael Briggs?" said the taller of the two men.

"That's me."

The two men sat down, almost in unison.

"Are you the manufacturer of the virus known as codename: Whisperer?"

"Manufacturer? I haven't heard it put quite like that. I drafted it, formulated it, created it, and when I was told to go and use it I got royally fucked over for it, but I guess you guys already know that," said Briggs.

"Did that virus cause the creation of a swarm of venomous spiders?" said the tall man.

"That's my understanding of it, yes."

"Could you tell me, sir, how that was allowed to happen?"

Briggs sighed. He had been over this story a thousand times. "Look, the virus had a large biological element to it. It was a basic lifeform, programmed to bond to spider DNA and change it so that the life cycle of the spiders was shortened considerably. Nobody and I mean nobody could have predicted what the virus did the moment it was released."

"Would you care to enlighten us?" said the shorter man.

"I don't know for sure, because I was never given the opportunity to dissect and study any of the mutations, but the theory that I have is that the biological element of the virus became rogue. It decided that it wanted to survive. It became the primary lifeforce in every spider that it infected, but it was still young, it was still learning. It must have grown far quicker than it was ready to, which is why the spiders were mutated. The concentration of the virus was far too strong. It should have been withdrawn and reconstructed and made to be weaker and more docile, but I never had the chance to do any of the studies, nor any of the modifications, because I have been kept here ever since it happened."

"Newtown was bombed, Doctor Briggs. Surely that virus would have been destroyed in the fire, am I correct?"

"No, you are not correct. You would have had to destroy it on a cellular level. Just burning it would have created residue that would have been carried by the smoke in the fire or the remains of any of those spiders. You would have had to clean that site as you would with a town littered with radiation. As long as it is there on a cellular level, it will survive."

There was a silence in the room for a few moments, the two men gave each other a look. They both stood up.

"You need to come with us Doctor Briggs," said shorter man.

Briggs crossed his arms, "Like hell I will, you owe me a damn explanation as to why you are here, who you are working for and why the hell you are so interested in the Whisperer. Why don't you arrest me? Take me in front of a judge, charge me with buggering sheep if that's what gives you a hard-on. Five years I have been sat in here and suddenly you two clowns show up and tell me I have to go with you? Fuck-a-doodle-doo. You can kiss my fat one."

"We anticipated that you might give us that answer," said tall man.

An arm suddenly went around Briggs' neck. Tall man and shorter man pounced on him before he could even begin to struggle. He felt the sting of a needle in his upper arm, the same thing that he had felt over a dozen times since he had arrived on the Tulip Suite. He was going to sleep and there was nothing he could do about it.

He gave up even trying to struggle, he waited for the drug to smash through the blood supply in his brain, and a moment later the off switch inside his head was clicked.

The darkness enveloped him again.

3.

The murky image began to swim in front of his eyes. He knew what it was from the moment it began to come out of the fog, like a ship about to crash into the rocks. The murkiness took shape, showing him the broken residential street, littered with the remains of human bodies and broken giant spiders. The stench of the decay filled his nose, making his stomach turn over and his throat tighten. This time, he wasn't wearing the protective suit, he didn't have the small rifle containing the tranquilizer dart. He was utterly exposed.

He turned his head slightly and saw the writhing, stinking mass of spiders, clumped together to build a protective tower up into the sky, such were the sheer numbers of them. He knew what was waiting inside for him, he had seen it in his nightmares so many times since the day it had happened.

Sure enough, the tower of spiders began to fall, their bloated and stretched bodies slapping against the tarmac. Some of them broke open on impact, splashing the ground with a sickly red and yellow pus. Some of them landed on their backs and were unable to get themselves back on their feet. The rest began to charge towards him. He braced himself for the stinging bites, the paralysis, the torrent of festering creatures to embrace him. Instead, they ran past him as if he was invisible.

He heard the shrieking roar. He felt his blood turn cold. It was coming for him all over again. It was….

Bang…

The image in front of his eyes began to falter.

Bang…

The image vanished. He began to feel a burning sensation against his right cheek.

Whack….

His eyes popped open. Shorter man was standing over him, his hand raised. It took Briggs a moment to realise that Shorter had been slapping him in the face to bring him around. His right cheek felt like it had been doused in hot water. There was a coppery taste of his own blood in his mouth. He tried to stand up, but his arms wouldn't move. The rattling of metal on metal brought to him the realisation that he had been cuffed to the arms of the chair he was sitting on.

"Just take it easy," said Shorter.

Briggs, safe in the knowledge that he wasn't going anywhere relaxed and sat back in the chair. He looked around the room he was in. He knew straight away that he was no longer on the ward, but instead inside some kind of police interview room. There was a large mirror on the wall to his left that he knew was two-way. There was a camera in the top-left corner, its red light illuminated just to let him know that everything was going on the record. At the very least, it offered him a small layer of protection from immediate harm. He kept an eye on that light, because if it winked out at any moment then he would likely be in trouble.

Shorter went and stood at the side of the door opposite Taller. A moment later the door opened and a squat man, wearing an obviously custom-made suit waddled in through the open space. Briggs knew him straight away. He had seen him on the television often enough. It was Bernard

Layfield. It was the Prime Minister of Great Britain.

There had been an election two years ago, and Layfield had never been off the television. His bald head, accentuated by the horseshoe of hair around the sides and the back of his skull, looked perpetually sweaty. He looked like a man that was permanently overheating, not just by the pressure of the job, but by an appalling diet that obviously consisted of too many mixed grills and vintage wine. Every time Briggs had seen him on the television, ranting about the raging amounts of government debt, and the high levels of unemployment, he wondered to himself how a man in such dreadful shape could possibly have lived for so long. He had wondered how he didn't just drop dead in the middle of another one of his rambling speeches, delivered with the gusto of an experienced blowhard. It had also crossed his mind that Layfield must have been a terribly smelly man who, no matter how many times a day he showered, must have stunk like a pig taking a bath in a variety of turds.

Layfield squeezed himself into the chair opposite Briggs. They were separated by a large metal table that Briggs guessed had been bolted to the floor. Briggs was a little star-struck by Layfield's arrival, but the feeling was doubled over by an overwhelming sense of revulsion. He had never cared for Layfield, or his policies, or anything about the man. But he had struck a chord with the British people, the disenchanted and disenfranchised poor folk, who had been desperate for change. His victory couldn't have been called anything else other than a landslide. Briggs had been watching the election coverage all night when it had happened. He saw the jubilant, sweaty Layfield shaking hands with other well-suited people, kissing women on the cheek, and puffing out his cheeks as if the whole event had overwhelmed him.

And, here he was now, sitting right in front of him, looking just as sweaty and out of breath as he had done on television. A faint waft of bodily odor, encased in a thin seal of deodorant and matching aftershave, met Briggs' nostrils. He had been absolutely spot on about the way that he had smelled, so he could be pretty certain that his other judgments on Layfield were on the money.

"I take it that you know who I am," said Layfield. He laced his hands together on the table in front of him.

"I've seen you on the box once or twice, but no more than that. I can't stand the smell of bullshit, see?" said Briggs. Shorter stepped forwards and raise his hand. Layfield put up an arm to stop him.

"Leave it be," he warned. "It's quite alright. If I was in his situation I would be angry too."

Shorter returned to his position next to the door. Layfield started to speak again, but Briggs cut him off.

"It's all bullshit isn't it?" he said.

Layfield's eyes began to twitch. "You had better explain that statement to me."

"Before I say anything more, could you release one of my hands so I can smoke?" said Briggs.

Layfield took a snoring breath. "I don't see why not, but be warned Briggs, these men are armed, you try anything…. *anything,* and they will blow you apart. You be nice and I'll be nice right back 'K?" he said. The prick almost sounded magnanimous. Briggs offered him a nod. Layfield gestured to the men stood behind him and taller stepped forwards, pulling a key out of his pocket. He unhooked Briggs' left hand and then brought out a pack of cigarettes from his other pocket. He offered one to Briggs and then clicked a light to it with a cheap looking lighter. Briggs dragged and then chugged out smoke in Layfield's direction. Layfield's expression didn't change as the smoke billowed around him.

"That's a really nasty habit you have there, Doctor Briggs," said Layfield.

Briggs shrugged and took another hit off his smoke. "Well, if you live the life that I've had for the last five years then there isn't much else for you to do other than pick up shitty habits."

Layfield smiled briefly, then his face returned to his television face, one devoid of all emotion. A closed book.

"Your case has been very unique Doctor. We have never had an event like the one that happened in Newtown in the history of this great country. Many, many lives were lost that day, both in the town and in the hospital where the outbreak began. The repercussions of that day were felt throughout the world. Most people didn't even believe it, even when it was reported on television. Even the people who had loved ones killed, they didn't believe it. The story, to them, was so far-fetched, so ridiculous that they largely rejected it. It was only the people who were there and saw it with their own eyes that gave it any credibility. But, the masses have shouted them down over the years, to a point where the truthers are now considered conspiracy theorists and that *you* Doctor Briggs were responsible for unleashing bio-chemical weapons both in the hospital and in Newtown. We kept you in the Tulip Suite for your own protection."

Briggs stared at him wide-eyed, his cigarette forgotten between his fingers, and then he burst out laughing. Layfield smiled politely as he laughed. He laughed until tears ran out of his eyes and spilled down his cheeks. Eventually, the laughter dried up and Briggs wiped his streaming eyes with his sleeve. He took another pull on his cigarette and then he mashed it out on the table in front of him.

"So, let me get this straight. It wasn't the government that kept me locked up, it was the *people?*" said Briggs.

Layfield shrugged. "If that's the way you want to look at it."

"It wasn't the people that gave me that assignment. It wasn't the people that *refused* to listen to me when that virus went rogue. It was you, and your kind. You bombed Newtown, you wiped it off the face of the earth, and you tried to take me out too. You lot kept me locked up all these years, and now I'm hearing about terrorist attacks all over the television, and just like magic, your fat arse is suddenly sitting in front of me trying to justify your position on why I have been locked away ever since. Why don't you just knock off the bullshit and tell me why you are here and more importantly, why *I* am here," said Briggs. He sat back in his chair, trying not to breathe the horribly sweaty air in the room.

Shorter stepped forwards again. "Why don't you just show some fuckin' respect," he growled.

"Go fuck yourself," Briggs retorted. Shorter stepped forwards and was again cut off by Layfield who sent him back to his post by the door.

Layfield leaned forwards. "Alright Doctor Briggs, I'm going to level with you," he said. Out of the corner of his eye, Briggs saw the red light on top of the camera blink out. Some heavy shit was about to go down, he thought to himself.

"There have been some major incidents, all of them within the town of Layton. I don't know how good your geography is Doctor Briggs, but Layton sits just six miles from where Newtown once stood. During the explosion, most of the homes in Layton lost their windows, such was the force of the blast. The first incident happened in Layton General Hospital. Two people, one a civilian, the other a police officer were in an isolation ward together. The girl had suffered a broken leg and the officer had lost part of his arm in an accident of unknown origin. Both of these people were bitten by a spider during the course of the day. The hospital staff would have been none the wiser, but the same morning, a three-year-old child died as a result of a similar bite and the investigating officer handed in a specimen that he found at the scene."

"It was a spider, wasn't it? A mutated spider of some sort," said Briggs.

"Not mutated at all Doctor Briggs. It was almost a perfect example of a British house spider. But it was one of those spiders that inflicted the bite on the officer in the hospital."

"Did it kill him? Did he die?" said Briggs.

"No Doctor, he didn't," said Layfield. He lowered his head for a moment, the sweat on the bald spot was beginning to run small rivers down the shiny skin.

"What happened to him?"

"He changed Doctor Briggs. He became something we haven't seen before. As did the girl with the broken leg," said Layfield. He rummaged in his inside pocket and brought out his mobile phone. He tapped the screen half a dozen times and then slid the phone across the table. Briggs picked it up and had a look at the image on the screen.

The world swam in front of his eyes. His heart began to pound, almost right out of his chest. His lungs began to spasm, stopping the regular pull of breaths and replacing them with dog-like panting. He threw the phone onto the table, the metallic bang echoing around the sparse room. He pinched his eyes shut, trying to get the image from the phone screen out of his mind, but it was as if the image was burned into his eyes, the same way that staring at the sun would leave a blind spot in every image you looked at thereafter.

    It was a picture of the girl that Layfield had been talking about. The picture looked like it had been taken in a long hallway, which Briggs had assumed had been the corridor of the hospital. The girl was standing right in the middle of the corridor, the torn remains of her hospital gown clinging to her body. It had been shredded by the extra limbs that had grown out of the sides of her lower chest and abdomen. The new legs were pressed against the walls at either side, lifting the human legs off the floor. He had only looked at the picture for a moment, but he saw the broken leg and the metal bar that had been surgically attached to it to hold it together. He also saw the image that came out of the dark corner of his mind and overlay itself onto the picture on Layfield's phone. The two were almost indistinguishable.

"Are you going to tell me what that is?" said Layfield.

"How did you get that picture?" said Briggs. His voice had picked up a very distinguished wobble.

"It was taken by one of the staff and forwarded by the investigating D.C.I. He was the one that had been working on the case. It was taken inside that hospital today. Are you going to tell me what it is?"

Briggs took a deep breath. "I need another cigarette," he said.

After he had been obliged he sat back in his chair. He had managed to settle himself down again. He had been dreaming about this moment, when they all came crawling back to him because the virus had returned, but now that it looked like it was happening he felt no joy, no sense of revenge, nothing. It was the biggest anti-climax of his whole life. The only thing that he felt was a hollow, empty fear that felt like it ran through his entire middle.

"Well?" said Layfield.

Briggs dragged on his cigarette. He supposed that if he told this fat little fuck what he wanted to know then perhaps he might put him back in the Tulip Suite for the rest of his days. He thought that it might be the safest place to be, but he knew deep down that they would get in. They always got in when you least expected them to.

"It's a hybrid," he said and blew out smoke. Layfield still looked like he had no clue.

"The Whisperer…. The virus was only supposed to bond itself to spider DNA. But the one factor that I didn't even think about was the fact that the virus would evolve so quickly. The moment it was released, in a gaseous form, it began to mutate, it began to evolve. It took on a survival instinct. Every living thing on this earth has to evolve to survive, right?"

Layfield shrugged.

"There were elements of the virus that accelerated the life cycle of spiders, so their numbers would be culled. They were at such high levels that they were beginning to wipe out the bee population, and you don't need me to tell you how much of a disaster for the environment that would have been. But, as I say, the virus had its own ideas. By the time I got inside the spider nest in Newtown, the next stage had already begun. It had found a way to bond to human DNA and to fuse the two together, creating a new type of species that could host the virus, give it life."

He pointed at Layfield's phone. "That, right there is proof of what I am telling you. When you killed Newtown, that virus survived. It took a little time, but it started to grow again, and I'm betting it has gotten a little smarter this time. All you did by blowing it up was to press the reset switch, force it to start again. All it needed to do was to bond to its first arachnid host and then it would have been away."

Briggs leaned forwards as far as his cuffed hand would let him. "Those spiders that bit those people are infected with it, all of them. God knows how many more there are. The spider to human ratio is something like two-point-eight-million-to-one. From the looks of it, only one bite is needed for that virus to bond to a human and turn them into *that*" he said, tapping the table.

There was quiet in the room for a moment. The clock on the wall buzzed, insect-like in the silence.

"Can you prove any of these….these… things that you're saying?" said Layfield.

"Not sitting here with a cuff on my arm I can't. But I can tell you, nobody knows that virus as I do. I'm telling you right now, whether you choose to believe me, or you choose to go and put me back on that ward until I'm old and grey, that virus is going to turn into a plague very quickly. From the looks of things, it has already made a start," said Briggs.

Silence again. Briggs could almost see the cogs in Layfield's head turning over. He was surprised that the sweat on there wasn't starting to sizzle.

"What if I could offer you your old job back," said Layfield.

And there it was. There had been the moment he had been waiting for, for five long years. Five years of nightmares, five years of eating the same appalling food at the same times every day. Five years of being told when he could go for a cigarette when he could go to bed, when he had to get up in the morning and five years of Doctor Fucking Low.

He had been right all along. He knew he had been right, but as the time had passed he had begun to believe it less and less, but here it was, right in front of him. He finally had the axe, the question was whether or not he was going to grind it. He thought he might sharpen it a little.

"I was told that the Environmental Services Agency was a figment of my imagination. It is going to take something very special to win you my trust again after what you have put me through," said Briggs.

Layfield offered a pained smile. "I quite understand your position, Doctor Briggs. But you have to understand, that we had no idea what it was that we were dealing with. It wasn't inconceivable that you had, if you pardon the phrase, doctored that virus to behave in a way that nobody had predicted. At least that was the information that was being passed around in the government at that time."

Briggs opened his mouth to protest but Layfield held up his hand to silence him. "Rest assured Doctor Briggs, I do not represent that government. Do I believe what they have said about you? Having met you, I'm not so sure."

"So, what's the deal?" said Briggs.

"We have an offer for you. You come back to work for us. You find a cure for this...virus of yours. If you get the job done, then we let you go with a new identity, a relocation and more money than you could possibly spend in your lifetime," said Layfield. He sat back in his chair and folded his arms across his considerable middle.

"What about my reputation?"

"I'm afraid that is the one sacrifice that you will have to make. The country needs its Bogeyman, and they have chosen you for that particular honor. I can't deny them that."

"And if I say no?"

"Do you really think that is a possibility?" said Layfield, cocking his head slightly to the left.

Briggs mulled it over. Layfield had him by the short hairs, and he knew it. What choice did he have? At least he might have a shot at some sort of life after it was all over. He thought about going to Hawaii and spending the rest of his days sipping cocktails by the beach. Perhaps he would watch the sun go down every evening, perhaps he could meet a girl....perhaps.

He leaned forward and offered his free hand to Layfield.

"We have a deal?" said Layfield.

"It had better be a lot of money. I have plans."

"You won't be disappointed," said Layfield. He reached over the desk with his own pudgy hand and they shook.

4.

The Environmental Services Agency was real alright. It always had been. Now, here he was heading back to the people who he had been told had been a figment of his imagination for five years. He had so many conflicting emotions over it he could barely focus on a single one of them. One thing he did know for sure, was that he had a lovely warm fuzzy feeling in the pit of his stomach, knowing that he would never be back on the Tulip Suite ever again. But, even that emotion was conflicted with a terrible sadness. He found himself missing his little room, missing his cigarette breaks, missing the regular food, missing the staff that had treated him well, and even the ones who had been dismissive of him. He had known about people becoming institutionalized. He had written a paper on it years ago during his university course, but he had never really believed that it was possible, but here he was, a living example of the very thing he didn't believe in.

Wasn't life funny? He guessed it was because a smile was breaking out over his face.

Ridiculous. Utterly ridiculous. Really, what did he have to smile about? He was basically still a prisoner. The choice he had been given hadn't been one with much of a back-out clause. If that was the case he would have told Layfield to cram his offer right up his arse, or at least he thought he would have. Again, the stir of confusion within him couldn't offer him a clear answer.

Then there was the virus.

Now there was something to think over, that virus that he had spent so long creating. It was basically his baby, and he had unleashed it on the world without a thought that it might try and counter its basic programming. Had it really tried to survive? Or had it just been rewritten by the effects of the pollutants in the atmosphere? He had to admit it, he was desperate to find out if it was still out there and causing trouble, in which case, it had adapted to survive. Now, if that was true, and he could prove that it was true….

He had created a new form of life.

He snapped his thoughts back to reality. He didn't know anything for sure yet. It didn't stop the thought dancing around his head.

How many men who walked this earth could say that they had created a new form of life, how many? None that he could think of. Yes, there were plenty of people who had *discovered* new forms of life, but how many had *actually created* a new form of life. It had the Nobel prize written all over it...

He held his breath for a moment and brought his mind back to front and center. He had to remember that this thing that he had created had caused a hell of a lot of people to die. It had caused a whole town to be wiped off the face of the earth, never to return. It had killed everyone in his team, those that he had called his friends. On top of that, it had caused the death of Lorna Johnson, the unfortunate woman who just happened to be in the wrong place at the wrong time. Looking at the bigger picture, they had all been fish out of water, she had just joined them as they flapped and gasped their way through the mutation of the virus and the Newtown spiders.

Just wait, he told himself. *Let's just see what we find.*

But there was the picture that Layfield had shown him. The picture from the hospital, the girl that had been mutated into a hybrid, just the same as the one that he had seen in Newtown. That *had* to be the virus. It just had to be. There was nothing else on this earth that could have caused that to happen, surely.

Oh, he could just drive himself mad.

"Three minutes to landing Doctor Briggs," said a voice suddenly in his ears. The headset he was wearing was cumbersome and uncomfortable, but the constant noise from the helicopter rotors made it impossible to communicate any other way. The voice had come from Lieutenant Monsun, who was sitting in the seat next to him. He had been assigned to escort him to the ESA. Briggs had found him to be the master of the poker face. Briggs had tried to crack him with a few jokes, but Monsun was having none of it. His stony face remained unimpressed with Briggs' shoddy attempts at humor. The only response he had got from Monsun had been a somewhat gruff "Very droll, sir," and nothing more. He had given Monsun up as a bad lot. Perhaps there would be some other like-minded scientists at the ESA that he could enjoy some laughs with.

The helicopter started to lose altitude quickly. Briggs gripped the sides of his seat and doubled over to combat the stomach drop. He wasn't the biggest fan of flying at the best of times, and this had been in first go in a helicopter. He wasn't above the idea that he would like to make this one his last. He pinched his eyes closed, wondering if they were about to slam into the ground, and then at least the whole sorry mess would be put to rest finally. Instead, he felt the drop slowing and the soft metallic *clunk* as the helicopter touched down.

"Let's go. Duck your head until we're clear, otherwise, you might get yourself a haircut," said Monsun.

Briggs nodded and then took off his headset. The door was opened by another soldier on the outside and Briggs stepped out. It was the freshest air that he had breathed in a long time, even over the smell of the burning fuel from the chopper. He dutifully ducked his head and allowed the soldier to lead him away from the whirring blades.

"Clear now, sir," said the soldier. Briggs thanked him, straightened himself up and took a moment to stretch.

The building was right next to the beach, a remote location that wasn't available to the general public. It was all government owned, and run by the military and the security around the place was tight as tight could be. Briggs breathed in, taking a good smell of that slightly salty sea air. Never had such a simple pleasure felt so wonderful in all his days. He began to feel his need to be back in the Tulip Suite start to falter. Perhaps tomorrow he might get a chance to walk on the beach, perhaps take off his shoes and feel the sand squish between his toes, that would be heavenly, absolutely heavenly.

"Let's go," said Monsun from behind him, breaking him out of his momentary fantasy.

Briggs saw the door in front of him. There was a guard on the door waving him over. He wasn't going to be given a moment to gather himself it would seem. He had a momentary fear that he was simply moving from one prison to another. It probably wasn't good to think like that, a man could drive himself crazy...

The light inside the building was such that it hurt Briggs' eyes. Every corridor seemed to blaze with a whiteness that was almost unbearable to look at. Had it been this bright the last time he was hear? Perhaps he had just been so used to it that he hadn't even noticed it anymore. Or, it could have been the fact that the Tulip Suite was in a state of such neglect that his eyes were not used to seeing a fresh paint job. He was being led down the corridor, the unknown soldier from the door in front and Monsun behind him. The corridor split into a left-hand turn and Briggs started down it, unconsciously heading to his old work area. Monsun corrected him with a rough shove.

"Watch it!" Briggs yelled at him. Monsun's expression never changed. He looked like a man who had done this kind of assignment a thousand times over. Briggs began to wonder to himself how many men Monsun had killed over his lifetime. He even opened his mouth to ask and then snapped it shut again. Some things, he thought, were better left unsaid.

As they carried on down the corridor, he realised that they were heading down to the conference room. He figured that his work was not going to begin right away. Hell, he wasn't even going to get a cup of coffee. Just as he suspected they made their way towards the front of the building, where all the offices were located, the nicely carpeted areas and glass walls, the space where business attire was compulsory, as was a decent set of qualifications. This was an area of the building that represented everything he hated about the people that he worked for. He didn't want to be involved in office politics or sucking up to the directors, it just wasn't him. He did, however, enjoy the facilities that were on offer. The odor of fresh coffee seemed to be ingrained in the very fabric of the building out here. The smell of it made his mouth water.

They headed for the conference room and Briggs caught sight of Layfield, our wonderful Prime Minister sitting at the head of the large, polished surface of the conference table. He sighed, not wanting to engage in another conversation with him. He wouldn't have even voted for him, never mind liked to have sat and had a chat with him. Doing it twice within a twenty-four-hour period was just not cricket. Nevertheless, he took a deep breath and allowed himself to be led into the room. Layfield stood up as he entered and offered his hand.

"Here he is, here's our man," he said. He almost sounded happy, almost. There was a definite tinge of shakiness in his voice. Briggs picked up on it. Layfield was worried. Whatever was going on out there, it was potentially catastrophic and he was the man in the hot seat. Briggs almost felt sorry for him, almost. He shook Layfield's hand which felt clammy and limp, like a dead fish. It was another sign that he was being pressed against the wall with his pants down. Layfield offered him a seat and he took the one nearest to him. He made Layfield even more nervous, he knew it and he took pleasure in it.

"Well, how does it feel to be back?" said Layfield, a big false grin across his face.

"It's like I never left," said Briggs with more than a hint of sarcasm.

"We have got everything in place for you to conduct your....research? Whatever it is that you do. The full capacity of this complex is at your disposal, plus anything that you need. You ask for it, it will be provided," said Layfield.

"I'll need an extra pair of hands and a guarantee that you won't interfere with my work. Oh, and I need confirmation of the promise you made to me. Call it a down payment if you like," said Briggs.

Layfield swallowed hard. His throat clicked audibly. "I will have a bank account set up in the next few hours, and ten percent of your final payoff deposited, will that suffice?"

"Good enough, now what about…."

"An assistant? Oh yes, I have an assistant for you Doctor Briggs. I anticipated that you might need some help and encouragement. I need a pair of eyes on you Doc, just to make sure that you uphold *your* end of the deal. That's the way it's going to be." said Layfield. He sounded like he had a little bass in his voice again. Now it was Briggs' turn to be a little on edge.

"What are you up to?" said Briggs.

"Doctor Briggs, you should have more faith in me. I'm just making sure that we have all our cards on the table before we set out on this little project together. Have a little faith," said Layfield. He smiled, which put another dab of fear in Briggs' guts. He tried to put Layfield on the back-foot again.

"So, what's the latest with your little terrorist situation?"

The smile dropped from Layfield's face as if someone had slapped it right off. "The town of Layton is in the process of being evacuated. Reports are coming in of spiders coming up out of the drains and running people out of their homes. The army is setting up a border on the nearby city of Hemmington and all the towns that are immediately around Layton. They have flamethrowers and other heavy artillery to deal with the problem. It will be contained until you come up with a solution. There are many, many casualties so far Doctor."

"Looks like you really are getting butt-fucked eh? Good luck getting voted in next time," said Briggs.

That got Layfield mad. He stood up out of his chair. "You show me some *respect* Briggs, show me some damn *respect.* I could still have you back in that hospital at any moment, and don't you *bloody well forget it,"* he roared. His rotund cheeks had turned an ugly shade of scarlet with the force of his shouting.

He stood there for a moment, gathering himself, opening and closing his fists in an effort to calm down. After a moment he spoke again, his voice was back to its usual calm and monotonous tone. "All of the facilities are ready for you to begin your work. All of the samples are at your disposal. I suggest that you get on with the job Doctor Briggs."

Layfield got up to leave, but Briggs stood in his way. The two soldiers at the door stiffened.

"You just make sure that you make good on your promise. You see, I don't trust you an inch, and I have absolutely no reason to change my mind on that," said Briggs. There was a decent blob of anger in his belly, but he needed to keep a lid on it, at least for now.

Layfield said nothing. Briggs stepped aside and let him walk away. If he never saw him again it would have suited him just fine.

"Come with me," said Monsun. "Time to have a look at your new office." He still had his poker face on. Briggs wondered if that guy even knew what an emotion was.

Monsun turned and made his way out of the door. Briggs dutifully followed and they were backed up by the two soldiers that had been guarding the door. Briggs already knew the way, but he allowed Monsun to lead him anyway. There was no need to cause a fuss with men who were carrying guns after all. Before long they were standing outside the double doors that lead into Briggs' old laboratory.

"All yours Doc," said Monsun with his customary warmth.

Briggs pushed through the doors and had a look around. All of the old equipment he had used the last time he was here was gone, all of it replaced with newer and more up-to-date items. The department that he had left behind all those years ago had operated on a shoe-string budget, and everything he had to work with at the time had given the impression that they had found most of it in a second-hand shop. This setup, however, looked as though there was some serious money behind it. A fella, a smart fella might have thought to himself that they had got this room ready for the eventuality that they might be needing it again. As the thought raced around his head, something felt like it had clicked into place for him. It was no wonder they had kept him in that hospital the way that they had, they had an idea that the virus might come back too. But, a fat bastard like Layfield wouldn't have been able to work that one out by himself, he would have needed minds much superior to his to put that particular jigsaw together. Someone else had been mowing his lawn whilst he had been away, that was for sure. The more he looked around the room, the more he saw the evidence. The equipment was new, that was for sure, but it had all the markings of equipment that was subject to daily tinkering. He felt a snap of mild irritation at the idea of someone else being in his lab.

"You must be Doctor Briggs," said a voice from behind him. He turned around and saw that a woman had come into the room behind him whilst he had been mourning the passing of his exclusivity. She had the look of a woman that had yet to reach thirty, and yet she brimmed with confidence. She was dressed in a pin-striped trouser suit and she was clutching a large folder to her chest. Her brown eyes, set behind a pair of rimless spectacles, sparkled with, what Briggs suspected to be, a vast intelligence. He had a pretty good idea that she had been the one that had been picking his nose whilst he wasn't looking. If he was right, then he guessed he would let it go for now.

"Yes, that's me," he said.

"I've been looking forward to meeting you finally," she said, putting the folder on the counter. "I have read all your research on metaphysical biology, really brilliant stuff."

She was talking at a speed that was a little too fast and gesticulating wildly as she did so. It took Briggs a moment to realise that she was star-struck. She was a fan.

"Did you understand it all?" he said.

"Yessir," she spluttered. "I wrote a dissertation on it. I got top marks too. When I got posted here, it was the week after, y'know, Newtown. They said I had to disseminate your work, find out all about it."

"Do you think that you have a grasp on it now? Sorry, what's your name?"

She fanned herself with her hands for a moment, another overdone gesture. "Oh, yes of course… Becky…er, Willis. Doctor Becky Willis," she said holding out her hand. Briggs shook it gently. The hand was slick and clammy with sweat.

"It's a pleasure to meet you Doctor Becky Willis," said Briggs, giving her a smile. He was hoping that once the novelty had worn off that she would calm down a little. He wouldn't be able to tolerate the fawning for very long.

"Likewise," bellowed Willis.

Briggs thought it over for a moment and then he said, "Would you like to get a cup of coffee, and we can bring each other up to speed. We can't do anything until we get to know each other a little."

"Yeah…..oh my….yes I would love to. I'll show you where the canteen is," said Willis. Briggs was going to tell her that he already knew, but for the second time that day, he allowed himself to be lead through the complex that he had called home for so many years.

5.

The laboratory wasn't the only thing that had been substantially improved whilst he had been away. Before, there had only been one choice of coffee, the same watery, flavorless rubbish every single day. Now they had a much more sophisticated machine that dispensed every type of coffee that you could possibly want. It took Briggs a few moments to decide which one he actually fancied. He opted for a caramel cappuccino, in the end, not having any idea if he would actually like it or not. There was a bigger selection of food too, just from the vending machines that were on offer. The counter service was closed at this unsociable hour, but Willis assured Briggs that the food was of the highest standard, and he would find out once the catering staff arrived the next day. They settled themselves onto the table nearest the large windows. There wasn't much to see out of the windows other than the orange glow of the outside lighting. Briggs was momentarily surprised to see a soldier slowly walking across the bottom of the window. Willis saw the surprise on his face.

"Walkways, all around the complex," she said through a mouthful of cheese and ham sandwich. "Security around here got real tight after Newtown." She paused to swallow. "The internet blew up with conspiracy theories, most of which centered around the government. It wasn't difficult to make the link between you and them, with a little fishing around of course, at least until somebody started scrubbing."

Briggs had just unwrapped a chicken and bacon panini. It was halfway to his mouth when he realised what Willis had said. It paused in his hands.

"Scrubbing?" he said.

"Oh, yeah, scrubbing. It's when a tech guy removes all evidence from the internet, all videos, articles, everything. There were so many videos out there it was impossible for the government to put out their version of the story and get people to buy into it. They almost pushed the kill switch to get rid of it all," said Willis. She folded the last of her sandwich into her mouth. Briggs had a suspicion that she was from working-class stock, one that had risen far above any expectation that had been put upon her. People from a higher etiquette would have probably eaten that sandwich with a knife and fork.

"I thought that the kill switch was just a rumor. I didn't think anyone had the power to take out the whole internet," said Briggs. He took a bite of his panini. After five years of hospital food, he felt as if his entire set of taste buds were having an almighty orgasm. He had never had food taste so good and he doubted he ever would again.

"I'm only going off what I had heard around this place. I'm a natural earwigger, goes with the territory. I don't know anything for sure, except that all evidence of what went on has vanished into thin air. Everything except, of course, the work that you did here, and the work I have done since."

Briggs set down his sandwich. "Tell me what you know."

Willis sipped her coffee. "Me tell you?" she giggled, "Ok. The virus you created, The Whisperer was designed to speed up the metabolic rate of all breeds of British spider. The motive is to thin out their numbers and stop them from snacking on the common honey bee, which would have caused the ecological balance of the world to be out of whack."

Briggs laughed, she had a way with words that tickled his funny bone.

Willis smiled pleasantly at him whilst he laughed. She waited for him to stop before she carried on.

"I'm willing to guess that you don't really know what happened to it when it was released, or do you?" she said.

"I have a theory, but it's all I have."

"Tell me your theory," she said. She had set her sandwich down and was giving him her full attention.

"Ok. I think that the virus tried to survive, it mutated to try and break free of its programming. The moment we set it loose, it was like setting a bird free, all it wanted to do was fly," said Briggs.

"That's pretty good. In a way you're right, but there is more to it than that," said Willis and took a gulp of her coffee.

"Well, don't keep me in suspenders," said Briggs and Willis giggled.

"It wasn't the virus that tried to survive, it was the spiders," she said and drank more coffee.

Briggs mulled it over for a moment. He leaned forward and folded his arms on the table. "How is that possible?"

"If you catch a cold, what is the first thing that happens?" she went on without allowing Briggs to answer. "Your body attacks the invading virus as best it can. Depending on the virus the body will go to more and more extreme lengths, that's why you get a fever or septic toes, or your teeth fall out. The reaction to that virus when it invaded the body of those spiders was as extreme as it comes. That's why they mutated. The reaction to the virus caused it, not the virus itself."

Briggs sat back again. He was floored. Such was his high opinion of the virus that it never occurred to him that it wasn't the cause of the mutations.

"Do you have any proof?" he said.

"I have one of them," she said.

"Come again?"

"I have one of the Newtown spiders. It's dead, but I still have it. I believe it was the one that killed the fireman, at least, that's what they told me," said Willis and drank more coffee. She looked up at Briggs who was sat in front of her open-mouthed.

"You wanna see it? I can show you if you like, then I have to get some sleep, I'm knackered," she said curtly.

"Sure," said Briggs, and he did. There was a slug of apprehension crawling in his guts, but the curiosity of seeing one of the beasts again was far stronger.

"Let's go, bring your coffee," she said pushing her chair back and standing up.

"You couldn't part me from it," he said picking up his plastic cup.

She led him back towards the lab, but this time they carried on past the doors and into the next room. She clicked a switch on the wall and the room lit up. The lighting was a dim orange glow, just enough to see inside. Briggs knew it was to preserve any samples that they had inside, the light would cause them to degenerate.

Willis closed the door behind them. The room was lined with large enclosed jars filled with a clear greenish liquid. Inside the jars were different types of insects and creatures, one of them was, what looked like, a Labrador, permanently frozen in the liquid with its now pale tongue hanging out the side of its mouth. Willis led him down the grotesque museum exhibits to the end jar.

"Here you go," she said and pointed to the jar at the end of the row.

Briggs looked at the jar and he felt his breath stop for a moment. The flashbacks of Newtown bolted briefly through his mind. He shook them off as best he could and he took a step closer to the creature in the jar. It was one of the Newtown spiders alright. Its outer skin looked like it had been stretched and torn from the mutations. Its abdomen was heavily swollen, like a boil that was ready to burst open at any moment. The spider floated in the fluid, its legs (which had been worn away a little through the passage of time) waved to him slowly through the glass. The back legs had grown far beyond the capacity of normality. They dangled down from the spider's body like two pieces of grotesque cord. He felt mildly unwell looking at it, and yet his scientific brain wanted so badly to understand it. To know what made it tick.

"What do you think? I mean, I never saw one of these when it was alive 'cept when the videos were online, but I always thought that they looked sort of fake anyway," said Willis.

"They were a lot more menacing when they moved, believe me. I never want to be put in that kind of situation again," said Briggs. He misted over for a moment, remembering the tower of spiders in Newtown, remembering the sound that they made, all of them rustling together as they tried to hold formation. He felt a shiver coming up his neck, he suppressed it as much as he could but Willis saw it.

"It must have been pretty tough," said Willis. She reached for his hand and gave it a squeeze, after a moment he squeezed back and offered her a smile.

"Whatever is happening now, I'm sure we can work it out between us. As a species, we have come up with some pretty hot solutions to most of the worst diseases in the world, I'm sure we can manage this one too," said Willis.

"The solution? I know about the solution, don't you worry about that," said Briggs.

"You have an idea?" said Willis, her face lighting up.

"You could say that all in good time," he said.

"I saw the pictures, y'know, the pictures of the girl….the infected girl. What had happened to her?"

"The virus has had five years to regroup. Personally? I think it has evolved. I only saw its bond to one human host the last time it happened, and I don't know anything for sure, but I think she was bitten and somehow survived. The bites from these spiders," he gestured to the specimen tank, " was enough to paralyze a fully grown human. They used human bodies to gestate more like them, the whole process took less than a few minutes. I think the girl I saw in Newtown had been bitten but didn't get impregnated….. I think. I didn't stick around to find out."

"I wouldn't have done either," said Willis. She still had hold of his hand and was now rubbing her thumb up and down his finger. "But, we can start tomorrow. We should go and get some sleep. There are a couple of bunks at the back of the building we can get our heads down on."

He thought about sleep for a moment. He wouldn't have even entertained the idea half-an-hour ago, and yet at even the mention of it, he felt waves of tiredness begin to wash over him. He nodded at Willis and she led him out of the room. Neither of them noticed that they were still holding hands.

She led him to the rear of the complex and into the on-call room. It contained what was as close to a comfortable home setting as you were likely to get in the circumstances. There was a long sofa, a television mounted to the wall and a large single bed that had been made up with a prissiness that was unbecoming of a government-financed operation.

"There is another one next door. If you need anything there is an intercom next to the door here," said Willis.

"Ok, well, I will leave you in peace and tomorrow we can get started," said Briggs and he moved to leave. Willis stepped in front of him.

"Can I just say Doctor Briggs, it is an honor to meet you finally. I feel like I have known you for years already," she said.

"Likewise," said Briggs.

Willis hesitated for a moment, there was a little colour building in her cheeks.

"I wondered…. If you want to, y'know. Spend the rest of the night with me?" she stuttered.

Briggs opened his mouth, ready to turn down her offer, that he was older than her, that she was a work colleague. Excuse, after excuse danced on the edge of his tongue. But instead, he said nothing. He put out his arms and encircled her waist. He pulled her in close and for the first time in a very long time, Briggs felt the wonderful intoxicating feel of female flesh again.

His staying power had not improved a jot.

6.

Despite his best efforts to play night watchman, Braden had fallen asleep. His head had dropped forwards and he began to drool down his shirt. He had a broken and vague dream that he had been on a large yacht in a harbor that looked like it had been plucked right out of a big budget movie. Every single possible cliché was present, from the champagne glasses sitting on a tray on the deck to the ridiculous captain's uniform that he was wearing. After he had woken up the last remnants of the dream hung around in his mind for a few moments and then they evaporated. He had been waiting for Mary and Jax to turn up so that they could sail away to the middle of the ocean, the only place that they could be safe from the events that had happened on land. The residue of the dream made him wonder if they would be better off on their own without Trent's help. At the moment, he couldn't even entertain that idea, they needed him and his off-road vehicle to get to safety. Once that had happened then Braden was going to weigh up their options. He didn't really believe in the idea that a dream could tell you which direction to go in your life, but then again, he didn't believe a lot of things were possible until a few years ago. He couldn't quite put his finger on what it was about Trent that was bugging him. He had always found Trent to be mildly irritating at the best of times. He was polite to him as the next-door neighbor, that hadn't been a problem. There had been times when he had seen him and Mary talking over the garden fence. Mary laughed at his weak jokes just a little bit too easily for his liking. Trent certainly wasn't that funny. Perhaps it was the fact that good ol' Trent didn't seem to have an ounce of fat on his body. He even cleaned his big-ass car without his shirt on, which drew more than a few admiring glances from the local female (and some of the male) population. Perhaps it was the fact that he had pulled them out of danger instead of Braden doing it himself. Did he really have that much of an ego? Did he really have to be the alpha male in any given situation? Probably he did, after all, he had been fighting to stay on top his entire professional career. Now he was facing the possibility of having to stay on top within the confines of his own marriage. He was out of his element here and he knew it. He was no good with the great outdoors or survival instincts that didn't involve fucking people over in one way or another. In his own mind, he was putting Trent on notice. Sorry buddy, but you gotta go.

He looked around him and saw that they were still parked up. Not long before he had nodded off, they had gone off road again and parked up in some woodland that Braden didn't even know existed.

Trent had the CB radio headset on his head. He was listening out, being the watchman, ready to move at a moment's notice. After just a few minutes of Braden being back in the land of the living, Trent took off the headset and handed it back to Braden.

"Here, keep listening. Those bastards are on the move."

He started the engine and got them moving again. There was also a strange and pungent smell that Braden recognized from his younger days of all night partying and excess. He looked over at Trent. He had his window open a little and he was smoking a home-made cigarette that obviously didn't just contain tobacco. Trent looked like he was a guy that was just out for a Sunday drive rather than fleeing the hoards that had come out of the ground that used to be a town. A voice suddenly blared in Braden's left ear, causing him to jerk and draw in a sudden breath. It was just the headset. Someone had said something unintelligible.

"Anything happening on that radio?" said Trent. His voice had taken on a drawling husky tone from the special cigarette that he had been smoking.

"Nothing interesting. Where are we heading?" said Braden.

"I thought we might hole up at the ranger's station for a little while, try and get our bearings a little, otherwise we will just end up driving around until we run out of fuel."

"I don't know if you have noticed, but there is a hell of a lot of hungry spiders coming out of the ground, and we are on the menu. What makes you think we would be safe there?" said Braden. There was a strong tinge of sarcasm in his voice, but it was obvious that Trent was far too stoned to notice.

"Look, it's right out in the middle of nowhere, it has big metal doors and double thick windows, they won't be able to get in. There's food, water, and a generator, everything we'll need for now. Take it easy chief, I know what I'm doing," said Trent and took another deep drag from his joint. The ashes fell off the end and landed in his lap. He brushed them away absent-mindedly.

Braden wanted to yell at him, chew him out, shake him and tell him that they would die in that little shack, they needed to get away from all of the major cities. They should head for the coast, they would be safe there and perhaps they could find themselves a decent sized boat that they could get away from the land with. That was a plan, but again he wasn't driving and this wasn't his car. He would put his plan into operation at the nearest available opportunity. That might even involve taking Trent's car if necessary. Yes. That was the best idea. He had to sit on his thoughts for now. As soon as he could, he was going to take charge. It was a far better option than leaving the lives of his family up to this pothead. He kept his mouth shut and watched out of the front window at the view opening up in front of them. They were cresting the summit of Layton Valley. They could see in all directions from here. Braden began to grind his teeth together hard. To the far right was Hemmington City. The next town over was the site of the new and improved Newtown which had still been under construction right up until this latest disaster had struck. The most shocking part of the view was what used to be the village of Layton itself. The entire town had been wiped from the face of the earth only to be replaced by a gaping black hole in the ground that looked to Braden like it was capable of sucking the light out of the remains of the day. The shimmying blackness of spider bodies had been spread out as far and as wide as they could see from this vantage point. The part that made Braden feel like his heart was about to break out of his chest was the fact that they could see a dozen or so spiders that were so large that from all the way up here you could make them out clearly. They looked to be moving pretty slowly, but Braden knew that due to their sheer size that they were covering a lot of ground in a short space of time. The car turned to the right and off the main road that they were on. They started to head up at a steep angle. The road below them wasn't paved and it pulled at the wheels threatening to take them back down to look at that nightmarish view again. Trent squeezed the pedal a little harder and the car picked up the pace. The road leveled off and then they were inside a pretty dense woodland. Just up ahead was a building that looked like a house that had been a piece of flat-pack furniture. It certainly didn't look to Braden like it was a safe place to hole up. He could quite easily imagine the spiders breaking through those walls as easily as paper.

"You're not seriously telling me that this is a safe place are you?" said Braden.

"This little place has withstood some of the worst conditions that you could imagine. It has even had a tree fall on it once, didn't even scratch it," said Trent and uttered a barking cough. He pitched the end of his joint into the ashtray and pulled the car up just outside the shack.

"Here we are ladies," he said to Mary. Jax was still asleep on her chest and was snoring steadily. Trent turned off the engine. Everywhere felt suddenly far too quiet. A few hours of hell on earth would generally do that to you, but all the same, it felt strange and unearthly after everything that had gone on.

Trent undid his seatbelt and opened his door. He stepped out of the car and began to stretch. Mary moved Jax over and got out herself. She raised her arms to the sky and her spine crackled.

"Braden, can you come and get Jax?" she said.

Braden got out of the car without saying a word. He still wasn't convinced about the safety aspect of the ranger's station, and he wouldn't ever change his mind. He went to the rear door, undid Jax's seatbelt and then gathered her up in his arms. It was amazing how heavy she was getting. He could still remember holding her in the crook of his elbow when she had been a baby.

Trent went and put his key into the door of the station and opened it up. "There's a bed in here, you can put her on there," said Trent. Braden dutifully headed over and went inside. It was amazingly spacious inside and there looked to be a lot of potentially useful equipment in there. He went over to the far-right corner where there was a bunk bed. He carefully laid Jax out as gently as he could. She clucked, turned over and carried on snoring.

Mary walked in through the door, her arms folded across her chest and a pensive look across her face. Trent bobbed in and out of the door laying down a backpack and other equipment that he had stashed in the back of his car. Finally, he pulled the door closed with a hollow clang and he shot the bolts across at the top and the bottom.

"Make yourselves at home. I don't know about any of you, but I could use a cup of tea and a biscuit," said Trent.

Probably got the munchies from all that pot you have been smoking, thought Braden.

Mary started to go to her knees. She was sucking wind quickly, her chest rising and falling rapidly. Braden wanted to go to her and make sure that she was alright. But he found himself rooted to the spot, unable to get his brain into gear enough to help her. Trent looked at him and then at Mary. He went over to her and knelt down. He put his hands on either shoulder.

"*Can't……breathe…..I…..I…*" said Mary.

"It's just delayed shock is all, you're hyperventilating," said Trent. He got hold of her chin and tipped her head up to look at him.

"Look at me, Mary. I want you to breathe with me ok? In through the nose and out through the mouth," said Trent. He began a slow controlled breathing, all the time keeping his eyes locked on Mary's. She struggled at first, snatching in the air too quickly, but soon she picked up his rhythm and her breathing began to slow to a more controlled pace. There was high colour in her cheeks and a sweat was starting to break on her forehead.

Trent breathed with her for five minutes, until her heart rate had slowed down enough for her to be back in control again. All the time Braden was watching them with a gnawing tinge of bright green jealousy crawling around in his guts. He wanted to go over and shove Trent right on his arse and sort Mary out himself. The only thing that was stopping him was the fact that he thought that Trent would probably beat the shit out of him right in front of his wife and daughter. He was certainly built enough to do it. The veins in his exposed arms were popping almost out of his skin. If he was going to outdo this guy, he would have to use his mind, his *intelligence* to outwit him. He was helping Mary to her feet. She wobbled backward a little and Trent caught her around her waist to stop her falling over. Braden didn't know for sure if he was just imagining things but for a moment, it looked to him like their eyes locked. A smile ghosted at the corners of Mary's mouth and that was more than enough to get Braden moving. He strode forwards and encircled his own arm around Mary's shoulders.

"Here, come and sit down," he said and offered her a weak smile.

"Sure," she said and allowed Braden to take her to one of the sofas that lined the wall behind them. Trent nodded at them and went over to the back door. He opened it up and went out, closing the door behind him.

"Are you alright?" said Braden, holding Mary's hand in his.

"I'm fine, it's all just a lot to take in that's all," she said.

"I know, but we are safe for now at least. Are you sure that you're ok?"

"I'm *fine* Braden, stop fussing," she snapped. He let go of her hand and wandered over to the desk. This wasn't the time nor the place to start an argument with her. If he began rowing then he had an idea that he wouldn't stop until they were both screaming at each other. That wouldn't help their situation at all. There was a rumbling coming from somewhere and then the sound went up a notch and stayed there. A moment later Trent came back through the door. He threw a switch on the wall and all of the equipment began to power up.

"I just powered up the generator so we can get a better idea of our situation," said Trent. He started to turn on all of the computers that were littered across the desks. There was a screen up on the wall in front of them. It looked to Braden like it was the same size as their television.

"There are cameras rigged up on all sides, we can see everything that's going on out there. I have links to all live satellite views of the surrounding areas, radio contact with anyone within a hundred-mile radius. We should be able to get a better idea of just how far this is going. But, I just have one question, Braden."

"Shoot."

"Spiders? Big fucking spiders? Where the hell did they come from? Are they the same ones that took out Newtown?"

"They're not the same, they're different. They're better, faster and stronger this time. I'm pretty sure that this is all related, but I have no idea how. I…."

Braden broke off. The screen on the wall had finished powering up. It was split evenly into four feeds representing the corners of the station. He could see the car parked outside and the road that they had come in on.

"Oh Jesus," he said.

The road had been partially blotted out. There was a large cluster of black spiders coming up the road towards the car. Right in the middle of them was a spider so big that they could only see the legs touching down on the floor. The black spiders scattered out of the way each time a leg came down. Trent whirled around and looked at the screen.

"Shit. Better cut the generator. It makes a fair amount of noise," he said.

He started for the door and Braden caught him by the arm. "You can't go out there," he said.

"No time for arguments," said Trent and snatched his arm away. He ran out of the door leaving it open behind him. Braden toyed with the idea of pulling the door shut behind him and leaving him out there. Instead, he stood still, closing and unclosing his fists. The hum from the generator died and a moment later Trent came back in through the door. He slammed it shut behind him, his face contorted into an expression of deep concern.

"They're trying to get in at the back. They won't be able to get through, but it's not going to stop them trying," said Trent.

He went around the back of the desk and brought out a cricket bat. He handed it to Braden. "Just in case anything gets in here," he said and brought out another, slightly smaller bat. "I have them here just in case anyone tries to break in. The police ain't gonna get here in a hurry," he said.

The windows began to get dark as spider bodies started to cloud over the glass.

"Christ," said Mary and she ran over to the bed where Jax was still sleeping. She curled up on the bunk with her.

"Get down," said Trent, pulling Braden to the floor. Trent began to crawl to one of the sofas. Braden went with him. They sat up at the foot of the sofa, their backs pressing against the cushions of the seat. The light in the room that had been coming in through the windows was almost completely gone. The spiders were almost completely covering the windows, all of them still moving forwards. Trent and Braden could see the windows reflected in the screen on the opposite side of the room. They could see the spiders moving across the glass, some of them slipping a little. They were horrendously large. larger than the ones Braden had encountered in the house on Corsica Road. There was an added thudding to the constant rustling noise that was going on all around them. Braden knew that it was the giant spider that had been lumbering up the path. The giant spider sounded like it was on the outside edge of the wall they were against. Braden wasn't even aware of it, but he was holding his breath. Something banged on the roof above them and pieces of dust and dirt rained down from the ceiling and tinkled on the hard, wooden floor. Something in the ceiling creaked to a point where Braden was certain that the roof was going to come down on them. He gritted his teeth and covered his head with his hands expecting the crushing weight to come crashing down on him at any moment. Instead, the ceiling creaked again and then it went quiet. Outside they could hear trees being pushed over. They crashed to the floor causing the station to shake even more. The giant spider sounded like it was moving away. Braden began to breathe a little more normal now that the threat was passing. The spiders on the windows began to thin out a little. Some of them stopped moving and sat on the glass trying to keep a foothold on the slippery pane. Braden could see them slowly sliding down the glass and then scramble around to try and get a grip on it again. They would get a grip on the glass and then start sliding again. The hammering of their huge spindly legs sent a shiver down Braden's spine.

He didn't know how long they sat there waiting for the spiders to go away. At one point Jax woke up and let out a high-pitched shriek which was cut off by Mary clapping a hand over her mouth.

"Why aren't they going?" said Mary. Her voice was rising in volume. She was scared, she was ready to go running around the room pulling her hair out and losing her mind. Trent crawled over to her and climbed onto the bed.

"We'll just wait. We'll wait for them to go away. They can't get in here, this place is tight. It's built to withstand the worst weather conditions in the world, a few spiders won't be a problem, I promise you," said Trent.

As Braden watched on, Trent stroked his wife's upper leg and gave it a friendly pat. Mary smiled at him and covered his hand with hers. Braden felt that horrible bubble of jealousy again. This was all getting too familiar for his liking. It filled every cell in his body with a burning hatred for Trent and his good car, his muscled arms, his stupid rangers station. It didn't matter to Braden that he had pulled them right out of harm's way, all he could see was a man who kept on putting his hands on his wife right in front of him and worse than that, she was offering no resistance. In fact, she was encouraging him.

Trent came back over to where Braden was still sitting on the floor and picked up his bat. He turned back to Mary.

"Don't you worry, I won't let them get in here," he said to Mary. She smiled at him in a way that she used to smile at Braden. His blood began to boil. His temper flared and he scooped up his own bat that was on the floor next to him. He stood up and swung the bat as hard as he could at the back of Trent's left knee. The sound of Trent's knee joint being burst out of place by the impact of the bat was like a gunshot that echoed all around the room. Trent doubled over, clawing at his leg and screaming a horrible crackling bellow that made Braden want to cover his ears. Jax covered her face and began to sob uncontrollably. Mary jumped up off the bed and began screaming at Braden, asking him what the fuck he thought he was doing. He brandished the bat at her.

"Sit down Mary, just sit the fuck down," he growled at her. He looked to Mary like he had finally lost his mind. A cold ice-block of fear was sitting in her guts. Jax had backed into the corner of the bed and was sitting with her knees up to hide her face and her hands were covering her ears. Mary sat down on the edge of the bunk.

Braden circled around so that Trent could see him. He was breathing hard and clutching at his shattered knee.

"Now then, I want the truth from you. I saw how you were touching Mary, and I saw the look in her eye. You were very quick to pile us all into your car and bring us here. So, as I said, I want the truth from you," said Braden. His voice was shaking and close to cracking.

"I….I…don't know what you're talking about," said Trent, his breaths coming in short, sharp snaps.

Braden raised the bat up again. Trent put up his hand and cowered.

"Alright….alright…I'll tell you," he said.

"Trent, don't. Please don't," said Mary.

Braden raised the bat over his head. "Last chance," he said.

"Me and Mary have been seeing each other," Trent blurted.

For a moment, the words wouldn't get into Braden's head. He slowly lowered the bat. All of his anger, all of his resentment had burned away and it had been replaced by a numbing sense of disbelief. The strength felt like it was running out of his body and that at any moment he was going to crumple up and drop to the floor. His legs began to shake at first and then the shaking made its way up his body. It reached his face and his mouth began to gibber silently. Trent turned a little to his left and then threw up on the floor next to him. The pain from his broken knee was becoming too hard for him to bear.

"Say that again," said Braden in a weak voice.

"Braden, stop it. Let's talk about it," said Trent, wiping his mouth with his sleeve.

Braden appeared not to hear him. He turned slowly around to Mary who was still sat on the bed with tears running down her face.

"He's lying. I want him to say it again and then I'm going to smash his face in for *lying*," said Braden.

"He's not lying," said Mary in a breathless voice, one that was so quiet that Braden couldn't hear her through the sound of his heart thumping in his ears.

"What did you say? *What the fuck did you say?*"

"He's not lying," said Mary. She was almost pleading this time.

Braden felt the anger come back again, bubbling up from his guts. He turned to Trent and raised the bat again, letting out a guttural roar as he did so. Treat wrapped his arm around his head to try and protect himself from the impending blow. But, it didn't arrive. Braden lowered the bat. He had caught sight of the few remaining spiders that were still jostling for position on the window.

"I have a better idea, a much better idea for a shit-weasel like you," growled Braden through gritted teeth. He dropped the bat and went to the front door of the station. He undid the bolts at the top and the bottom and turned the catch so that the door was unlocked.

"What are you going to do? *What are you going to do?*" said Trent. His voice was rising and rising. He knew exactly what Braden was going to do.

Braden came over to Trent. He bent down and hooked an arm under Trent's chin.

"You like to play with my wife? With my *fucking wife?* Well, You can go and play with those fucking spiders, you piece of shit," roared Braden. He began to drag Trent towards the door. Trent outweighed Braden by around three stones and his body was thick with outdoor muscle. Dragging him across the floor was almost impossible, almost. But, Braden was angry and his anger gave him just enough strength to pull Trent across the polished wooden floor. He didn't hear Mary shouting at him to stop, he didn't hear Jax screaming. He didn't see Mary getting up off the bunk and grabbing the bat off the floor and he didn't see her bringing the bat down on the side of his head until the last moment before it hit.

Braden was knocked clean out. His legs stiffened for a moment and then they buckled, spilling him to the floor. Trent dropped to the floor gasping and clawing at his throat. Mary stood for a moment, the bat still in her hand. Then the dawning realization of what she had done began to sink in. She dropped the bat as if it was suddenly hot and wiped her hands on her jeans as if it could clean away what she had done to Braden. What else could she have done? Braden was going to open the door and try to put Trent out there, he would have been killed. Not to mention the fact that the open door would have let the spiders inside and that would have been it for all of them. Her strongest urge was to protect Trent. It was true that she had been seeing him for quite a while now. Every time that Braden didn't come home she would invite Trent around to share in a bottle of wine and listen to his stories of the shit that he got up to whilst he was working. She had confessed to him that she was thinking of leaving Braden and he had listened attentively and reassured her that starting over again wasn't quite as daunting a prospect as she thought. He himself had been through a pretty messy divorce, but once the dust had settled, he had ended up with a life that was far more satisfying than it ever had been before. He held her hands, he told her that everything would be alright and that she had to believe in herself. He told her that she was a strong and beautiful woman and…..and then she had leaned in and kissed him. He hadn't responded at first and she had begun to think that she had just sabotaged the best friendship that she had managed to forge in a long time. But his resistance had melted away quickly. Then his hands were all over her, those strong hands that she had fantasized about. She had wanted it to happen for such a long time, with every glance out of the window of her bedroom into his garden, watching him digging and planting, to every stolen glance when he had been going up the path to his front door, looking at how tired and slightly grubby looking he was after a hard day's work. He did something that Braden had never done in all the years that they had been together, he came home at the same time every night. She tried to imagine what that would have been like, to have a man that came home regularly. She fantasized about him getting straight into the shower, perhaps even inviting her to come in with him so she could scrub his back. The things she could do with a man like that were beyond her imagination. But she wanted to try and keep the bare threads of their family together. Jax loved her dad and it would be terrible for her to see him go, or at least that was how she was thinking at the time.

The moment that his lips met hers, she knew that she was going down a road that went against everything that she believed in. She had always thought that a cheater was the worst thing anybody could be. If they were married, they were married and that was that there were no shades of grey on that issue. However, once he had gone home that night and she was sat on the sofa drinking the last of the wine that they had shared, closing her eyes and still feeling his lips enclosing around her nipple and his hardness pushing inside her with an urgency that she hadn't felt for such a long time, she had realized that the issue was not as simple as it appeared on the surface. She was justifying the pleasure that she had got from it which seemed like a million miles away from the hurt and the loneliness that came from being with Braden. She sat on the sofa, telling herself that she deserved a little happiness, didn't she? She didn't want to look back on her life in fifty years' time and have a bunch of regrets, did she? She certainly didn't want to be on her deathbed wondering how wonderful it would have been if she had the guts to actually sleep with a man that she found interesting to talk to and attractive, did she?

She had spent the next day wandering around the house, cleaning rooms that didn't need cleaning, and unable to close down the thoughts in her mind that all circulated around Trent and what they had done right there on the couch just last night. A part of her was deeply regretting it because she had become one of the things that she had always been taught to hate. But, there was another bigger part of her that wanted to go around to his door and get a second helping. Her body felt like it was aching all over and that the only cure for that terrible ache was another passionate session with him. Eventually, she had got up the nerve to go. Braden was out working and Jax was at school, giving her a good three hours before she was due to go and pick her up. Trent's car was in the driveway. She went out of the house and knocked on his door, with her heart thumping like mad in her chest, making every breath that came out of her mouth shake uncontrollably. Nobody came to the door at first and she was about to leave when she heard footsteps on the other side of the door. A moment later, Trent pulled the door open. He was dressed in a loose t-shirt and baggy jogging bottoms. He hesitated for a moment as if he was never expecting to see her ever again and then he reached out, grabbed her hand and pulled her gently inside. The moment the door was closed they were upon each other, her hands going up to his hair and pulling on it with urgency and passion. His lips were on hers and his tongue was darting in and out of her mouth. He reached down and pulled her leggings down to her knees. Her panties came down with them and she kicked them off along with her shoes. His hands went to each of her thighs and they lifted her up with ease parting her legs on the way. She felt his hardness pressing against her through his loose trousers. Her hands went down and uncovered him, ready for him to find his way inside her again. Her ache for him began to spiral out of control, her first orgasm exploding from deep within her the moment his hardness pushed against her. He drove himself inside her, pressing her up against the wall. His hips hammered against her and his fingers dug into the soft flesh of her buttocks. He exploded within her, holding his breath as the spasms rocked his body. She felt that deep warmth spread out inside her, giving her everything that her body had been aching for since last night. His eyes met hers and they both smiled at each other, their breaths coming in deep, quick pants from their exertions. He carried her over to his couch and kissed her again, slowly and more carefully this time. It made her tingle in places that she never even knew you could get tingles in. It felt good and it felt right and from that moment on, whenever the opportunity presented itself, she would go to his house and indulge herself as much as she possibly could.

At no point in her life did she ever think that she would be in the situation that she was in right now, standing over her unconscious husband, that she had whacked over the head with a bat, and her lover who was lay on the floor with his knee all bent out of shape. Add to that the fact that there were spiders that were the size of dogs trying to hang onto the windows and the fact that they were miles from any kind of civilization, and you had all the makings of a pretty bad day at Black Rock.

Her first priority was Jax. She was sobbing uncontrollably on the bunk. She hadn't heard her sob like that before, not in a way that sounded like she was utterly terrified. She had to bring her back from the edge, otherwise, she might do something careless and put herself and all of them in danger. She squatted down in front of Jax, got hold of her hands and held them in hers. Jax's chest was snatching in sobs. Her face was red, blotchy and stained with tears.

"Hey kiddo, hey there champ. How are you doing?"

"I……want…..to….go….home," said Jax between the sobs.

"I know you do kiddo, I do too, and we will as soon as it's safe," said Mary, although she was pretty sure, given everything that had happened to them that their home had been swallowed up by the earth.

"Why….did…you…..hit…..dad?"

Mary paused for a moment, picking her words very carefully. "He hurt Trent, and he was going to take him outside. I couldn't let him do that. I had to stop him. He'll be alright, I didn't hit him very hard," she said. It felt like she had hit him pretty hard. The sound that the bat made when it connected with his skull sounded pretty hard too.

"I'm….scared," said Jax.

"I know sweetie, but we will be safe in here. Those spiders won't be able to get in, you can trust me on that."

Jax nodded and wiped her face with her hand. She reached her arms out and grabbed onto her mother's neck. Mary hugged her back, wishing that she could take it all away for her.

"I need some help here," said Trent from behind her.

Mary let Jax go and looked her in the eyes. "I have to go and help Trent, then we will get this place up and running. Everything is going to be just fine, trust me ok?"

Jax nodded, "Ok."

Mary went over to Trent who had just finished pulling himself back so that he could lean his back against one of the sofas. He was sweating profusely, mostly due to the pain he was in. He clutched at his wounded knee. It looked like it had swollen pretty badly.

"Is it broken?" said Mary.

"I don't know. It might just be dislocated. I'm going to see if I can pop it all back into place. If it doesn't work, then I'll know if it's broken or not," said Trent.

"What can I do?" said Mary.

"You need to get your hands under my ankle. When I tell you to, you need to pull it upwards as hard as you can. I'm going to push on the kneecap at the same time," said Trent. He leaned forwards, hooked his fingers under his knee and placed his thumbs lightly on the swollen top of the joint.

Mary went to his ankle, squatted down and hooked her hands under it just like Trent had said.

"Ready?" he said and Mary nodded. She was hoping that she didn't throw up. Her stomach wasn't so strong when it came to bones. Even the sound of somebody popping their knuckles was enough to make her want to heave.

"On three," said Trent and Mary nodded again.

He counted to three and Mary pulled the leg up hard. At exactly the same moment Trent pushed down with all his might on his kneecap. There was resistance at first from both ends and then there was a sickening crunch and Trent's leg popped out straight again. Trent put his head back and roared through clenched teeth. The chords on his neck were standing out and the skin was turning almost purple with the effort of his yelling. After a moment, he began to breathe again in short, sharp bursts. Mary could see the relief on his face as the pain started to ebb away. His leg looked far more normal than it had done a few moments earlier.

"Did it work?" said Mary. Her initial nausea had passed over enough for her to be able to talk again. She would probably be dreaming about the noise that came from Trent's knee for months to come. She needed to push it out of her mind for now.

Trent felt around the knee wincing a little and then he flexed the joint. It caused him some pain, but the joint was mobile again.

"Looks good. I just need to tape it up so it doesn't blow out again."

"Do we have anything here that would do the job?"

"Yep, out the back door is the utility room. There is some black tape, pretty strong stuff. You'll have to raid the draws. I don't know exactly where it is," said Trent.

Mary hesitated for a moment. Trent could read her mind. She was worried about the spiders.

"Don't worry. The outer door is closed. They can't get in here, I promise," he said. Mary tried a smile, but it didn't quite work. She headed for the door, tipping Jax a wink as she went by. Jax looked like she had been through the mill. The things she had seen in the last few hours were far beyond anything a child of her age should have experienced. Mary was worried that it all might have a negative effect on her. The world that all of them had known had taken a big old kick in the nuts and it was never going to be the same for any of them ever again.

She went out of the back door and into the utility room. To the right of her was the outer door and Trent had been accurate in his description of it. The door was solid metal just like the one at the front and it was fastened shut by a large set of bolts at the top and the bottom. The generator sat on the floor against the wall, an exhaust hose reaching up to a flue in the wall at the side of the door. Next to them and right in front of her were two sets of metal drawers that Trent had told her about.

There was still a pretty sizable prickle of fear running up and down her back. She wanted to get back inside just as quickly as she could. She tore the draws open, throwing things out of them left and right. The panic was rising quickly in her, even though in her logical mind, there was no way for the spiders to get in. She got to the third draw down and found two large rolls of black duct tape. She snatched them up and went back into the main room, slamming the door behind her. The moment that the door was closed, she felt her heart rate start to slow down again. God knows why. Her worst nightmare was sitting right here in this room. Her husband who she had whacked around the head with a cricket bat and her on-the-side lover with a dicky knee was in the same room along with her daughter. Never mind the murderous spiders outside, this was bad enough for anyone to deal with. She went over to Trent and handed him the rolls of tape. He gingerly pulled up his trouser leg and uncovered the knee. The skin around it was starting to look like a party balloon and it was turning a nasty black colour. Trent took one of the rolls, picked out the end of the tape and began wrapping his leg, just above and below the injury. Then he wrapped the tape hard around his knee, grimacing, every time the tape touched the kneecap. When he was done, he tossed the roll to one side and lowered his trouser leg. He began to crawl his way back up the sofa. He got his good leg under him and he pushed his way up to his feet. He carefully put the wounded leg down. He winced as a bolt of pain came shooting up from the knee. On the plus side, he could stand on it. He tried a few paces around the room.

"How is it?" said Mary.

"Hurts. But it isn't giving out. I think we got it," said Trent, still hobbling around in a big circle. He looked down at the floor at Braden, who was beginning to stir. Mary had knocked him cold, but from what Trent could see, there was no permanent damage.

"What shall we do about him?" said Trent.

Mary shrugged, "I don't know. I don't blame him for being angry."

Trent looked down at him thoughtfully. "I'll try and talk to him. We are no good to each other swinging weapons with all the shit that's going on out there," he said, jerking a thumb at the window.

Braden started to try and get himself off the floor. Mary quickly got the cricket bats and moved them out of harm's way.

"Hit me....can't believe you hit me….." he was saying. He was climbing up the sofa, just like Trent was a moment earlier.

Mary felt a flash of irritation. He was complaining about the fact that he got whacked around the head? Hadn't he put out Trent's knee in the same way? She wanted to chew him out about it, but instead, she bit her tongue. She looked around at Jax. She was staring a hole in father, a deep frown set upon her smooth face. Mary had seen that look before when Braden had fucked up by not coming home on time or had broken yet another promise to her.

"She was stopping you doing something that you would have regretted," said Trent.

"Well, you would stick up for her wouldn't you, you bastard," said Braden. He had managed to maneuver himself into a sitting position on the sofa. His had was rubbing his temple where the bat had made contact with him. The blood that had been trickling out of the cut had started to dry out, and it was flaking off and dropping onto his shoulder like scarlet dandruff.

"If you had opened that door then we would all have been dead by now, you, your wife, and your daughter," said Trent.

"Don't you ever speak to me about my daughter, you hear me? You hear me? you home-wrecking cunt?" Braden roared suddenly. Jax flinched, the sound of her father's raised voice had built in the reflexive fear over the years.

Trent sighed. He was trying to keep his temper in check. Really, he just wanted to go over to him, grip him and try and shake some reasoning and sense into him. But, after all, he had been fucking his wife, and that gave him no moral high ground whatsoever.

"We have a bigger problem right now that's outside these walls, and it's much bigger than the issues that we have in here right now. There will come a time when we can settle those differences, and it ain't now," said Trent.

"Fuck…."

"We need to make sure that we are going to be safe, and then we can have this out, just you and me," said Trent.

Braden said nothing, he just stared at Trent with baleful hatred in his eyes.

"Come on Braden, you're a smart man. You know I'm talking sense. Once everything is straight then we can sort things out between us, anyway that you like, ok?"

The burning hate in Braden's eyes softened a little. Trent was right about that, Braden was a smart cookie. No-one could take that away from him. Perhaps he would bide his time. Perhaps he would wait. Perhaps he would feed that wife-stealing shit bag to the spiders as soon as he got a chance. He would hit him when he least expected it. And he would watch him get bitten. He would watch him be made into one of those horrendous mutilated corpses that he saw inside the house on Corsica Road. Then he would make Mary pay for her mistake. Hell, yes he would. He could feel the love he had for her starting to muddy and curdle. Trent had poured a healthy dose of sugar into his fuel tank. Mary wasn't the perfect beautiful woman that he once knew. She was something corrupted, something dirty, something he had lost all his respect for. She was just like all the others with their loose morals. He could have done the same thing to her on many different occasions, but he had always resisted. It was the one thing that he could offer her that was consistent, his undying loyalty to her. Yes, he had been absent for a vast amount of time during their marriage, but he had always been faithful to her. There had been many opportunities for him to fall from grace from both sexes, but he had never taken them up on it. He would always put Mary's face, her sweet and innocent face up in his mind and that would be enough for him to turn it down. He had risked his arse to get the story of the century, which was going to pay him enough for them to both retire. He had risked his life, and this was how he was being repaid. Now here was the arsehole that had been keeping his bed warm telling him how it was going to be. He could just cave his fucking head in right now, just grab one of those bats and start hitting, and keep on hitting until he was nothing more than a pile of smashed brains on the floor. But his daughter was sitting just across the room. It was bad enough that she had seen him hit Trent already, what would it mean if he beat Trent to death right in front of her. She would see him as a murderer. She would never trust him again as long as she lived and he couldn't live with that, not ever. But, an accident. If Trent had an accident, then it wouldn't be his fault, not at all. If he played along with it then Trent wouldn't suspect a thing and then when the moment was right…..

His anger dissipated a little. It would be smart under the circumstances to play the long game. "Ok," he mumbled, his steely gaze never leaving Trent.

"Good stuff," said Trent. "Mary, we need to get the generator back up and running again. I could do with you just taking a look outside the window and seeing just how many of our little friends are still out there."

Mary nodded and then went over to the window. There was another sofa underneath it and she carefully knelt on the arm of it so that she could get close to the glass. There was a spider on the outside that was still half covering the window. One of its legs was still tapping and sliding, trying to get a good grip, otherwise, the spider was still. Mary looked over the large black body and through the long spindly legs and saw the woodland outside. She took in a sharp breath. Every one of the trees outside had large webs strung up between the trunks and the branches. In the middle of some of them, the spiders were sitting as if they were waiting for something to come along that they could possibly eat. She really didn't want to hazard a guess what was on their menu. There were a few of them still crawling around on the floor, but far less of them than there were half-an-hour ago when they had first arrived.

"They're still out there, but they're pretty spread out," said Mary.

Trent walked, his damaged leg rigid, to the console where his computer and radio were situated. "Right, I need to get that generator on, then we can try and find out more about what is going on out there," he said.

Mary nodded at him and he hobbled over to the back door. He opened it up and went through to the utility room.

Mary looked over at Braden who was sat silently in his seat, he was still rubbing at the knot on his temple. He looked tired and pissed off.

"Are you alright?" she said.

Braden shrugged and said nothing.

"I'm sorry I hit you, but I didn't want you doing something stupid," said Mary.

Braden mumbled something from behind his hand.

"What?"

"I said, I'm good at doing stupid things, aren't I? Just like getting married to you, you fucking whore," he said in a raspy voice that he barely recognized as his own.

Mary walked right up to him and slapped him hard across his face. Her hand began to fizz from the impact with Braden's cheek. She stood in front of him, shaking with a combination of anger and fear.

"Don't you *dare* speak to me like that in front of our daughter," she hissed at him. A single tear welled in her eye and ran down her face. Braden said nothing. He dropped his head forwards a little so he didn't have to make eye contact with her. His hand came back up and began rubbing the side of his head again. Mary walked away from him and went and sat next to Jax on the bunk. Jax was sat with her head down, just like her father. Mary put an arm around her and kissed the top of her head. Just like her father, she had no response. Mary was almost to the point where she just wanted to shout and scream at the both of them, and she nearly did it, but the click and hum of the generator snapped her out of the moment. Her eyes darted to the window and she saw that the spiders that had been sitting pretty still were jumped into action by the sound of the generator. They darted up and down the window and then they disappeared from view. Trent came hobbling in from the back, pulling the door shut behind him. He went over to the desk and powered up the computer. He grabbed a headset from the radio and put it on his head. He clicked some buttons on the radio console and began mumbling into the microphone which was hanging from one of the earpieces in front of his mouth. He went to work on the computer and then a picture came on the screen attached to the wall.

"This is us. It's a satellite picture of everything around us, and…." He broke off. Something was coming through on the radio. He mumbled something else into the microphone and then lowered the earphones to his neck.

"There is a full-scale evacuation going on in the area right now. People that survived Layton are dotted around the area. If we can make it to the Layton dam then they will airlift us out of here. I think it will be our best option," said Trent.

"How far is it from here?" said Mary.

"About three miles," said Trent.

"We can make it. Three miles is nothing," said Mary.

Trent went back to his computer, he clicked around a little and then the image on the screen changed. It was more of the local landscape. Trent got up out of his chair and went over to the screen to get a better look.

"Yes, we can make it. However, it's going to be risky…."

"Where are they going to take us," said Braden suddenly.

"Military base, about eighty miles from here," said Trent.

Braden fell silent again. He went back to rubbing the lump on his temple. He had a look of a man that had been utterly defeated.

"We have to get to the car. But I think it's too far away from the door for you to get to, and how are you going to drive with your leg the way it is," said Mary.

"Can you drive?" said Trent.

"Yes, but I never go over thirty," said Mary. She shrugged her shoulders as if to say *That's all I got.*

"Well, I guess I'll have to teach you how to drive my way," said Trent.

Braden felt himself prickle again. Anything that sounded a little like flirting between them made him want to go and take to Trent with the bat again. But he had to go along with what was going on otherwise he was going to end up being left here to fend for himself. He didn't see any indicator in here of any food anywhere around. He bit his tongue instead.

"You'll have to go and move the car closer to the door," said Trent.

"You want me to go out there? No way," said Mary.

Trent looked over at Braden, "How about it?"

Braden looked over at Mary. The pinched look on her face elicited a tiny spark of sympathy somewhere deep inside him. His love for her wasn't completely dead yet. Give it time, and he was sure that it would be. There was too much raw emotion around the whole issue right now. "I'll go with you, Two people would be safer than one," he heard himself say. He stood up and went over to where Mary had thrown the cricket bats and he picked one of them up. Braden went over to Trent who cowered slightly as he approached.

"Relax. It's for them," said Braden pointing at the window. "I'm going to need your keys."

Trent fished in his pocket and held them out for Braden. Braden took them and started to head for the door. He turned back and looked at Mary. "You had better shut the door behind us."

Mary nodded at him.

"Take care of Jax," he said.

"I will, I promise," said Trent

"Let's do this then," said Braden. Mary picked up the other bat and then went with him to the door. Braden pulled the bolts over and turned the catch under the handle. He stuffed the keys into his pocket and raised the bat in his hand. He pressed the handle down and pulled the door open.

Both of them jumped backward. There was a huge spider stuck to the outside of the door. Braden reflexively swung the bat. It struck the spider dead center in the middle of its body, knocking it off the door. It hit the floor on its back and its legs began to flail as it tried to right itself. Jax screamed and climbed onto the top bunk to try and get away. Braden brought the bat down and hit the spider again. It impacted the top half of the spiders' body causing it to break right across its middle. A stream of pink fluid began to bubble out of the split in the spiders' body. The spiders' flailing intensified for a moment, flicking the pink fluid in all directions. Some of it got onto Trent, who frantically began to wipe it off. Some of it got into his mouth and he bent over and began to spit on the floor and retch noisily.

Braden brought the bat down again and again until the spider lay still. "Come on," he said to Mary. He kicked the dead spider as hard as he could, sending it sliding across the floor and out of the doorway. They went outside and Mary pulled the door shut behind them.

The ground outside the station was mercifully spider free, but every tree out there had been strung up with silky webs. Braden saw a squirrel that had been caught up in one of them. It wriggled and pulled at its trapped legs, causing the web to shimmer and vibrate. A huge spider came darting down the web and fell upon the squirrel. It sank its fangs into the squirrel's head. The animal threw its body around, trying desperately to escape and then, as Braden looked on, it froze. The squirrel's body shriveled up, like a balloon losing its air and then it drifted downwards from the web as if it was no heavier than a feather. The spider sat in the web for a moment longer and then scuttled off back to its hiding place. Braden turned away from it, feeling mildly sickened at what he had just seen. He focused his attention on the car and he saw, with his heart sinking into his stomach that one of the spider webs had been attached to the roof. If they disturbed it then they would be attacked in just the same way that that poor squirrel had been. Between here and the car, the path had a few of the webs attached to some of the loose rocks that lined the edges of it.

"Don't touch the webs, whatever you do," said Braden. Mary nodded and readjusted her grip on the bat. They began to move slowly forwards. The air outside felt like it was unnaturally still, there wasn't a breeze blowing, or a bird call anywhere that they could hear. It felt like they were walking through a graveyard rather than an area of natural beauty. They went single file. Mary taking up the rear. Their legs moved dangerously close to the strands of web laid out at the sides of the path. Braden checked each one of his steps that he was taking, making sure that he was well away from the strings that could get them killed. At one point a stone overturned under his foot, causing him to momentarily be off-balance. His arms came up to steady himself, nearly putting the bat right into one of the strands of web. Mary hissed in a breath behind him and grabbed hold of his shoulder to steady him. He managed to get his balance back, and both of them started to breathe again.

"That was too close," whispered Braden. Mary said nothing. Her heart was hammering so fast that she thought she would go into cardiac arrest at any moment. Braden started to move forward again, slowly and more carefully than before, if that was possible. They were just a few feet away from the car and Braden fished the keys out of his pocket. Braden felt an extra surge of urgency, he was so close to being safe that his body wanted him to abandon the stealthy approach and bomb straight for the door and safety.

A sound from above caught his ear. It sounded like there were branches in the trees breaking somewhere. His head snapped upwards. His vision was momentarily blocked by the hazy glare of the sun above the trees and then he saw it. One of the spiders that had set up home in the upper branches of the trees must have lost its grip, it was falling through the trees. Most of the branches it hit broke, such was the size of the monster. It tumbled and span towards the earth at a terrifying rate. It landed four feet away from where Mary and Braden were stood. It landed right side up and then began to shuffle around in a half circle. Its front legs had struck the ground first causing them to be bent and broken out of shape. Mary uttered a high-pitched scream at the same time that Braden let out a bellow of terror. They both began to bolt for the car. The impact of the spider hitting the ground and the scream from both of them vibrated through every one of the webs that had been attached to the ground. Spiders began to scuttle down the trees and into the middle of their webs. Braden pressed the button to unlock the door and the car let out a beep and the lights on the tail flashed twice to let them know it was open. Mary was in the car first, tearing the door open and then pulling it shut behind her. Braden managed to get his door open just as a huge spider thumped down onto the roof of the car. Such was Braden's height that he was face to face with the back end of the spider. It shuffled around with lightning speed until it was facing him. Braden managed to duck down and throw himself into the car just as the spider launched itself forwards to bite him. Braden stretched out and grabbed the door handle. He pulled it shut just as the spider was beginning to make its way down from the roof and into the open door. The impact of the door onto the spider trapped its head and its forelegs inside the car. The rest of the spider's body fell to the floor outside leaving the severed piece dangling on the inside of the door. The still-twitching legs tickled and stroked Braden's arm and his face, making him jump and yell out in disgust.

"Get us out of here!" shrieked Mary. More of the spiders were dropping to the floor and making their way quickly towards the car. Some of them were already climbing up the sides and were trying to bite at the windows, spraying a clear fluid from their fangs. The liquid ran down the window until it touched the paintwork which began to fizz and sizzle.

Braden fumbled the key into the slot and fired up the engine. Another spider dropped down onto the bonnet of the car. Braden shoved the car into reverse and hammered the pedal down. The car pulled backward, causing some of the spiders to get thrown from the vehicle. Braden saw in the rear-view mirror that the road behind them was covered with spiders. The car bumped and shook as it ran over them. Some of them were broken and flattened by the weight of the car. Others had their legs mutilated and broken. Braden saw that there was no way that Trent and Jax were going to be able to get to the side doors of the car without being attacked and bitten. He kept the image of the squirrel in his mind, the way that he had seen it shrivel up like a prune and he imagined that happening to Jax. He gritted his teeth and hammered the pedal down harder. The car smashed through the door of the station and took a generous chunk of the wall out with it. Trent jumped up out of his chair and then fell to the floor. He scrambled to his feet as best he could with his bad knee. Jax jumped down off the top bunk and ran behind Trent. Debris and injured spiders were littering the floor.

Inside the car, Braden found the button to release the boot lid which began to rise upwards slowly. Trent grabbed hold of Jax and shuffled towards the open boot. Mary and Braden were yelling at Jax to get in the car. She finally bolted forwards and dived into the boot. She climbed straight over onto the back seat and then onto Mary's knee where she threw her arms around Mary's neck and buried her head into her shoulder. Trent was nearly at the back of the car. He was reaching out for it, ready to get in.

Braden saw him coming, and he shoved the car into gear and he hit the gas. The car pulled away and Trent fell forwards onto the ground. He yelled out once, just once before two of the spiders were upon him. One climbed onto his head, leaned forward and sunk its fangs into Trent. One fang impaled itself into the bridge of Trent's nose, the other went through his eyelid and straight through the soft meat of his eyeball. He screamed until his vocal cords ruptured and a glut of blood came up out of his throat. Another bite landed halfway up the back of his neck. The concentrated venom from the larger spider dissolving the flesh and the bones away. His carotid artery gave out, sending a jet of blood in all directions. Trent's severed head was dragged away by one of the spiders, his face was frozen in that final scream and stayed that way until it was ingested.

They were a mile away when Mary realized that Trent wasn't in the car.

"What happened to him? Did they get him?" wailed Mary.

"They got him," Braden lied. If Mary had looked over at him she would have seen a smile threatening to break out over Braden's face.

7.

Doctor Briggs woke up in Willis' bunk in the ESA complex just three hours after he had finally gone to sleep. Willis had been his first sexual encounter for over five years, and he had made the absolute most of it that he could. They would probably have gone on a little longer had they not both been fighting off the urge to sleep, but they had both succumbed. He had been a little surprised to find that she was already up and about when he had awoken. It would seem that she needed even less sleep than he did. He could get along with her just fine. He even entertained the idea of extending her an invitation to Hawaii when all of this had been put to sleep.

The first thing that came to his mind once he had gathered himself enough was that his sleep had been uninterrupted by dreams of any sort, at least none that he could recall. He wasn't soaked with his own sweat as he usually was when he woke up in the morning and he had been allowed to come out of his sleep a little more naturally, rather than being torn from his sleep by visions of hell playing before his eyes. He swung his legs out of the bed and sat on the edge of it for a moment. He couldn't decide if he was looking forward to his first full day of work in such a long time or not.

He stood up and walked around the little room for a few moments. He toyed with the idea of putting the television on for a few moments and finding out what was going on out in the big bad world, and then he decided against it. He thought it might be better if he knew as little as possible. The invention of the virus in the first place had taken him just under four years, at least to get it to a point where the host wasn't killed by it, now he had to find a way to make it go away? Did they really think that he had invented the thing without a failsafe? It was all dependent on how much the virus had evolved. The behavior of the spiders that were infected was the key to his diagnosis.

First things first though, he had to sort himself out a change of clothes. Off-hand he went to one of the drawers next to the bed and pulled it open, not expecting to find anything in there, however it was full almost to the brim of all colours of t-shirt. He looked at them for a moment, taken aback by their mere presence and then he closed the drawer again. He tried the next one down and found five pairs of neatly folded jeans and in the bottom one, several sets of underwear and socks. He pulled out an item from each of the drawers, checked the sizes and wasn't surprised to find that they were all matched to him. It began to dawn in his head, as he dressed in the new gear, just how much planning had gone into all of this? It wasn't a spur of the moment arrangement at all. He couldn't even muster any surprise within himself. Nothing that had Layfield's hands in it would ever be totally clean. If that man dipped his hands in shit they would come out cleaner than they had done before.

He smiled to himself and wondered what on earth he could have for breakfast before he got started. He found himself looking forward to seeing Willis again. He couldn't help but find himself attracted to her. He put that down to the fact that he hadn't felt the welcoming warmth of female skin for a very long time. He hadn't felt much of an appetite for any of that nonsense whilst he was in the hospital, but that was probably to do with the drugs that they had been giving him. They had tried to kill his free will with them and they had pretty much failed on that front. They *had* succeeded in killing his dick stone dead, he had to give them that one. Still, perhaps now that the medical regime had been all but forgotten and the affection that Willis had shown him so far, he might start getting a little of his fire back. He was mulling the idea of Hawaii over in his mind. That would be the perfect way to retire, with nothing but warm weather, cocktails and beautiful people all around him. Sounded pretty perfect to him, oh hell yes.

He headed to the door, stopping only to have a quick glance in the full-length mirror to see how he looked in his new gear. He pulled the door open with a view to going and finding Willis, but he was surprised to find her on the other side of the door. She jumped back a little and let out a little squeal of surprise.

"Oh, I just went for a shower, I didn't run out on you I promise. I was just gonna invite you out for breakfast," she said.

"Well, I could eat the arse out of a dead elephant, if you pardon the expression," said Briggs.

Willis giggled, covering her mouth as she did so. The gesture made her look even younger. Briggs scolded himself a little for sleeping with her. Dirty old man.

"May I escort you, ma'am," he said, a little flirtatiously despite his internal dialogue. He offered an arm out to her.

"I'd be delighted sir," she said and linked his outstretched arm. They started down the hallway and towards the canteen. As they got closer Briggs caught the aroma of freshly cooked bacon. His stomach groaned and growled like a dying ogre. He could see himself becoming some sort of food obsessive, having lived on overcooked, dry crap for so long. He might even get fat, not that he minded. There were worse things in life than being fat, that was for sure, being hungry was far worse. He picked up the pace a little.

"Hey, what's your hurry?" said Willis.

"Oh, just hungry. Too many years on hospital food, you know."

"Hospital food? What happened? Did you have an accident?" said Willis.

Briggs looked at her to see if she was joking. If she was, she certainly was a good actor. "Did they not tell you where I've been for all these years?"

Willis shook her head.

"Well then, I have a hell of a story to tell you over breakfast," said Briggs.

And tell her he did, all of it, as they both made their way through a full English each with extra toast. Briggs found himself impressed that Willis liked to eat. She wasn't one of those girls that were so self-obsessed that she would just munch on a salad in a vain attempt to stay thin for another day. She listened to his story about the end of Newtown, the capture and incarceration into the Tulip Suite and his repeated meetings with Doctor Low, the arsehole who had tried relentlessly to get him to confess to terrorism. When he was done, she sat back in her chair and shook her head.

"Why would you agree to come back here? I'd have told them to shove it up their ass," she said and Briggs laughed.

"Well, let's just say that if I do my duty for my country I will have enough coin to retire on, and that will be compensation enough for me," said Briggs.

"Fuck me. How much?" said Willis.

"I'm not allowed to specify. But it's a lot."

"I might ask for a pay rise, see how they like that," said Willis. Briggs laughed again and shook his head.

"I'll tell you what, when we get this shit sorted then I'll make sure you get what you deserve too, how does that suit you?" said Briggs.

The frown across Willis' face smoothed out into her trademark toothy smile. "You got a deal, mister," she said and stuck out her hand which Briggs shook.

"Ok partner. I suppose we had better get started. The sooner we get it done the sooner we can retire," said Briggs.

**

They made it back into the lab. The room was flooded with lots of natural light that was coming in through the windows. It lent the room a more appealing ambiance than the gloom of the evening before. Something caught Briggs' eye from the moment that they walked in. There was a rectangular shape on the workbench to his right. It looked rectangular, it was hard to see fully because the item was covered with a large cloth. Briggs looked at Willis who offered nothing more than a shrug that told him she had no idea what it was.

"Looks like we have been given a present to celebrate our first day together," said Briggs. He went over to it and whipped the cloth off it in one smooth motion. When they saw what was underneath they both took a step backward.

"Woop, shit," yelped Willis.

Woop shit was absolutely right. Under the cloth, there was a clear plastic specimen box, and inside were around a dozen black house spiders. The moment that Briggs took the cloth away they swarmed in his direction and began to clamber over each other to try and get to him. There was no grip for them on the slick inside of the tank, but it didn't stop them trying. They frantically ran over each other, tried to climb the box and fell back down again. It looked like a small collection of blackened hatred being driven mad by its insane instinct to get to them. They showed no sign of resting or calming down and watching it reminded Briggs of some of the inmates at the Tulip Suite, still fighting and squirming, even though they knew that they were outnumbered and their fate was inevitable. It was the behavior of something that had given over its natural instincts and had moved down a step into a primeval instinct to fight and survive.

Psychosis.

The word echoed through his mind. He tried to push it away, but it wasn't going anywhere. He turned to Willis, and she took a step backward. She must have seen something on his face.

"Wha....What is it?" she said.

"Come closer, watch them. Then you can tell me," he said.

He picked up the cloth and draped it over the tank again. "Now watch them." He whipped the cloth away and the spiders ran towards Briggs again, falling and clambering over themselves to try and get out of the tank. Willis watched them, a sneer of disgust on her face.

"They're acting like… like… animals" said Willis.

"Exactly. They have no control over themselves."

Willis pondered it for a moment. Briggs was hoping that she would put the dots together.

"It's the virus. It's driven them insane. It's taken away their basic instinct and turned them into… this," she said pointing at the tank.

"They could have attacked at any time. Why now? Why are they behaving like this now?"

Willis offered a shrug. "There must have been a trigger point?"

"Correct. Layfield told me that there had been a little girl killed yesterday morning. I have to know if they were already aggressive or if this behavior started to happen afterward," said Briggs. He had begun to pace up and down the room, not knowing what to do with himself.

"We can't change this biologically can we?" said Willis.

"I fear that it is already too late for that. If this virus has evolved to become dominant, overriding all the natural instincts of its host, then no, there is nothing we can do to fully stop it. We could come up with a vaccine to treat the earlier stage of the virus, that's no problem, but this is highly evolved. This is now a new form of parasitical life, and I think it's moving onto humans.," said Briggs.

"You said we could treat the earlier stage. We could stop it from spreading any further, couldn't we? We could, couldn't we?" said Willis. There was a tone of anxiety in her voice.

"Yes, we can. We can stop it from spreading, and then all that the powers that be have to worry about is containing the evolved spiders," said Briggs.

"Where do we start?"

Briggs stopped pacing. He opened his mouth and closed it again.

"What is it?" said Willis.

"When I put together the building blocks of the Whisperer, I needed a DNA strand that could be easily altered to mimic that of a spider. I needed DNA that was flexible enough to bond to its host. I used...." He broke off for a moment, his throat working and his lips moving silently.

"Tell me," said Willis.

"I used my own DNA."

"Christ, what were you thinking?" said Willis.

"Oh, there's more. I had to get the virus passed through quarantine before it could be used out in the open. That included a human trial to make sure that it didn't affect them. I couldn't find a volunteer, so I tested it on myself."

Willis said nothing, she looked at him open-mouthed. "So that means..."

Briggs nodded. "I'm already infected, have been for five years and that also means that I have immunity. The cure for all of this is running around in my veins. I think the powers that be knew it and that's why I'm still alive."

Willis was stunned into silence. She began to pace up and down the room. "OK, that's good isn't it? That's a good thing. We need to synthesize whatever is in your bloodstream and then we have got it right?"

"Again, it depends on how far the virus has evolved. We need to speak to boots on the ground, people who were there, and we need to collect more samples. Hybrid ones if we can get them. Then we can start studying the reaction between my immune blood and the blood of an infected. That's our key to finding the cure."

"I'll make some phone calls," said Willis. She started for the door and then paused.

"Briggs. Are we too late?" she said.

Briggs offered her a smile. "No, it's not too late. We just need to know what we're dealing with before we engage the science. It might not be too late just yet, but we have to move fast before it spreads too far," he said.

Willis nodded and then pushed her way out of the doors. Briggs was left alone, looking at the box of spiders that had been left on the table, watching them still trying to escape. One of them looked like it had rolled over onto its back and died, perhaps exhausted by its efforts.

They are willing to die to get to us, he thought.

That was when the first sliver of fear began to edge its way into his insides.

8.

Hemmington Central Park had been modeled on Central Park in Manhattan, New York. The planning council at the time had been very keen to bring some of that American vibrancy and financial economy to the north of England. By trying to replicate the layout of such a booming city, it was thought that the workforce and the inhabitants would have been inspired to create such levels of success just by having their own version of the city that they had seen on television, or visited on holiday at some point. The plans were passed by the fawning, sycophantic planning committee, so lost in their own arrogance that they didn't scrutinise the numbers closely enough. The building of Central Park in the center of Hemmington had been finished on time but had almost bankrupted the council, who then had to scrimp and save on housing projects and office space. The park was fantastic, it had to be said, but the problem was that Hemmington was so poor that it only managed to take on contracts for telesales companies and debt collection agencies. The workforce was largely unskilled and was driven to indulge themselves in all manner of mind-altering substances of an evening. During the weekend it was even worse, and pretty soon the park had become a gathering point for the young and disaffected that weren't old enough to be contained within the relative safety of the many pubs and night spots that littered the town. Soon the beautiful park that had swallowed the council's budget whole had begun to look rather shabby around the edges. It was still the best part of the whole city, a rough diamond stuck slap bang in the middle of a dirt pile.

It was the park that had become a makeshift base for the military, much to the displeasure of the natives, who were becoming increasingly restless. To compound matters, the internet had stopped working and all mobile phones had become nothing more than pretty little black slabs in the pockets of the irritated masses. Some of the call centers had tried to carry on as normal but had found that their phone lines were patchy at best and none of their computers could communicate with each other, so they had begrudgingly sent the workforce home until further notice. The vast majority of them had decided to go to the pub instead, to have a nice cold pint and to await news of what the hell was actually happening.

The helicopter carrying Thompson and Cindy landed on the main playing field, well away from the center of the park where the military was still in the process of putting up large tents and marquees to accommodate the influx of people that they had managed to evacuate from Layton and the surrounding areas.

Thompson and Cindy were escorted from the helicopter to the edge of the field. Thompson was in pretty bad shape from his exertions on the road. He was still struggling to get a deep breath into his lungs without his ribs howling in pain. At the moment, that pain was just fine, because they had made it here alive and they had escaped the wall of spiders that was heading for the city. The moment the helicopter had crossed over the airspace above the large roadblock that had been put in place, the army had given it to the spiders with everything they had. Long blasts of flame had swept across the wall of scuttling bodies, setting scores of them alight, vaporizing the ones that were nearest the front. Explosions went off, throwing hundreds of them into the air. The rattling of gunfire underscored the assault. Thousands of bullets were fired into the rolling mass of spiders, shredding them, obliterating them. The fight carried on for just over ten minutes and then the wall of oncoming spiders stopped. They stopped dead in their tracks. The firing continued for another thirty seconds and then began to die out as the soldiers began to realise what was happening.

Corporal Keller bellowed to the other soldiers to cease fire. "Save it, save the ammo," he yelled into his radio. There were a few more bursts of gunfire and then the guns fell silent. Keller stood up on the barricade, looking out over the road. The black carpet of spiders had stopped their advance. It was still in a state of perpetual movement, rippling and writhing, but they didn't move forward, not one inch.

Keller grabbed his radio and jumped down from the top of the barricade. "Ma'am we have stopped them for now. They're still here but they are not advancing any further. We have limited ammunition until the next drop gets here, over."

The radio hissed, "Affirmative. Ammunition drop ETA one hour. Possible chemical weapons inbound too. Hold your position, over," said Brigadier Taber.

"Holding position, confirmed, over, out," said Keller. He climbed up the barricade again and had another look at the spiders covering the road. He didn't even want to try and estimate how many of them there were. From his vantage point, it looked like there were millions of them.

Why aren't they attacking? He thought. It wasn't as if they didn't have them totally outnumbered. They could have held them off for a little while but they would surely overrun them. They could climb over the barricades, continue down the road and into the city. They could go up the edges of the road, up the grassy verges on either side and try and get to the flamethrowers on the top of each verge. They could do if they wanted, so why were they waiting? What were they waiting for?

A signal. They're waiting for a signal, thought Keller. He grabbed the radio again and switched to the short-range frequency. "Listen up everyone, keep an eye on them. If they come forward again, give them everything you have."

He looked out over the spiders, knowing full well that this battle, this *war* was only just beginning. It wasn't a case of if, it was a case of when.

**

Thompson and Cindy made it to the makeshift medical center in the middle of the park. The park was absolutely brimming with people, most of which looked lost an unsure of what they were supposed to do with themselves. They were brought inside the tent which was lined with fold-out beds, the kind that wouldn't have looked out of place on a holiday camp. Every bed had a body in it. Some were totally still, some of them writhed and moaned in pain. At the front of the tent, there was a fold-out table with an army officer sat behind the desk, a laptop open in front of him. He looked up when he saw Thompson and Cindy walk inside.

"Names please?"

"Gerald Arthur Thompson, Cindy Thompson," said Cindy.

The officer took more details, dates of birth, address, national insurance number, blood type, everything.

"So, you're from Layton? Did you have any encounters with spiders whilst you were in Layton, were either of you bitten?" said the officer.

"We encountered, yes. I'm a D.C.I. I was investigating the death of a young girl just yesterday morning, I think it was a spider that killed her," said Thompson.

The officer tapped the information into the computer, pressed another button and then closed the lid. "Were you on Corsica Road in Layton yesterday?" said the officer.

"That's right. That's where the little girl lived, and two other victims," said Thompson. He was getting out of breath again.

"Are you injured in any way, sir?"

"Yes, he had a fall, his ribs, back and his wrist are messed up," said Cindy.

"Right then sir, you must come with me. We need to get you comfortable as soon as we can."

The officer led them out of the tent and growled something into his radio. He turned to Thompson. "We have all been asked to look out for you. You were there at the start of all of this, you need to answer some questions if that's ok. We need all the intelligence that we can get at the moment."

"Of course," Thompson gasped.

"Don't worry, we will get you all fixed up first. I can't have you in pain. There's a car coming for you to take you to the Hurst Centre. It's a private hospital. The best that we have," said the officer.

Thompson wanted to protest. He hated the idea of private healthcare when there were so many in need, but the pain caressing his body made him shut right up and accept whatever help he was offered. Besides he had never really had the VIP treatment before in his life and he wasn't about to stop that from happening now.

"Please, take a seat, make yourselves as comfortable as you can. The car will be here to pick you up in a few minutes," said the officer and showed them to a small row of deckchairs. Cindy tried to help Thompson into the chair, but he ended up losing his balance and crashing down into the seat with a wince.

"Sorry," said Cindy, but he waved it off and patted the seat next to him for her to sit in. She lowered herself onto the edge of her seat and took one of Thompson's hands in her own. "Are you alright? Really, I mean," she said.

Thompson offered her a smile through his pain and his sweating. "I'm alright. I've had worse, trust me."

"Try to rest up a little," she said and kissed his hand. "You are my hero after all."

Thompson laughed, clutching his ribs to try and stop them from moving. Cindy sat back in her chair and scratched at her leg.

Thompson leaned back tentatively, trying to take the strain off all of his muscles in his mid-section. He managed to move into a position that was actually pretty comfortable. He breathed a sigh of relief and had a look at the world around him. The park looked like it had seen better days. There was a large amount of graffiti on every concrete surface, some of it pretty good and others that made bold, simple and misspelled proclamations. 'Fuck the tory's' being one of the most dominant. Pretty much every bit of grass had someone sitting on it, some alone, some in a pair, lots of families trying to make the most of the situation they had been in. The evacuation of Layton must have happened pretty fast in Thompson's opinion. He had just been lucky that they had got out first before anything had a chance to happen to them. Christ, if he had been a few minutes later then it would be a much different story for them right now. He knew one thing for sure, to get an evacuation done so quickly and to get so many people out, it had to have been planned in advance, ready to go at a moment's notice. They had been planning for this, that was what Thompson thought, they had been planning for it for years.

      The tower blocks that surrounded the park looked like big uneven concrete teeth poking up into the skyline. Thompson could see the green stripes of Suicide Towers from where he was sitting. He had been inside that tower block when he had been on the case of a man that had been driven mad by the noise coming from his neighbors flat. He had knocked on the door of the neighbor and then took a baseball bat to the noisy buggers' knees. He had insisted that it had been an act of self-defense and that if he had tried to tolerate the noise for much longer, he would have ended up caving his neighbors head in with that bat. It didn't even occur to the hapless man that even after he had put his neighbor in a wheelchair, that the noise he could hear continued as he sat in the police cell waiting to be charged. Of course, the noise was inside his head rather than coming through the admittedly paper-thin walls inside those flats.

Thompson shook his head and smiled. The number of people that he had dealt with over the years had been large and varied. Never a dull moment, never the same day twice. That was the nature of the job. He certainly had never had a day like today, or yesterday. Yep, it was another one for the books, if there were any books left of course. His eyes were beginning to feel heavy and despite the coolness in the air, he felt as if he could just go for a decent nap right about now. He was about to shuffle himself into a decent napping position when he heard an unrest beginning to build amongst the masses of people. There was a combination of shouting and the beeping of a car horn. The officer came over to them again.

"Your car is here Mr. Thompson. Please come with me," he said.

Thompson winced as he pulled himself back out of the chair again. Cindy did her best to support him, but she wasn't strong enough to take any of his weight. His spine crackled as he got to his feet. It was stiffening up on him something rotten. He had never really considered himself as an old man, but today he felt every inch of it. The officer led them around the medical tent and back towards the main path that ran through the middle of the park. It led from the edge of the main road right up to the most central point where the bandstand stood. However, in their way was a lot of irritable and very vocal people. A path had been forged through the seething masses by some very heavily armed soldiers. As they walked through Thompson could pick up on little snatches of the unrest.

….want to call my wife….

….need to check in….

….tell us what's happening…..

…..won't talk to us….

By the time he got to the car, a very plush dark green Jaguar with blacked out windows, the type of car a president might get around in, he had a pretty good idea of the mood of the people. They weren't telling them anything and somehow they had taken down the internet too so they couldn't get information from any other source either.

Not bad for an old man, he thought to himself.

They got into the car and it began to drive out of the park. The soft leather seats were much more inviting than the deck chairs they had been sitting on a few moments earlier. Thompson felt another wave of sleepiness wash over him. He resisted it, only because his copper's eye was restless. He wanted to have a look around, see what other clues he could find. He was still on the job after all.

Despite himself and his strong instincts, he was asleep before the car had even got to the park gates.

9.

Three hours after Thompson had arrived at the Hurst Centre, and was being wheeled in, still fast asleep, for assessment, Briggs and Willis were in the air aboard a helicopter and heading for Hemmington City. They were being escorted again by Monsun, who still hadn't found any humor deep with his soul. If he had then he was still doing a pretty damn good job of hiding it. He was, however, forthcoming with information of the spider outbreak that had happened in Layton.

"Hemmington City is holding. The spiders have got as far as the barricade but they can't get inside. Our boys have got too much to hit them with," said Monsun through their headsets.

"What about the other directions? They won't just go for Hemmington, there's Hale Peak, Hurndell, Denway. They surround Layton don't they?" said Briggs.

"Every town and village surrounding Layton has a military presence. There are too many spiders to keep them contained in Layton, and we don't want a repeat of what happened to Newtown either. The tactic is to draw them all out of Layton and attack them when they are exposed with lower-level explosions, flamethrowers, and anything else we can hit them with without causing major damage. Hell, we are even talking about using a pesticide on them," said Monsun.

"What about the hybrids?" said Briggs.

"What?" said Monsun.

"The human spiders from the hospital. Have you taken them out yet?"

Monsun was quiet for a moment. Briggs tried to read his stony face to no avail.

"They haven't been found yet," said Monsun.

"You're fucking kidding me, right?"

"I'm not in the business of telling lies Doctor Briggs," said Monsun.

"Humans spliced with spider DNA that contains a virus so aggressive that it causes the most incredible mutations any of us have ever seen. It turns people who have been bitten into large spider-like monsters that tower probably eight-to-ten feet tall and you've lost them? Jesus Christ," said Briggs sitting back in his seat and folding his arms across his chest. He looked at Monsun. His eye caught it, it caught the tight pursing of Monsun's lips and the baleful, murderous look in his eye, just for a fleeting second.

He had gotten under Monsun's skin. He was human after all. He smiled to himself a little. He still had the ability to piss people off, therefore he was still relevant, at least to himself.

"We will find them," said Monsun.

Briggs said nothing. He had an idea that Monsun was just toeing the line. He wasn't going to tell him anything truthful without putting a spin on the whole thing.

"I think when the time is right, they will show themselves again," said Willis. Monsun offered her a polite nod.

"So, who is this person we're going to see?" said Briggs.

"Gerald Thompson. He was the investigating officer on the case of Lottie Richmond who died yesterday morning of severe anaphylaxis. He is in the Hurst Centre with some minor injuries he sustained as he was escaping from Layton. Apparently, his partner is one of the Hybrids that our friend here lost," said Willis.

Monsun's lips pursed again and Briggs stifled a laugh. "Sounds like we could learn something from him. Hopefully, it will give us a little insight as to that we are dealing with."

Monsun sat forward suddenly and pushed the forefingers of his right hand against his earphones. He was listening to a transmission that Briggs and Willis weren't a party to. He shielded his mouth as he spoke into the radio. The conversation went on for a few moments and then he dropped his hand again.

"Well Briggs, I think you might be surplus to requirements," said Monsun, back in their ears again.

"How do you figure that?"

"The spiders that had made it to the outskirts of Hemmington have gone. They must have retreated. We drove them away," he said. The ghost of a smile flickered around the corner of his mouth.

Briggs looked over at Willis and then back to Monsun. "I wouldn't be so sure of that." He said.

10.

Brigadier Taber had gone over to the south barricade the moment that she heard the report that the spiders had gone. She had found Keller who was still standing on top of the barricade, a pair of binoculars stuck to his face. He was scanning the horizon, looking for any sign of their return. Taber climbed up to where he was standing. The road in front of them was almost completely clear. Some sections of the tarmac had been cratered by some of the explosions. Pieces of ash floated around the air, carried by the breeze that was washing down the road. Cars still littered one side of the road where they had been abandoned, some of them still burning from the carnage that had ensued earlier.

"What happened?" said Taber.

"It was the strangest thing. They never moved for two hours, not one bit, and then they suddenly started dispersing. They went in all directions, most of 'em went back up the road. It happened so fast that we didn't even have time to react. If I didn't know better, I would have said that they were signaled to move," said Keller.

"Did you sweep the perimeter? They could be trying to find a way in," said Taber.

"It was the first thing we did. All the barricades are reporting no sightings, and that's not just here, that's at all the barricades within fifty miles. They haven't seen anything. It's like they just vanished off the face of the earth," said Keller.

Taber shot him a look, "Several thousand aggressive spiders do *not* just vanish Keller. They have to be somewhere." She tapped a button on the headset she was wearing. "I need a chopper in the air right now with every piece of surveillance equipment that you have. We need to find those spiders, and we need to find them now," she yelled.

She climbed down from the barrier again and leveled a finger at Keller. "You, keep looking and don't leave that spot. I want every barricade to stay on high alert, you got that Keller? You see anything with more legs than you and I don't get to hear about it then I will feed you to those fuckers myself, do we understand each other?"

"Crystal clear Ma'am," said Keller.

"Good," said Taber and walked away. There were some big and tough soldiers that gave way to Taber as she walked through. She had to prove herself over and over again to get the ranking that she had, and she didn't give an inch to anyone. She was about as tough and hard-boiled as they came. If she said she was going to feed him to the spiders herself then he was pretty certain that she would go through with it too.

Keller turned his attention back to the road, scanning it with the binoculars. But there wasn't a thing moving out there, not a single thing.

11.

The Hurst Centre had its own landing pad on the roof. From the ground, the place looked like a stately home, albeit a very modern stately home. It was surrounded by almost perfectly kept gardens. You would have to look long and hard to find a blade of grass out of whack or a stray, uncut leaf on one of the many hedgerows that bordered them. The Hurst Centre was the kind of place where just walking through the main gates made your own personal stock feel like it was rising sharply. If you weren't wearing an expensive suit then you were likely to feel a little out of place.

Stepping inside the building from the roof doorway, Briggs thought to himself that it would have been a much more pleasant experience if he had been incarcerated in a place just like this one instead of the relative poverty of the Tulip Suite. There would have been no crappy, overcooked fish and stale, dry chips here. It would have been eggs benedict, fresh mushroom soup and caviar and crackers for a snack. Still, he had no energy to keep yanking on that lever. He had a job to do after all. An aging, but very well turned-out female doctor escorted them to the room where Gerald Thompson was staying.

"He's very tired, so please go easy on him. His wife is a little…. defensive shall we say?" said the doctor.

Briggs nodded to indicate his understanding. The doctor went through the large oak door and into the room to announce Briggs' arrival. There were a few muffled voices and then the doctor waved them in.

"Ten minutes, that's all I can give you at the moment," said the doctor to Briggs.

"We might need…" began Willis, but Briggs cut her off.

"Ten minutes is fine, thank you," he said.

They went into the room and the door was pulled closed behind them. Thompson was sat up in the bed, propped up by more pillows than Briggs had ever seen in one bed. His face looked pale and pained, that of a man who had been through something of a personal war. His eyes scanned Briggs suspiciously. Thompson knew who he was, Briggs had no doubt about that. Thompson's wife sat on the chair next to the bed. She looked pissed off and tired. She was steadily scratching at her knee with her long nails and giving Briggs a look that would have stopped a clock.

"Listen, I'm really sorry to intrude on you like this. My name is…"

"Briggs. You're Doctor Michael Briggs. I know who you are, I know exactly who the fuck you are. I'm giving you exactly thirty seconds to get the fuck out of here," rasped Thompson.

"I need to talk to you about what happened yesterday, it's important…."

"Important? I'll tell you what's fucking important, a little girl was killed yesterday. Three years old she was, just three years old. My partner got bitten too and he turned into something…." He broke off, struggling with his emotions for a moment. He composed himself and then carried on. "He turned into something monstrous, a killer, a *murderer*. That man had a family, kids for Christ's sake. This all has to do with what happened in Newtown, hasn't it? It has to, otherwise, you wouldn't be here right now. I know you Briggs and I know what you did, now I swear to almighty God, if you don't leave there's going to be trouble."

"Please," said Willis. "Please, can you just hear us out, just for a few minutes."

"Lady, I don't know what lies he has told you, but he is a killer. If you want to keep on living then you do yourself a favor and get as far away from him as possible," said Thompson.

"Believe whatever you want Thompson, it doesn't matter. I need to talk to you about what happened and I'm not leaving until you tell me," said Briggs. His patience was wearing a little thin. He didn't have time for this bullshit.

"Fine. If you won't leave, then I will," said Thompson. He started to get out of the bed.

"Gerald…." moaned Cindy.

"No, I'm not staying here sharing a space with *him*." He roared. He gingerly stood up, pulled open one of the drawers next to the bed and began to get himself dressed. He pulled on his trousers without bothering to remove the bed robe he had been given to wear.

"Gerald," whined Cindy again. She started to get out of her chair, leveling a finger at Briggs. "If he hurts himself, I'm holding you responsible."

Cindy stood up with the intention of escorting Gerald out of the room. She managed just one step and then froze. A look of utter horror and fear tore across her face. Gerald, who had taken off the bed robe and was in the process of buttoning up his shirt saw her freeze.

"Cindy, what is it? Cindy?..."

Briggs went to try and help her, but Thompson shoved him out of the way. He staggered backward, almost taking Willis out with him.

"Get away from her," Thompson growled. He staggered around the bed towards Cindy.

Cindy tried to step towards him, but a horrible wet crunching noise came from her leg. She tried to catch herself on the edge of the bed but she couldn't keep her grip, she began to spill forwards. She would have had a violent impact with the wooden floor had Thompson not made it to her in time. He caught her under the arms and pulled her back up, his face grimacing in the awful pain from his ribs and back. They were under a pressure bandage to limit the movement and he was doped on painkillers, but taking the weight of his wife still caused an incredible amount of agony. He didn't care about the pain, all he cared about was getting Cindy on the bed. He hauled her up and lay her down on the pillows. He began to move away but she gripped onto him.

"Gerald, I'm sorry," she whispered. "I'm so sorry."

"What on earth do you have to be sorry for? I'll get the doctor they'll….."

"It's too late Gerald. I love you….. Mr. Policeman," she said and then she smiled.

"What? What are you talking about? I'll get the doctor and…" and then his foot kicked something on the floor.

"Oh Jesus," said Briggs. Willis clapped her hand over her mouth.

Cindy Thompson's leg had come away from the rest of her body, just above the knee. It had slipped seamlessly out of the bottom of her jeans when Gerald had lifted her onto the bed. Gerald turned and looked at the floor. He saw the leg, that beautiful smooth leg that he had stroked as it lay across him every evening whilst they watched television, lying on the ground. The severed end was covered with the same rotting green flesh that had been present on Wells' arm when it had come loose. She had been bitten, she had been infected and that meant only one thing.

Cindy closed her eyes and began to shake and convulse.

The change had begun.

12.

Keller had asked for a chair to be brought up to the top of the barricade. He had been scanning the horizon, looking for any activity, but he hadn't seen a damn thing. Not a twitch, not a scuttle, just nothing. Everything was quiet and deserted. Now he was sat with his binoculars in his lap, smoking a cigarette and making the most of the orders that he had been given. Most of the fires that had been burning on the road had pretty much gone out. It was a fine day, a little cool, but fine nonetheless. Now and again he would radio Taber and tell her nothing was happening. He did it to a point where Taber had roared down the radio only to report to her if something actually happened. If he did it again she was going to come right over there and cram his radio up his arse. He Roger'd that one with a smirk, happy that he had gotten under her skin a little.

Such was his complacency that he had started to nod off in his seat and by the time the commotion in Centre Park began to happen he was almost fully asleep.

**

The anger amongst the people in the park, mostly about the fact that not a single mobile phone or app would connect to the network, was just starting to tip over to the point where the military was having to pull their guns on the gathering crowds to keep them back. Some of them gathered rocks, bottles and large sticks to brandish at them. It was looking increasingly likely that things were going to get ugly.

But then there was a soft *poom* from behind them. It was followed by the clang and hissing of glass hitting the floor. Some of the people towards the back of the mob heard it and turned their heads up towards Suicide Towers. Then they saw it. They saw the creature climbing out of the hole that had once housed a window. A good portion of the concrete around it and a generous chunk of the cladding had been torn away. The creature clung to the side of the white and green striped tower, its leg span big enough to cover four whole floors. From where the people were standing it looked like the biggest spider there had ever been on the face of the earth. If any of them had been a little closer, they would have seen that the creature still had some of the facial features and the smooth dark-skinned body of the late Doctor Ochre. The creature ran to the top of the tower, moving with a speed that was both graceful and terrifying to the people that saw it.

The people at the back of the mob began to scream and point. Some of them took videos and pictures with their otherwise useless mobile phones. The terror rippled through the crowd until they were all looking up at the tower. Some of the soldiers saw it and they began to mobilise, coordinating their operations to go and get the monster at the top of the tower.

But it was too late. The spiders were already ahead of them.

The monster on the tower began to emit a sound. Such was its volume that the mass of panic was dropped suddenly into silence. All of them stood, their heads craned up to the tower, listening to that strange noise.

Click-click

Click-click

Click-click.

The sound echoed all around the city, bouncing off the walls of all the tower blocks, off the floors of the roads and pavements. It vibrated through everything.

Subtly at first and then with increasing fury, the ground beneath Hemmington City began to shake. People fell to the floor, some of them clinging onto the vibrating ground. Some tried to run, but their feet were thrown out from under them. Buildings began to split, the cracks running up from the ground, popping windows like over-inflated balloons, showering the streets and the people in shards of glass. Fingers, toes and a few noses were sheared off by the falling glass. Even the combined screams of the people of Hemmington could drown out the noise.

The field in the middle of the park, which had been turned into the base for the army began to distort. The middle of the field began to rise up, turning itself into a hill, tipping over the tents and marquees, forcing vehicles to roll away from it or to tip over onto their sides.

Then everything stopped.

The silence was broken by the screams of the wounded and the muttering of people as they got up off the floor. They saw the ground that had been pushed upwards into a grassy peak in the middle. They came close to it, again with their mobile phones out, snapping pictures, taking videos. The silence prevailed just long enough, just long enough for everyone to drop their guard a little. Then the creature on the tower let out an ear-piercing screech, an inhuman roar that caused the masses to collectively put their hands over their ears.

Then the ground lurched.

The grassy hill in the middle of the park suddenly burst open. Chunks of grass and dirt flew in all directions hitting people, killing some, blinding others. Those that weren't injured saw the fountain of black erupt from the new hole in the middle of the park. It shot thirty feet in the air and rained down again. Then the panic that had been brewing inside the people in the park came to the surface as they saw what the black chunks raining down were. Legs uncurled, fangs flexed, ready to bite.

The spiders had scattered from the road and gone down into the drains, the sewers and the old tunnels that had been under the city for a hundred years. Thousands, millions of them came streaming out of the hole in the floor. The people tried to run, but the spiders were too fast and too large in number. They swarmed over the screaming people, biting, injecting them with their poison.

    The creature on the tower started to roar.

13.

Cindy was starting to convulse just as the ground underneath them began to shake.

Briggs stepped forwards and grabbed Thompson by his arm. "Let's get out of here," he yelled, trying to pull Thompson away. Thompson yanked his arm out of Briggs' grip.

"Leave me the fuck alone," he yelled.

"She's changing, isn't she? She's becoming one of them," said Willis.

"I won't let it happen, I won't let her become one of those things," yelled Thompson.

"Come on, we can get you out of here. We have a helicopter…."

"I'm *not leaving her like this do you understand? I have to take care of her.*" He screamed at Briggs.

Briggs didn't quite understand what he was talking about, but Willis knew. She went out of the door, looked up and saw Monsun in the corridor. He was growling into his radio trying to find out what the hell was going on. Willis shouted him.

"What is it?" he yelled over the noise of the ground shaking. Windows were bursting all over the building and the noise was incredible.

"We have an infected. You need to deal with it," yelled Willis.

Monsun cocked his gun and headed for the room. Willis pushed through the door and fell down. She crawled across the ground until she had found a wall to lean on next to Briggs.

Thompson was at the foot of the bed. He had a cut over his right eye and blood was streaming down his cheek. He looked up and saw Monsun, and he saw Monsun's gun.

Thompson was about to yell at Monsun to give him a gun, but it was at that moment that the ground stopped shaking. Monsun looked at the woman on the bed and he hissed in a breath. He raised his gun towards her.

"*No, please*. Please, let me….let me….she's my wife," said Thompson his hand raised.

Monsun drew a pistol from his belt. He clicked off the safety and looked at Thompson.

"I'm a police officer," said Thompson.

Monsun handed him the pistol.

Thompson pointed it at Cindy.

Cindy had two new appendages growing out of her upper abdomen. Blood was arching out of the new holes in her body. Her one remaining leg drummed the bed and kicked out in pain. Her eyes were rolling back in her head and a steady stream of foam was running out of her mouth. A horrible choking, gurgling sound was coming from her throat. Her hands began to split open, spilling green mucus onto the pure white bed linen. Chunks of skin dropped and slapped to the wooden floor. Cindy's wedding finger fell off, and the ring she had worn since the day they had been married came free and rolled under the bed. Cindy let out a deep, guttural roar. Whatever it was on that bed, it wasn't Cindy anymore. It was an abomination.

He pulled the trigger, just once. The bullet blew out one of Cindy's eyes and tore the back of her head off. Blood and clear spinal fluid was thrown all over the wall behind her and began to run down the pristine white pillows.

Thompson lowered the gun. He let out a scream of dreadful anguish and turned away from her.

"I'm sorry Thompson," said Briggs. "I'm so sorry. There was nothing anyone could have done, it was…."

"For the best?" said Thompson in a raspy and broken voice. "I know what's for the best," he said.

He raised the gun up again and fired. The shot hit Briggs in his shoulder. Willis let out a scream of terror and backed away from him as fast as she could. Briggs clawed at the wound, unable to register the fact that he was hurt. Blood dribbled onto the wooden floor beneath him. He held out his bloody hand towards Thompson, a smile of disbelief breaking on his face.

"I….I…..I'm….."

Thompson fired the gun over and over. Briggs' body was twisted and thrown in every direction as the bullets smashed home, tearing arteries and smashing through bones. The final shot caught him in the bridge of his nose. He went down, his mouth fell open spilling a river of his own blood and brain fragments into his lap.

Thompson fired again, but the gun clicked, letting him know it was empty. Thompson handed the gun back to Monsun.

"I owed him that," said Thompson.

"No argument here," said Monsun. "A lot of people owed him that."

"You don't know what you've done," said Willis.

"What did you say?" said Monsun.

"You don't know what you've *done,*" screamed Willis.

"What is she talking about?" said Thompson.

Monsun shrugged, "Beats the hell out of me."

Willis put her hands on her head and began to pull at her own hair. *"You don't know what you've doooooone,"* She screamed, over and over again. She looked down at the battered body of Briggs. She saw the blood. That precious blood of his, running all over the floor.

"She's in shock, that's all. She's....."

Monsun was cut off by the window breaking inwards. A torrent of spiders flooded in through the broken pane. Monsun raised his rifle and began to fire his gun as fast as he could. He took some of them down, but they were outnumbered. Around four-hundred-thousand to one.

Willis closed her eyes tight and put her hands over her ears. She waited for the sting of the bites to come, but after a few moments, she realised that they had stopped. She cautiously opened her eyes again. The room was flooded with spiders. They had bitten Monsun and Thompson to the point where they couldn't move. They lay on the floor, twitching occasionally, snoring in breaths. The spiders had stopped just in front of where Willis was stood. One of them ran up her front, right up to the crook of her neck. She held her breath, not wanting to move an inch, desperate to swipe the spider away. It ran onto her face, its legs tickling her skin and then it stopped for a moment, its feelers tapping the surface of her nose, sampling, tasting.

Then it jumped, spreading its legs out as it fell. The moment it hit the floor the rest of the swarm began to retreat, back out of the broken window again. A few moments later the room was empty. Willis backed up into the wall. She slid down, covered her face and started to cry.

Outside the Hurst center, the spiders began to pile up on top of each other. More and more of them came, turning themselves into a huge organic tower, surrounding the building in a black, festering cocoon.

The spider had sensed something about Willis. It had tasted it in the sweat coming out of her pores. She had mated recently, and the chemical changes in her body had already begun. She had mated with a carrier, and her child was going to be the next generation, the new queen.

14.

Two helicopters were flying over Hemmington when the tower of spiders began to build itself. One of them was carrying survivors that had been evacuated from Layton Valley. The large chopper had already been told to divert away from Hemmington, it was now unsafe, not fit for habitation. It was a war zone according to the reports coming out of there. Mary Benson could see what was going on down in Hemmington. Jax wanted to look, but she said no, it would give her more nightmares. Most of the ground had turned into a black writhing carpet of spiders. From the sky, they could see the incoming wave of bigger spiders that had flooded out of the ground in Layton. Every populated area below them was a no-go. They were going to have to go further afield if they were going to stand any chance of survival. The word going around the twenty-or-so people in the back of the large helicopter was that they were heading for the coast.

Ironic that it had been Braden Benson's plan all along. It was just a pity he wasn't allowed to see it happen.

Mary wasn't going to let him get away with killing Trent, not a chance in hell. He had been her last gasp of having something in her life that gave her real joy and meaning and what Braden had done to him was as good as murder. She knew that he had driven away without him. She knew he had condemned Trent to death. He had to suffer the consequences of his actions once and for all.

They had made it to the Layton dam with seconds to spare. The spiders weren't far behind them when they pulled the car up just a few feet from the waiting chopper. The moment the car pulled over, Mary was out of the door and snatching Jax up into her arms. She made it to the chopper first, loading Jax on and then stepping aboard herself. She saw Braden running, his gangly legs flapping around as he charged forwards. She waited until he was near enough for him to hear her and she suddenly yelled out.

"He's been bitten."

Braden had heard it. His face had creased over in puzzlement. He tried to get on the chopper, but the people on board kicked him away. He fought them, screaming and begging them to let him on. Then a soldier had come forwards and shot him three times. Jax hadn't seen it. She was unaware that the fuss was about her Dad. She had asked her where he was when they had lifted off. Mary had told her that he had to go and do his own thing again. She had heard that one so many times before. After today, she would never hear it again. They headed for the coast. Mary wondered what she could possibly get up to now that she had finally broken free. The possibilities were endless, as long as they took care of those bastard spiders.

The second helicopter contained Brigadier Taber. She was looking down at the mass of spiders assembling around the Hurst Centre. Keller, the smart arse, was on board too. She needed his eyes, not that she would ever admit it to him, the little puke.

"That's the same, isn't it? That's the same as Newtown. I seen the pictures, Ma'am," he said, pointing down at the spider tower below them.

"Yes it is," said Taber. She clicked the button on the headset to the open channel. "All units to the Hurst Centre. Give 'em everything you got, all chemical, then get back to your sweeps," she said.

Not on my fuckin' watch, she mumbled under her breath.

Epilogue.

Out in the woodlands, not far from Layton Valley the decapitated body of the Wells creature lay out in the sun. A steady hum of flies hung around the remains of the beast. The severed head was less than three feet away, and it almost looked as if it had a little smirk on its face.

Three hours earlier, the mutation formally known as Wells had found the Katie Underwood mutation in the woodlands. She had purposely found a quiet place to be and she had begun to emit a pheromone that proved to be as intoxicating to Wells as the smell of freshly fried doughnuts. When he found her, the smell had become as addictive as any drug he had ever experienced in his life. It ran through his broken body, bringing it to life, making it tingle with a desire that he had never felt before in all his time as a human. The Katie thing turned away and held its rear end upwards towards him. Small fragments of his human mind and instincts were still flickering deep within his psyche as his mutated genitalia was pushed inside hers and gripped with a firmness and a pleasure that he had seldom enjoyed before. The explosive and prolonged orgasm he had experienced had probably been one of the best moments of his life. It had almost seemed worth it, worth the unrelenting agony of his new body.

But it was also the last thing that he ever did. The Katie thing pulled away from his deflating hardness, turned around and bit off his head in one fell swoop, sending a jet of blackened blood skywards. She waited for a few hours, making sure that the gift he had given her was ready to proceed and then she squatted over his stiffening corpse and laid her stinking, fertilized eggs onto the body of Wells. When they hatched, they were going to feast on the body of their father.

The new breed was about to be born.

Printed by Amazon Italia Logistica S.r.l.
Torrazza Piemonte (TO), Italy